OXFORD WORLD'S CLASSICS

*For over 100 years Oxford World's Classics have brought
readers closer to the world's great literature. Now with over 700
titles—from the 4,000-year-old myths of Mesopotamia to the
twentieth century's greatest novels—the series makes available
lesser-known as well as celebrated writing.*

*The pocket-sized hardbacks of the early years contained
introductions by Virginia Woolf, T. S. Eliot, Graham Greene,
and other literary figures which enriched the experience of reading.
Today the series is recognized for its fine scholarship and
reliability in texts that span world literature, drama and poetry,
religion, philosophy and politics. Each edition includes perceptive
commentary and essential background information to meet the
changing needs of readers.*

OXFORD WORLD'S CLASSICS

JACK LONDON

The Son of the Wolf
Tales of the Far North

Edited with an Introduction and Notes by
CHARLES N. WATSON, JR.

OXFORD

UNIVERSITY PRESS

OXFORD

UNIVERSITY PRESS

Great Clarendon Street, Oxford OX2 6DP

Oxford University Press is a department of the University of Oxford.
It furthers the University's objective of excellence in research, scholarship,
and education by publishing worldwide in

Oxford New York

Athens Auckland Bangkok Bogotá Buenos Aires Calcutta
Cape Town Chennai Dar es Salaam Delhi Florence Hong Kong Istanbul
Karachi Kuala Lumpur Madrid Melbourne Mexico City Mumbai
Nairobi Paris São Paulo Singapore Taipei Tokyo Toronto Warsaw

with associated companies in Berlin Ibadan

Oxford is a registered trade mark of Oxford University Press
in the UK and in certain other countries

British Library Cataloguing in Publication Data

Data available

Library of Congress Cataloging in Publication Data

London, Jack, 1876–1916.
The son of the wolf : tales of the Far North / Jack London;
edited with an introduction by Charles N. Watson, Jr.
p. cm.—(Oxford world's classics)
Includes bibliographical references.
1. Klondike River Valley (Yukon)—Gold discoveries—Fiction.
2. Yukon Territory—Social life and customs—Fiction. 3. Adventure
stories, American. I. Watson, Charles N., 1939– . II. Title.
III. Series.
PS3523.O46S72 1996 813'.52—dc20 95–3673

ISBN 0–19–283486–X (pbk.)

3 5 7 9 10 8 6 4

Printed in Great Britain by
Cox & Wyman Ltd.
Reading, Berkshire

CONTENTS

CONTENTS

FOR NANCE

INTRODUCTION

When the 21-year-old Jack London hoisted his gear aboard the steamship *Umatilla* at the San Francisco wharf on 25 July 1897, he was joining a motley collection of passengers embarking on one of the most colourful and in some ways most painful adventures of an era that had witnessed many such odysseys. Along with the century, the frontier spirit of the New World had pretty much run its course, as Frederick Jackson Turner had recently proclaimed in a celebrated 1893 address to the American Historical Association. The existence of open land and the dream of easy riches, Turner argued, had operated both as an incentive to the energetic individual and as a safety valve for social conflict. But now the continent had been crossed, the easy gold had been panned out, Indian resistance had been suppressed, the imperative of 'manifest destiny' had been fulfilled, and there were no more frontiers to conquer. Except the Klondike.

The Klondike gold rush of 1897 took its name from one of the many tributaries of the upper Yukon River in the Yukon Territory of north-western Canada. Prospectors had been panning these streams for years with only middling success until August of 1896, when an American, George Carmack, and two Indians called Skookum Jim and Tagish Charlie struck rich deposits in what was soon to be renamed Bonanza Creek. By the time word of the strike gravitated to the 'outside', the best claims had already been staked. But this discouraging news came too late: the gold fever had spread and the rush was on. Many men—and a few venturesome women—threw up their jobs, pawned their belongings or mortgaged their property, purchased wilderness outfits, and headed north with little idea of the hardships and disappointments that awaited them on the long trail to Dawson City, the prospectors' boom-town that had sprung to life at the confluence of the Yukon and the Klondike.

The young Jack London was better prepared for hardship than most. He was born out of wedlock in 1876 to the energetic but emotionally unstable Flora Wellman, who had migrated from her native Ohio and set up in San Francisco as a music teacher, lecturer on spiritualism, and conductor of seances. In 1875 she had been living with William H. Chaney, a sometime editor, lawyer, and politician, latterly a 'professor' of astrology and almost certainly the future writer's father. By the time of his son's birth Chaney had moved on, and several months later Wellman married a middle-aged widower, John London, who became a devoted stepfather to the boy, now renamed John Griffith London and always called Jack. The Londons' modest ventures in truck farming and storekeeping never seemed to prosper, and at the age of 10 Jack was delivering papers and taking odd jobs to help the family finances. Later he worked gruelling fourteen-hour shifts in a cannery for ten cents an hour; still later he shovelled coal in a power plant and worked in the stifling heat of a steam laundry.

By now the family had settled in Oakland, the smaller city on the eastern shore of San Francisco Bay. Here, for the remainder of his childhood and adolescence, London lived a kind of double life. On the one hand he was a voracious reader, slipping away at every opportunity to the Oakland Public Library to immerse himself in the literature of romantic adventure and popular rags-to-riches biography. But the realities of the Oakland waterfront soon led these venturesome impulses in more dangerous directions. He purchased a small sailboat and learned to navigate the treacherous Bay currents, acquired a taste for the hard-drinking rituals of the waterfront tavern, and eventually fell in with a group of oyster pirates who conducted night-time raids on the commercial beds of the Upper Bay. At the age of 17 he enlisted as an able-bodied seaman for a seven-month voyage on a seal-hunting schooner bound for Japan and the Bering Sea; and a year later he embarked on an even more dangerous excursion as a tramp, riding the rails eastward as far as New York City before finally being arrested for vagrancy near Niagara Falls and sentenced to thirty days in the county penitentiary—a harrowing experience he eventually recounted in *The Road* (1907).

Yet through all these escapades, as he later noted, he was

'never without a book', and he returned to California a confirmed socialist and a more serious student. Resuming his high-school studies at the age of 19, he began to write stories and sketches for the school paper. He enrolled for a semester at the nearby University of California at Berkeley but dropped out after one semester because the pace of his courses, he claimed, was too slow. Believing he could learn more on his own, he launched a campaign to form himself as a writer. Two years earlier he had won first prize in a writing contest sponsored by a San Francisco newspaper for a story called 'Typhoon Off the Coast of Japan', based on an episode during his seal-hunting voyage; and with this encouragement he now wrote voluminously, in every conceivable genre, and circulated his work to any newspaper or magazine that seemed remotely likely to accept it. There were no takers. By the summer of 1897, frustrated that his most dogged efforts had been fruitless, he was ready to try a fresh tack; and as the Klondike fever intensified, he joined the throngs of wayfarers, hoping for a big strike or, failing that, at least a new foundation for his literary ambitions.

After a change of steamers at Port Townsend, Washington, London completed the eight-day passage up the coast and found himself ashore at the tiny trading post of Dyea on the northern end of the Alaska panhandle, a few miles above Skagway and a stone's throw from an Indian village. The beach was littered with the outfits of thousands of would-be prospectors, all with the same goal of somehow transporting themselves and their supplies over the 3,600-foot Chilkoot Pass to the series of lakes that formed the headwaters of the Yukon River, which would eventually carry them to the Klondike. The rates charged by native packers were rising by the day, and London consequently determined to carry his outfit, load by load, on his own back. Now accompanied by three other hopeful Klondikers, he eventually completed the twenty-eight mile trek to Lake Lindemann (he usually spelled it *Linderman*), and along the way the group was joined by an elderly but indomitable man named Tarwater, who became the hero of the last of London's Northland tales, 'Like Argus of the Ancient Times'.

The trek over the Chilkoot had been both difficult and dangerous, and the hundreds of miles remaining between Lake Lindemann and Dawson City promised to be equally challenging. It took the group two weeks to fell trees and whipsaw them into the planks with which they could build a boat capable of navigating a series of windy lakes and whitewater rapids. On the stretch of the upper Yukon connecting lakes Marsh and Laberge, the group was forced to decide whether to risk a passage through the notoriously treacherous Box Canyon and White Horse Rapids or to play it safe with an overland portage. They took the risk, for by now it was late September and the big freeze-up was imminent. On the thirty-mile passage down Laberge they encountered their first snowstorm, and a variety of ice formations began to hamper their progress: slush ice moving in from the tributaries, rim ice along the banks, and anchor ice forming on the bottom and floating to the surface. They passed the Five Finger Rapids, named for its five great up-thrusting rocks, and by 9 October they had made it as far as the confluence of the Yukon and the Stewart, eighty miles upriver from Dawson, where they decided to hole up in an abandoned cabin for the winter.

If the success of the Northland venture had depended on the discovery of gold, it would have had to be written off as a relative failure. London and a companion explored nearby Henderson Creek, staked claims, and boated downriver to Dawson to record them; but the laborious process of winter mining apparently yielded little colour in their pans. During his six weeks in Dawson, London had ample opportunity to experience the saloon and dance-hall culture of this raw mining town, though the former oyster pirate, sailor, and cross-country tramp would have found little to be shocked by. Back in the Stewart River cabin he passed the time by reading Milton's *Paradise Lost* and Darwin's *Origin of Species*, arguing metaphysical questions with anyone who would take him on, soaking up the innumerable tales that circulated among the denizens of such isolated outposts, and undertaking the tasks required to survive a winter where a Fahrenheit temperature of twenty below zero was accounted warm and a cold snap sent the thermometer as low as minus seventy.

The frigid temperatures and occasional frayed tempers were bad enough, but what more seriously undermined his well-being was the absence of fresh fruit and vegetables. The consequence was the onset of scurvy, a vitamin-deficiency disease that causes the gums to bleed and the joints to swell and ache. If untreated, it will eventually prove fatal. Hence, by spring and the titanic break-up of the Yukon ice, described memorably in such tales as 'At the Rainbow's End', London was only too ready to abandon his mining claim, head for Dawson and temporary dietary relief, and finally, on 8 June, along with two companions, launch a small boat on a voyage of nearly 2,000 miles down the Yukon westward through Alaska to the Bering Sea. At the port town of St Michael's he caught a steamer on which he could shovel coal to earn his passage home.

In August of 1898 the returning adventurer was even more determined to succeed as a writer, and the man-killing effort he devoted to the task makes an absorbing story in its own right—a story he eventually told, with varying omissions and embellishments but with a fundamental emotional honesty, in two autobiographical texts: the novel *Martin Eden* (1909) and the alcoholic memoir *John Barleycorn* (1913). Turning down a chance at steady employment in the post office, he kept himself afloat through odd jobs and frequent trips to the pawnshop while rationing his sleep and spending long hours at his desk. He continued to try his hand at any kind of writing that might sell, persisting in a pattern that would remain with him for life: hack-work, frankly acknowledged as such, to pay the bills; and a more serious craft, driven by what he came to call a 'working philosophy of life'. Fittingly, his first breakthrough came in both modes at once. In December a magazine called *The Black Cat* paid him forty dollars for 'A Thousand Deaths', a horror story in the manner of Edgar Allan Poe; and the *Overland Monthly*, a reputable San Francisco magazine, offered him the munificent sum of five dollars for one of his Northland tales, 'To the Man on Trail'.

The *Overland*, in fact, urged him to send them more; and

when 'To the Man on Trail' was published, in January 1899, it was the first of a series of Northland fictions to appear in its pages in the ensuing months. London soon discovered that the impoverished *Overland* was readier to accept a story than to pay for it, but by then he was finding new outlets. His most significant success came in August, when the *Atlantic Monthly* accepted one of his longest tales, 'An Odyssey of the North', provided that he agree to shorten it by 3,000 words. He grumbled but made the cuts, for he could ill afford to pass up this entrée into the Eastern literary market-place. By November the prestigious Boston firm of Houghton Mifflin had accepted a group of the Northland tales for book publication, and they duly appeared on 7 April 1900 under the title *The Son of the Wolf: Tales of the Far North*. Two more collections and a novel, *A Daughter of the Snows*, quickly followed, and in 1903 his novella *The Call of the Wild* became an instant best-seller and established his enduring reputation as a chronicler of Northland adventure.

Complying with his new publisher's request for a fuller account of his life, London sent Houghton Mifflin a biographical sketch that stressed his lifelong self-construction as a poor boy who had struggled for success against formidable odds. Citing his early life of 'toil' in a 'long sordid list of occupations', he went on to sum up the frustrations he had faced as a would-be writer whose manner of life was unfavourable to literary pursuits: 'I have had no literary help or advice of any kind—just been sort of hammering around in the dark till I knocked holes through here and there and caught glimpses of daylight.' As he often did when describing his early struggles, London was inclined to exaggerate, since in actuality he had enjoyed the companionship and advice of a number of literary friends, especially Cloudesley Johns, a Los Angeles reporter and neophyte fiction writer with whom he carried on an intensive literary correspondence. His letters to Johns, along with the essays he began publishing on the literary market-place and the craft of fiction, can tell us much about the cultural milieu from which his career drew its formative impulses.

Ever since his experience of the ugly realities of prison life in 1894 London had considered himself a socialist, and throughout his life he advanced his strong if unorthodox socialist convictions in numerous essays and public lectures. But what motivated his socialism was not so much a commitment to economic egalitarianism and class struggle as a belief that the escape-route from poverty was open to the superior individual. His socialism thus existed in uneasy tension with an ethic drawn from Social Darwinism—a system of ideas developed especially by the British scientific philosopher Herbert Spencer, whose followers in the United States had become influential because their doctrine of the 'survival of the fittest' seemed to provide a rationale for the excesses of entrepreneurial capitalism. Though hardly an apologist for the Rockefellers and Vanderbilts, London strongly believed that life was a constant struggle against a hostile environment in which only the possessor of an exceptional will and imagination would thrive. Within a few years he was finding confirmation of his views in his reading of the German philosopher Friedrich Nietzsche, whose belief in the moral authority of superior power led to the concept of the overman, or superman. This *mélange* of powerful ideas might not have attained perfect intellectual coherence, but it did constitute a philosophical outlook that seemed true to what the young writer had experienced in the Northland.

Many of these ideas reflected the rising prestige of science, particularly evolutionary biology; and like many of his contemporaries, London was caught up in a belief system that was stimulating a reconceptualization of both the human condition and the nature of literary art. In fiction, the origins of the new movement lay chiefly in France, where in the 1850s and 1860s Gustave Flaubert, author of the controversial *Madame Bovary* (1857), presided over a literary circle that promoted the new credo of objectivity, stylistic precision, and authorial invisibility. By the 1870s Émile Zola, under the influence of the physiologist Claude Bernard, was taking these ideas one step further in a celebrated essay on the 'experimental novel'. According to this new literary 'naturalism', an author should write a novel with the detachment of

a scientist observing and recording the behaviour of laboratory animals. And animals is what Zola's characters typically
were: a collection of hereditary instincts and appetites doomed
to degenerate under the pressure of a sordid and inescapable
environment.

Jack London, who considered himself a rigorously scientific thinker, was influenced by such views but not bound
by them. Like his California contemporary Frank Norris,
he tempered the bleakness of literary naturalism with a considerable dose of romance. By 'romance' he did not mean a
saccharine sentimentality or the knights in shining armour so
prevalent in popular historical fiction. Rather, as he expressed
it in a 1903 essay on Rudyard Kipling, he believed in a
romance that would 'seize upon and press into enduring art-
forms the vital facts of our existence'. Rejecting the realism
of minute detail—what Norris had scornfully dismissed as
the 'drama of a broken teacup'—he insisted on a mode of
fiction in which realism's fidelity to fact ultimately gave way
to the poetic power of myth. Like his later autobiographical
hero Martin Eden, he sought 'an impassioned realism, shot
through with human aspiration and faith'.

For his mature development as a writer, London needed
not only a vision of life but a style and craft of fiction. For
these, as James I. McClintock has shown in an excellent
book on London's short stories, he turned primarily to Spencer and Kipling. Although many stylistic voices can be heard
in London's fiction at one time or another, Herbert Spencer's *Philosophy of Style* (1871) was perfectly positioned to
codify the qualities London sought. For Spencer the naturalistic philosopher, the inevitable metaphor for style was a
'mechanical apparatus'—a 'machine', which for maximum
communicative efficiency should run with the least possible
friction. The watchword was 'economy'—economy of the
writer's words and hence of the reader's mental energies.
This economy was best achieved through an Anglo-Saxon
rather than Latinate vocabulary, direct phrasing, and the dis-
tilling effect of a powerful metaphor.

Such a style had already been put to use by Kipling, best
known for his celebrations of British military and colonial

adventure in *Plain Tales from the Hills* (1888) and *Soldiers Three* (1895). As McClintock points out, many of London's earlier Northland stories followed Kipling's method of beginning with an introductory paragraph of didactic reflection, followed by the narrative as a case in point. Soon London was learning not only from Kipling but also from Joseph Conrad how to achieve a greater aesthetic distance and a more complex dramatic effect by concealing the authorial voice and making use of a narrative frame, in which a story is told by a character whose interactions with his listener(s) serve as a counterpoint to and implied commentary on the central tale. Such artistic self-consciousness was manifested with growing frequency in his letters to Cloudesley Johns. 'Don't you tell the reader', he insisted, but instead 'HAVE YOUR CHARACTERS TELL IT BY THEIR DEEDS, ACTIONS, TALK.' In another letter to Johns he revealed his increasing consciousness of what Henry James and his followers referred to as the *point of view* and which narrative theorists now call *focalization*: the angle and distance from which the reader is permitted to view the action. Illustrating from 'The Law of Life', his own story of an old Indian left to die, he explained how he determined on a suitable narrative method:

How do I approach the event? What point of view do I take? Why, the old Indian's, of course. . . . The reader listens with him to every familiar sound; hears the last draw away; feels the silence settle down. The old man wanders back into his past; the reader wanders with him—thus is the whole theme exploited through the soul of the Indian. . . . Don't you see, nothing, even the moralizing and generalizing, is done, save through him, in expressions of his experience.

The voice we hear in this passage is plainly that of a serious artist. But in these letters the amateur philosopher and professional craftsman alternate with another Jack London—one who virtually boasts of his willingness to turn out hackwork and compromise his artistic integrity to meet the demands of the market-place. In fact, London was fond of proclaiming that he wrote only for money; and although there is ample evidence that his motivation was more complex, it is true that he found an outlet for his writing only after the trial-and-error process of mastering the tastes of the reading public and the editorial preferences of popular magazines. He was fortunate to have begun his career during a golden age of magazine publishing, when such monthlies as *The Atlantic*, *Harper's*, *The Century*, and *McClure's* exerted a powerful influence on American middle-class culture. The *Overland* may have been run on a shoestring but other magazines paid their writers well, and London was proud of his eventual ability to command ten cents a word from the magazines as well as top royalties from his book publishers. Following Mark Twain in his penchant for speculative business ventures, he described himself to one editor as a 'writer who is a business man'—a literary entrepreneur who could outplay the capitalists at their own game.

In a sense, then, London's struggle to become a successful professional writer was only another version of the kind of conflict he had repeatedly encountered in the Northland: a dogged persistence—sometime triumphant, sometimes futile—against a hostile environment and seemingly impossible odds. To put it another way, such conflict implies an initially unequal balance of power, which London's protagonists struggle to redress. In some stories the power-struggle is elemental, a stark contest between one human being and an indifferent or hostile land. When the conflict acquires a more complex human dimension, it then becomes more political, in the sense that the struggle for power in human society is always political in the broadest meaning of the term, whether along the lines of gender or ethnic identity or social class. The Northland provided London with a rich environment in which to record the interplay of all these forces, as his first book, *The Son of the Wolf*, reveals with particular clarity.

The Son of the Wolf offers an early example of a fictional genre which in the twentieth century was to become increasingly prominent, especially among American writers: a sequence of loosely related stories. Less than a novel but more than a miscellaneous collection, this genre exists in a tension between its centripetal sources of unity—continuity of setting, a central theme, and often a recurring protagonist—and its centrifugal diversity. James Joyce's *Dubliners* (1914) is a partial instance, though it lacks a central recurring character. In the United States, the most prominent examples would be Sherwood Anderson's *Winesburg, Ohio* (1919), Ernest Hemingway's *In Our Time* (1925), and William Faulkner's *Go Down, Moses* (1942). In London's collection the Northland itself, whether as passive backdrop or active antagonist, is a continually powerful presence; and seven of the nine tales involve, more or less centrally, an unofficial arbiter of frontier justice in the person of Malemute Kid. Indeed, justice—achieved or denied—is a central concern of this first volume.

All of these ingredients—environment, character, and theme—are present in the fine opening tale, 'The White Silence'. As the story begins, Malemute Kid, accompanied by his old friend Mason and the latter's Indian wife, Ruth, is driving a dog-sled across the frozen land with a six-day supply of food and 200 miles yet to traverse. Here the odds against them are evoked in what is perhaps London's most resonant depiction of the insidiously implacable Northland environment:

Nature has many tricks wherewith she convinces man of his finity, —the ceaseless flow of the tides, the fury of the storm, the shock of the earthquake, the long roll of heaven's artillery,—but the most tremendous, the most stupefying of all, is the passive phase of the White Silence. All movement ceases, the sky clears, the heavens are as brass; the slightest whisper seems sacrilege, and man becomes timid, affrighted at the sound of his own voice. Sole speck of life journeying across the ghostly wastes of a dead world, he trembles at his audacity, realizes that his is a maggot's life, nothing more. Strange thoughts arise unsummoned, and the mystery of all things strives for utterance.

As Earle Labor points out in one of the best books on London's life and writings, this Melvillean passage raises the action to the archetypal level of myth. Just as the White Whale, for Melville's Ishmael, is charged with the 'dumb blankness, full of meaning, in a wide landscape of snows', the White Silence of the North becomes for London the blank page on which 'the mystery of all things strives for utterance'.

But the conflict in this tale is not only between humanity and the environment. It also pits the human characters against each other and sets up a sequence of conflicts within their own hearts and minds. Early in the narrative the Sisyphean labours of the trail are captured in a poignant moment when one of the dogs, weakened by hunger, falls in the traces immediately after drawing the sled to the top of a steep bank, thus causing the entire outfit—dogs, sled, and people—to tumble back to the bottom, where they are forced to begin the climb again. The enraged Mason savagely whips the stricken dog until Malemute Kid intervenes and cuts her out of the traces. Thereafter, if she cannot keep up with the sled, as an act of mercy she will be shot. Hardly has this episode concluded when Mason himself becomes the wounded animal. Grievously injured by a falling tree and unable to travel, he must leave to Malemute Kid the ethical dilemma of whether to remain with him until he dies or to put an end to his agony with a rifle shot.

In these events the oddly peripheral role of the wife signals yet another dimension of the tale: the prominence and intensity of the bond between the two men—a bond that recent theorists of gender and sexualities such as Eve Kosofsky Sedgwick have referred to as 'homosocial desire'. As the mortally injured Mason reminisces about his past, his reflections 'were as Greek to Ruth, but the Kid understood and felt', for two men who have 'shared their bed with death' achieve a communion almost beyond words. Their five years together, the Kid recalls, have 'knitted the bonds of comradeship'. Indeed, so close had they grown that he had 'often been conscious of a vague jealousy of Ruth, from the first time she had come between'. The parting between husband and wife is heartfelt but brief; and as Ruth heads the dogsled down the trail, it is the Kid who attends the dying man in his final hours, waiting with his rifle to grant him the release he has pleaded for—the bullet that constitutes as true an act of love as the figurative 'little death' which, in fantasy or reality, consummates a Renaissance love poem.

The love triangle portrayed in 'The White Silence' gives way in the second tale—the title narrative 'The Son of the

Wolf'—to a more conventional love plot centred on the cultural conflict between the indigenous tribes and the white interlopers. This, then, is the first of many London tales in which relations between men and women become entangled with the politics of race, social class, and contemporary notions of national destiny. In this heyday of Anglo-American imperialism, London did not escape the influence of such chauvinistic slogans as Kipling's celebration of the 'white man's burden' or the transformation of the American doctrine of 'manifest destiny' into a defence of white supremacy. These racist elements in London's fiction cannot be wished away. They were part of the political air he breathed, and they appealed strongly to the psycho-social needs of a young man of questionable birth and impoverished childhood struggling to legitimate himself as a member-in-good-standing of American middle-class culture. Nevertheless, careful reading will often reveal in such narratives a more complex racial and sexual politics.

'The Son of the Wolf' is a case in point. In the central action, an American miner-frontiersman, Scruff Mackenzie, finding himself in need of a wife, proceeds to out-boast, out-wit, and finally out-fight an entire Indian tribe in order to make off with the chief's daughter, who easily succumbs to his magnetic power. But on closer examination this seemingly crude tale of Anglo-Saxon supremacy is found to be hedged with mock-heroic ironies and a more intriguing interplay of cultural perspectives. There is quiet mock-heroic humour in the depiction of Mackenzie 'mapping out a campaign' and musing on an appropriate name-change for his prospective bride, whose Indian name is Zarinska: 'He would possess her, make her his wife, and name her—ah, he would name her Gertrude! Having thus decided, he rolled over on his side and dropped off to sleep, a true son of his all-conquering race.' Soon their courtship display turns openly and almost humorously sexual, as Zarinska-soon-to-become-Gertrude 'took from her sewing-bag a moosehide sheath', then 'drew his great hunting-knife, gazed reverently along the keen edge . . . and shot it into place in its new home'.

This process of undercutting the heroic stature of the

all-conquering white man is given a more telling dimension
when he must argue for his prospective bride before a council of tribal elders. The result is a study in comparative cultural
mythology, as Mackenzie pits his narrative of Anglo-Saxon
destiny against the tribal shaman's transformation of two
of the central myths of Western culture: the Greek myth of
Prometheus and the biblical story of the Fall:

The singing and the dancing ceased, and the Shaman flared up in
rude eloquence. Through the sinuosities of their vast mythology, he
worked cunningly upon the credulity of his people. The case was
strong. Opposing the creative principles as embodied in the Crow
and the Raven, he stigmatized Mackenzie as the Wolf, the fighting
and the destructive principle. Not only was the combat of these
forces spiritual, but men fought, each to his totem. They were
the children of Jelchs, the Raven, the Promethean firebringer;
Mackenzie was the child of the Wolf, or, in other words, the Devil.
For them to bring a truce to this perpetual warfare, to marry their
daughters to the arch-enemy, were treason and blasphemy of the
highest order. No phrase was harsh, nor figure vile, enough in branding Mackenzie as a sneaking interloper and emissary of Satan.

Is Mackenzie an Adam to this primitive Eve—perhaps even
a messiah to this benighted people? Or is he the Satanic
interloper—the principle of destruction? When our hero
invokes as the Kiplingesque 'Law of the Wolf' a standard of
justice ten times harsher than the biblical standard of 'an eye
for an eye' ('*Whoso taketh the life of one Wolf* [that is, white
person], *the forfeit shall ten of his people pay*'), is the tale
promoting Anglo-Saxon supremacy or mocking it? As an
attentive observer of the ethnic politics of the Northland—
and as a careful reader of the early South Seas narratives of
Melville—London was prepared to infuse his story of racial
and sexual conquest with a more balanced sense of cultural
relativity. The central irony is that the Indian shaman is able
to turn Western mythology upside-down and create an alternative myth of the frontier that is credible in its own right
and considerably less flattering to the white American ego.
  As Mackenzie enters the council, the young Indian woman, Zarinska, is stationed a step to his rear: 'her proper
place.' If there is irony in this statement it is difficult to

detect; the focus here is so exclusively on race and the Indian woman so clearly a stock figure that the issue of gender remains muted. In many other tales, however, traditional conceptions of the role of women are openly challenged. Indeed, almost by definition, any woman—native or white—who braves the hardships of the Northland winter while coping with the ways of men is of a mettle more formidable than that of her Southland counterpart. In 'The Priestly Prerogative', for example, it is the deceptively 'slender, girlish' Grace Bentham who has instigated her husband's Northland venture and, while pretending to walk the requisite step behind, actually 'broke trail for him when no one was looking'. Only a 'clever woman' could thus 'fill out the many weak places in an inefficient man, by her own indomitability reinforce his vacillating nature, infuse her ambitious soul into his, and spur him on to great achievements'. When she eventually contemplates leaving her husband for another man, she is dissuaded by a priest on the grounds that the child of her unsanctioned union will some day hear the world 'fling a tender name in his face'. Yet this disappointingly sentimental climax is not the last word, for when the priest encounters the husband, his admiration for Grace leads him to exercise his 'priestly prerogative' by concealing her defection with an unaccustomed lie. Thus, if contemporary readers were to be denied the commingled shock and satisfaction they had experienced when Ibsen's Nora walked out on her husband at the end of *A Doll's House*, they at least could find in Grace Bentham the first of London's many sympathetic—and occasionally complex—representations of the 'New Woman'.

In the remaining tales of *The Son of the Wolf*—and in the other Northland tales selected for this volume—readers will find many changes rung on these themes of conflict and contrast, desire thwarted or fulfilled, justice bestowed or denied. 'In a Far Country', for example, relentlessly chronicles the deterioration of two hapless 'Incapables' who mistakenly imagine themselves equal to the isolation and hardship of a Northland winter. In 'The Men of Forty-Mile' and 'To the Man on Trail', Malemute Kid dispenses crude but unerring justice in tales which, though slight, exhibit the charm of good 'local colour' fiction; and even the tale that is perhaps the weakest of these early efforts, 'The Wife of a King', possesses a certain interest for its depiction, in an awkward social comedy, of an Indian wife's struggle to regain the respect of the white husband who has abandoned her. 'The Wisdom of the Trail' is notable for another portrait of a seemingly fragile woman of unsuspected strength, a quality that deeply impresses Sitka Charley, the Indian trailmaster whose adoption of white values governs his adjudication of the fate of two Indian packers who have broken the law of the trail by consuming more than their share of the dwindling rations. The volume then concludes with one of London's richest fictions, 'An Odyssey of the North', in which the Indian Naass's tale of his pursuit of the white sailor who has stolen his bride rises to the incantatory power of epic poetry, though the heightened romanticism of this quest is rendered credible by a narrative frame that keeps it anchored in the mundane world.

In the later Northland tales the troubled relations between natives and whites remain a dominant concern. London's first-hand knowledge of native culture may have been limited, but Indian perspectives are nevertheless powerfully imagined, not only in 'The Law of Life' but in the bitter ironies and black humour of 'The League of the Old Men' and 'The White Man's Way'. Three other tales—'The Great Interrogation', 'The Story of Jees Uck', and 'The Marriage of Lit-lit'—are noteworthy for their contrasting views of the ethics of the sexual liaisons between a white man and an Indian woman. Though all of these tales contain vestiges of the racial and sexual ideology of the times, each of them also finds ways to call this conventional wisdom into question, and each illustrates London's continuing interest in unconventionally strong women. Also to be found here are narratives of endurance or disaster on the long trail: 'Grit of Women', 'At the Rainbow's End', 'Love of Life', 'Finis', and 'Like Argus of the Ancient Times'. The last of these, written a scant two months before London's death in November 1916, reveals in the death-and-rebirth experience of old John

Tarwater his belated fascination with the psychology of C. G. Jung—especially the theory of the libido as the vital force driving the process of human individuation, and the notion that the unconscious mind is a repository of cultural symbols, or archetypes, of fundamental human experiences.

With the notable exception of 'Like Argus of the Ancient Times', in his later years London wrote less Northland fiction and little that was praiseworthy. The first section of the novel *Burning Daylight* (1910) is set in the North and exhibits some of his former power, though it mainly reworks old materials and themes; and the collection *Smoke Bellew* (1912), a recycling of the Malemute Kid idea in the person of the title character, rarely rises above the level of hack-work. By 1907, in fact, London's preoccupations had changed. His two-year voyage to Hawaii and the South Sea Islands had given him ample new material to exploit, and after his return to California in 1909 he devoted himself largely to the development of his ranch at Glen Ellen, in Sonoma County, north of San Francisco Bay. Here his back-to-the-land impulses and his fascination with scientific agriculture played a role in several of his novels and a few of his short stories; but the experiential force of his Northland excursion, so powerfully generative for the younger writer, was essentially spent. The Northland fiction remains, however, his most enduring legacy—a unique body of work that continues to attract new generations of readers. Even those dimensions of his fiction that so clearly—and at times unflatteringly—mark him as a man of his era simulaneously reveal him as one of its most discerning interpreters. Perhaps the present volume can help to bring this feature of his work more fully to light.

NOTE ON THE TEXT

The text of each tale has been set from a photocopy of the first printing of the first American edition of the book in which it initially appeared. In this I have followed the example Earle Labor, Robert C. Leitz, III, and I. Milo Shepard, editors of *The Complete Short Stories of Jack London* (Stanford, 1993), who point out that the editors of the book collections followed London's own corrected manuscripts, whereas the magazine texts often contained unauthorized alterations based on house styling or editorial taste. In this collection the only deviations from the first-edition texts are the correction of the rare typographical error and the introduction of such British conventions as the elimination of the period after an abbreviated title ('Dr', 'St', etc.) and the substitution of single for double quotation marks. I am grateful to the staff of the Special Collections Department of the Syracuse University Libraries for supplying me with photocopies of those first editions of London texts that were not in my own collection.

First periodical publication for each tale is listed below, along with first book publication for tales collected in volumes other than *The Son of the Wolf*.

'To the Man on Trail'. *Overland Monthly*, 33 (Jan. 1899), 36–40.

'The White Silence'. *Overland Monthly*, 33 (Feb. 1899), 138–42.

'The Son of the Wolf'. *Overland Monthly*, 33 (Apr. 1899), 335–43.

'The Men of Forty-Mile'. *Overland Monthly*, 33 (May 1899), 388, 401–5.

'In a Far Country'. *Overland Monthly*, 33 (June 1899), 540–9.

'The Priestly Prerogative'. *Overland Monthly*, 34 (July 1899), 59–65.

'The Wife of a King'. *Overland Monthly*, 34 (Aug. 1899), 112–19.

'The Wisdom of the Trail'. *Overland Monthly*, 34 (Dec. 1899), 541–4.

'An Odyssey of the North'. *Atlantic Monthly*, 85 (Jan. 1900), 85–100.

'Grit of Women'. *McClure's Magazine*, 15 (Aug. 1900), 324–30. Collected in *The God of His Fathers and Other Stories* (New York: McClure, Phillips, 1900).

'The Great Interrogation'. *Ainslee's Magazine*, 6 (Dec. 1900), 394–402. Collected in *The God of His Fathers*.

'The Law of Life'. *McClure's Magazine*, 16 (Mar. 1901), 435–8. Collected in *Children of the Frost* (New York: Macmillan, 1902).

'At the Rainbow's End'. *Pittsburgh Leader* (24 Mar. 1901), 31. Collected in *The God of His Fathers*.

'The Story of Jees Uck'. *The Smart Set*, 8 (Sept. 1902), 57–70. Collected in *The Faith of Men and Other Stories* (New York: Macmillan, 1904).

'The League of the Old Men'. *Brandur Magazine*, 1 (4 Oct. 1902), 7–11. Collected in *Children of the Frost*.

'The Marriage of Lit-lit'. *Frank Leslie's Popular Monthly*, 56 (Sept. 1903), 461–8. Collected in *The Faith of Men*.

'Love of Life'. *McClure's Magazine*, 26 (Dec. 1905), 144–58; *Blackwood's Magazine*, 178 (Dec. 1905), 765–80. Collected in *Love of Life and Other Stories* (New York: Macmillan, 1907).

'The White Man's Way'. *Sunday Magazine of the New York Tribune* (4 Nov. 1906), 3–4. Collected in *Love of Life*.

'Morganson's Finish'. *Success Magazine*, 10 (May 1907), 311–14, 371–6. Collected as 'Finis' in *The Turtles of Tasman* (New York: Macmillan, 1916).

'Like Argus of the Ancient Times'. *Hearst's Magazine*, 31 (Mar. 1917), 176–8, 214–16. Collected in *The Red One* (New York: Macmillan, 1918).

SELECT BIBLIOGRAPHY

The standard bibliography of writings by and about London, now in need of updating, is *Jack London: A Bibliography* (Georgetown, Calif., 1966; augmented Millwood, NY, 1973), by Hensley C. Woodbridge, John London, and George H. Tweney. Also useful are Dale L. Walker and James E. Sisson, III, *The Fiction of Jack London: A Chronological Bibliography* (El Paso, 1972), and Joan R. Sherman's *Jack London: A Reference Guide* (Boston, 1977). Although no collection of the complete works currently exists, a three-volume edition of *The Complete Short Stories of Jack London* (Stanford, 1993) has been carefully edited by Earle Labor, Robert C. Leitz, III, and I. Milo Shepard. The same editors have produced the three-volume *Letters of Jack London* (Stanford, 1988), an invaluable resource for the London student. Though each has its biases and limitations, the most useful biographies are Richard O'Connor's *Jack London: A Biography* (Boston, 1964), Andrew Sinclair's *Jack: A Biography of Jack London* (New York, 1977), Russ Kingman's *A Pictorial Life of Jack London* (New York, 1979), and Clarice Stasz's *American Dreamers: Charmian and Jack London* (New York, 1988). *The Book of Jack London* (New York, 1921) is a worshipful two-volume life by the novelist's second wife, Charmian Kittredge London, which must be used with great caution but nevertheless contains important information and perspectives, as does *Jack London and His Times* (New York, 1939; repr. Seattle, 1968), by the novelist's daughter Joan London, who intermixes biography, personal recollection, and depiction of her father's milieu from a leftist perspective. Another early study of London's socialist writings is Philip S. Foner's *Jack London: American Rebel* (New York, 1947), and a more recent book on the same topic is Carolyn Johnston's *Jack London—An American Radical?* (Westport, Conn., 1984). Further scholarly resources are Dale L. Walker's *Jack London: No Mentor But Myself* (Port Washington, NY, 1979), a collection of letters, reviews, and essays on writing and writers; and David Mike Hamilton's '*The Tools of My Trade': The Annotated Books in Jack London's Library* (Seattle, 1986).

Though necessarily brief, the best combination of biography and critical interpretation can be found in Earle Labor's *Jack London* (New York, 1974), now available in a revised edition (New York, 1994) written with Jeanne Campbell Reesman. Essential to an understanding of the Northland writings in the context of the early life and career are Franklin Walker, *Jack London and the Klondike* (San Marino, Calif., 1966), and James I. McClintock, *White Logic: Jack London's Short Stories* (Grand Rapids, Mich., 1975). Other critical interpretations of the Northland fictions—mainly the longer ones— can be found in Joan D. Hedrick, *Solitary Comrade: Jack London and His Work* (Chapel Hill, NC, 1982); Charles N. Watson, Jr., *The Novels of Jack London: A Reappraisal* (Madison, Wis., 1983); and James Lundquist, *Jack London: Adventures, Ideas, and Fiction* (New York, 1987). Finally, three new books of importance to the Northland work are Jacqueline Tavernier-Courbin's *The Call of the Wild: A Naturalistic Romance* (New York, 1994), Daniel Dyer's *The Call of the Wild: A Reader's Companion* (Norman, Okla., 1995), and Jonathan Auerbach's *Male Call: Becoming Jack London* (Durham, NC, 1996).

A CHRONOLOGY OF JACK LONDON

1876   Born out of wedlock on 12 January in San Francisco to Flora Wellman, music teacher and spiritualist; father is almost certainly William Henry Chaney, an astrologer and former lawyer and journalist; in September Wellman marries John London, names son John Griffith London.

1878   Londons move to Oakland; John London runs grocery store.

1881   Grocery business fails; Londons move to farm in Alameda.

1882   Londons move to small ranch in San Mateo County, south of San Francisco.

1884   Londons move to small ranch in Livermore Valley east of San Francisco Bay; John London's efforts to raise chickens are unsuccessful.

1886   Londons move back to Oakland; Flora London runs boarding-house; Jack delivers newspapers, works on ice wagon and in bowling alley, begins reading at Oakland Public Library.

1891   Graduates from Cole Grammar School, works in cannery, buys sailboat and begins sailing on Bay; becomes oyster pirate.

1892   Serves as deputy with California Fish Patrol.

1893   Sails for seven months on seal-hunting schooner *Sophia Sutherland* to Japan and Bering Sea; works in jute mill; wins first prize in newspaper contest for story 'Typhoon Off the Coast of Japan'.

1894   Shovels coal in power plant; begins eight-month cross-country tramping journey as member of Kelly's Army (western contingent of Coxey's Army of Unemployed). Arrested for vagrancy near Niagara Falls, New York; serves thirty-day sentence in Erie County Penitentiary.

1895   Attends Oakland High School, contributes stories and articles to school paper; falls in love with Mabel Applegarth.

1896   Drops out of high school; joins Socialist Labor Party, becomes frequent soap-box speaker for socialist cause; crams for entrance exams for University of California at Berkeley, enrolls for Fall semester.

1897   Withdraws from Berkeley after one semester; works on writing; works in Belmont Academy laundry; joins Klondike gold rush, spends six weeks in Dawson City, stakes claim on Henderson Creek.

1898 Spends winter in cabin at confluence of Yukon and Stewart rivers; spends spring in Dawson; sails skiff down Yukon River to Bering Sea, arriving home in August; first Northland tale, 'To the Man on Trail', accepted by *Overland Monthly* in December.

1899 Seven more Northland tales published by *Overland*; 'An Odyssey of the North' accepted by *Atlantic Monthly*; meets Anna Strunsky.

1900 In April marries Bessie Maddern. Publishes *The Son of the Wolf.*

1901 Daughter Joan born in January; unsuccessful Social Democratic candidate for mayor of Oakland; falls in love with Anna Strunsky. Publishes *The God of His Fathers*, Northland tales.

1902 Begins correspondence with George P. Brett of Macmillan Company, editor of most of his subsequent books; moves to nearby Piedmont; lives in East End of London to research *The People of the Abyss*; daughter Becky born in October. Publishes *A Daughter of the Snows*, Northland novel; *The Children of the Frost*, Northland tales; *The Cruise of the Dazzler*, children's adventure novel.

1903 Begins love affair with Charmian Kittredge; separates from his wife and moves back to Oakland. Publishes *The Call of the Wild*, Northland novella; with Anna Strunsky publishes *The Kempton–Wace Letters*, epistolary dialogue on love.

1904 Covers Russo-Japanese War in Korea for Hearst newspapers; Bessie London files for divorce. Publishes *The Faith of Men*, Northland tales; *The Sea-Wolf*, novel.

1905 Buys 130-acre Hill Ranch near Glen Ellen in Sonoma County; makes socialist lecture tour through Midwest and East; in November marries Charmian Kittredge; travels to Jamaica and Cuba. Publishes *War of the Classes*, socialist essays; *The Game*, prize-fight novella; *Tales of the Fish Patrol*, children's adventure stories.

1906 Begins construction of ketch *Snark* for projected seven-year voyage around the world; covers San Francisco earthquake for *Collier's* magazine. Publishes *Moon-Face*, short stories; *White Fang*, Northland novel; *Scorn of Women*, Northland play.

1907 Sails *Snark* from Oakland to Hawaii, Marquesas Islands, and Tahiti. Publishes *Before Adam*, novel of prehistoric life; *Love of Life*, Northland tales; *The Road*, tramp sketches.

1908 Sails *Snark* to Solomon Islands; hospitalized in Sydney, Australia, for treatment of assorted tropical illnesses and double fistula. Publishes *The Iron Heel*, novel of socialist revolution.

1909 Sells *Snark* and takes passage home on freighter, with stops in Ecuador and Panama. Publishes *Martin Eden*, autobiographical novel.

1910 Plans construction of Wolf House; spends three weeks at Carmel artists' colony; daughter Joy born in June, lives only thirty-eight hours; purchases sailboat *Roamer*, cruises on Sacramento and San Joaquin rivers. Publishes *Lost Face*, Northland stories; *Revolution*, socialist essays; *Burning Daylight*, Northland and business novel; *Theft*, play.

1911 Takes wagon trip through northern California and southern Oregon. Publishes *When God Laughs*, short stories; *Adventure*, Solomon Islands novel; *The Cruise of the Snark*, travel sketches; *South Sea Tales*, short stories.

1912 Spends winter in New York; briefly leaves Macmillan for Century Company; takes five-month voyage around Cape Horn on clipper *Dirigo*. Publishes *The House of Pride*, Hawaiian stories; *A Son of the Son*, South Seas tales; *Smoke Bellew*, Northland tales.

1913 Resumes publishing with Macmillan; nearly completed Wolf House destroyed by fire. Publishes *The Night-Born*, short stories; *The Abysmal Brute*, prize-fight novella; *John Barleycorn*, alcoholic memoir.

1914 Covers Mexican Revolution for *Collier's* until forced home by acute dysentery. Publishes *The Strength of the Strong*, short stories; *The Mutiny of the Elsinore*, sea novel.

1915 Spends five month in Hawaii. Publishes *The Scarlet Plague*, novella of return to barbarism; *The Star Rover*, prison novel featuring out-of-body experiences.

1916 Spends six months in Hawaii; resigns from Socialist Party; dies on 22 November; cause of death given as uremia and renal colic, later alleged to have been complicated by (possibly accidental) self-administered overdose of morphine; more recent theories assign cause to stroke and heart failure or complications of lupus. Publishes *The Little Lady of the Big House*, novel; *The Turtles of Tasman*, short stories; *The Acorn-Planter*, play.

1917 Posthumous publication of *Jerry of the Islands*, dog story set mainly in South Seas; *Michael, Brother of Jerry*, sequel.

1918 Posthumous publication of *Hearts of Three*, adventure novel; *The Red One*, short stories.

1919 Posthumous publication of *On the Makaloa Mat*, short stories.

1922 Posthumous publication of *Dutch Courage*, children's adventure tales.

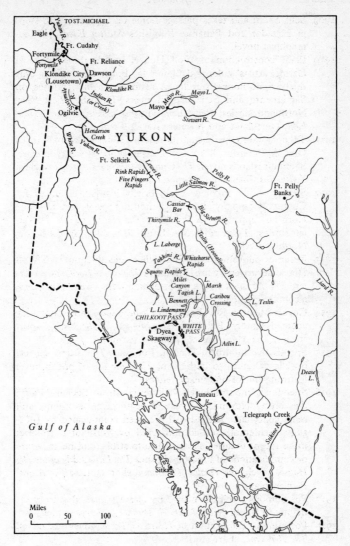

The Klondike

THE SON OF THE WOLF

Tales of the Far North

TO
THE SONS OF THE WOLF
WHO SOUGHT THEIR HERITAGE AND
LEFT THEIR BONES AMONG THE
SHADOWS OF THE
CIRCLE

THE WHITE SILENCE

'Carmen won't last more than a couple of days.' Mason spat out a chunk of ice and surveyed the poor animal ruefully, then put her foot in his mouth and proceeded to bite out the ice which clustered cruelly between the toes.

'I never saw a dog with a highfalutin' name that ever was worth a rap,' he said, as he concluded his task and shoved her aside. 'They just fade away and die under the responsibility. Did ye ever see one go wrong with a sensible name like Cassiar, Siwash, or Husky? No, sir! Take a look at Shookum here, he's'—

Snap! The lean brute flashed up, the white teeth just missing Mason's throat.

'Ye will, will ye?' A shrewd clout behind the ear with the butt of the dogwhip stretched the animal in the snow, quivering softly, a yellow slaver dripping from its fangs.

'As I was saying, just look at Shookum, here—he's got the spirit. Bet ye he eats Carmen before the week's out.'

'I'll bank another proposition against that,' replied Malemute Kid,* reversing the frozen bread placed before the fire to thaw. 'We'll eat Shookum before the trip is over. What d' ye say, Ruth?'

The Indian woman settled the coffee with a piece of ice, glanced from Malemute Kid to her husband, then at the dogs, but vouchsafed no reply. It was such a palpable truism that none was necessary. Two hundred miles of unbroken trail in prospect, with a scant six days' grub for themselves and none for the dogs, could admit no other alternative. The two men and the woman grouped about the fire and began their meagre meal. The dogs lay in their harnesses, for it was a midday halt, and watched each mouthful enviously.

'No more lunches after to-day,' said Malemute Kid. 'And we've got to keep a close eye on the dogs,—they're getting vicious. They'd just as soon pull a fellow down as not, if they get a chance.'

'And I was president of an Epworth* once, and taught in

the Sunday school.' Having irrelevantly delivered himself of
this, Mason fell into a dreamy contemplation of his steaming
moccasins, but was aroused by Ruth filling his cup. 'Thank
God, we've got slathers of tea! I've seen it growing, down in
Tennessee. What wouldn't I give for a hot corn pone just
now! Never mind, Ruth; you won't starve much longer, nor
wear moccasins either.'

The woman threw off her gloom at this, and in her eyes
welled up a great love for her white lord,—the first white
man she had ever seen,—the first man whom she had known
to treat a woman as something better than a mere animal or
beast of burden.

'Yes, Ruth,' continued her husband, having recourse to
the macaronic jargon in which it was alone possible for them
to understand each other; 'wait till we clean up and pull for
the Outside. We'll take the White Man's canoe and go to the
Salt Water. Yes, bad water, rough water,—great mountains
dance up and down all the time. And so big, so far, so far
away,—you travel ten sleep, twenty sleep, forty sleep' (he
graphically enumerated the days on his fingers), 'all the time
water, bad water. Then you come to great village, plenty
people, just the same mosquitoes next summer. Wigwams
oh, so high,—ten, twenty pines. Hi-yu skookum!'*

He paused impotently, cast an appealing glance at Malemute Kid, then laboriously placed the twenty pines, end on
end, by sign language. Malemute Kid smiled with cheery
cynicism; but Ruth's eyes were wide with wonder, and
with pleasure; for she half believed he was joking, and such
condescension pleased her poor woman's heart.

'And then you step into a—a box, and pouf! up you go.'
He tossed his empty cup in the air by way of illustration, and
as he deftly caught it, cried: 'And biff! down you come. Oh,
great medicine-men! You go Fort Yukon, I go Arctic City,*
—twenty-five sleep,—big string, all the time,—I catch him
string,—I say, "Hello, Ruth! How are ye?"—and you say, "Is
that my good husband?"—and I say "Yes,"—and you say,
"No can bake good bread, no more soda,"—then I say, "Look
in cache, under flour; good-by." You look and catch plenty
soda. All the time you Fort Yukon, me Arctic City. Hi-yu
medicine-man!'

Ruth smiled so ingenuously at the fairy story, that both men burst into laughter. A row among the dogs cut short the wonders of the Outside, and by the time the snarling combatants were separated, she had lashed the sleds and all was ready for the trail.

'Mush! Baldy! Hi! Mush on!' Mason worked his whip smartly, and as the dogs whined low in the traces, broke out the sled with the gee-pole.* Ruth followed with the second team, leaving Malemute Kid, who had helped her start, to bring up the rear. Strong man, brute that he was, capable of felling an ox at a blow, he could not bear to beat the poor animals, but humored them as a dog-driver rarely does,—nay, almost wept with them in their misery.

'Come, mush on there, you poor sore-footed brutes!' he murmured, after several ineffectual attempts to start the load. But his patience was at last rewarded, and though whimpering with pain, they hastened to join their fellows.

No more conversation; the toil of the trail will not permit such extravagance. And of all deadening labors, that of the Northland trail is the worst. Happy is the man who can weather a day's travel at the price of silence, and that on a beaten track.

And of all heart-breaking labors, that of breaking trail is the worst. At every step the great webbed shoe sinks till the snow is level with the knee. Then up, straight up, the deviation of a fraction of an inch being a certain precursor of disaster, the snowshoe must be lifted till the surface is cleared; then forward, down, and the other foot is raised perpendicularly for the matter of half a yard. He who tries this for the first time, if haply he avoids bringing his shoes in dangerous propinquity and measures not his length on the treacherous footing, will give up exhausted at the end of a hundred yards; he who can keep out of the way of the dogs for a whole day may well crawl into his sleeping-bag with a clear conscience and a pride which passeth all understanding; and he who travels twenty sleeps on the Long Trail is a man whom the gods may envy.

The afternoon wore on, and with the awe, born of the White Silence, the voiceless travelers bent to their work.

Nature has many tricks wherewith she convinces man of his finity,—the ceaseless flow of the tides, the fury of the storm, the shock of the earthquake, the long roll of heaven's artillery,—but the most tremendous, the most stupefying of all, is the passive phase of the White Silence. All movement ceases, the sky clears, the heavens are as brass; the slightest whisper seems sacrilege, and man becomes timid, affrighted at the sound of his own voice. Sole speck of life journeying across the ghostly wastes of a dead world, he trembles at his audacity, realizes that his is a maggot's life, nothing more. Strange thoughts arise unsummoned, and the mystery of all things strives for utterance. And the fear of death, of God, of the universe, comes over him,—the hope of the Resurrection and the Life, the yearning for immortality, the vain striving of the imprisoned essence,—it is then, if ever, man walks alone with God.

So wore the day away. The river took a great bend, and Mason headed his team for the cut-off across the narrow neck of land. But the dogs balked at the high bank. Again and again, though Ruth and Malemute Kid were shoving on the sled, they slipped back. Then came the concerted effort. The miserable creatures, weak from hunger, exerted their last strength. Up—up—the sled poised on the top of the bank; but the leader swung the string of dogs behind him to the right, fouling Mason's snowshoes. The result was grievous. Mason was whipped off his feet; one of the dogs fell in the traces; and the sled toppled back, dragging everything to the bottom again.

Slash! the whip fell among the dogs savagely, especially upon the one which had fallen.

'Don't, Mason,' entreated Malemute Kid; 'the poor devil's on its last legs. Wait and we'll put my team on.'

Mason deliberately withheld the whip till the last word had fallen, then out flashed the long lash, completely curling about the offending creature's body. Carmen—for it was Carmen—cowered in the snow, cried piteously, then rolled over on her side.

It was a tragic moment, a pitiful incident of the trail,—a dying dog, two comrades in anger. Ruth glanced solicitously from man to man. But Malemute Kid restrained himself, though there was a world of reproach in his eyes, and bending over the dog, cut the traces. No word was spoken. The teams were double-spanned and the difficulty overcome; the sleds were under way again, the dying dog dragging herself along in the rear. As long as an animal can travel, it is not shot, and this last chance is accorded it,—the crawling into camp, if it can, in the hope of a moose being killed.

Already penitent for his angry action, but too stubborn to make amends, Mason toiled on at the head of the cavalcade, little dreaming that danger hovered in the air. The timber clustered thick in the sheltered bottom, and through this they threaded their way. Fifty feet or more from the trail towered a lofty pine. For generations it had stood there, and for generations destiny had had this one end in view,— perhaps the same had been decreed of Mason.

He stooped to fasten the loosened thong of his moccasin. The sleds came to a halt and the dogs lay down in the snow without a whimper. The stillness was weird; not a breath rustled the frost-encrusted forest; the cold and silence of outer space had chilled the heart and smote the trembling lips of nature. A sigh pulsed through the air,—they did not seem to actually hear it, but rather felt it, like the premoni- tion of movement in a motionless void. Then the great tree, burdened with its weight of years and snow, played its last part in the tragedy of life. He heard the warning crash and attempted to spring up, but almost erect, caught the blow squarely on the shoulder.

The sudden danger, the quick death,—how often had Malemute Kid faced it! The pine needles were still quivering as he gave his commands and sprang into action. Nor did the Indian girl faint or raise her voice in idle wailing, as might many of her white sisters. At his order, she threw her weight on the end of a quickly extemporized handspike, easing the pressure and listening to her husband's groans, while Malemute Kid attacked the tree with his axe. The steel rang merrily as it bit into the frozen trunk, each stroke being accompanied by a forced, audible respiration, the 'Huh!' 'Huh!' of the woodsman.

At last the Kid laid the pitiable thing that was once a man in the snow. But worse than his comrade's pain was the dumb anguish in the woman's face, the blended look of hopeful, hopeless query. Little was said; those of the Northland are early taught the futility of words and the inestimable value of deeds. With the temperature at sixty-five below zero, a man cannot lie many minutes in the snow and live. So the sled-lashings were cut, and the sufferer, rolled in furs, laid on a couch of boughs. Before him roared a fire, built of the very wood which wrought the mishap. Behind and partially over him was stretched the primitive fly,—a piece of canvas, which caught the radiating heat and threw it back and down upon him,—a trick which men may know who study physics at the fount.

And men who have shared their bed with death know when the call is sounded. Mason was terribly crushed. The most cursory examination revealed it. His right arm, leg, and back, were broken; his limbs were paralyzed from the hips; and the likelihood of internal injuries was large. An occasional moan was his only sign of life.

No hope; nothing to be done. The pitiless night crept slowly by,—Ruth's portion, the despairing stoicism of her race, and Malemute Kid adding new lines to his face of bronze. In fact, Mason suffered least of all, for he spent his time in Eastern Tennessee, in the Great Smoky Mountains, living over the scenes of his childhood. And most pathetic was the melody of his long-forgotten Southern vernacular, as he raved of swimming-holes and coon-hunts and water-melon raids. It was as Greek to Ruth, but the Kid understood and felt,—felt as only one can feel who has been shut out for years from all that civilization means.

Morning brought consciousness to the stricken man, and Malemute Kid bent closer to catch his whispers.

'You remember when we foregathered on the Tanana, four years come next ice-run? I didn't care so much for her then. It was more like she was pretty, and there was a smack of excitement about it, I think. But d' ye know, I've come to think a heap of her. She's been a good wife to me, always at my shoulder in the pinch. And when it comes to trading, you know there isn't her equal. D' ye recollect the time she shot the Moosehorn Rapids to pull you and me off that rock, the bullets whipping the water like hailstones?—and the time of the famine at Nuklukyeto?*—or when she raced the ice-run to bring the news? Yes, she's been a good wife to me, better 'n that other one. Didn't know I'd been there? Never told you, eh? Well, I tried it once, down in the States. That's why I'm here. Been raised together, too. I came away to give her a chance for divorce. She got it.

'But that's got nothing to do with Ruth. I had thought of cleaning up and pulling for the Outside next year,—her and I,—but it's too late. Don't send her back to her people, Kid. It's beastly hard for a woman to go back. Think of it!—nearly four years on our bacon and beans and flour and dried fruit, and then to go back to her fish and cariboo. It's not good for her to have tried our ways, to come to know they're better 'n her people's, and then return to them. Take care of her, Kid,—why don't you,—but no, you always fought shy of them,—and you never told me why you came to this country. Be kind to her, and send her back to the States as soon as you can. But fix it so as she can come back,—liable to get homesick, you know.

'And the youngster—it's drawn us closer, Kid. I only hope it is a boy. Think of it!—flesh of my flesh, Kid. He mustn't stop in this country. And if it's a girl, why she can't. Sell my furs; they'll fetch at least five thousand, and I've got as much more with the company. And handle my interests with yours. I think that bench claim* will show up. See that he gets a good schooling; and Kid, above all, don't let him come back. This country was not made for white men.

'I'm a gone man, Kid. Three or four sleeps at the best. You've got to go on. You must go on! Remember, it's my wife, it's my boy,—O God! I hope it's a boy! You can't stay by me,—and I charge you, a dying man, to pull on.'

'Give me three days,' pleaded Malemute Kid. 'You may change for the better; something may turn up.'

'No.'

'Just three days.'

'You must pull on.'

'Two days.'

'It's my wife and my boy, Kid. You would not ask it.'

'One day.'

'No, no! I charge'—

'Only one day. We can shave it through on the grub, and I might knock over a moose.'

'No,—all right; one day, but not a minute more. And Kid, don't—don't leave me to face it alone. Just a shot, one pull on the trigger. You understand. Think of it! Think of it! Flesh of my flesh, and I'll never live to see him!

'Send Ruth here. I want to say good-by and tell her that she must think of the boy and not wait till I'm dead. She might refuse to go with you if I didn't. Good-by, old man; good-by.

'Kid! I say—a—sink a hole above the pup, next to the slide. I panned out forty cents on my shovel there.

'And Kid!' he stooped lower to catch the last faint words, the dying man's surrender of his pride. 'I'm sorry—for—you know—Carmen.'

Leaving the girl crying softly over her man, Malemute Kid slipped into his *parka* and snowshoes, tucked his rifle under his arm, and crept away into the forest. He was no tyro in the stern sorrows of the Northland, but never had he faced so stiff a problem as this. In the abstract, it was a plain, mathematical proposition,—three possible lives as against one doomed one. But now he hesitated. For five years, shoulder to shoulder, on the rivers and trails, in the camps and mines, facing death by field and flood and famine, had they knitted the bonds of their comradeship. So close was the tie, that he had often been conscious of a vague jealousy of Ruth, from the first time she had come between. And now it must be severed by his own hand.

Though he prayed for a moose, just one moose, all game seemed to have deserted the land, and nightfall found the exhausted man crawling into camp, light-handed, heavy-hearted. An uproar from the dogs and shrill cries from Ruth hastened him.

Bursting into the camp, he saw the girl in the midst of the snarling pack, laying about her with an axe. The dogs had broken the iron rule of their masters and were rushing the grub. He joined the issue with his rifle reversed, and the hoary game of natural selection* was played out with all the ruthlessness of its primeval environment. Rifle and axe went up and down, hit or missed with monotonous regularity; lithe bodies flashed, with wild eyes and dripping fangs; and man and beast fought for supremacy to the bitterest conclusion. Then the beaten brutes crept to the edge of the firelight, licking their wounds, voicing their misery to the stars.

The whole stock of dried salmon had been devoured, and perhaps five pounds of flour remained to tide them over two hundred miles of wilderness. Ruth returned to her husband, while Malemute Kid cut up the warm body of one of the dogs, the skull of which had been crushed by the axe. Every portion was carefully put away, save the hide and offal, which were cast to his fellows of the moment before.

Morning brought fresh trouble. The animals were turning on each other. Carmen, who still clung to her slender thread of life, was downed by the pack. The lash fell among them unheeded. They cringed and cried under the blows, but refused to scatter till the last wretched bit had disappeared, —bones, hide, hair, everything.

Malemute Kid went about his work, listening to Mason, who was back in Tennessee, delivering tangled discourses and wild exhortations to his brethren of other days.

Taking advantage of neighboring pines, he worked rapidly, and Ruth watched him make a cache similar to those sometimes used by hunters to preserve their meat from the wolverines and dogs. One after the other, he bent the tops of two small pines toward each other and nearly to the ground, making them fast with thongs of moosehide. Then he beat the dogs into submission and harnessed them to two of the sleds, loading the same with everything but the furs which enveloped Mason. These he wrapped and lashed tightly about him, fastening either end of the robes to the bent pines. A single stroke of his hunting-knife would release them and send the body high in the air.

Ruth had received her husband's last wishes and made no struggle. Poor girl, she had learned the lesson of obedience well. From a child, she had bowed, and seen all women bow, to the lords of creation, and it did not seem in the nature of things for woman to resist. The Kid permitted her one outburst of grief, as she kissed her husband,—her own people had no such custom,—then led her to the foremost sled and helped her into her snowshoes. Blindly, instinctively, she took the gee-pole and whip, and 'mushed' the dogs out on the trail. Then he returned to Mason, who had fallen into a coma; and long after she was out of sight, crouched by the fire, waiting, hoping, praying for his comrade to die.

It is not pleasant to be alone with painful thoughts in the White Silence. The silence of gloom is merciful, shrouding one as with protection and breathing a thousand intangible sympathies; but the bright White Silence, clear and cold, under steely skies, is pitiless.

An hour passed,—two hours,—but the man would not die. At high noon, the sun, without raising its rim above the southern horizon, threw a suggestion of fire athwart the heavens, then quickly drew it back. Malemute Kid roused and dragged himself to his comrade's side. He cast one glance about him. The White Silence seemed to sneer, and a great fear came upon him. There was a sharp report; Mason swung into his aerial sepulchre; and Malemute Kid lashed the dogs into a wild gallop as he fled across the snow.

THE SON OF THE WOLF

Man rarely places a proper valuation upon his womankind, at least not until deprived of them. He has no conception of the subtle atmosphere exhaled by the sex feminine so long as he bathes in it; but let it be withdrawn, and an ever-growing void begins to manifest itself in his existence, and he becomes hungry, in a vague sort of way, for a something so indefinite that he cannot characterize it. If his comrades have no more experience than himself, they will shake their heads dubiously and dose him with strong physic. But the hunger will continue and become stronger; he will lose interest in the things of his every-day life and wax morbid; and one day, when the emptiness has become unbearable, a revelation will dawn upon him.

In the Yukon country, when this comes to pass, the man usually provisions a poling-boat, if it be summer, and if winter harnesses his dogs, and heads for the Southland. A few months later, supposing him to be possessed of a faith in the country, he returns with a wife to share with him in that faith, and incidentally in his hardships. This but serves to show the innate selfishness of man. It also brings us to the trouble of 'Scruff' Mackenzie, which occurred in the old days, before the country was stampeded and staked by a tidal-wave of *che-cha-quas*,* and when the Klondike's only claim to notice was its salmon fisheries.

Scruff Mackenzie bore the ear-marks of a frontier birth and a frontier life. His face was stamped with twenty-five years of incessant struggle with nature in her wildest moods,—the last two, the wildest and hardest of all, having been spent in groping for the gold which lies in the shadow of the Arctic Circle. When the yearning sickness came upon him he was not surprised, for he was a practical man and had seen other men thus stricken. But he showed no sign of his malady, save that he worked harder. All summer he fought mosquitoes and washed the sure-thing bars of the Stuart River for a double grub-stake.* Then he floated a raft of house-logs down the Yukon to Forty Mile,* and put together as comfortable a cabin as any the camp could boast of. In fact, it showed such cosy promise that many men elected to be his partner and to come and live with him. But he crushed their aspirations with rough speech, peculiar for its strength and brevity, and bought a double supply of grub from the trading-post.

As has been noted, Scruff Mackenzie was a practical man. If he wanted a thing he usually got it, but in doing so, went no farther out of his way than was necessary. Though a son of toil and hardship, he was averse to a journey of six hundred miles on the ice, a second of two thousand miles on the ocean, and still a third thousand miles or so to his last stamping-grounds,—all in the mere quest of a wife. Life was too short. So he rounded up his dogs, lashed a curious freight to his sled, and faced across the divide whose westward slopes were drained by the head-reaches of the Tanana.

He was a sturdy traveler, and his wolf-dogs could work harder and travel farther on less grub than any other team in the Yukon. Three weeks later he strode into a hunting-camp of the Upper Tanana Sticks.* They marveled at his temerity; for they had a bad name and had been known to kill white men for as trifling a thing as a sharp axe or a broken rifle. But he went among them single-handed, his bearing being a delicious composite of humility, familiarity, *sang-froid*, and insolence. It required a deft hand and deep knowledge of the barbaric mind effectually to handle such diverse weapons; but he was a past master in the art, knowing when to conciliate and when to threaten with Jove-like wrath.

He first made obeisance to the Chief Thling-Tinneh,* presenting him with a couple of pounds of black tea and tobacco, and thereby winning his most cordial regard. Then he mingled with the men and maidens, and that night gave a *potlach*.* The snow was beaten down in the form of an oblong, perhaps a hundred feet in length and quarter as many across. Down the centre a long fire was built, while either side was carpeted with spruce boughs. The lodges were forsaken, and the fivescore or so members of the tribe gave tongue to their folk-chants in honor of their guest.

Scruff Mackenzie's two years had taught him the not many hundred words of their vocabulary, and he had likewise conquered their deep gutturals, their Japanese idioms, constructions, and honorific and agglutinative particles. So he made oration after their manner, satisfying their instinctive poetry-love with crude flights of eloquence and metaphorical contortions. After Thling-Tinneh and the Shaman had responded in kind, he made trifling presents to the menfolk, joined in their singing, and proved an expert in their fifty-two-stick gambling game.

And they smoked his tobacco and were pleased. But among the younger men there was a defiant attitude, a spirit of braggadocio, easily understood by the raw insinuations of the toothless squaws and the giggling of the maidens. They had known few white men, 'Sons of the Wolf,' but from those few they had learned strange lessons.

Nor had Scruff Mackenzie, for all his seeming carelessness, failed to note these phenomena. In truth, rolled in his sleeping-furs, he thought it all over, thought seriously, and emptied many pipes in mapping out a campaign. One maiden only had caught his fancy,—none other than Zarinska, daughter to the chief. In features, form, and poise, answering more nearly to the white man's type of beauty, she was almost an anomaly among her tribal sisters. He would possess her, make her his wife, and name her—ah, he would name her Gertrude! Having thus decided, he rolled over on his side and dropped off to sleep, a true son of his all-conquering race.

It was slow work and a stiff game; but Scruff Mackenzie manœuvred cunningly, with an unconcern which served to puzzle the Sticks. He took great care to impress the men that he was a sure shot and a mighty hunter, and the camp rang with his plaudits when he brought down a moose at six hundred yards. Of a night he visited in Chief Thling-Tinneh's lodge of moose and cariboo skins, talking big and dispensing tobacco with a lavish hand. Nor did he fail to likewise honor the Shaman; for he realized the medicine-man's influence with his people, and was anxious to make of him an ally. But that worthy was high and mighty, refused to be propitiated, and was unerringly marked down as a prospective enemy.

Though no opening presented for an interview with Zarinska, Mackenzie stole many a glance to her, giving fair warning of his intent. And well she knew, yet coquettishly surrounded herself with a ring of women whenever the men were away and he had a chance. But he was in no hurry; besides, he knew she could not help but think of him, and a few days of such thought would only better his suit.

At last, one night, when he deemed the time to be ripe, he abruptly left the chief's smoky dwelling and hastened to a neighboring lodge. As usual, she sat with squaws and maidens about her, all engaged in sewing moccasins and beadwork. They laughed at his entrance, and badinage, which linked Zarinska to him, ran high. But one after the other they were unceremoniously bundled into the outer snow, whence they hurried to spread the tale through all the camp.

His cause was well pleaded, in her tongue, for she did not know his, and at the end of two hours he rose to go.

'So Zarinska will come to the White Man's lodge? Good! I go now to have talk with thy father, for he may not be so minded. And I will give him many tokens; but he must not ask too much. If he say no? Good! Zarinska shall yet come to the White Man's lodge.'

He had already lifted the skin flap to depart, when a low exclamation brought him back to the girl's side. She brought herself to her knees on the bearskin mat, her face aglow with true Eve-light, and shyly unbuckled his heavy belt. He looked down, perplexed, suspicious, his ears alert for the slightest sound without. But her next move disarmed his doubt, and he smiled with pleasure. She took from her sewing-bag a moosehide sheath, brave with bright beadwork, fantastically designed. She drew his great hunting-knife, gazed reverently along the keen edge, half tempted to try it with her thumb, and shot it into place in its new home. Then she slipped the sheath along the belt to its customary resting-place, just above the hip.

For all the world, it was like a scene of olden time,—a lady and her knight. Mackenzie drew her up full height and swept her red lips with his mustache,—the, to her, foreign caress of the Wolf. It was a meeting of the stone age and the steel.

There was a thrill of excitement in the air as Scruff Mackenzie, a bulky bundle under his arm, threw open the flap of Thling-Tinneh's tent. Children were running about in the open, dragging dry wood to the scene of the *potlach*, a babble of women's voices was growing in intensity, the young men were consulting in sullen groups, while from the Shaman's lodge rose the eerie sounds of an incantation.

The chief was alone with his blear-eyed wife, but a glance sufficed to tell Mackenzie that the news was already old. So he plunged at once into the business, shifting the beaded sheath prominently to the fore as advertisement of the betrothal.

'O Thling-Tinneh, mighty chief of the Sticks and the land of the Tanana, ruler of the salmon and the bear, the moose and the cariboo! The White Man is before thee with a great purpose. Many moons has his lodge been empty, and he is lonely. And his heart has eaten itself in silence, and grown hungry for a woman to sit beside him in his lodge, to meet him from the hunt with warm fire and good food. He has heard strange things, the patter of baby moccasins and the sound of children's voices. And one night a vision came upon him, and he beheld the Raven, who is thy father, the great Raven, who is the father of all the Sticks. And the Raven spake to the lonely White Man, saying: "Bind thou thy moccasins upon thee, and gird thy snowshoes on, and lash thy sled with food for many sleeps and fine tokens for the Chief Thling-Tinneh. For thou shalt turn thy face to where the midspring sun is wont to sink below the land, and journey to this great chief's hunting-grounds. There thou shalt make big presents, and Thling-Tinneh, who is my son, shall become to thee as a father. In his lodge there is a maiden into whom I breathed the breath of life for thee. This maiden shalt thou take to wife."

'O Chief, thus spake the great Raven; thus do I lay many presents at thy feet; thus am I come to take thy daughter!'

The old man drew his furs about him with crude

consciousness of royalty, but delayed reply while a youngster crept in, delivered a quick message to appear before
the council, and was gone.

'O White Man, whom we have named Moose-Killer, also
known as the Wolf, and the Son of the Wolf! We know thou
comest of a mighty race; we are proud to have thee our
potlach-guest; but the king-salmon does not mate with the
dog-salmon, nor the Raven with the Wolf.'

'Not so!' cried Mackenzie. 'The daughters of the Raven
have I met in the camps of the Wolf,—the squaw of Mortimer,
the squaw of Tregidgo, the squaw of Barnaby, who came
two ice-runs back, and I have heard of other squaws, though
my eyes beheld them not.'

'Son, your words are true; but it were evil mating, like the
water with the sand, like the snowflake with the sun. But met
you one Mason and his squaw? No? He came ten ice-runs
ago,—the first of all the Wolves. And with him there was a
mighty man, straight as a willow-shoot, and tall; strong as
the bald-faced grizzly, with a heart like the full summer moon;
his'—

'Oh!' interrupted Mackenzie, recognizing the well-known
Northland figure,—'Malemute Kid!'

'The same,—a mighty man. But saw you aught of the
squaw? She was full sister to Zarinska.'

'Nay, Chief; but I have heard. Mason—far, far to the north,
a spruce-tree, heavy with years, crushed out his life beneath.
But his love was great, and he had much gold. With this,
and her boy, she journeyed countless sleeps toward the winter's noonday sun, and there she yet lives,—no biting frost,
no snow, no summer's midnight sun, no winter's noonday
night.'

A second messenger interrupted with imperative summons
from the council. As Mackenzie threw him into the snow, he
caught a glimpse of the swaying forms before the council-
fire, heard the deep basses of the men in rhythmic chant,
and knew the Shaman was fanning the anger of his people.
Time pressed. He turned upon the chief.

'Come! I wish thy child. And now. See! here are tobacco,
tea, many cups of sugar, warm blankets, handkerchiefs, both

good and large; and here, a true rifle, with many bullets and much powder.'

'Nay,' replied the old man, struggling against the great wealth spread before him. 'Even now are my people come together. They will not have this marriage.'

'But thou art chief.'

'Yet do my young men rage because the Wolves have taken their maidens so that they may not marry.'

'Listen, O Thling-Tinneh! Ere the night has passed into the day, the Wolf shall face his dogs to the Mountains of the East and fare forth to the Country of the Yukon. And Zarinska shall break trail for his dogs.'

'And ere the night has gained its middle, my young men may fling to the dogs the flesh of the Wolf, and his bones be scattered in the snow till the springtime lay them bare.'

It was threat and counter-threat. Mackenzie's bronzed face flushed darkly. He raised his voice. The old squaw, who till now had sat an impassive spectator, made to creep by him for the door. The song of the men broke suddenly, and there was a hubbub of many voices as he whirled the old woman roughly to her couch of skins.

'Again I cry—listen, O Thling-Tinneh! The Wolf dies with teeth fast-locked, and with him there shall sleep ten of thy strongest men,—men who are needed, for the hunting is but begun, and the fishing is not many moons away. And again, of what profit should I die? I know the custom of thy people; thy share of my wealth shall be very small. Grant me thy child, and it shall all be thine. And yet again, my brothers will come, and they are many, and their maws are never filled; and the daughters of the Raven shall bear children in the lodges of the Wolf. My people are greater than thy people. It is destiny. Grant, and all this wealth is thine.'

Moccasins were crunching the snow without. Mackenzie threw his rifle to cock, and loosened the twin Colts in his belt.

'Grant, O Chief!'

'And yet will my people say no.'

'Grant, and the wealth is thine. Then shall I deal with thy people after.'

'The Wolf will have it so. I will take his tokens,—but I would warn him.'

Mackenzie passed over the goods, taking care to clog the rifle's ejector, and capping the bargain with a kaleidoscopic silk kerchief. The Shaman and half a dozen young braves entered, but he shouldered boldly among them and passed out.

'Pack!' was his laconic greeting to Zarinska as he passed her lodge and hurried to harness his dogs. A few minutes later he swept into the council at the head of the team, the woman by his side. He took his place at the upper end of the oblong, by the side of the chief. To his left, a step to the rear, he stationed Zarinska,—her proper place. Besides, the time was ripe for mischief, and there was need to guard his back.

On either side, the men crouched to the fire, their voices lifted in a folk-chant out of the forgotten past. Full of strange, halting cadences and haunting recurrences, it was not beautiful. 'Fearful' may inadequately express it. At the lower end, under the eye of the Shaman, danced half a score of women. Stern were his reproofs to those who did not wholly abandon themselves to the ecstasy of the rite. Half hidden in their heavy masses of raven hair, all disheveled and falling to their waists, they slowly swayed to and fro, their forms rippling to an ever-changing rhythm.

It was a weird scene; an anachronism. To the south, the nineteenth century was reeling off the few years of its last decade; here flourished man primeval, a shade removed from the prehistoric cave-dweller, a forgotten fragment of the Elder World. The tawny wolf-dogs sat between their skin-clad masters or fought for room, the firelight cast backward from their red eyes and slavered fangs. The woods, in ghostly shroud, slept on unheeding. The White Silence, for the moment driven to the rimming forest, seemed ever crushing inward; the stars danced with great leaps, as is their wont in the time of the Great Cold; while the Spirits of the Pole trailed their robes of glory athwart the heavens.

Scruff Mackenzie dimly realized the wild grandeur of the setting as his eyes ranged down the fur-fringed sides in quest of missing faces. They rested for a moment on a newborn babe, suckling at its mother's naked breast. It was forty below,—seventy and odd degrees of frost. He thought of the tender women of his own race, and smiled grimly. Yet from the loins of some such tender woman had he sprung with a kingly inheritance,—an inheritance which gave to him and his dominance over the land and sea, over the animals and the peoples of all the zones. Single-handed against fivescore, girt by the Arctic winter, far from his own, he felt the prompting of his heritage, the desire to possess, the wild danger-love, the thrill of battle, the power to conquer or to die.

The singing and the dancing ceased, and the Shaman flared up in rude eloquence. Through the sinuosities of their vast mythology, he worked cunningly upon the credulity of his people. The case was strong. Opposing the creative principles as embodied in the Crow and the Raven, he stigmatized Mackenzie as the Wolf, the fighting and the destructive principle. Not only was the combat of these forces spiritual, but men fought, each to his totem. They were the children of Jelchs, the Raven, the Promethean fire-bringer;* Mackenzie was the child of the Wolf, or, in other words, the Devil. For them to bring a truce to this perpetual warfare, to marry their daughters to the arch-enemy, were treason and blasphemy of the highest order. No phrase was harsh, nor figure vile, enough in branding Mackenzie as a sneaking interloper and emissary of Satan. There was a subdued, savage roar in the deep chests of his listeners as he took the swing of his peroration.

'Ay, my brothers, Jelchs is all-powerful! Did he not bring heaven-born fire that we might be warm? Did he not draw the sun, moon, and stars from their holes that we might see? Did he not teach us that we might fight the Spirits of Famine and of Frost? But now Jelchs is angry with his children, and they are grown to a handful, and he will not help. For they have forgotten him, and done evil things, and trod bad trails, and taken his enemies into their lodges to sit by their fires. And the Raven is sorrowful at the wickedness of his children; but when they shall rise up and show they have come back, he will come out of the darkness to aid them. O brothers! the

Fire-Bringer has whispered messages to thy Shaman; the same shall ye hear. Let the young men take the young women to their lodges; let them fly at the throat of the Wolf; let them be undying in their enmity! Then shall their women become fruitful, and they shall multiply into a mighty people! And the Raven shall lead great tribes of their fathers and their fathers' fathers from out of the North; and they shall beat back the Wolves till they are as last year's camp-fires; and they shall again come to rule over all the land! 'Tis the message of Jelchs, the Raven.'

This foreshadowing of the Messiah's coming brought a hoarse howl from the Sticks as they leaped to their feet. Mackenzie slipped the thumbs of his mittens, and waited. There was a clamor for the Fox, not to be stilled till one of the young men stepped forward to speak.

'Brothers! The Shaman has spoken wisely. The Wolves have taken our women, and our men are childless. We are grown to a handful. The Wolves have taken our warm furs, and given for them evil spirits which dwell in bottles, and clothes which come not from the beaver or the lynx, but are made from the grass. And they are not warm, and our men die of strange sicknesses. I, the Fox, have taken no woman to wife; and why? Twice have the maidens which pleased me gone to the camps of the Wolf. Even now have I laid by skins of the beaver, of the moose, of the cariboo, that I might win favor in the eyes of Thling-Tinneh, that I might marry Zarinska, his daughter. Even now are her snowshoes bound to her feet, ready to break trail for the dogs of the Wolf. Nor do I speak for myself alone. As I have done, so has the Bear. He, too, had fain been the father of her children, and many skins has he cured thereto. I speak for all the young men who know not wives. The Wolves are ever hungry. Always do they take the choice meat at the killing. To the Ravens are left the leavings.

'There is Gugkla!' he cried, brutally pointing out one of the women, who was a cripple. 'Her legs are bent like the ribs of a birch canoe. She cannot gather wood nor carry the meat of the hunters. Did the Wolves choose her?'

'Ai! ai!' vociferated his tribesmen.

'There is Moyri, whose eyes are crossed by the Evil Spirit. Even the babes are affrighted when they gaze upon her, and it is said the bald-face* gives her the trail. Was she chosen?'

Again the cruel applause rang out.

'And there sits Pischet. She does not hearken to my words. Never has she heard the cry of the chit-chat, the voice of her husband, the babble of her child. She lives in the White Silence. Cared the Wolves aught for her? No! Theirs is the choice of the kill; ours is the leavings.

'Brothers, it shall not be! No more shall the Wolves slink among our camp-fires. The time is come.'

A great streamer of fire, the aurora borealis, purple, green, and yellow, shot across the zenith, bridging horizon to horizon. With head thrown back and arms extended, he swayed to his climax.

'Behold! The spirits of our fathers have arisen and great deeds are afoot this night!'

He stepped back, and another young man somewhat diffidently came forward, pushed on by his comrades. He towered a full head above them, his broad chest defiantly bared to the frost. He swung tentatively from one foot to the other. Words halted upon his tongue, and he was ill at ease. His face was horrible to look upon, for it had at one time been half torn away by some terrific blow, At last he struck his breast with his clenched fist, drawing sound as from a drum, and his voice rumbled forth as the surf from an ocean cavern.

'I am the Bear,—the Silver-Tip and the Son of the Silver-Tip! When my voice was yet as a girl's, I slew the lynx, the moose, and the cariboo; when it whistled like the wolverines from under a cache, I crossed the Mountains of the South and slew three of the White Rivers; when it became as the roar of the Chinook,* I met the bald-faced grizzly, but gave no trail.'

At this he paused, his hand significantly sweeping across his hideous scars.

'I am not as the Fox. My tongue is frozen like the river. I cannot make great talk. My words are few. The Fox says great deeds are afoot this night. Good! Talk flows from his tongue like the freshets of the spring, but he is chary of deeds. This night shall I do battle with the Wolf. I shall slay him, and Zarinska shall sit by my fire. The Bear has spoken.'

Though pandemonium raged about him, Scruff Mackenzie held his ground. Aware how useless was the rifle at close quarters, he slipped both holsters to the fore, ready for action, and drew his mittens till his hands were barely shielded by the elbow gauntlets. He knew there was no hope in attack *en masse*, but true to his boast, was prepared to die with teeth fast-locked. But the Bear restrained his comrades, beating back the more impetuous with his terrible fist. As the tumult began to die away, Mackenzie shot a glance in the direction of Zarinska. It was a superb picture. She was leaning forward on her snowshoes, lips apart and nostrils quivering, like a tigress about to spring. Her great black eyes were fixed upon her tribesmen, in fear and in defiance. So extreme the tension, she had forgotten to breathe. With one hand pressed spasmodically against her breast and the other as tightly gripped about the dogwhip, she was as turned to stone. Even as he looked, relief came to her. Her muscles loosened; with a heavy sigh she settled back, giving him a look of more than love.

Thling-Tinneh was trying to speak, but his people drowned his voice. Then Mackenzie strode forward. The Fox opened mouth to a piercing yell, but so savagely did Mackenzie whirl upon him that he shrank back, his larynx all a-gurgle with suppressed sound. His discomfiture was greeted with roars of laughter, and served to soothe his fellows to a listening mood.

'Brothers! The White Man, whom ye have chosen to call the Wolf, came among you with fair words. He was not like the Innuit;* he spoke not lies. He came as a friend, as one who would be a brother. But your men have had their say, and the time for soft words is past. First, I will tell you that the Shaman has an evil tongue and is a false prophet, that the messages he spake are not those of the Fire-Bringer. His ears are locked to the voice of the Raven, and out of his own head he weaves cunning fancies, and he has made fools of you. He has no power. When the dogs were killed and eaten, and your stomachs were heavy with untanned hide and strips of moccasins; when the old men died, and the old women died, and the babes at the dry dugs of the mothers died; when the land was dark, and ye perished as do the salmon in the fall; ay, when the famine was upon you, did the Shaman bring reward to your hunters? did the Shaman put meat in your bellies? Again I say, the Shaman is without power. Thus! I spit upon his face!'

Though taken aback by the sacrilege, there was no uproar. Some of the women were even frightened, but among the men there was an uplifting, as though in preparation or anticipation of the miracle. All eyes were turned upon the two central figures. The priest realized the crucial moment, felt his power tottering, opened his mouth in denunciation, but fled backward before the truculent advance, upraised fist, and flashing eyes of Mackenzie. He sneered and resumed.

'Was I stricken dead? Did the lightning burn me? Did the stars fall from the sky and crush me? Pish! I have done with the dog. Now will I tell you of my people, who are the mightiest of all the peoples, who rule in all the lands. At first we hunt as I hunt, alone. After that we hunt in packs; and at last, like the cariboo-run, we sweep across all the land. Those whom we take into our lodges live; those who will not come die. Zarinska is a comely maiden, full and strong, fit to become the mother of Wolves. Though I die, such shall she become; for my brothers are many, and they will follow the scent of my dogs. Listen to the Law of the Wolf: *Whoso taketh the life of one Wolf, the forfeit shall ten of his people pay.* In many lands has the price been paid; in many lands shall it yet be paid.

'Now will I deal with the Fox and the Bear. It seems they have cast eyes upon the maiden. So? Behold, I have bought her! Thling-Tinneh leans upon the rifle; the goods of purchase are by his fire. Yet will I be fair to the young men. To the Fox, whose tongue is dry with many words, will I give of tobacco five long plugs. Thus will his mouth be wetted that he may make much noise in the council. But to the Bear, of whom I am well proud, will I give of blankets two; of flour, twenty cups; of tobacco, double that of the Fox; and if he fare with me over the Mountains of the East, then will I give him a rifle, mate to Thling-Tinneh's. If not? Good! The Wolf is weary of speech. Yet once again will he say the Law: *Whoso taketh the life of one Wolf, the forfeit shall ten of his people pay.*'

Mackenzie smiled as he stepped back to his old position, but at heart he was full of trouble. The night was yet dark. The girl came to his side, and he listened closely as she told of the Bear's battle-tricks with the knife.

The decision was for war. In a trice, scores of moccasins were widening the space of beaten snow by the fire. There was much chatter about the seeming defeat to the Shaman; some averred he had but withheld his power, while others conned past events and agreed with the Wolf. The Bear came to the centre of the battle-ground, a long naked hunting-knife of Russian make in his hand. The Fox called attention to Mackenzie's revolvers; so he stripped his belt, buckling it about Zarinska, into whose hands he also intrusted his rifle. She shook her head that she could not shoot,—small chance had a woman to handle such precious things.

'Then, if danger come by my back, cry aloud, "My husband!" No; thus, "My husband!"'

He laughed as she repeated it, pinched her cheek, and reëntered the circle. Not only in reach and stature had the Bear the advantage of him, but his blade was longer by a good two inches. Scruff Mackenzie had looked into the eyes of men before, and he knew it was a man who stood against him; yet he quickened to the glint of light on the steel, to the dominant pulse of his race.

Time and again he was forced to the edge of the fire or the deep snow, and time and again, with the foot tactics of the pugilist, he worked back to the centre. Not a voice was lifted in encouragement, while his antagonist was heartened with applause, suggestions, and warnings. But his teeth only shut the tighter as the knives clashed together, and he thrust or eluded with a coolness born of conscious strength. At first he felt compassion for his enemy; but this fled before the primal instinct of life, which in turn gave way to the lust of slaughter. The ten thousand years of culture fell from him,* and he was a cave-dweller, doing battle for his female.

Twice he pricked the Bear, getting away unscathed; but the third time caught, and to save himself, free hands closed on fighting hands, and they came together. Then did he realize the tremendous strength of his opponent. His muscles were knotted in painful lumps, and cords and tendons threatened to snap with the strain; yet nearer and nearer came the Russian steel. He tried to break away, but only weakened himself. The fur-clad circle closed in, certain of and anxious to see the final stroke. But with wrestler's trick, swinging partly to the side, he struck at his adversary with his head. Involuntarily the Bear leaned back, disturbing his centre of gravity. Simultaneous with this, Mackenzie tripped properly and threw his whole weight forward, hurling him clear through the circle into the deep snow. The Bear floundered out and came back full tilt.

'O my husband!' Zarinska's voice rang out, vibrant with danger.

To the twang of a bow-string, Mackenzie swept low to the ground, and a bone-barbed arrow passed over him into the breast of the Bear, whose momentum carried him over his crouching foe. The next instant Mackenzie was up and about. The Bear lay motionless, but across the fire was the Shaman, drawing a second arrow.

Mackenzie's knife leaped short in the air. He caught the heavy blade by the point. There was a flash of light as it spanned the fire. Then the Shaman, the hilt alone appearing without his throat, swayed a moment and pitched forward into the glowing embers.

Click! click!—the Fox had possessed himself of Thling-Tinneh's rifle and was vainly trying to throw a shell into place. But he dropped it at the sound of Mackenzie's laughter.

'So the Fox has not learned the way of the plaything? He is yet a woman. Come! Bring it, that I may show thee!'

The Fox hesitated.

'Come, I say!'

He slouched forward like a beaten cur.

'Thus, and thus; so the thing is done.' A shell flew into place and the trigger was at cock as Mackenzie brought it to shoulder.

'The Fox has said great deeds were afoot this night, and he spoke true. There have been great deeds, yet least among them were those of the Fox. Is he still intent to take Zarinska to his lodge? Is he minded to tread the trail already broken by the Shaman and the Bear? No? Good!'

Mackenzie turned contemptuously and drew his knife from the priest's throat.

'Are any of the young men so minded? If so, the Wolf will take them by two and three till none are left. No? Good! Thling-Tinneh, I now give thee this rifle a second time. If in the days to come thou shouldst journey to the Country of the Yukon, know thou that there shall always be a place and much food by the fire of the Wolf. The night is now passing into the day. I go, but I may come again. And for the last time, remember the Law of the Wolf!'

He was supernatural in their sight as he rejoined Zarinska. She took her place at the head of the team, and the dogs swung into motion. A few moments later they were swallowed up by the ghostly forest. Till now Mackenzie had waited; he slipped into his snowshoes to follow.

'Has the Wolf forgotten the five long plugs?'

Mackenzie turned upon the Fox angrily; then the humor of it struck him.

'I will give thee one short plug.'

'As the Wolf sees fit,' meekly responded the Fox, stretching out his hand.

THE MEN OF FORTY-MILE

When Big Jim Belden ventured the apparently innocuous proposition that mush-ice was 'rather pecooliar,' he little dreamed of what it would lead to. Neither did Lon McFane, when he affirmed that anchor-ice was even more so; nor did Bettles, as he instantly disagreed, declaring the very existence of such a form to be a bugaboo.

'An' ye'd be tellin' me this,' cried Lon, 'after the years ye've spint in the land! An' we atin' out the same pot this many's the day!'

'But the thing's agin reason,' insisted Bettles. 'Look you, water's warmer than ice'—

'An' little the difference, once ye break through.'

'Still it's warmer, because it ain't froze. An' you say it freezes on the bottom?'

'Only the anchor-ice, David, only the anchor-ice. An' have ye niver drifted along, the water clear as glass, whin suddin, belike a cloud over the sun, the mushy ice comes bubblin' up an' up, till from bank to bank an' bind to bind it's drapin' the river like a first snowfall?'

'Unh hunh! more'n once when I took a doze at the steering-oar. But it allus come out the nighest side-channel, an' not bubblin' up an' up.'

'But with niver a wink at the helm?'

'No; nor you. It's agin reason. I'll leave it to any man!'

Bettles appealed to the circle about the stove, but the fight was on between himself and Lon McFane.

'Reason or no reason, it's the truth I'm tellin' ye. Last fall, a year gone, 'twas Sitka Charley* and meself saw the sight, droppin' down the riffle ye'll remember below Fort Reliance.* An' regular fall weather it was,—the glint o' the sun on the golden larch an' the quakin' aspens; an' the glister of light on ivery ripple; an' beyond, the winter an' the blue haze of the North comin' down hand in hand. It's well ye know the same, with a fringe to the river an' the ice formin' thick in the eddies,—an' a snap an' sparkle to the air, an' ye a-feelin' it through all yer blood, a-takin' new lease of life with ivery suck of it. 'Tis then, me boy, the world grows small an' the wandther-lust lays ye by the heels.

'But it's meself as wandthers. As I was sayin', we a-paddlin', with niver a sign of ice, barrin' that by the eddies, when the Injin lifts his paddle an' sings out, "Lon McFane! Look ye below! So have I heard, but niver thought to see!" As ye know, Sitka Charley, like meself, niver drew first breath in the land; so the sight was new. Then we drifted, with a head over ayther side, peerin' down through the sparkly water. For the world like the days I spint with the pearlers, watchin' the coral banks a-growin' the same as so many gardens under the sea. There it was, the anchor-ice, clingin' an' clusterin' to ivery rock, after the manner of the white coral.

'But the best of the sight was to come. Just after clearin' the tail of the riffle, the water turns quick the color of milk, an' the top of it in wee circles, as when the graylin' rise in the spring or there's a splatter of wet from the sky. 'Twas the anchor-ice comin' up. To the right, to the lift, as far as iver a man cud see, the water was covered with the same. An' like so much porridge it was, slickin' along the bark of the canoe, stickin' like glue to the paddles. It's many's the time I shot the selfsame riffle before, and it's many's the time after, but niver a wink of the same have I seen. 'Twas the sight of a lifetime.'

'Do tell!' dryly commented Bettles. 'D' ye think I'd b'lieve such a yarn? I'd ruther say the glister of light'd gone to your eyes, and the snap of the air to your tongue.'

''Twas me own eyes that beheld it, an' if Sitka Charley was here, he'd be the lad to back me.'

'But facts is facts, an' they ain't no gittin' round 'em. It ain't in the nature of things for the water furtherest away from the air to freeze first.'

'But me own eyes'—

'Don't git het up over it,' admonished Bettles, as the quick Celtic anger began to mount.

'Then yer not after belavin' me?'

'Sence you're so blamed forehanded about it, no; I'd b'lieve nature first, and facts.'

'Is it the lie ye'd be givin' me?' threatened Lon. 'Ye'd better be askin' that Siwash* wife of yours. I'll lave it to her, for the truth I spake.'

Bettles flared up in sudden wrath. The Irishman had unwittingly wounded him; for his wife was the half-breed daughter of a Russian fur-trader, married to him in the Greek Mission of Nulato, a thousand miles or so down the Yukon, thus being of much higher caste than the common Siwash, or native, wife. It was a mere Northland nuance, which none but the Northland adventurer may understand.

'I reckon you kin take it that way,' was his deliberate affirmation.

The next instant Lon McFane had stretched him on the floor, the circle was broken up, and half a dozen men had stepped between.

Bettles came to his feet, wiping the blood from his mouth. 'It hain't new, this takin' and payin' of blows, and don't you never think but that this will be squared.'

'An' niver in me life did I take the lie from mortal man,' was the retort courteous. 'An' it's an avil day I'll not be to hand, waitin' an' willin' to help ye lift yer debts, barrin' no manner of way.'

'Still got that 38–55?'

Lon nodded.

'But you'd better git a more likely calibre. Mine'll rip holes through you the size of walnuts.'

'Niver fear; it's me own slugs smell their way with soft noses, an' they'll spread like flapjacks against the coming out beyand. An' when'll I have the pleasure of waitin' on ye? The water-hole's a strikin' locality.'

''Tain't bad. Jest be there in an hour, and you won't set long on my coming.'

Both men mittened and left the Post, their ears closed to the remonstrances of their comrades. It was such a little thing; yet with such men, little things, nourished by quick tempers and stubborn natures, soon blossomed into big things. Besides, the art of burning to bed-rock* still lay in the womb of the future, and the men of Forty-Mile, shut in by the long Arctic winter, grew high-stomached with over-eating and enforced idleness, and became as irritable as do the bees in the fall of the year when the hives are overstocked with honey.

There was no law in the land. The Mounted Police was also a thing of the future. Each man measured an offense and meted out the punishment in as much as it affected himself. Rarely had combined action been necessary, and never in all the dreary history of the camp had the eighth article of the Decalogue* been violated.

Big Jim Belden called an impromptu meeting. Scruff Mackenzie was placed as temporary chairman, and a messenger dispatched to solicit Father Roubeau's good offices. Their position was paradoxical, and they knew it. By the right of might could they interfere to prevent the duel; yet such action, while in direct line with their wishes, went counter to their opinions. While their rough-hewn, obsolete ethics recognized the individual prerogative of wiping out blow with blow, they could not bear to think of two good comrades, such as Bettles and McFane, meeting in deadly battle. Deeming the man who would not fight on provocation a dastard, when brought to the test it seemed wrong that he should fight.

But a scurry of moccasins and loud cries, rounded off with a pistol-shot, interrupted the discussion. Then the storm-doors opened and Malemute Kid entered, a smoking Colt's in his hand and a merry light in his eye.

'I got him.' He replaced the empty shell, and added, 'Your dog, Scruff.'

'Yellow Fang?' Mackenzie asked.

'No; the lop-eared one.'

'The devil! Nothing the matter with him.'

'Come out and take a look.'

'That's all right, after all. Guess he's got 'em, too. Yellow Fang came back this morning and took a chunk out of him, and came near to making a widower of me. Made a rush for Zarinska, but she whisked her skirts in his face and escaped with the loss of the same and a good roll in the snow. Then he took to the woods again. Hope he don't come back. Lost any yourself?'

'One—the best one of the pack—Shookum. Started amuck this morning, but didn't get very far. Ran foul of Sitka

Charley's team, and they scattered him all over the street. And now two of them are loose and raging mad; so you see he got his work in. The dog census will be small in the spring if we don't do something.'

'And the man census, too.'

'How's that? Who's in trouble now?'

'Oh, Bettles and Lon McFane had an argument, and they'll be down by the water-hole in a few minutes to settle it.'

The incident was repeated for his benefit, and Malemute Kid, accustomed to an obedience which his fellow men never failed to render, took charge of the affair. His quickly formulated plan was explained, and they promised to follow his lead implicitly.

'So you see,' he concluded, 'we do not actually take away their privilege of fighting; and yet I don't believe they'll fight when they see the beauty of the scheme. Life's a game, and men the gamblers. They'll stake their whole pile on the one chance in a thousand. Take away that one chance, and— they won't play.'

He turned to the man in charge of the Post. 'Storekeeper, weigh out three fathoms of your best half-inch manila.'

'We'll establish a precedent which will last the men of Forty-Mile to the end of time,' he prophesied. Then he coiled the rope about his arm and led his followers out of doors, just in time to meet the principals.

'What danged right'd he to fetch my wife in?' thundered Bettles to the soothing overtures of a friend. ''Twa'n't called for,' he concluded decisively. ''Twa'n't called for,' he reiterated again and again, pacing up and down and waiting for Lon McFane.

And Lon McFane—his face was hot and tongue rapid as he flaunted insurrection in the face of the Church. 'Then, father,' he cried, 'it's with an aisy heart I'll roll in me flamy blankets, the broad of me back on a bed of coals. Niver shall it be said Lon McFane took a lie 'twixt the teeth without iver liftin' a hand! An' I'll not ask a blessin'. The years have been wild, but it's the heart was in the right place.'

'But it's not the heart, Lon,' interposed Father Roubeau; 'it's pride that bids you forth to slay your fellow man.'

'Yer Frinch,' Lon replied. And then, turning to leave him, 'An' will ye say a mass if the luck is against me?'

But the priest smiled, thrust his moccasined feet to the fore, and went out upon the white breast of the silent river. A packed trail, the width of a sixteen-inch sled, led out to the water-hole. On either side lay the deep, soft snow. The men trod in single file, without conversation; and the black-stoled priest in their midst gave to the function the solemn aspect of a funeral. It was a warm winter's day for Forty-Mile,—a day in which the sky, filled with heaviness, drew closer to the earth, and the mercury sought the unwonted level of twenty below. But there was no cheer in the warmth. There was little air in the upper strata, and the clouds hung motionless, giving sullen promise of an early snowfall. And the earth, unresponsive, made no preparation, content in its hibernation.

When the water-hole was reached, Bettles, having evidently reviewed the quarrel during the silent walk, burst out in a final ''Twa'n't called for,' while Lon McFane kept grim silence. Indignation so choked him that he could not speak.

Yet deep down, whenever their own wrongs were not uppermost, both men wondered at their comrades. They had expected opposition, and this tacit acquiescence hurt them. It seemed more was due them from the men they had been so close with, and they felt a vague sense of wrong, rebelling at the thought of so many of their brothers coming out, as on a gala occasion, without one word of protest, to see them shoot each other down. It appeared their worth had diminished in the eyes of the community. The proceedings puzzled them.

'Back to back, David. An' will it be fifty paces to the man, or double the quantity?'

'Fifty,' was the sanguinary reply, grunted out, yet sharply cut.

But the new manila, not prominently displayed but casually coiled about Malemute Kid's arm, caught the quick eye of the Irishman and thrilled him with a suspicious fear.

'An' what are ye doin' with the rope?'

'Hurry up!' Malemute Kid glanced at his watch. 'I've a

batch of bread in the cabin, and I don't want it to fall. Besides, my feet are getting cold.'

The rest of the men manifested their impatience in various suggestive ways.

'But the rope, Kid? It's bran' new, an' sure yer bread's not that heavy it needs raisin' with the like of that?'

Bettles by this time had faced around. Father Roubeau, the humor of the situation just dawning on him, hid a smile behind his mittened hand.

'No, Lon; this rope was made for a man.' Malemute Kid could be very impressive on occasion.

'What man?' Bettles was becoming aware of a personal interest.

'The other man.'

'An' which is the one ye'd mane by that?'

'Listen, Lon,—and you, too, Bettles! We've been talking this little trouble of yours over, and we've come to one conclusion. We know we have no right to stop your fighting'—

'True for ye, me lad!'

'And we're not going to. But this much we can do, and shall do,—make this the only duel in the history of Forty-Mile, set an example for every *che-cha-qua* that comes up or down the Yukon. The man who escapes killing shall be hanged to the nearest tree. Now, go ahead!'

Lon smiled dubiously, then his face lighted up. 'Pace her off, David,—fifty paces, wheel, an' niver a cease firin' till a lad's down for good. 'Tis their hearts'll niver let them do the deed, an' it's well ye should know it for a true Yankee bluff.'

He started off with a pleased grin on his face, but Malemute Kid halted him.

'Lon! It's a long while since you first knew me?'

'Many's the day.'

'And you, Bettles?'

'Five year next June high water.'

'And have you once, in all that time, known me to break my word? Or heard of me breaking it?'

Both men shook their heads, striving to fathom what lay beyond.

'Well, then, what do you think of a promise made by me?'

'As good as your bond,' from Bettles.

'The thing to safely sling yer hopes of heaven by,' promptly indorsed Lon McFane.

'Listen! I, Malemute Kid, give you my word—and you know what that means—that the man who is not shot stretches rope within ten minutes after the shooting.' He stepped back as Pilate might have done after washing his hands.*

A pause and a silence came over the men of Forty-Mile. The sky drew still closer, sending down a crystal flight of frost,—little geometric designs, perfect, evanescent as a breath, yet destined to exist till the returning sun had covered half its northern journey. Both men had led forlorn hopes in their time,—led, with a curse or a jest on their tongues, and in their souls an unswerving faith in the God of Chance. But that merciful deity had been shut out from the present deal. They studied the face of Malemute Kid, but they studied as one might the Sphinx. As the quiet minutes passed, a feeling that speech was incumbent on them began to grow. At last the howl of a wolf-dog cracked the silence from the direction of Forty-Mile. The weird sound swelled with all the pathos of a breaking heart, then died away in a long-drawn sob.

'Well I be danged!' Bettles turned up the collar of his mackinaw jacket and stared about him helplessly.

'It's a gloryus game yer runnin', Kid,' cried Lon McFane. 'All the percentage to the house an' niver a bit to the man that's buckin'. The Devil himself 'd niver tackle such a cinch—and damned if I do.'

There were chuckles, throttled in gurgling throats, and winks brushed away with the frost which rimed the eye-lashes, as the men climbed the ice-notched bank and started across the street to the Post. But the long howl had drawn nearer, invested with a new note of menace. A woman screamed round the corner. There was a cry of, 'Here he comes!' Then an Indian boy, at the head of half a dozen frightened dogs, racing with death, dashed into the crowd. And behind came Yellow Fang, a bristle of hair and a flash of gray. Everybody but the Yankee fled. The Indian boy had tripped and fallen. Bettles stopped long enough to grip him by the slack of his furs, then headed for a pile of cordwood already occupied by a number of his comrades. Yellow Fang, doubling after one of the dogs, came leaping back. The fleeing animal, free of the rabies but crazed with fright, whipped Bettles off his feet and flashed on up the street. Malemute Kid took a flying shot at Yellow Fang. The mad dog whirled a half airspring, came down on his back, then, with a single leap, covered half the distance between himself and Bettles.

But the fatal spring was intercepted. Lon McFane leaped from the woodpile, countering him in midair. Over they rolled, Lon holding him by the throat at arm's length, blinking under the fetid slaver which sprayed his face. Then Bettles, revolver in hand and coolly waiting a chance, settled the combat.

"Twas a square game, Kid,' Lon remarked, rising to his feet and shaking the snow from out his sleeves; 'with a fair percentage to meself that bucked it.'

That night, while Lon McFane sought the forgiving arms of the Church in the direction of Father Roubeau's cabin, Malemute Kid and Scruff Mackenzie talked long to little purpose.

'But would you,' persisted Mackenzie, 'supposing they had fought?'

'Have I ever broken my word?'

'No; but that isn't the point. Answer the question. Would you?'

Malemute Kid straightened up. 'Scruff, I've been asking myself that question ever since, and'—

'Well?'

'Well, as yet, I haven't found the answer.'

IN A FAR COUNTRY

When a man journeys into a far country, he must be prepared to forget many of the things he has learned, and to acquire such customs as are inherent with existence in the new land; he must abandon the old ideals and the old gods, and oftentimes he must reverse the very codes by which his conduct has hitherto been shaped. To those who have the protean faculty of adaptability, the novelty of such change may even be a source of pleasure; but to those who happen to be hardened to the ruts in which they were created, the pressure of the altered environment is unbearable, and they chafe in body and in spirit under the new restrictions which they do not understand. This chafing is bound to act and react, producing divers evils and leading to various misfortunes. It were better for the man who cannot fit himself to the new groove to return to his own country; if he delay too long, he will surely die.

The man who turns his back upon the comforts of an elder civilization, to face the savage youth, the primordial simplicity of the North, may estimate success at an inverse ratio to the quantity and quality of his hopelessly fixed habits. He will soon discover, if he be a fit candidate, that the material habits are the less important. The exchange of such things as a dainty menu for rough fare, of the stiff leather shoe for the soft, shapeless moccasin, of the feather bed for a couch in the snow, is after all a very easy matter. But his pinch will come in learning properly to shape his mind's attitude toward all things, and especially toward his fellow man. For the courtesies of ordinary life, he must substitute unselfishness, forbearance, and tolerance. Thus, and thus only, can he gain that pearl of great price,—true comradeship. He must not say 'Thank you;' he must mean it without opening his mouth, and prove it by responding in kind. In short, he must substitute the deed for the word, the spirit for the letter.

When the world rang with the tale of Arctic gold, and the

lure of the North gripped the heartstrings of men, Carter
Weatherbee threw up his snug clerkship, turned the half of
his savings over to his wife, and with the remainder bought
an outfit. There was no romance in his nature,—the bondage of commerce had crushed all that; he was simply tired
of the ceaseless grind, and wished to risk great hazards in
view of corresponding returns. Like many another fool, dis-
daining the old trails used by the Northland pioneers for a
score of years, he hurried to Edmonton* in the spring of the
year; and there, unluckily for his soul's welfare, he allied
himself with a party of men.

There was nothing unusual about this party, except its
plans. Even its goal, like that of all other parties, was the
Klondike. But the route it had mapped out to attain that
goal took away the breath of the hardiest native, born and
bred to the vicissitudes of the Northwest. Even Jacques
Baptiste, born of a Chippewa woman and a renegade *voyageur*
(having raised his first whimpers in a deerskin lodge north of
the sixty-fifth parallel, and had the same hushed by blissful
sucks of raw tallow), was surprised. Though he sold his
services to them and agreed to travel even to the never-
opening ice, he shook his head ominously whenever his advice
was asked.

Percy Cuthfert's evil star must have been in the ascendant,
for he, too, joined this company of argonauts. He was an
ordinary man, with a bank account as deep as his culture,
which is saying a good deal. He had no reason to embark on
such a venture,—no reason in the world, save that he suffered from an abnormal development of sentimentality. He
mistook this for the true spirit of romance and adventure.
Many another man has done the like, and made as fatal a
mistake.

The first break-up of spring found the party following the
ice-run of Elk River. It was an imposing fleet, for the outfit
was large, and they were accompanied by a disreputable
contingent of half-breed *voyageurs* with their women and
children. Day in and day out, they labored with the bateaux
and canoes, fought mosquitoes and other kindred pests, or
sweated and swore at the portages. Severe toil like this lays

a man naked to the very roots of his soul, and ere Lake Athabasca* was lost in the south, each member of the party had hoisted his true colors.

The two shirks and chronic grumblers were Carter Weatherbee and Percy Cuthfert. The whole party complained less of its aches and pains than did either of them. Not once did they volunteer for the thousand and one petty duties of the camp. A bucket of water to be brought, an extra armful of wood to be chopped, the dishes to be washed and wiped, a search to be made through the outfit for some suddenly indispensable article,—and these two effete scions of civilization discovered sprains or blisters requiring instant attention. They were the first to turn in at night, with a score of tasks yet undone; the last to turn out in the morning, when the start should be in readiness before the breakfast was begun. They were the first to fall to at meal-time, the last to have a hand in the cooking; the first to dive for a slim delicacy, the last to discover they had added to their own another man's share. If they toiled at the oars, they slyly cut the water at each stroke and allowed the boat's momentum to float up the blade. They thought nobody noticed; but their comrades swore under their breaths and grew to hate them, while Jacques Baptiste sneered openly and damned them from morning till night. But Jacques Baptiste was no gentleman.

At the Great Slave, Hudson Bay dogs were purchased, and the fleet sank to the guards with its added burden of dried fish and pemmican.* Then canoe and bateau answered to the swift current of the Mackenzie, and they plunged into the Great Barren Ground. Every likely-looking 'feeder' was prospected, but the elusive 'pay-dirt' danced ever to the north. At the Great Bear,* overcome by the common dread of the Unknown Lands, their *voyageurs* began to desert, and Fort of Good Hope saw the last and bravest bending to the tow-lines as they bucked the current down which they had so treacherously glided. Jacques Baptiste alone remained. Had he not sworn to travel even to the never-opening ice?

The lying charts, compiled in main from hearsay, were now constantly consulted. And they felt the need of hurry, for the sun had already passed its northern solstice and was leading the winter south again. Skirting the shores of the bay, where the Mackenzie disembogues into the Arctic Ocean, they entered the mouth of the Little Peel River. Then began the arduous up-stream toil, and the two Incapables fared worse than ever. Tow-line and pole, paddle and tump-line, rapids and portages,—such tortures served to give the one a deep disgust for great hazards, and printed for the other a fiery text on the true romance of adventure. One day they waxed mutinous, and being vilely cursed by Jacques Baptiste, turned, as worms sometimes will. But the half-breed thrashed the twain, and sent them, bruised and bleeding, about their work. It was the first time either had been man-handled.

Abandoning their river craft at the headwaters of the Little Peel, they consumed the rest of the summer in the great portage over the Mackenzie watershed to the West Rat. This little stream fed the Porcupine, which in turn joined the Yukon where that mighty highway of the North countermarches on the Arctic Circle. But they had lost in the race with winter, and one day they tied their rafts to the thick eddy-ice and hurried their goods ashore. That night the river jammed and broke several times; the following morning it had fallen asleep for good.

'We can't be more 'n four hundred miles from the Yukon,' concluded Sloper,* multiplying his thumb nails by the scale of the map. The council, in which the two Incapables had whined to excellent disadvantage, was drawing to a close.

'Hudson Bay Post, long time ago. No use um now.' Jacques Baptiste's father had made the trip for the Fur Company in the old days, incidentally marking the trail with a couple of frozen toes.

'Sufferin' cracky!' cried another of the party. 'No whites?'

'Nary white,' Sloper sententiously affirmed; 'but it's only five hundred more up the Yukon to Dawson. Call it a rough thousand from here.'

Weatherbee and Cuthfert groaned in chorus.

'How long'll that take, Baptiste?'

The half-breed figured for a moment. 'Workum like hell, no man play out, ten—twenty—forty—fifty days. Um babies come' (designating the Incapables), 'no can tell. Mebbe when hell freeze over; mebbe not then.'

The manufacture of snowshoes and moccasins ceased. Somebody called the name of an absent member, who came out of an ancient cabin at the edge of the camp-fire and joined them. The cabin was one of the many mysteries which lurk in the vast recesses of the North. Built when and by whom, no man could tell. Two graves in the open, piled high with stones, perhaps contained the secret of those early wanderers. But whose hand had piled the stones?

The moment had come. Jacques Baptiste paused in the fitting of a harness and pinned the struggling dog in the snow. The cook made mute protest for delay, threw a handful of bacon into a noisy pot of beans, then came to attention. Sloper rose to his feet. His body was a ludicrous contrast to the healthy physiques of the Incapables. Yellow and weak, fleeing from a South American fever-hole, he had not broken his flight across the zones, and was still able to toil with men. His weight was probably ninety pounds, with the heavy hunting-knife thrown in, and his grizzled hair told of a prime which had ceased to be. The fresh young muscles of either Weatherbee or Cuthfert were equal to ten times the endeavor of his; yet he could walk them into the earth in a day's journey. And all this day he had whipped his stronger comrades into venturing a thousand miles of the stiffest hardship man can conceive. He was the incarnation of the unrest of his race, and the old Teutonic stubbornness, dashed with the quick grasp and action of the Yankee, held the flesh in the bondage of the spirit.

'All those in favor of going on with the dogs as soon as the ice sets, say ay.'

'Ay!' rang out eight voices,—voices destined to string a trail of oaths along many a hundred miles of pain.

'Contrary minded?'

'No!' For the first time the Incapables were united without some compromise of personal interests.

'And what are you going to do about it?' Weatherbee added belligerently.

'Majority rule! Majority rule!' clamored the rest of the party.

'I know the expedition is liable to fall through if you don't come,' Sloper replied sweetly; 'but I guess, if we try real hard, we can manage to do without you. What do you say, boys?'

The sentiment was cheered to the echo.

'But I say, you know,' Cuthfert ventured apprehensively; 'what's a chap like me to do?'

'Ain't you coming with us?'

'No-o.'

'Then do as you damn well please. We won't have nothing to say.'

'Kind o' calkilate yuh might settle it with that canoodlin' pardner of yourn,' suggested a heavy-going Westerner from the Dakotas, at the same time pointing out Weatherbee. 'He'll be shore to ask yuh what yur a-goin' to do when it comes to cookin' an' gatherin' the wood.'

'Then we'll consider it all arranged,' concluded Sloper. 'We'll pull out to-morrow, if we camp within five miles,— just to get everything in running order and remember if we've forgotten anything.'

The sleds groaned by on their steel-shod runners, and the dogs strained low in the harnesses in which they were born to die. Jacques Baptiste paused by the side of Sloper to get a last glimpse of the cabin. The smoke curled up pathetically from the Yukon stovepipe. The two Incapables were watching them from the doorway.

Sloper laid his hand on the other's shoulder.

'Jacques Baptiste, did you ever hear of the Kilkenny cats?'*

The half-breed shook his head.

'Well, my friend and good comrade, the Kilkenny cats fought till neither hide, nor hair, nor yowl, was left. You understand?—till nothing was left. Very good. Now, these two men don't like work. They won't work. We know that. They'll be all alone in that cabin all winter,—a mighty long, dark winter. Kilkenny cats,—well?'

The Frenchman in Baptiste shrugged his shoulders, but the Indian in him was silent. Nevertheless, it was an eloquent shrug, pregnant with prophecy.

* * *

Things prospered in the little cabin at first. The rough badinage of their comrades had made Weatherbee and Cuthfert
conscious of the mutual responsibility which had devolved
upon them; besides, there was not so much work after all for
two healthy men. And the removal of the cruel whip-hand,
or in other words the bulldozing half-breed, had brought
with it a joyous reaction. At first, each strove to outdo the
other, and they performed petty tasks with an unction which
would have opened the eyes of their comrades who were
now wearing out bodies and souls on the Long Trail.

All care was banished. The forest, which shouldered in
upon them from three sides, was an inexhaustible woodyard.
A few yards from their door slept the Porcupine, and a hole
through its winter robe formed a bubbling spring of water,
crystal clear and painfully cold. But they soon grew to find
fault with even that. The hole would persist in freezing up,
and thus gave them many a miserable hour of ice-chopping.
The unknown builders of the cabin had extended the side-
logs so as to support a cache at the rear. In this was stored
the bulk of the party's provisions. Food there was, without
stint, for three times the men who were fated to live upon it.
But the most of it was of the kind which built up brawn and
sinew, but did not tickle the palate. True, there was sugar in
plenty for two ordinary men; but these two were little else
than children. They early discovered the virtues of hot water
judiciously saturated with sugar, and they prodigally swam
their flapjacks and soaked their crusts in the rich, white syr-
up. Then coffee and tea, and especially the dried fruits, made
disastrous inroads upon it. The first words they had were
over the sugar question. And it is a really serious thing when
two men, wholly dependent upon each other for company,
begin to quarrel.

Weatherbee loved to discourse blatantly on politics, while
Cuthfert, who had been prone to clip his coupons* and
let the commonwealth jog on as best it might, either ignored
the subject or delivered himself of startling epigrams. But
the clerk was too obtuse to appreciate the clever shaping of
thought, and this waste of ammunition irritated Cuthfert.
He had been used to blinding people by his brilliancy, and

it worked him quite a hardship, this loss of an audience. He felt personally aggrieved and unconsciously held his mutton-head companion responsible for it.

Save existence, they had nothing in common,—came in touch on no single point. Weatherbee was a clerk who had known naught but clerking all his life; Cuthfert was a master of arts, a dabbler in oils, and had written not a little. The one was a lower-class man who considered himself a gentleman, and the other was a gentleman who knew himself to be such. From this it may be remarked that a man can be a gentleman without possessing the first instinct of true comradeship. The clerk was as sensuous as the other was æsthetic, and his love adventures, told at great length and chiefly coined from his imagination, affected the supersensitive master of arts in the same way as so many whiffs of sewer gas. He deemed the clerk a filthy, uncultured brute, whose place was in the muck with the swine, and told him so; and he was reciprocally informed that he was a milk-and-water sissy and a cad. Weatherbee could not have defined 'cad' for his life; but it satisfied its purpose, which after all seems the main point in life.

Weatherbee flatted every third note and sang such songs as 'The Boston Burglar' and 'The Handsome Cabin Boy,' for hours at a time, while Cuthfert wept with rage, till he could stand it no longer and fled into the outer cold. But there was no escape. The intense frost could not be endured for long at a time, and the little cabin crowded them—beds, stove, table, and all—into a space of ten by twelve. The very presence of either became a personal affront to the other, and they lapsed into sullen silences which increased in length and strength as the days went by. Occasionally, the flash of an eye or the curl of a lip got the better of them, though they strove to wholly ignore each other during these mute periods. And a great wonder sprang up in the breast of each, as to how God had ever come to create the other.

With little to do, time became an intolerable burden to them. This naturally made them still lazier. They sank into a physical lethargy which there was no escaping, and which made them rebel at the performance of the smallest chore.

One morning when it was his turn to cook the common breakfast, Weatherbee rolled out of his blankets, and to the snoring of his companion, lighted first the slush-lamp* and then the fire. The kettles were frozen hard, and there was no water in the cabin with which to wash. But he did not mind that. Waiting for it to thaw, he sliced the bacon and plunged into the hateful task of bread-making. Cuthfert had been slyly watching through his half-closed lids. Consequently there was a scene, in which they fervently blessed each other, and agreed, thenceforth, that each do his own cooking. A week later, Cuthfert neglected his morning ablutions, but none the less complacently ate the meal which he had cooked. Weatherbee grinned. After that the foolish custom of washing passed out of their lives.

As the sugar-pile and other little luxuries dwindled, they began to be afraid they were not getting their proper shares, and in order that they might not be robbed, they fell to gorging themselves. The luxuries suffered in this gluttonous contest, as did also the men. In the absence of fresh vegetables and exercise, their blood became impoverished, and a loathsome, purplish rash crept over their bodies. Yet they refused to heed the warning. Next, their muscles and joints began to swell, the flesh turning black, while their mouths, gums, and lips took on the color of rich cream. Instead of being drawn together by their misery, each gloated over the other's symptoms as the scurvy took its course.

They lost all regard for personal appearance, and for that matter, common decency. The cabin became a pigpen, and never once were the beds made or fresh pine boughs laid underneath. Yet they could not keep to their blankets, as they would have wished; for the frost was inexorable, and the fire box consumed much fuel. The hair of their heads and faces grew long and shaggy, while their garments would have disgusted a ragpicker. But they did not care. They were sick, and there was no one to see; besides, it was very painful to move about.

To all this was added a new trouble,—the Fear of the North. This Fear was the joint child of the Great Cold and the Great Silence, and was born in the darkness of December, when the sun dipped below the southern horizon for good. It affected them according to their natures. Weatherbee fell prey to the grosser superstitions, and did his best to resurrect the spirits which slept in the forgotten graves. It was a fascinating thing, and in his dreams they came to him from out of the cold, and snuggled into his blankets, and told him of their toils and troubles ere they died. He shrank away from the clammy contact as they drew closer and twined their frozen limbs about him, and when they whispered in his ear of things to come, the cabin rang with his frightened shrieks. Cuthfert did not understand,—for they no longer spoke,—and when thus awakened he invariably grabbed for his revolver. Then he would sit up in bed, shivering nervously, with the weapon trained on the unconscious dreamer. Cuthfert deemed the man going mad, and so came to fear for his life.

His own malady assumed a less concrete form. The mysterious artisan who had laid the cabin, log by log, had pegged a wind-vane to the ridge-pole. Cuthfert noticed it always pointed south, and one day, irritated by its steadfastness of purpose, he turned it toward the east. He watched eagerly, but never a breath came by to disturb it. Then he turned the vane to the north, swearing never again to touch it till the wind did blow. But the air frightened him with its unearthly calm, and he often rose in the middle of the night to see if the vane had veered,—ten degrees would have satisfied him. But no, it poised above him as unchangeable as fate. His imagination ran riot, till it became to him a fetich. Sometimes he followed the path it pointed across the dismal dominions, and allowed his soul to become saturated with the Fear. He dwelt upon the unseen and the unknown till the burden of eternity appeared to be crushing him. Everything in the Northland had that crushing effect,—the absence of life and motion; the darkness; the infinite peace of the brooding land; the ghastly silence, which made the echo of each heart-beat a sacrilege; the solemn forest which seemed to guard an awful, inexpressible something, which neither word nor thought could compass.

The world he had so recently left, with its busy nations

and great enterprises, seemed very far away. Recollections occasionally obtruded,—recollections of marts and galleries and crowded thoroughfares, of evening dress and social functions, of good men and dear women he had known,—but they were dim memories of a life he had lived long centuries agone, on some other planet. This phantasm was the Reality. Standing beneath the wind-vane, his eyes fixed on the polar skies, he could not bring himself to realize that the Southland really existed, that at that very moment it was a-roar with life and action. There was no Southland, no men being born of women, no giving and taking in marriage. Beyond his bleak sky-line there stretched vast solitudes, and beyond these still vaster solitudes. There were no lands of sunshine, heavy with the perfume of flowers. Such things were only old dreams of paradise. The sunlands of the West and the spicelands of the East, the smiling Arcadias and blissful Islands of the Blest,—ha! ha! His laughter split the void and shocked him with its unwonted sound. There was no sun. This was the Universe, dead and cold and dark, and he its only citizen. Weatherbee? At such moments Weatherbee did not count. He was a Caliban,* a monstrous phantom, fettered to him for untold ages, the penalty of some forgotten crime.

He lived with Death among the dead, emasculated by the sense of his own insignificance, crushed by the passive mastery of the slumbering ages. The magnitude of all things appalled him. Everything partook of the superlative save himself,—the perfect cessation of wind and motion, the immensity of the snow-covered wilderness, the height of the sky and the depth of the silence. That wind-vane,—if it would only move. If a thunderbolt would fall, or the forest flare up in flame. The rolling up of the heavens as a scroll, the crash of Doom—anything, anything! But no, nothing moved; the Silence crowded in, and the Fear of the North laid icy fingers on his heart.

Once, like another Crusoe,* by the edge of the river he came upon a track,—the faint tracery of a snowshoe rabbit on the delicate snow-crust. It was a revelation. There was life in the Northland. He would follow it, look upon it, gloat over it. He forgot his swollen muscles, plunging through the deep snow in an ecstasy of anticipation. The forest swallowed him up, and the brief midday twilight vanished; but he pursued his quest till exhausted nature asserted itself and laid him helpless in the snow. There he groaned and cursed his folly, and knew the track to be the fancy of his brain; and late that night he dragged himself into the cabin on hands and knees, his cheeks frozen and a strange numbness about his feet. Weatherbee grinned malevolently, but made no offer to help him. He thrust needles into his toes and thawed them out by the stove. A week later mortification set in.

But the clerk had his own troubles. The dead men came out of their graves more frequently now, and rarely left him, waking or sleeping. He grew to wait and dread their coming, never passing the twin cairns without a shudder. One night they came to him in his sleep and led him forth to an appointed task. Frightened into inarticulate horror, he awoke between the heaps of stones and fled wildly to the cabin. But he had lain there for some time, for his feet and cheeks were also frozen.

Sometimes he became frantic at their insistent presence, and danced about the cabin, cutting the empty air with an axe, and smashing everything within reach. During these ghostly encounters, Cuthfert huddled into his blankets and followed the madman about with a cocked revolver, ready to shoot him if he came too near. But, recovering from one of these spells, the clerk noticed the weapon trained upon him. His suspicions were aroused, and thenceforth he, too, lived in fear of his life. They watched each other closely after that, and faced about in startled fright whenever either passed behind the other's back. This apprehensiveness became a mania which controlled them even in their sleep. Through mutual fear they tacitly let the slush-lamp burn all night, and saw to a plentiful supply of bacon-grease before retiring. The slightest movement on the part of one was sufficient to arouse the other, and many a still watch their gazes countered as they shook beneath their blankets with fingers on the trigger-guards.

What with the Fear of the North, the mental strain, and the ravages of the disease, they lost all semblance of humanity, taking on the appearance of wild beasts, hunted and desperate. Their cheeks and noses, as an aftermath of the freezing, had turned black. Their frozen toes had begun to drop away at the first and second joints. Every movement brought pain, but the fire box was insatiable, wringing a ransom of torture from their miserable bodies. Day in, day out, it demanded its food,—a veritable pound of flesh,—and they dragged themselves into the forest to chop wood on their knees. Once, crawling thus in search of dry sticks, unknown to each other they entered a thicket from opposite sides. Suddenly, without warning, two peering death's-heads confronted each other. Suffering had so transformed them that recognition was impossible. They sprang to their feet, shrieking with terror, and dashed away on their mangled stumps; and falling at the cabin door, they clawed and scratched like demons till they discovered their mistake.

Occasionally they lapsed normal, and during one of these sane intervals, the chief bone of contention, the sugar, had been divided equally between them. They guarded their separate sacks, stored up in the cache, with jealous eyes; for there were but a few cupfuls left, and they were totally devoid of faith in each other. But one day Cuthfert made a mistake. Hardly able to move, sick with pain, with his head swimming and eyes blinded, he crept into the cache, sugar canister in hand, and mistook Weatherbee's sack for his own.

January had been born but a few days when this occurred. The sun had some time since passed its lowest southern declination, and at meridian now threw flaunting streaks of yellow light upon the northern sky. On the day following his mistake with the sugar-bag, Cuthfert found himself feeling better, both in body and in spirit. As noontime drew near and the day brightened, he dragged himself outside to feast on the evanescent glow, which was to him an earnest of the sun's future intentions. Weatherbee was also feeling somewhat better, and crawled out beside him. They propped themselves in the snow beneath the moveless wind-vane, and waited.

The stillness of death was about them. In other climes,

when nature falls into such moods, there is a subdued air of expectancy, a waiting for some small voice to take up the broken strain. Not so in the North. The two men had lived seeming æons in this ghostly peace. They could remember no song of the past; they could conjure no song of the future. This unearthly calm had always been,—the tranquil silence of eternity.

Their eyes were fixed upon the north. Unseen, behind their backs, behind the towering mountains to the south, the sun swept toward the zenith of another sky than theirs. Sole spectators of the mighty canvas, they watched the false dawn slowly grow. A faint flame began to glow and smoulder. It deepened in intensity, ringing the changes of reddish-yellow, purple, and saffron. So bright did it become that Cuthfert thought the sun must surely be behind it,—a miracle, the sun rising in the north! Suddenly, without warning and without fading, the canvas was swept clean. There was no color in the sky. The light had gone out of the day. They caught their breaths in half-sobs. But lo! the air was a-glint with particles of scintillating frost, and there, to the north, the wind-vane lay in vague outline on the snow. A shadow! A shadow! It was exactly midday. They jerked their heads hurriedly to the south. A golden rim peeped over the mountain's snowy shoulder, smiled upon them an instant, then dipped from sight again.

There were tears in their eyes as they sought each other. A strange softening came over them. They felt irresistibly drawn toward each other. The sun was coming back again. It would be with them to-morrow, and the next day, and the next. And it would stay longer every visit, and a time would come when it would ride their heaven day and night, never once dropping below the sky-line. There would be no night. The ice-locked winter would be broken; the winds would blow and the forests answer; the land would bathe in the blessed sunshine, and life renew. Hand in hand, they would quit this horrid dream and journey back to the Southland. They lurched blindly forward, and their hands met,—their poor maimed hands, swollen and distorted beneath their mittens.

But the promise was destined to remain unfulfilled. The Northland is the Northland, and men work out their souls by strange rules, which other men, who have not journeyed into far countries, cannot come to understand.

An hour later, Cuthfert put a pan of bread into the oven, and fell to speculating on what the surgeons could do with his feet when he got back. Home did not seem so very far away now. Weatherbee was rummaging in the cache. Of a sudden, he raised a whirlwind of blasphemy, which in turn ceased with startling abruptness. The other man had robbed his sugar-sack. Still, things might have happened differently, had not the two dead men come out from under the stones and hushed the hot words in his throat. They led him quite gently from the cache, which he forgot to close. That consummation was reached; that something they had whispered to him in his dreams was about to happen. They guided him gently, very gently, to the woodpile, where they put the axe in his hands. Then they helped him shove open the cabin door, and he felt sure they shut it after him,—at least he heard it slam and the latch fall sharply into place. And he knew they were waiting just without, waiting for him to do his task.

'Carter! I say, Carter!'

Percy Cuthfert was frightened at the look on the clerk's face, and he made haste to put the table between them.

Carter Weatherbee followed, without haste and without enthusiasm. There was neither pity nor passion in his face, but rather the patient, stolid look of one who has certain work to do and goes about it methodically.

'I say, what's the matter?'

The clerk dodged back, cutting off his retreat to the door, but never opening his mouth.

'I say, Carter, I say; let's talk. There's a good chap.'

The master of arts was thinking rapidly, now, shaping a skillful flank movement on the bed where his Smith & Wesson lay. Keeping his eyes on the madman, he rolled backward on the bunk, at the same time clutching the pistol.

'Carter!'

The powder flashed full in Weatherbee's face, but he swung his weapon and leaped forward. The axe bit deeply at the base of the spine, and Percy Cuthfert felt all consciousness of his lower limbs leave him. Then the clerk fell heavily upon him, clutching him by the throat with feeble fingers. The sharp bite of the axe had caused Cuthfert to drop the pistol, and as his lungs panted for release, he fumbled aimlessly for it among the blankets. Then he remembered. He slid a hand up the clerk's belt to the sheath-knife; and they drew very close to each other in that last clinch.

Percy Cuthfert felt his strength leave him. The lower portion of his body was useless. The inert weight of Weatherbee crushed him,—crushed him and pinned him there like a bear under a trap. The cabin became filled with a familiar odor, and he knew the bread to be burning. Yet what did it matter? He would never need it. And there were all of six cupfuls of sugar in the cache,—if he had foreseen this he would not have been so saving the last several days. Would the wind-vane ever move? It might even be veering now. Why not? Had he not seen the sun to-day? He would go and see. No; it was impossible to move. He had not thought the clerk so heavy a man.

How quickly the cabin cooled! The fire must be out. The cold was forcing in. It must be below zero already, and the ice creeping up the inside of the door. He could not see it, but his past experience enabled him to gauge its progress by the cabin's temperature. The lower hinge must be white ere now. Would the tale of this ever reach the world? How would his friends take it? They would read it over their coffee, most likely, and talk it over at the clubs. He could see them very clearly. 'Poor Old Cuthfert,' they murmured; 'not such a bad sort of a chap, after all.' He smiled at their eulogies, and passed on in search of a Turkish bath. It was the same old crowd upon the streets. Strange, they did not notice his moosehide moccasins and tattered German socks! He would take a cab. And after the bath a shave would not be bad. No; he would eat first. Steak, and potatoes, and green things,—how fresh it all was! And what was that? Squares of honey, streaming liquid amber! But why did they bring so much?

Ha! ha! he could never eat it all. Shine! Why certainly. He put his foot on the box. The bootblack looked curiously up at him, and he remembered his moosehide moccasins and went away hastily.

Hark! The wind-vane must be surely spinning. No; a mere singing in his ears. That was all,—a mere singing. The ice must have passed the latch by now. More likely the upper hinge was covered. Between the moss-chinked roof-poles, little points of frost began to appear. How slowly they grew! No; not so slowly. There was a new one, and there another. Two—three—four; they were coming too fast to count. There were two growing together. And there, a third had joined them. Why, there were no more spots. They had run together and formed a sheet.

Well, he would have company. If Gabriel ever broke the silence of the North, they would stand together, hand in hand, before the great White Throne. And God would judge them, God would judge them!

Then Percy Cuthfert closed his eyes and dropped off to sleep.

'Dump it in.'

'But I say, Kid, isn't that going it a little too strong? Whiskey and alcohol's bad enough; but when it comes to brandy and pepper-sauce and'—

'Dump it in. Who's making this punch, anyway?' And Malemute Kid smiled benignantly through the clouds of steam. 'By the time you've been in this country as long as I have, my son, and lived on rabbit-tracks and salmon-belly, you'll learn that Christmas comes only once per annum. And a Christmas without punch is sinking a hole to bedrock with nary a pay-streak.'

'Stack up on that fer a high cyard,' approved Big Jim Belden, who had come down from his claim on Mazy May to spend Christmas, and who, as every one knew, had been living the two months past on straight moose-meat. 'Hain't fergot the *hooch* we-uns made on the Tanana, hev yeh?'

'Well, I guess yes. Boys, it would have done your hearts good to see that whole tribe fighting drunk—and all because of a glorious ferment of sugar and sour dough. That was before your time,' Malemute Kid said as he turned to Stanley Prince, a young mining expert who had been in two years. 'No white women in the country then, and Mason wanted to get married. Ruth's father was chief of the Tananas, and objected, like the rest of the tribe. Stiff? Why, I used my last pound of sugar; finest work in that line I ever did in my life. You should have seen the chase, down the river and across the portage.'

'But the squaw?' asked Louis Savoy, the tall French-Canadian, becoming interested; for he had heard of this wild deed, when at Forty Mile the preceding winter.

Then Malemute Kid, who was a born raconteur, told the unvarnished tale of the Northland Lochinvar.* More than one rough adventurer of the North felt his heartstrings draw closer, and experienced vague yearnings for the sunnier pastures of the Southland, where life promised something more than a barren struggle with cold and death.

'We struck the Yukon just behind the first ice-run,' he concluded, 'and the tribe only a quarter of an hour behind. But that saved us; for the second run broke the jam above and shut them out. When they finally got into Nuklukyeto, the whole Post was ready for them. And as to the foregathering, ask Father Roubeau here: he performed the ceremony.'

The Jesuit took the pipe from his lips, but could only express his gratification with patriarchal smiles, while Protestant and Catholic vigorously applauded.

'By gar!' ejaculated Louis Savoy, who seemed overcome by the romance of it. 'La petite squaw; mon Mason brav. By gar!'

Then, as the first tin cups of punch went round, Bettles the Unquenchable sprang to his feet and struck up his favorite drinking song:—

> There's Henry Ward Beecher*
> And Sunday-school teachers,
>   All drink of the sassafras root;
> But you bet all the same,
> If it had its right name,
>   It's the juice of the forbidden fruit.

> Oh the juice of the forbidden fruit,

roared out the Bacchanalian chorus,—

> Oh the juice of the forbidden fruit;
>   But you bet all the same,
>   If it had its right name,
> It's the juice of the forbidden fruit.

Malemute Kid's frightful concoction did its work; the men of the camps and trails unbent in its genial glow, and jest and song and tales of past adventure went round the board. Aliens from a dozen lands, they toasted each and all. It was the Englishman, Prince, who pledged 'Uncle Sam, the precocious infant of the New World;' the Yankee, Bettles, who drank to 'The Queen, God bless her;' and together, Savoy and Meyers, the German trader, clanged their cups to Alsace and Lorraine.

Then Malemute Kid arose, cup in hand, and glanced at

the greased-paper window, where the frost stood full three inches thick. 'A health to the man on trail this night; may his grub hold out; may his dogs keep their legs; may his matches never miss fire.'

Crack! Crack!—they heard the familiar music of the dogwhip, the whining howl of the Malemutes, and the crunch of a sled as it drew up to the cabin. Conversation languished while they waited the issue.

'An old-timer; cares for his dogs and then himself,' whispered Malemute Kid to Prince, as they listened to the snapping jaws and the wolfish snarls and yelps of pain which proclaimed to their practiced ears that the stranger was beating back their dogs while he fed his own.

Then came the expected knock, sharp and confident, and the stranger entered. Dazzled by the light, he hesitated a moment at the door, giving to all a chance for scrutiny. He was a striking personage, and a most picturesque one, in his Arctic dress of wool and fur. Standing six foot two or three, with proportionate breadth of shoulders and depth of chest, his smooth-shaven face nipped by the cold to a gleaming pink, his long lashes and eyebrows white with ice, and the ear and neck flaps of his great wolfskin cap loosely raised, he seemed, of a verity, the Frost King, just stepped in out of the night. Clasped outside his mackinaw jacket, a beaded belt held two large Colt's revolvers and a hunting-knife, while he carried, in addition to the inevitable dogwhip, a smokeless rifle of the largest bore and latest pattern. As he came forward, for all his step was firm and elastic, they could see that fatigue bore heavily upon him.

An awkward silence had fallen, but his hearty 'What cheer, my lads?' put them quickly at ease, and the next instant Malemute Kid and he had gripped hands. Though they had never met, each had heard of the other, and the recognition was mutual. A sweeping introduction and a mug of punch were forced upon him before he could explain his errand.

'How long since that basket-sled, with three men and eight dogs, passed?' he asked.

'An even two days ahead. Are you after them?'

'Yes; my team. Run them off under my very nose, the cusses. I've gained two days on them already,—pick them up on the next run.'

'Reckon they'll show spunk?' asked Belden, in order to keep up the conversation, for Malemute Kid already had the coffee-pot on and was busily frying bacon and moose-meat.

The stranger significantly tapped his revolvers.

'When'd yeh leave Dawson?'

'Twelve o'clock.'

'Last night?'—as a matter of course.

'To-day.'

A murmur of surprise passed round the circle. And well it might; for it was just midnight, and seventy-five miles of rough river trail was not to be sneered at for a twelve hours' run.

The talk soon became impersonal, however, harking back to the trails of childhood. As the young stranger ate of the rude fare, Malemute Kid attentively studied his face. Nor was he long in deciding that it was fair, honest, and open, and that he liked it. Still youthful, the lines had been firmly traced by toil and hardship. Though genial in conversation, and mild when at rest, the blue eyes gave promise of the hard steel-glitter which comes when called into action, especially against odds. The heavy jaw and square-cut chin demonstrated rugged pertinacity and indomitability. Nor, though the attributes of the lion were there, was there wanting the certain softness, the hint of womanliness, which bespoke the emotional nature.

'So thet's how me an' the ol' woman got spliced,' said Belden, concluding the exciting tale of his courtship. '"Here we be, dad," sez she. "An' may yeh be damned," sez he to her, an' then to me, "Jim, yeh—yeh git outen them good duds o' yourn; I want a right peart slice o' thet forty acre ploughed 'fore dinner." An' then he turns on her an' sez, "An' yeh, Sal; yeh sail inter them dishes." An' then he sort o' sniffled an' kissed her. An' I was thet happy,—but he seen me an' roars out, "Yeh, Jim!" An' yeh bet I dusted fer the barn.'

'Any kids waiting for you back in the States?' asked the stranger.

'Nope; Sal died 'fore any come. Thet's why I'm here.'

Belden abstractedly began to light his pipe, which had failed to go out, and then brightened up with, 'How 'bout yerself, stranger,—married man?'

For reply, he opened his watch, slipped it from the thong which served for a chain, and passed it over. Belden pricked up the slush-lamp, surveyed the inside of the case critically, and swearing admiringly to himself, handed it over to Louis Savoy. With numerous 'By gars!' he finally surrendered it to Prince, and they noticed that his hands trembled and his eyes took on a peculiar softness. And so it passed from horny hand to horny hand—the pasted photograph of a woman, the clinging kind that such men fancy, with a babe at the breast. Those who had not yet seen the wonder were keen with curiosity; those who had, became silent and retrospective. They could face the pinch of famine, the grip of scurvy, or the quick death by field or flood; but the pictured semblance of a stranger woman and child made women and children of them all.

'Never have seen the youngster yet,—he's a boy, she says, and two years old,' said the stranger as he received the treasure back. A lingering moment he gazed upon it, then snapped the case and turned away, but not quick enough to hide the restrained rush of tears.

Malemute Kid led him to a bunk and bade him turn in.

'Call me at four, sharp. Don't fail me,' were his last words, and a moment later he was breathing in the heaviness of exhausted sleep.

'By Jove! he's a plucky chap,' commented Prince. 'Three hours' sleep after seventy-five miles with the dogs, and then the trail again. Who is he, Kid?'

'Jack Westondale. Been in going on three years, with nothing but the name of working like a horse, and any amount of bad luck to his credit. I never knew him, but Sitka Charley told me about him.'

'It seems hard that a man with a sweet young wife like his should be putting in his years in this God-forsaken hole, where every year counts two on the outside.'

'The trouble with him is clean grit and stubbornness. He's cleaned up twice with a stake, but lost it both times.'

Here the conversation was broken off by an uproar from Bettles, for the effect had begun to wear away. And soon the bleak years of monotonous grub and deadening toil were being forgotten in rough merriment. Malemute Kid alone seemed unable to lose himself, and cast many an anxious look at his watch. Once he put on his mittens and beaver-skin cap, and leaving the cabin, fell to rummaging about in the cache.

Nor could he wait the hour designated; for he was fifteen minutes ahead of time in rousing his guest. The young giant had stiffened badly, and brisk rubbing was necessary to bring him to his feet. He tottered painfully out of the cabin, to find his dogs harnessed and everything ready for the start. The company wished him good luck and a short chase, while Father Roubeau, hurriedly blessing him, led the stampede for the cabin; and small wonder, for it is not good to face seventy-four degrees below zero with naked ears and hands.

Malemute Kid saw him to the main trail, and there, gripping his hand heartily, gave him advice.

'You'll find a hundred pounds of salmon-eggs on the sled,' he said. 'The dogs will go as far on that as with one hundred and fifty of fish, and you can't get dog-food at Pelly, as you probably expected.' The stranger started, and his eyes flashed, but he did not interrupt. 'You can't get an ounce of food for dog or man till you reach Five Fingers, and that's a stiff two hundred miles. Watch out for open water on the Thirty Mile River, and be sure you take the big cut-off above Le Barge.'*

'How did you know it? Surely the news can't be ahead of me already?'

'I don't know it; and what's more, I don't want to know it. But you never owned that team you're chasing. Sitka Charley sold it to them last spring. But he sized you up to me as square once, and I believe him. I've seen your face; I like it. And I've seen—why, damn you, hit the high places for salt water and that wife of yours, and'—Here the Kid unmittened and jerked out his sack.

'No; I don't need it,' and the tears froze on his cheeks as he convulsively gripped Malemute Kid's hand.

'Then don't spare the dogs; cut them out of the traces as

fast as they drop; buy them, and think they're cheap at ten dollars a pound. You can get them at Five Fingers, Little Salmon, and the Hootalinqua.* And watch out for wet feet,' was his parting advice. 'Keep a-traveling up to twenty-five, but if it gets below that, build a fire and change your socks.'

Fifteen minutes had barely elapsed when the jingle of bells announced new arrivals. The door opened, and a mounted policeman of the Northwest Territory entered, followed by two half-breed dog-drivers. Like Westondale, they were heavily armed and showed signs of fatigue. The half-breeds had been born to the trail, and bore it easily; but the young policeman was badly exhausted. Still, the dogged obstinacy of his race held him to the pace he had set, and would hold him till he dropped in his tracks.

'When did Westondale pull out?' he asked. 'He stopped here, didn't he?' This was supererogatory, for the tracks told their own tale too well.

Malemute Kid had caught Belden's eye, and he, scenting the wind, replied evasively, 'A right peart while back.'

'Come, my man; speak up,' the policeman admonished.

'Yeh seem to want him right smart. Hez he ben gittin' cantankerous down Dawson way?'

'Held up Harry McFarland's for forty thousand; exchanged it at the P. C. store* for a check on Seattle; and who's to stop the cashing of it if we don't overtake him? When did he pull out?'

Every eye suppressed its excitement, for Malemute Kid had given the cue, and the young officer encountered wooden faces on every hand.

Striding over to Prince, he put the question to him. Though it hurt him, gazing into the frank, earnest face of his fellow countryman, he replied inconsequentially on the state of the trail.

Then he espied Father Roubeau, who could not lie. 'A quarter of an hour ago,' the priest answered; 'but he had four hours' rest for himself and dogs.'

'Fifteen minutes' start, and he's fresh! My God!' The poor fellow staggered back, half fainting from exhaustion and disappointment, murmuring something about the run from Dawson in ten hours and the dogs being played out.

Malemute Kid forced a mug of punch upon him; then he turned for the door, ordering the dog-drivers to follow. But the warmth and promise of rest were too tempting, and they objected strenuously. The Kid was conversant with their French patois, and followed it anxiously.

They swore that the dogs were gone up; that Siwash and Babette would have to be shot before the first mile was covered; that the rest were almost as bad; and that it would be better for all hands to rest up.

'Lend me five dogs?' he asked, turning to Malemute Kid.

But the Kid shook his head.

'I'll sign a check on Captain Constantine* for five thousand,—here's my papers,—I'm authorized to draw at my own discretion.'

Again the silent refusal.

'Then I'll requisition them in the name of the Queen.'

Smiling incredulously, the Kid glanced at his well-stocked arsenal, and the Englishman, realizing his impotency, turned for the door. But the dog-drivers still objecting, he whirled upon them fiercely, calling them women and curs. The swart face of the older half-breed flushed angrily, as he drew himself up and promised in good, round terms that he would travel his leader off his legs, and would then be delighted to plant him in the snow.

The young officer—and it required his whole will—walked steadily to the door, exhibiting a freshness he did not possess. But they all knew and appreciated his proud effort; nor could he veil the twinges of agony that shot across his face. Covered with frost, the dogs were curled up in the snow, and it was almost impossible to get them to their feet. The poor brutes whined under the stinging lash, for the dog-drivers were angry and cruel; nor till Babette, the leader, was cut from the traces, could they break out the sled and get under way.

'A dirty scoundrel and a liar!' 'By gar! him no good!' 'A thief!' 'Worse than an Indian!' It was evident that they were angry—first, at the way they had been deceived; and second, at the outraged ethics of the Northland, where honesty, above all, was man's prime jewel. 'An' we gave the cuss a hand, after knowin' what he'd did.' All eyes were turned accusingly upon Malemute Kid, who rose from the corner where he had been making Babette comfortable, and silently emptied the bowl for a final round of punch.

'It's a cold night, boys,—a bitter cold night,' was the irrelevant commencement of his defense. 'You've all traveled trail, and know what that stands for. Don't jump a dog when he's down. You've only heard one side. A whiter man than Jack Westondale never ate from the same pot nor stretched blanket with you or me. Last fall he gave his whole clean-up, forty thousand, to Joe Castrell, to buy in on Dominion. To-day he'd be a millionaire. But while he stayed behind at Circle City, taking care of his partner with the scurvy, what does Castrell do? Goes into McFarland's, jumps the limit, and drops the whole sack. Found him dead in the snow the next day. And poor Jack laying his plans to go out this winter to his wife and the boy he's never seen. You'll notice he took exactly what his partner lost,—forty thousand. Well, he's gone out; and what are you going to do about it?'

The Kid glanced round the circle of his judges, noted the softening of their faces, then raised his mug aloft. 'So a health to the man on trail this night; may his grub hold out; may his dogs keep their legs; may his matches never miss fire. God prosper him; good luck go with him; and'—

'Confusion to the Mounted Police!' cried Bettles, to the crash of the empty cups.

THE PRIESTLY PREROGATIVE

This is the story of a man who did not appreciate his wife; also, of a woman who did him too great an honor when she gave herself to him. Incidentally, it concerns a Jesuit priest who had never been known to lie. He was an appurtenance, and a very necessary one, to the Yukon country; but the presence of the other two was merely accidental. They were specimens of the many strange waifs which ride the breast of a gold rush or come tailing along behind.

Edwin Bentham and Grace Bentham were waifs; they were also tailing along behind, for the Klondike rush of '97 had long since swept down the great river and subsided into the famine-stricken city of Dawson. When the Yukon shut up shop and went to sleep under a three-foot ice-sheet, this peripatetic couple found themselves at the Five Finger Rapids, with the City of Gold still a journey of many sleeps to the north.

Not a few cattle had been butchered at this place in the fall of the year, and the offal made a goodly heap. The three fellow *voyageurs* of Edwin Bentham and wife gazed upon this deposit, did a little mental arithmetic, caught a certain glimpse of a bonanza, and decided to remain. And all winter they sold sacks of bones and frozen hides to the famished dog-teams. It was a modest price they asked, a dollar a pound, just as it came. Six months later, when the sun came back and the Yukon awoke, they buckled on their heavy money-belts and journeyed back to the Southland, where they yet live and lie mightily about the Klondike they never saw.

But Edwin Bentham—he was an indolent fellow, and had he not been possessed of a wife, would have gladly joined issues in the dog-meat speculation. As it was, she played upon his vanity, told him how great and strong he was, how a man such as he certainly was could overcome all obstacles and of a surety obtain the Golden Fleece.* So he squared his jaw, sold his share in the bones and hides for a sled and one dog, and turned his snowshoes to the north. Needless to state, Grace Bentham's snowshoes never allowed his tracks to grow cold. Nay, ere their tribulations had seen three days, it was the man who followed in the rear, and the woman who broke trail in advance. Of course, if anybody hove in sight, the position was instantly reversed. Thus did his manhood remain virgin to the travelers who passed like ghosts on the silent trail. There are such men in this world.

How such a man and such a woman came to take each other for better and for worse is unimportant to this narrative. These things are familiar to us all, and those people who do them, or even question them too closely, are apt to lose a beautiful faith which is known as Eternal Fitness.

Edwin Bentham was a boy, thrust by mischance into a man's body,—a boy who could complacently pluck a butterfly, wing from wing, or cower in abject terror before a lean, nervy fellow, not half his size. He was a selfish cry-baby, hidden behind a man's mustache and stature, and glossed over with a skin-deep veneer of culture and conventionality. Yes; he was a clubman and a society man,—the sort that grace social functions and utter inanities with a charm and unction which are indescribable; the sort that talk big, and cry over a toothache; the sort that put more hell into a woman's life by marrying her than can the most graceless libertine that ever browsed in forbidden pastures. We meet these men every day, but we rarely know them for what they are. Second to marrying them, the best way to get this knowledge is to eat out of the same pot and crawl under the same blanket with them for—well, say a week; no greater margin is necessary.

To see Grace Bentham was to see a slender, girlish creature; to know her was to know a soul which dwarfed one's own, yet retained all the elements of the eternal feminine. This was the woman who urged and encouraged her husband in his Northland quest, who broke trail for him when no one was looking, and cried in secret over her weakling woman's body.

So journeyed this strangely assorted couple down to old Fort Selkirk, then through five-score miles of dismal wilderness to Stuart River. And when the short day left them, and the man lay down in the snow and blubbered, it was the woman who lashed him to the sled, bit her lips with the pain of her aching limbs, and helped the dog haul him to Malemute Kid's cabin. Malemute Kid was not at home, but Meyers, the German trader, cooked great moose-steaks and shook up a bed of fresh pine boughs.

Lake, Langham, and Parker were excited, and not unduly so when the cause was taken into account.

'Oh, Sandy! Say, can you tell a porter-house from a round? Come out and lend us a hand, anyway!' This appeal emanated from the cache, where Langham was vainly struggling with divers quarters of frozen moose.

'Don't you budge from those dishes!' commanded Parker.

'I say, Sandy—there's a good fellow—just run down to the Missouri Camp and borrow some cinnamon,' begged Lake.

'Oh! oh! hurry up! Why don't'—But the crash of meat and boxes, in the cache, abruptly quenched this peremptory summons.

'Come now, Sandy; it won't take a minute to go down to the Missouri'—

'You leave him alone,' interrupted Parker. 'How am I to mix the biscuits if the table isn't cleared off?'

Sandy paused in indecision, till suddenly the fact that he was Langham's 'man' dawned upon him. Then he apologetically threw down the greasy dishcloth, and went to his master's rescue.

These promising scions of wealthy progenitors had come to the Northland in search of laurels, with much money to burn, and a 'man' apiece. Luckily for their souls, the other two men were up the White River in search of a mythical quartz-ledge;* so Sandy had to grin under the responsibility of three healthy masters, each of whom was possessed of peculiar cookery ideas. Twice that morning had a disruption of the whole camp been imminent, only averted by immense concessions from one or the other of these knights of the chafing-dish. But at last their mutual creation, a really dainty dinner, was completed. Then they sat down to a three-cornered game of 'cut-throat,'—a proceeding which did away with all *casus belli* for future hostilities, and permitted the victor to depart on a most important mission.

This fortune fell to Parker, who parted his hair in the middle, put on his mittens and bear-skin cap, and stepped over to Malemute Kid's cabin. And when he returned, it was in the company of Grace Bentham and Malemute Kid,—the former very sorry her husband could not share with her their hospitality, for he had gone up to look at the Henderson Creek* mines, and the latter still a trifle stiff from breaking trail down the Stuart River. Meyers had been asked, but had declined, being deeply engrossed in an experiment of raising bread from hops.

Well, they could do without the husband; but a woman— why, they had not seen one all winter, and the presence of this one promised a new hegira in their lives. They were college men and gentlemen, these three young fellows, yearning for the flesh-pots they had been so long denied. Probably Grace Bentham suffered from a similar hunger; at least, it meant much to her, the first bright hour in many weeks of darkness.

But that wonderful first course, which claimed the versatile Lake for its parent, had no sooner been served than there came a loud knock at the door.

'Oh! Ah! Won't you come in, Mr Bentham?' said Parker, who had stepped to see who the newcomer might be.

'Is my wife here?' gruffly responded that worthy.

'Why, yes. We left word with Mr Meyers.' Parker was exerting his most dulcet tones, inwardly wondering what the deuce it all meant. 'Won't you come in? Expecting you at any moment, we reserved a place. And just in time for the first course, too.'

'Come in, Edwin, dear,' chirped Grace Bentham from her seat at the table.

Parker naturally stood aside.

'I want my wife,' reiterated Bentham hoarsely, the intonation savoring disagreeably of ownership.

Parker gasped, was within an ace of driving his fist into the face of his boorish visitor, but held himself awkwardly in check. Everybody rose. Lake lost his head and caught himself on the verge of saying, 'Must you go?'

Then began the farrago of leave-taking. 'So nice of you' —'Awfully sorry'—'By Jove! how things did brighten'— 'Really now, you'—'Thank you ever so much'—'Nice trip to Dawson'—etc.

In this wise the lamb was helped into her jacket and led to the slaughter. Then the door slammed, and they gazed woefully upon the deserted table.

'Damn!' Langham had suffered disadvantages in his early training, and his oaths were weak and monotonous. 'Damn!' he repeated, vaguely conscious of the incompleteness and vainly struggling for a more virile term.

It is a clever woman who can fill out the many weak places in an inefficient man, by her own indomitability reinforce his vacillating nature, infuse her ambitious soul into his, and spur him on to great achievements. And it is indeed a very clever and tactful woman who can do all this, and do it so subtly that the man receives all the credit and believes in his inmost heart that everything is due to him and him alone.

This is what Grace Bentham proceeded to do. Arriving in Dawson with a few pounds of flour and several letters of introduction, she at once applied herself to the task of pushing her big baby to the fore. It was she who melted the stony heart and wrung credit from the rude barbarian who presided over the destiny of the P. C. Company; yet it was Edwin Bentham to whom the concession was ostensibly granted. It was she who dragged her baby up and down creeks, over benches and divides, and on a dozen wild stampedes; yet everybody remarked what an energetic fellow that Bentham was. It was she who studied maps, and catechised miners, and hammered geography and locations into his hollow head, till everybody marveled at his broad grasp of the country and knowledge of its conditions. Of course, they said the wife was a brick, and only a few wise ones appreciated and pitied her.

She did the work; he got the credit and reward. In the Northwest Territory a married woman cannot stake or record a creek, bench, or quartz claim;* so Edwin Bentham went down to the Gold Commissioner and filed on Bench Claim 23, second tier, of French Hill. And when April came they were washing out a thousand dollars a day, with many, many such days in prospect.

At the base of French Hill lay Eldorado Creek,* and on a creek claim stood the cabin of Clyde Wharton. At present he was not washing out a diurnal thousand dollars; but his dumps grew, shift by shift, and there would come a time when those dumps would pass through his sluice-boxes, depositing in the riffles, in the course of half a dozen days, several hundred thousand dollars. He often sat in that cabin, smoked his pipe, and dreamed beautiful little dreams,—dreams in which neither the dumps nor the half-ton of dust in the P. C. Company's big safe played a part.

And Grace Bentham, as she washed tin dishes in her hillside cabin, often glanced down into Eldorado Creek, and dreamed,—not of dumps nor dust, however. They met frequently, as the trail to the one claim crossed the other, and there is much to talk about in the Northland spring; but never once, by the light of an eye nor the slip of a tongue, did they speak their hearts.

This is as it was at first. But one day Edwin Bentham was brutal. All boys are thus; besides, being a French Hill king now, he began to think a great deal of himself and to forget all he owed to his wife. On this day, Wharton heard of it, and waylaid Grace Bentham, and talked wildly. This made her very happy, though she would not listen, and made him promise to not say such things again. Her hour had not come.

But the sun swept back on its northern journey, the black of midnight changed to the steely color of dawn, the snow slipped away, the water dashed again over the glacial drift, and the wash-up began. Day and night the yellow clay and scraped bed-rock hurried through the swift sluices, yielding up its ransom to the strong men from the Southland. And in that time of tumult came Grace Bentham's hour.

To all of us such hours at some time come,—that is, to us who are not too phlegmatic. Some people are good, not from inherent love of virtue, but from sheer laziness. Those of us who know weak moments may understand.

Edwin Bentham was weighing dust over the bar of the saloon at the Forks—altogether too much of his dust went over that pine board—when his wife came down the hill and slipped into Clyde Wharton's cabin. Wharton was not expecting her, but that did not alter the case. And much subsequent misery and idle waiting might have been avoided, had not Father Roubeau seen this and turned aside from the main creek trail.

'My child'—

'Hold on, Father Roubeau! Though I'm not of your faith, I respect you; but you can't come in between this woman and me!'

'You know what you are doing?'

'Know! Were you God Almighty, ready to fling me into eternal fire, I'd bank my will against yours in this matter.'

Wharton had placed Grace on a stool and stood belligerently before her.

'You sit down on that chair and keep quiet,' he continued, addressing the Jesuit. 'I'll take my innings now. You can have yours after.'

Father Roubeau bowed courteously and obeyed. He was an easy-going man and had learned to bide his time. Wharton pulled a stool alongside the woman's, smothering her hand in his.

'Then you do care for me, and will take me away?'

Her face seemed to reflect the peace of this man, against whom she might draw close for shelter.

'Dear, don't you remember what I said before? Of course I'—

'But how can you?—the wash-up?'

'Do you think that worries? Anyway, I'll give the job to Father Roubeau, here. I can trust him to safely bank the dust with the company.'

'To think of it!—I'll never see him again.'

'A blessing!'

'And to go—Oh, Clyde, I can't! I can't!'

'There, there; of course you can. Just let me plan it. You see, as soon as we get a few traps together, we'll start, and'—

'Suppose he comes back?'

'I'll break every'—

'No, no! No fighting, Clyde! Promise me that.'

'All right! I'll just tell the men to throw him off the claim. They've seen how he's treated you, and haven't much love for him.'

'You mustn't do that. You mustn't hurt him.'

'What then? Let him come right in here and take you away before my eyes?'

'No-o,' she half whispered, stroking his hand softly.

'Then let me run it, and don't worry. I'll see he doesn't get hurt. Precious lot he cared whether you got hurt or not! We won't go back to Dawson. I'll send word down for a couple of the boys to outfit and pole a boat up the Yukon. We'll cross the divide and raft down the Indian River to meet them. Then'—

'And then?'

Her head was on his shoulder. Their voices sank to softer cadences, each word a caress. The Jesuit fidgeted nervously.

'And then?' she repeated.

'Why, we'll pole up, and up, and up, and portage the White Horse Rapids and the Box Cañon.'

'Yes?'

'And the Sixty-Mile River; then the lakes, Chilcoot, Dyea, and Salt Water.'

'But, dear, I can't pole a boat.'

'You little goose! I'll get Sitka Charley; he knows all the good water and best camps, and he is the best traveler I ever met, if he is an Indian. All you'll have to do, is to sit in the middle of the boat, and sing songs, and play Cleopatra, and fight—no, we're in luck; too early for mosquitoes.'

'And then, O my Antony?'*

'And then a steamer, San Francisco, and the world! Never to come back to this cursed hole again. Think of it! The world, and ours to choose from!* I'll sell out. Why, we're rich! The Waldworth Syndicate will give me half a million for what's left in the ground, and I've got twice as much in the dumps and with the P. C. Company. We'll go to the Fair in Paris in 1900. We'll go to Jerusalem, if you say so. We'll buy an Italian palace, and you can play Cleopatra to your heart's content. No, you shall be Lucretia, Acte,* or anybody your little heart sees fit to become. But you mustn't, you really mustn't'—

'The wife of Cæsar shall be above reproach.'

'Of course, but'—

'But I won't be your wife, will I, dear?'

'I didn't mean that.'

'But you'll love me just as much, and never even think— oh! I know you'll be like other men; you'll grow tired, and— and'—

'How can you? I'—

'Promise me.'

'Yes, yes; I do promise.'

'You say it so easily, dear; but how do you know?—or I know? I have so little to give, yet it is so much. Oh, Clyde! promise me you won't?'

'There, there! You mustn't begin to doubt already. Till death do us part, you know.'

'Think! I once said that to—to him, and now?'

'And now, little sweetheart, you're not to bother about such things any more. Of course, I never, never will, and'—

And for the first time, lips trembled against lips. Father Roubeau had been watching the main trail through the window, but could stand the strain no longer. He cleared his throat and turned around.

'Your turn now, Father!' Wharton's face was flushed with the fire of his first embrace. There was an exultant ring to his voice as he abdicated in the other's favor. He had no doubt as to the result. Neither had Grace, for a smile played about her mouth as she faced the priest.

'My child,' he began, 'my heart bleeds for you. It is a pretty dream, but it cannot be.'

'And why, Father? I have said yes.'

'You knew not what you did. You did not think of the oath you took, before your God, to that man who is your husband. It remains for me to make you realize the sanctity of such a pledge.'

'And if I do realize, and yet refuse?'

'Then God'—

'Which God? My husband has a God which I care not to worship. There must be many such.'

'Child! unsay those words! Ah! you do not mean them. I understand. I, too, have had such moments.' For an instant he was back in his native France, and a wistful, sad-eyed face came as a mist between him and the woman before him.

'Then, Father, has my God forsaken me? I am not wicked above women. My misery with him has been great. Why should it be greater? Why shall I not grasp at happiness? I cannot, will not, go back to him!'

'Rather is your God forsaken. Return. Throw your burden upon Him, and the darkness shall be lifted. Oh, my child'—

'No; it is useless; I have made my bed and so shall I lie. I will go on. And if God punishes me, I shall bear it somehow. You do not understand. You are not a woman.'

'My mother was a woman.'

'But'—

'And Christ was born of woman.'

She did not answer. A silence fell. Wharton pulled his mustache impatiently and kept an eye on the trail. Grace leaned her elbow on the table, her face set with resolve. The smile had died away. Father Roubeau shifted his ground.

'You have children?'

'At one time I wished—but now—no. And I am thankful.'

'And a mother?'

'Yes.'

'She loves you?'

'Yes.' Her replies were whispers.

'And a brother?—no matter, he is a man. But a sister?'

Her head drooped a quavering yes.

'Younger? Very much?'

'Seven years.'

'And you have thought well about this matter? About them? About your mother? And your sister? She stands on the threshold of her woman's life, and this wildness of yours may mean much to her. Could you go before her, look upon her fresh young face, hold her hand in yours, or touch your cheek to hers?'

To his words, her brain formed vivid images, till she cried out, 'Don't! don't!' and shrank away as do the wolf-dogs from the lash.

'But you must face all this; and better it is to do it now.'

In his eyes, which she could not see, there was a great compassion, but his face, tense and quivering, showed no relenting. She raised her head from the table, forced back the tears, struggled for control.

'I shall go away. They will never see me, and come to forget me. I shall be to them as dead. And—and I will go with Clyde—to-day.'

It seemed final. Wharton stepped forward, but the priest waved him back.

'You have wished for children?'

A silent yes.

'And prayed for them?'

'Often.'

'And have you thought, if you should have children?' Father Roubeau's eyes rested for a moment on the man by the window.

A quick light shot across her face. Then the full import dawned upon her. She raised her hand appealingly, but he went on.

'Can you picture an innocent babe in your arms? A boy? The world is not so hard upon a girl. Why, your very breast would turn to gall! And you could be proud and happy of your boy, as you looked on other children?'—

'Oh, have pity! Hush!'

'A scapegoat'—

'Don't! don't! I will go back!' She was at his feet.

'A child to grow up with no thought of evil, and one day the world to fling a tender name in his face!'

'O my God! my God!'

She groveled on the floor. The priest sighed and raised her to her feet. Wharton pressed forward, but she motioned him away.

'Don't come near me, Clyde! I am going back!' The tears were coursing pitifully down her face, but she made no effort to wipe them away.

'After all this? You cannot! I will not let you!'

'Don't touch me!' She shivered and drew back.

'I will! You are mine! Do you hear? You are mine!' Then he whirled upon the priest. 'Oh what a fool I was to ever let you wag your silly tongue! Thank your God you are not a common man, for I'd— But the priestly prerogative must be exercised, eh? Well, you have exercised it. Now get out of my house, or I'll forget who and what you are!'

Father Roubeau bowed, took her hand, and started for the door. But Wharton cut them off.

'Grace! You said you loved me?'

'I did.'

'And you do now?'

'I do.'

'Say it again.'

'I do love you, Clyde; I do.'

'There, you priest!' he cried. 'You have heard it, and with those words on her lips you would send her back to live a lie and a hell with that man?'

But Father Roubeau whisked the woman into the inner room and closed the door. 'No words!' he whispered to Wharton, as he struck a casual posture on a stool. 'Remember, for her sake,' he added.

The room echoed to a rough knock at the door; then the latch raised and Edwin Bentham stepped in.

'Seen anything of my wife?' he asked, as soon as salutations had been exchanged.

Two heads nodded negatively.

'I saw her tracks down from the cabin,' he continued tentatively, 'and they broke off, just opposite here, on the main trail.'

His listeners looked bored.

'And I—I thought'—

'She was here!' thundered Wharton.

The priest silenced him with a look. 'Did you see her tracks leading up to this cabin, my son?' Wily Father Roubeau—he had taken good care to obliterate them as he came up the same path an hour before.

'I didn't stop to look, I'—His eyes rested suspiciously on

the door to the other room, then interrogated the priest. The latter shook his head; but the doubt seemed to linger.

Father Roubeau breathed a swift, silent prayer, and rose to his feet. 'If you doubt me, why'—He made as though to open the door.

A priest could not lie. Edwin Bentham had heard this often, and believed it. 'Of course not, Father,' he interposed hurriedly. 'I was only wondering where my wife had gone, and thought maybe—I guess she's up at Mrs Stanton's on French Gulch. Nice weather, isn't it? Heard the news? Flour's gone down to forty dollars a hundred, and they say the *che-cha-quas* are flocking down the river in droves. But I must be going; so good-by.'

The door slammed, and from the window they watched him take his quest up French Gulch.

A few weeks later, just after the June high-water, two men shot a canoe into mid-stream and made fast to a derelict pine. This tightened the painter and jerked the frail craft along as would a tow-boat. Father Roubeau had been directed to leave the Upper Country and return to his swarthy children at Minook. The white men had come among them, and they were devoting too little time to fishing, and too much to a certain deity whose transient habitat was in countless black bottles. Malemute Kid also had business in the Lower Country,* so they journeyed together.

But one, in all the Northland, knew the man Paul Roubeau, and that man was Malemute Kid. Before him alone did the priest cast off the sacerdotal garb and stand naked. And why not? These two men knew each other. Had they not shared the last morsel of fish, the last pinch of tobacco, the last and inmost thought, on the barren stretches of Bering Sea, in the heart-breaking mazes of the Great Delta, on the terrible winter journey from Point Barrow to the Porcupine?*

Father Roubeau puffed heavily at his trail-worn pipe, and gazed on the red-disked sun, poised sombrely on the edge of the northern horizon. Malemute Kid wound up his watch. It was midnight.

'Cheer up, old man!' The Kid was evidently gathering up

a broken thread. 'God surely will forgive such a lie. Let me give you the word of a man who strikes a true note:—

If She have spoken a word, remember thy lips are sealed,
And the brand of the Dog is upon him by whom is the secret revealed.
If there be trouble to Herward, and a lie of the blackest can clear,
Lie, while thy lips can move or a man is alive to hear.

Father Roubeau removed his pipe and reflected. 'The man speaks true, but my soul is not vexed with that. The lie and the penance stand with God; but—but'—

'What then? Your hands are clean.'

'Not so. Kid, I have thought much, and yet the thing remains. I knew, and I made her go back.'

The clear note of a robin rang out from the wooded bank, a partridge drummed the call in the distance, a moose lunged noisily in an eddy, but the twain smoked on in silence.

THE WISDOM OF THE TRAIL

Sitka Charley had achieved the impossible. Other Indians might have known as much of the wisdom of the trail as did he; but he alone knew the white man's wisdom, the honor of the trail, and the law. But these things had not come to him in a day. The aboriginal mind is slow to generalize, and many facts, repeated often, are required to compass an understanding. Sitka Charley, from boyhood, had been thrown continually with white men, and as a man he had elected to cast his fortunes with them, expatriating himself, once and for all, from his own people. Even then, respecting, almost venerating their power, and pondering over it, he had yet to divine its secret essence—the honor and the law. And it was only by the cumulative evidence of years that he had finally come to understand. Being an alien, when he did know he knew it better than the white man himself; being an Indian, he had achieved the impossible.

And of these things had been bred a certain contempt for his own people,—a contempt which he had made it a custom to conceal, but which now burst forth in a polyglot whirlwind of curses upon the heads of Kah-Chucte and Gowhee. They cringed before him like a brace of snarling wolf-dogs, too cowardly to spring, too wolfish to cover their fangs. They were not handsome creatures. Neither was Sitka Charley. All three were frightful-looking. There was no flesh to their faces; their cheek bones were massed with hideous scabs which had cracked and frozen alternately under the intense frost; while their eyes burned luridly with the light which is born of desperation and hunger. Men so situated, beyond the pale of the honor and the law, are not to be trusted. Sitka Charley knew this; and this was why he had forced them to abandon their rifles with the rest of the camp outfit ten days before. His rifle and Captain Eppingwell's were the only ones that remained.

'Come, get a fire started,' he commanded, drawing out the precious match box with its attendant strips of dry birch bark.

The two Indians fell sullenly to the task of gathering dead branches and underwood. They were weak, and paused often, catching themselves, in the act of stooping, with giddy motions, or staggering to the centre of operations with their knees shaking like castanets. After each trip they rested for a moment, as though sick and deadly weary. At times their eyes took on the patient stoicism of dumb suffering; and again the ego seemed almost bursting forth with its wild cry, 'I, I, I want to exist!'—the dominant note of the whole living universe.

A light breath of air blew from the south, nipping the exposed portions of their bodies and driving the frost, in needles of fire, through fur and flesh to the bones. So, when the fire had grown lusty and thawed a damp circle in the snow about it, Sitka Charley forced his reluctant comrades to lend a hand in pitching a fly. It was a primitive affair,— merely a blanket, stretched parallel with the fire and to windward of it, at an angle of perhaps forty-five degrees. This shut out the chill wind, and threw the heat backward and down upon those who were to huddle in its shelter. Then a layer of green spruce boughs was spread, that their bodies might not come in contact with the snow. When this task was completed, Kah-Chucte and Gowhee proceeded to take care of their feet. Their ice-bound moccasins were sadly worn by much travel, and the sharp ice of the river jams had cut them to rags. Their Siwash socks were similarly conditioned, and when these had been thawed and removed, the dead-white tips of the toes, in the various stages of mortification, told their simple tale of the trail.

Leaving the two to the drying of their footgear, Sitka Charley turned back over the course he had come. He, too, had a mighty longing to sit by the fire and tend his complaining flesh, but the honor and the law forbade. He toiled painfully over the frozen field, each step a protest, every muscle in revolt. Several times, where the open water between the jams had recently crusted, he was forced to miserably accelerate his movements as the fragile footing swayed and threatened beneath him. In such places death was quick and easy; but it was not his desire to endure no more.

His deepening anxiety vanished as two Indians dragged into view round a bend in the river. They staggered and panted like men under heavy burdens; yet the packs on their backs were a matter of but few pounds. He questioned them eagerly, and their replies seemed to relieve him. He hurried on. Next came two white men, supporting between them a woman. They also behaved as though drunken, and their limbs shook with weakness. But the woman leaned lightly upon them, choosing to carry herself forward with her own strength. At sight of her, a flash of joy cast its fleeting light across Sitka Charley's face. He cherished a very great regard for Mrs Eppingwell. He had seen many white women, but this was the first to travel the trail with him. When Captain Eppingwell proposed the hazardous undertaking and made him an offer for his services, he had shaken his head gravely; for it was an unknown journey through the dismal vastnesses of the Northland, and he knew it to be of the kind that try to the uttermost the souls of men. But when he learned that the Captain's wife was to accompany them, he had refused flatly to have anything further to do with it. Had it been a woman of his own race he would have harbored no objections; but these women of the Southland—no, no, they were too soft, too tender, for such enterprises.

Sitka Charley did not know this kind of woman. Five minutes before, he did not even dream of taking charge of the expedition; but when she came to him with her wonderful smile and her straight clean English, and talked to the point, without pleading or persuading, he had incontinently yielded. Had there been a softness and appeal to mercy in the eyes, a tremble to the voice, a taking advantage of sex, he would have stiffened to steel; instead her clear-searching eyes and clear-ringing voice, her utter frankness and tacit assumption of equality, had robbed him of his reason. He felt, then, that this was a new breed of woman; and ere they had been trail-mates for many days, he knew why the sons of such women mastered the land and the sea, and why the sons of his own womankind could not prevail against them. *Tender and soft!* Day after day he watched her, muscle-weary, exhausted, indomitable, and the words beat in upon him in a perennial refrain. *Tender and soft!* He knew her feet had been born to easy paths and sunny lands, strangers to the moccasined pain of the North, unkissed by the chill lips of the frost, and he watched and marveled at them twinkling ever through the weary day.

She had always a smile and a word of cheer, from which not even the meanest packer was excluded. As the way grew darker she seemed to stiffen and gather greater strength, and when Kah-Chucte and Gowhee, who had bragged that they knew every landmark of the way as a child did the skin-bales of the tepee, acknowledged that they knew not where they were, it was she who raised a forgiving voice amid the curses of the men. She had sung to them that night, till they felt the weariness fall from them and were ready to face the future with fresh hope. And when the food failed and each scant stint was measured jealously, she it was who rebelled against the machinations of her husband and Sitka Charley, and demanded and received a share neither greater nor less than that of the others.

Sitka Charley was proud to know this woman. A new richness, a greater breadth, had come into his life with her presence. Hitherto he had been his own mentor, had turned to right or left at no man's beck; he had moulded himself according to his own dictates, nourished his manhood regardless of all save his own opinion. For the first time he had felt a call from without for the best that was in him. Just a glance of appreciation from the clear-searching eyes, a word of thanks from the clear-ringing voice, just a slight wreathing of the lips in the wonderful smile, and he walked with the gods for hours to come. It was a new stimulant to his manhood; for the first time he thrilled with a conscious pride in his wisdom of the trail; and between the twain they ever lifted the sinking hearts of their comrades.

The faces of the two men and the woman brightened as they saw him, for after all he was the staff they leaned upon. But Sitka Charley, rigid as was his wont, concealing pain and pleasure impartially beneath an iron exterior, asked them the welfare of the rest, told the distance to the fire, and continued on the back-trip. Next he met a single Indian, unburdened, limping, lips compressed, and eyes set with the pain of a foot in which the quick fought a losing battle with the dead. All possible care had been taken of him, but in the last extremity the weak and unfortunate must perish, and Sitka Charley deemed his days to be few. The man could not keep up for long, so he gave him rough cheering words. After that came two more Indians, to whom he had allotted the task of helping along Joe, the third white man of the party. They had deserted him. Sitka Charley saw at a glance the lurking spring in their bodies, and knew they had at last cast off his mastery. So he was not taken unawares when he ordered them back in quest of their abandoned charge, and saw the gleam of the hunting-knives that they drew from the sheaths. A pitiful spectacle, three weak men lifting their puny strength in the face of the mighty vastness; but the two recoiled under the fierce rifle-blows of the one, and returned like beaten dogs to the leash. Two hours later, with Joe reeling between them and Sitka Charley bringing up the rear, they came to the fire, where the remainder of the expedition crouched in the shelter of the fly.

'A few words, my comrades, before we sleep,' Sitka Charley said, after they had devoured their slim rations of unleavened bread. He was speaking to the Indians, in their own tongue, having already given the import to the whites. 'A few words, my comrades, for your own good, that ye may yet perchance live. I shall give you the law; on his own head be the death of him that breaks it. We have passed the Hills of Silence, and we now travel the head-reaches of the Stuart. It may be one sleep, it may be several, it may be many sleeps, but in time we shall come among the Men of the Yukon, who have much grub. It were well that we look to the law. To-day, Kah-Chucte and Gowhee, whom I commanded to break trail, forgot they were men, and like frightened children ran away. True, they forgot; so let us forget. But hereafter let them remember. If it should happen they do not'—He touched his rifle carelessly, grimly. 'To-morrow they shall carry the flour and see that the white man Joe lies not down by the trail. The cups of flour are counted; should so much as an ounce be wanting at nightfall— Do ye understand? Today there were others that forgot. Moose-Head and Three-Salmon left the white man Joe to lie in the snow. Let them forget no more. With the light of day shall they go forth and break trail. Ye have heard the law. Look well, lest ye break it.'

Sitka Charley found it beyond him to keep the line close up. From Moose-Head and Three-Salmon, who broke trail in advance, to Kah-Chucte, Gowhee, and Joe, it straggled out over a mile. Each staggered, fell, or rested, as he saw fit. The line of march was a progression through a chain of irregular halts. Each drew upon the last remnant of his strength and stumbled onward till it was expended, but in some miraculous way there was always another last remnant. Each time a man fell, it was with the firm belief that he would rise no more; yet he did rise, and again, and again. The flesh yielded, the will conquered; but each triumph was a tragedy. The Indian with the frozen foot, no longer erect, crawled forward on hand and knee. He rarely rested, for he knew the penalty exacted by the frost. Even Mrs Eppingwell's lips were at last set in a stony smile, and her eyes, seeing, saw not. Often, she stopped, pressing a mittened hand to her heart, gasping and dizzy.

Joe, the white man, had passed beyond the stage of suffering. He no longer begged to be let alone, prayed to die; but was soothed and content under the anodyne of delirium. Kah-Chucte and Gowhee dragged him on roughly, venting upon him many a savage glance or blow. To them it was the acme of injustice. Their hearts were bitter with hate, heavy with fear. Why should they cumber their strength with his weakness? To do so, meant death; not to do so—and they remembered the law of Sitka Charley, and the rifle.

Joe fell with greater frequency as the daylight waned, and so hard was he to raise that they dropped farther and farther behind. Sometimes all three pitched into the snow, so weak had the Indians become. Yet on their backs was life, and strength, and warmth. Within the flour-sacks were all the potentialities of existence. They could not but think of this, and it was not strange, that which came to pass. They had fallen by the side of a great timber-jam where a thousand cords of firewood waited the match. Near by was an air hole through the ice. Kah-Chucte looked on the wood and the water, as did Gowhee; then they looked on each other. Never a word was spoken. Gowhee struck a fire; Kah-Chucte filled a tin cup with water and heated it; Joe babbled of things in another land, in a tongue they did not understand. They mixed flour with the warm water till it was a thin paste, and of this they drank many cups. They did not offer any to Joe; but he did not mind. He did not mind anything, not even his moccasins, which scorched and smoked among the coals.

A crystal mist of snow fell about them, softly, caressingly, wrapping them in clinging robes of white. And their feet would have yet trod many trails had not destiny brushed the clouds aside and cleared the air. Nay, ten minutes' delay would have been salvation. Sitka Charley, looking back, saw the pillared smoke of their fire, and guessed. And he looked ahead at those who were faithful, and at Mrs Eppingwell.

'So, my good comrades, ye have again forgotten that you were men? Good. Very good. There will be fewer bellies to feed.'

Sitka Charley retied the flour as he spoke, strapping the pack to the one on his own back. He kicked Joe till the pain broke through the poor devil's bliss and brought him doddering to his feet. Then he shoved him out upon the trail and started him on his way. The two Indians attempted to slip off.

'Hold, Gowhee! And thou, too, Kah-Chucte! Hath the flour given such strength to thy legs that they may outrun the swift-winged lead? Think not to cheat the law. Be men for the last time, and be content that ye die full-stomached. Come, step up, back to the timber, shoulder to shoulder. Come!'

The two men obeyed, quietly, without fear; for it is the future which presses upon the man, not the present.

'Thou, Gowhee, hast a wife and children and a deer-skin lodge in the Chippewyan.* What is thy will in the matter?'

'Give thou her of the goods which are mine by the word of the Captain—the blankets, the beads, the tobacco, the box which makes strange sounds after the manner of the white men. Say that I did die on the trail, but say not how.'

'And thou, Kah-Chucte, who hast nor wife nor child?'

'Mine is a sister, the wife of the Factor at Koshim. He beats her, and she is not happy. Give thou her the goods which are mine by the contract, and tell her it were well she go back to her own people. Shouldst thou meet the man, and be so minded, it were a good deed that he should die. He beats her, and she is afraid.'

'Are ye content to die by the law?'

'We are.'

'Then good-by, my good comrades. May ye sit by the well-filled pot in warm lodges, ere the day is done.'

As he spoke, he raised his rifle, and many echoes broke the silence. Hardly had they died away, when other rifles spoke in the distance. Sitka Charley started. There had been more than one shot, yet there was but one other rifle in the party. He gave a fleeting glance at the men who lay so quietly, smiled viciously at the wisdom of the trail, and hurried on to meet the Men of the Yukon.

THE WIFE OF A KING

I

Once, when the Northland was very young, the social and civic virtues were remarkable alike for their paucity and their simplicity. When the burden of domestic duties grew grievous, and the fireside mood expanded to a constant protest against its bleak loneliness, the adventurers from the Southland, in lieu of better, paid the stipulated prices and took unto themselves native wives. It was a foretaste of Paradise to the women, for it must be confessed that the white rovers gave far better care and treatment to them than did their Indian copartners. Of course, the white men themselves were satisfied with such deals, as were also the Indian men for that matter. Having sold their daughters and sisters for cotton blankets and obsolete rifles, and traded their warm furs for flimsy calico and bad whiskey, the sons of the soil promptly and cheerfully succumbed to quick consumption and other swift diseases correlated with the blessings of a superior civilization.

It was in these days of Arcadian simplicity that Cal Galbraith journeyed through the land and fell sick on the Lower River. It was a refreshing advent in the lives of the good Sisters of the Holy Cross,* who gave him shelter and medicine; though they little dreamed of the hot elixir infused into his veins by the touch of their soft hands and their gentle ministrations. Cal Galbraith became troubled with strange thoughts, which clamored for attention till he laid eyes on the Mission girl, Madeline. Yet he gave no sign, biding his time patiently. He strengthened with the coming spring, and when the sun rode the heavens in a golden circle, and the joy and throb of life were in all the land, he gathered his still weak body together and departed.

Now Madeline, the Mission girl, was an orphan. Her white father had failed to give a bald-faced grizzly the trail one day, and had died quickly. Then her Indian mother, having no man to fill the winter cache, had tried the hazardous experiment of waiting till the salmon-run on fifty pounds of flour and half as many of bacon. After that the baby, Chook-ra, went to live with the good Sisters, and to be thenceforth known by another name.

But Madeline still had kinsfolk, the nearest being a dissolute uncle who outraged his vitals with inordinate quantities of the white man's whiskey. He strove daily to walk with the gods, and incidentally his feet sought shorter trails to the grave. When sober he suffered exquisite torture. He had no conscience. To this ancient vagabond Cal Galbraith duly presented himself, and they consumed many words and much tobacco in the conversation that followed. Promises were also made; and in the end the old heathen took a few pounds of dried salmon and his birch-bark canoe, and paddled away to the Mission of the Holy Cross.

It is not given the world to know what promises he made and what lies he told,—the Sisters never gossip; but when he returned, upon his swarthy chest there was a brass crucifix, and in his canoe his niece Madeline. That night there was a grand wedding and a *potlach*; so that for two days to follow there was no fishing done by the village. But in the morning Madeline shook the dust of the Lower River from her moccasins, and with her husband, in a poling-boat, went to live on the Upper River in a place known as the Lower Country. And in the years which followed she was a good wife, sharing her husband's hardships and cooking his food. And she kept him in straight trails, till he learned to save his dust and to work mightily. In the end, he struck it rich, and built a cabin in Circle City;* and his happiness was such that men who came to visit him in his home circle became restless at the sight of it and envied him greatly.

But the Northland began to mature, and social amenities to make their appearance. Hitherto, the Southland had sent forth its sons; but it now belched forth a new exodus, this time of its daughters. Sisters and wives they were not; but they did not fail to put new ideas in the heads of the men, and to elevate the tone of things in ways peculiarly their own. No more did the squaws gather at the dances, go roaring down the centre in the good, old Virginia reels, or make merry with jolly 'Dan Tucker.'* They fell back on their native stoicism, and uncomplainingly watched the rule of their white sisters from the cabins.

Then another exodus came over the mountains from the prolific Southland. This time it was of women that became mighty in the land. Their word was law; their law was steel. They frowned upon the Indian wives, while the other women became mild and walked humbly. There were cowards who became ashamed of their ancient covenants with the daughters of the soil, who looked with a new distaste upon their dark-skinned children; but there were also others— men—who remained true and proud of their aboriginal vows. When it became the fashion to divorce the native wives, Cal Galbraith retained his manhood, and in so doing felt the heavy hand of the women who had come last, knew least, but who ruled the land.

One day, the Upper Country, which lies far above Circle City, was pronounced rich. Dog-teams carried the news to Salt Water; golden argosies freighted the lure across the North Pacific; wires and cables sang with the tidings; and the world heard for the first time of the Klondike River and the Yukon Country.

Cal Galbraith had lived the years quietly. He had been a good husband to Madeline, and she had blessed him. But somehow discontent fell upon him; he felt vague yearnings for his own kind, for the life he had been shut out from,— a general sort of desire, which men sometimes feel, to break out and taste the prime of living. Besides, there drifted down the river wild rumors of the wonderful Eldorado, glowing descriptions of the city of logs and tents, and ludicrous accounts of the *che-cha-quas* who had rushed in and were stampeding the whole country. Circle City was dead. The world had moved on up river and become a new and most marvelous world.

Cal Galbraith grew restless on the edge of things, and wished to see with his own eyes. So, after the wash-up, he weighed in a couple of hundred pounds of dust on the Company's big scales, and took a draft for the same on Dawson. Then he put Tom Dixon in charge of his mines, kissed Madeline goodby, promised to be back before the first mush-ice ran, and took passage on an up-river steamer.

Madeline waited,—waited through all the three months of daylight. She fed the dogs, gave much of her time to young Cal, watched the short summer fade away and the sun begin its long journey to the south. And she prayed much in the manner of the Sisters of the Holy Cross. The fall came, and with it there was mush-ice on the Yukon, and Circle City kings returning to the winter's work at their mines, but no Cal Galbraith. Tom Dixon received a letter, however, for his men sledded up her winter's supply of dry pine. The Company received a letter, for its dog-teams filled her cache with their best provisions, and she was told that her credit was limitless.

Through all the ages man has been held the chief instigator of the woes of woman; but in this case the men held their tongues and swore harshly at one of their number who was away, while the women failed utterly to emulate them. So, without needless delay, Madeline heard strange tales of Cal Galbraith's doings; also, of a certain Greek dancer who played with men as children did with bubbles. Now Madeline was an Indian woman, and further, she had no woman friend to whom to go for wise counsel. She prayed and planned by turns, and that night, being quick of resolve and action, she harnessed the dogs, and with young Cal securely lashed to the sled, stole away.

Though the Yukon still ran free, the eddy-ice was growing, and each day saw the river dwindling to a slushy thread. Save him who has done the like, no man may know what she endured in traveling a hundred miles on the rim-ice; nor may they understand the toil and hardship of breaking the two hundred miles of packed ice which remained after the river froze for good. But Madeline was an Indian woman, so she did these things, and one night there came a knock at Malemute Kid's door. Thereat he fed a team of starving dogs, put a healthy youngster to bed, and turned his attention to an exhausted woman. He removed her ice-bound moccasins while he listened to her tale, and stuck the point of his knife into her feet that he might see how far they were frozen.

Despite his tremendous virility, Malemute Kid was possessed of a softer, womanly element, which could win the confidence of a snarling wolf-dog or draw confessions from the most wintry heart. Nor did he seek them. Hearts opened to him as spontaneously as flowers to the sun. Even the priest, Father Roubeau, had been known to confess to him, while the men and women of the Northland were ever knocking at his door,—a door from which the latch-string hung always out. To Madeline, he could do no wrong, make no mistake. She had known him from the time she first cast her lot among the people of her father's race; and to her half-barbaric mind it seemed that in him was centred the wisdom of the ages, that between his vision and the future there could be no intervening veil.

There were false ideals in the land. The social strictures of Dawson were not synonymous with those of the previous era, and the swift maturity of the Northland involved much wrong. Malemute Kid was aware of this, and he had Cal Galbraith's measure accurately. He knew a hasty word was the father of much evil; besides, he was minded to teach a great lesson and bring shame upon the man. So Stanley Prince, the young mining expert, was called into the conference the following night, as was also Lucky Jack Harrington and his violin. That same night, Bettles, who owed a great debt to Malemute Kid, harnessed up Cal Galbraith's dogs, lashed Cal Galbraith, junior, to the sled, and slipped away in the dark for Stuart River.

II

'So; one—two—three, one—two—three. Now reverse! No, no! Start up again, Jack. See—this way.' Prince executed the movement as one should who has led the cotillion.

'Now; one—two—three, one—two—three. Reverse! Ah!

that's better. Try it again. I say, you know, you mustn't look at your feet. One—two—three, one—two—three. Shorter steps! You are not hanging to the gee-pole just now. Try it over. There! that's the way. One—two—three, one—two—three.'

Round and round went Prince and Madeline in an interminable waltz. The table and stools had been shoved over against the wall to increase the room. Malemute Kid sat on the bunk, chin to knees, greatly interested. Jack Harrington sat beside him, scraping away on his violin and following the dancers.

It was a unique situation, the undertaking of these three men with the woman. The most pathetic part, perhaps, was the businesslike way in which they went about it. No athlete was ever trained more rigidly for a coming contest, nor wolf-dog for the harness, than was she. But they had good material, for Madeline, unlike most women of her race, in her childhood had escaped the carrying of heavy burdens and the toil of the trail. Besides, she was a clean-limbed, willowy creature, possessed of much grace which had not hitherto been realized. It was this grace which the men strove to bring out and knock into shape.

'Trouble with her she learned to dance all wrong,' Prince remarked to the bunk, after having deposited his breathless pupil on the table. 'She's quick at picking up; yet I could do better had she never danced a step. But say, Kid, I can't understand this.' Prince imitated a peculiar movement of the shoulders and head,—a weakness Madeline suffered from in walking.

'Lucky for her she was raised in the Mission,' Malemute Kid answered. 'Packing, you know,—the head-strap. Other Indian women have it bad, but she didn't do any packing till after she married, and then only at first. Saw hard lines with that husband of hers. They went through the Forty Mile famine together.'

'But can we break it?'

'Don't know. Perhaps long walks with her trainers will make the riffle. Anyway, they'll take it out some, won't they, Madeline?'

The girl nodded assent. If Malemute Kid, who knew all things, said so, why, it was so. That was all there was about it.

She had come over to them, anxious to begin again. Harrington surveyed her in quest of her points, much in the same manner men do horses. It certainly was not disappointing, for he asked with sudden interest, 'What did that beggarly uncle of yours get anyway?'

'One rifle, one blanket, twenty bottles of *hooch*. Rifle broke.' She said this last scornfully, as though disgusted at how low her maiden-value had been rated.

She spoke fair English, with many peculiarities of her husband's speech, but there was still perceptible the Indian accent, the traditional groping after strange gutturals. Even this her instructors had taken in hand, and with no small success, too.

At the next intermission Prince discovered a new predicament.

'I say, Kid,' he said, 'we're wrong, all wrong. She can't learn in moccasins. Put her feet into slippers, and then on to that waxed floor—phew!'

Madeline raised a foot and regarded her shapeless house-moccasin dubiously. In previous winters, both at Circle City and Forty Mile, she had danced many a night away with similar footgear, and there had been nothing the matter. But now—well, if there was anything wrong it was for Malemute Kid to know, not her.

But Malemute Kid did know, and he had a good eye for measures; so he put on his cap and mittens and went down the hill to pay Mrs Eppingwell a call. Her husband, Clove Eppingwell, was prominent in the community as one of the great Government officials. The Kid had noted her slender little foot one night, at the Governor's Ball. And as he also knew her to be as sensible as she was pretty, it was no task to ask of her a certain small favor.

On his return, Madeline withdrew for a moment to the inner room. When she reappeared Prince was startled.

'By Jove!' he gasped. 'Who'd 'a' thought it! The little witch! Why, my sister'—

'Is an English girl,' interrupted Malemute Kid, 'with an

English foot. This girl comes of a small-footed race. Moccasins just broadened her feet healthily, while she did not misshape them by running with the dogs in her childhood.'

But this explanation failed utterly to allay Prince's admiration. Harrington's commercial instinct was touched, and as he looked upon the exquisitely turned foot and ankle, there ran through his mind the sordid list,—'one rifle, one blanket, twenty bottles of *hooch*.'

Madeline was the wife of a king, a king whose yellow treasure could buy outright a score of fashion's puppets; yet in all her life her feet had known no gear save red-tanned moosehide. At first she looked in awe at the tiny white satin slippers; but she quickly understood the admiration which shone, manlike, in the eyes of the men. Her face flushed with pride. For the moment she was drunken with her woman's loveliness; then she murmured, with increased scorn, 'And one rifle broke!'

So the training went on. Every day Malemute Kid led the girl out on long walks devoted to the correction of her carriage and the shortening of her stride. There was little likelihood of her identity being discovered, for Cal Galbraith and the rest of the Old-Timers were like lost children among the many strangers who had rushed into the land. Besides, the frost of the North has a bitter tongue, and the tender women of the South, to shield their cheeks from its biting caresses, were prone to the use of canvas masks. With faces obscured and bodies lost in squirrel-skin *parkas*, a mother and daughter, meeting on trail, would pass as strangers.

The coaching progressed rapidly. At first it had been slow, but later a sudden acceleration had manifested itself. This began from the moment Madeline tried on the white satin slippers, and in so doing found herself. The pride of her renegade father, apart from any natural self-esteem she might possess, at that instant received its birth. Hitherto, she had deemed herself a woman of an alien breed, of inferior stock, purchased by her lord's favor. Her husband had seemed to her a god, who had lifted her, through no essential virtues on her part, to his own godlike level. But she had never forgotten, even when young Cal was born, that she was not of his people. As he had been a god, so had his womankind been goddesses. She might have contrasted herself with them, but she had never compared. It might have been that familiarity bred contempt; however, be that as it may, she had ultimately come to understand these roving white men, and to weigh them. True, her mind was dark to deliberate analysis, but she yet possessed her woman's clarity of vision in such matters. On the night of the slippers she had measured the bold, open admiration of her three man friends; and for the first time comparison had suggested itself. It was only a foot and an ankle, but—but comparison could not, in the nature of things, cease at that point. She judged herself by their standards till the divinity of her white sisters was shattered. After all, they were only women, and why should she not exalt herself to their place? In doing these things she learned where she lacked, and with the knowledge of her weakness came her strength. And so mightily did she strive that her three trainers often marveled late into the night over the eternal mystery of woman.

In this way Thanksgiving night drew near. At irregular intervals Bettles sent word down from Stuart River regarding the welfare of young Cal. The time of their return was approaching. More than once a casual caller, hearing dance-music and the rhythmic pulse of feet, entered, only to find Harrington scraping away and the other two beating time or arguing noisily over a mooted step. Madeline was never in evidence, having precipitately fled to the inner room.

On one of these nights Cal Galbraith dropped in. Encouraging news had just come down from Stuart River, and Madeline had surpassed herself—not in walk alone, and carriage and grace, but in womanly roguishness. They had indulged in sharp repartee, and she had defended herself brilliantly; and then, yielding to the intoxication of the moment, and of her own power, she had bullied, and mastered, and wheedled, and patronized them with most astonishing success. And instinctively, involuntarily, they had bowed, not to her beauty, her wisdom, her wit, but to that indefinable something in woman to which man yields yet cannot name. The room was dizzy with sheer delight as she and Prince whirled through the last dance of the evening. Harrington was throwing in inconceivable flourishes, while Malemute Kid, utterly abandoned, had seized the broom and was executing mad gyrations on his own account.

At this instant the door shook with a heavy rap-rap, and their quick glances noted the lifting of the latch. But they had survived similar situations before. Harrington never broke a note. Madeline shot through the waiting door to the inner room. The broom went hurtling under the bunk, and by the time Cal Galbraith and Louis Savoy got their heads in, Malemute Kid and Prince were in each other's arms, wildly schottisching* down the room.

As a rule, Indian women do not make a practice of fainting on provocation, but Madeline came as near to it as she ever had in her life. For an hour she crouched on the floor, listening to the heavy voices of the men rumbling up and down in mimic thunder. Like familiar chords of childhood melodies, every intonation, every trick of her husband's voice, swept in upon her, fluttering her heart and weakening her knees till she lay half-fainting against the door. It was well she could neither see nor hear when he took his departure.

'When do you expect to go back to Circle City?' Malemute Kid asked simply.

'Haven't thought much about it,' he replied. 'Don't think till after the ice breaks.'

'And Madeline?'

He flushed at the question, and there was a quick droop to his eyes. Malemute Kid could have despised him for that, had he known men less. As it was, his gorge rose against the wives and daughters who had come into the land, and not satisfied with usurping the place of the native women, had put unclean thoughts in the heads of the men and made them ashamed.

'I guess she's all right,' the Circle City king answered hastily, and in an apologetic manner. 'Tom Dixon's got charge of my interests, you know, and he sees to it that she has everything she wants.'

Malemute Kid laid hand upon his arm, and hushed him suddenly. They had stepped without. Overhead, the aurora, a gorgeous wanton, flaunted miracles of color; beneath lay the sleeping town. Far below, a solitary dog gave tongue. The king again began to speak, but the Kid pressed his hand for silence. The sound multiplied. Dog after dog took up the strain till the full-throated chorus swayed the night. To him who hears for the first time this weird song, is told the first and greatest secret of the Northland; to him who has heard it often, it is the solemn knell of lost endeavor. It is the plaint of tortured souls, for in it is invested the heritage of the North, the suffering of countless generations—the warning and the requiem to the world's estrays.

Cal Galbraith shivered slightly as it died away in half-caught sobs. The Kid read his thoughts openly, and wandered back with him through all the weary days of famine and disease; and with him was also the patient Madeline, sharing his pains and perils, never doubting, never complaining. His mind's retina vibrated to a score of pictures, stern, clear-cut, and the hand of the Past drew back with heavy fingers on his heart. It was the psychological moment. Malemute Kid was half tempted to play his reserve card and win the game; but the lesson was too mild as yet, and he let it pass. The next instant they had gripped hands, and the king's beaded moccasins were drawing protests from the outraged snow as he crunched down the hill.

Madeline in collapse was another woman to the mischievous creature of an hour before, whose laughter had been so infectious and whose heightened color and flashing eyes had made her teachers for the while forget. Weak and nerveless, she sat in the chair just as she had been dropped there by Prince and Harrington. Malemute Kid frowned. This would never do. When the time of meeting her husband came to hand, she must carry things off with high-handed imperiousness. It was very necessary she should do it after the manner of white women, else the victory would be no victory at all. So he talked to her, sternly, without mincing of words, and initiated her into the weaknesses of his own sex, till she came to understand what simpletons men were after all, and why the word of their women was law.

A few days before Thanksgiving night, Malemute Kid made

another call on Mrs Eppingwell. She promptly overhauled her feminine fripperies, paid a protracted visit to the dry-goods department of the P. C. Company, and returned with the Kid to make Madeline's acquaintance. After that came a period such as the cabin had never seen before, and what with cutting, and fitting, and basting, and stitching, and numerous other wonderful and unknowable things, the male conspirators were more often banished the premises than not. At such times the Opera House* opened its double storm-doors to them. So often did they put their heads together, and so deeply did they drink to curious toasts, that the loungers scented unknown creeks of incalculable richness, and it is known that several *che-cha-quas* and at least one Old-Timer kept their stampeding packs stored behind the bar, ready to hit the trail at a moment's notice.

Mrs Eppingwell was a woman of capacity; so, when she turned Madeline over to her trainers on Thanksgiving night she was so transformed that they were almost afraid of her. Prince wrapped a Hudson Bay blanket about her with a mock reverence more real than feigned, while Malemute Kid, whose arm she had taken, found it a severe trial to resume his wonted mentorship. Harrington, with the list of purchase still running through his head, dragged along in the rear, nor opened his mouth once all the way down into the town. When they came to the back door of the Opera House they took the blanket from Madeline's shoulders and spread it on the snow. Slipping out of Prince's moccasins, she stepped upon it in new satin slippers. The masquerade was at its height. She hesitated, but they jerked open the door and shoved her in. Then they ran around to come in by the front entrance.

III

'Where is Freda?'* the Old-Timers questioned, while the *che-cha-quas* were equally energetic in asking who Freda was. The ballroom buzzed with her name. It was on everybody's lips. Grizzled 'sour-dough boys,' day-laborers at the mines but proud of their degree, either patronized the spruce-looking tenderfeet and lied eloquently,—the 'sour-dough boys' being specially created to toy with truth,—or gave them savage looks of indignation because of their ignorance. Perhaps forty kings of the Upper and Lower Countries were on the floor, each deeming himself hot on the trail and sturdily backing his judgment with the yellow dust of the realm. An assistant was sent to the man at the scales, upon whom had fallen the burden of weighing up the sacks, while several of the gamblers, with the rules of chance at their finger-ends, made up alluring books on the field and favorites.

Which was Freda? Time and again the Greek dancer was thought to have been discovered, but each discovery brought panic to the betting ring and a frantic registering of new wagers by those who wished to hedge. Malemute Kid took an interest in the hunt, his advent being hailed uproariously by the revelers, who knew him to a man. The Kid had a good eye for the trick of a step, and ear for the lilt of a voice, and his private choice was a marvelous creature who scintillated as the 'Aurora Borealis.' But the Greek dancer was too subtle for even his penetration. The majority of the gold-hunters seemed to have centred their verdict on the 'Russian Princess,' who was the most graceful in the room, and hence could be no other than Freda Moloof.

During a quadrille a roar of satisfaction went up. She was discovered. At previous balls, in the figure 'all hands round,' Freda had displayed an inimitable step and variation peculiarly her own. As the figure was called, the 'Russian Princess' gave the unique rhythm to limb and body. A chorus of I-told-you-so's shook the squared roof-beams, when lo! it was noticed that the 'Aurora Borealis' and another mask, the 'Spirit of the Pole,' were performing the same trick equally well. And when two twin 'Sun-Dogs' and a 'Frost Queen' followed suit, a second assistant was dispatched to the aid of the man at the scales.

Bettles came off trail in the midst of the excitement, descending upon them in a hurricane of frost. His rimed brows turned to cataracts as he whirled about; his mustache, still frozen, seemed gemmed with diamonds and turned the light in vari-colored rays; while the flying feet slipped on the chunks of ice which rattled from his moccasins and German socks. A Northland dance is quite an informal affair, the men of the creeks and trails having lost whatever fastidiousness they may have at one time possessed; and only in the high official circles are conventions at all observed. Here, caste carried no significance. Millionaires and paupers, dog-drivers and mounted policemen, joined hands with 'ladies in the centre,' and swept around the circle performing most remarkable capers. Primitive in their pleasures, boisterous and rough, they displayed no rudeness, but rather a crude chivalry as genuine as the most polished courtesy.

In his quest for the Greek dancer, Cal Galbraith managed to get into the same set with the 'Russian Princess,' toward whom popular suspicion had turned. But by the time he had guided her through one dance, he was willing not only to stake his millions that she was not Freda, but that he had had his arm about her waist before. When or where he could not tell, but the puzzling sense of familiarity so wrought upon him that he turned his attention to the discovery of her identity. Malemute Kid might have aided him instead of occasionally taking the 'Princess' for a few turns and talking earnestly to her in low tones. But it was Jack Harrington who paid the 'Russian Princess' the most assiduous court. Once he drew Cal Galbraith aside and hazarded wild guesses as to who she was, and explained to him that he was going in to win. This rankled the Circle City king, for man is not by nature monogamic, and he forgot both Madeline and Freda in the new quest.

It was soon noised about that the 'Russian Princess' was not Freda Moloof. Interest deepened. Here was a fresh enigma. They knew Freda though they could not find her, but here was somebody they had found and did not know. Even the women could not place her, and they knew every good dancer in the camp. Many took her for one of the official clique, indulging in a silly escapade. Not a few asserted she would disappear before the unmasking. Others were equally positive that she was the woman reporter of the Kansas City 'Star,' come to write them up at ninety dollars per column. And the men at the scales worked busily.

At one o'clock every couple took to the floor. The un-masking began amid laughter and delight, like that of care-free children. There was no end of oh's and ah's as mask after mask was lifted. The scintillating 'Aurora Borealis' became the brawny negress whose income from washing the community's clothes ran at about five hundred a month. The twin 'Sun-Dogs' discovered mustaches on their upper lips, and were recognized as brother fraction-kings of Eldorado. In one of the most prominent sets, and the slowest in uncov-ering, was Cal Galbraith with the 'Spirit of the Pole.' Oppo-site him was Jack Harrington and the 'Russian Princess.' The rest had discovered themselves, yet the Greek dancer was still missing. All eyes were upon the group. Cal Galbraith, in response to their cries, lifted his partner's mask. Freda's wonderful face and brilliant eyes flashed out upon them. A roar went up, to be hushed suddenly in the new and absorb-ing mystery of the 'Russian Princess.' Her face was still hid-den, and Jack Harrington was struggling with her. The dancers tittered on the tiptoes of expectancy. He crushed her dainty costume roughly, and then—and then the revelers exploded. The joke was on them. They had danced all night with a tabooed native woman.

But those that knew, and they were many, ceased abrupt-ly, and a hush fell upon the room. Cal Galbraith crossed over with great strides, angrily, and spoke to Madeline in polyglot Chinook. But she retained her composure, appar-ently oblivious to the fact that she was the cynosure of all eyes, and answered him in English. She showed neither fright nor anger, and Malemute Kid chuckled at her well-bred equanimity. The king felt baffled, defeated; his com-mon Siwash wife had passed beyond him.

'Come!' he said finally. 'Come on home.'

'I beg pardon,' she replied; 'I have agreed to go to sup-per with Mr Harrington. Besides, there's no end of dances promised.'

Harrington extended his arm to lead her away. He evinced not the slightest disinclination toward showing his back, but Malemute Kid had by this time edged in closer. The Cir-cle City king was stunned. Twice his hand dropped to his belt, and twice the Kid gathered himself to spring; but the retreating couple passed safely through the supper-room door, where canned oysters were spread at five dollars the plate. The crowd sighed audibly, broke up into couples, and followed them. Freda pouted and went in with Cal Galbraith; but she had a good heart and a sure tongue, and she spoiled his oysters for him. What she said is of no importance, but his face went red and white at intervals, and he swore repeatedly and savagely at himself.

The supper-room was filled with a pandemonium of voices, which ceased suddenly as Cal Galbraith stepped over to his wife's table. Since the unmasking considerable weights of dust had been placed as to the outcome. Everybody watched with breathless interest. Harrington's blue eyes were steady, but under the over-hanging tablecloth a Smith & Wesson* balanced on his knee. Madeline looked up, casually, with little interest.

'May—may I have the next round dance with you?' the king stuttered.

The wife of the king glanced at her card and inclined her head.

AN ODYSSEY OF THE NORTH

I

The sleds were singing their eternal lament to the creaking of the harnesses and the tinkling bells of the leaders; but the men and dogs were tired and made no sound. The trail was heavy with new-fallen snow, and they had come far, and the runners, burdened with flint-like quarters of frozen moose, clung tenaciously to the unpacked surface and held back with a stubbornness almost human. Darkness was coming on, but there was no camp to pitch that night. The snow fell gently through the pulseless air, not in flakes, but in tiny frost crystals of delicate design. It was very warm,—barely ten below zero,—and the men did not mind. Meyers and Bettles had raised their ear-flaps, while Malemute Kid had even taken off his mittens.

The dogs had been fagged out early in the afternoon, but they now began to show new vigor. Among the more astute there was a certain restlessness,—an impatience at the restraint of the traces, an indecisive quickness of movement, a sniffing of snouts and pricking of ears. These became incensed at their more phlegmatic brothers, urging them on with numerous sly nips on their hinderquarters. Those, thus chidden, also contracted and helped spread the contagion. At last, the leader of the foremost sled uttered a sharp whine of satisfaction, crouching lower in the snow and throwing himself against the collar. The rest followed suit. There was an ingathering of back-bands, a tightening of traces; the sleds leaped forward, and the men clung to the gee-poles, violently accelerating the uplift of their feet that they might escape going under the runners. The weariness of the day fell from them, and they whooped encouragement to the dogs. The animals responded with joyous yelps. They were swinging through the gathering darkness at a rattling gallop.

'Gee! Gee!' the men cried, each in turn, as their sleds

abruptly left the main-trail, heeling over on single runners like luggers on the wind.

Then came a hundred yards' dash to the lighted parchment window, which told its own story of the home cabin, the roaring Yukon stove, and the steaming pots of tea. But the home cabin had been invaded. Three-score huskies chorused defiance, and as many furry forms precipitated themselves upon the dogs which drew the first sled. The door was flung open, and a man, clad in the scarlet tunic of the Northwest Police, waded knee-deep among the furious brutes, calmly and impartially dispensing soothing justice with the butt end of a dog-whip. After that, the men shook hands; and in this wise was Malemute Kid welcomed to his own cabin by a stranger.

Stanley Prince, who should have welcomed him, and who was responsible for the Yukon stove and hot tea aforementioned, was busy with his guests. There were a dozen or so of them, as nondescript a crowd as ever served the Queen in the enforcement of her laws or the delivery of her mails. They were of many breeds, but their common life had formed of them a certain type,—a lean and wiry type, with trail-hardened muscles, and sun-browned faces, and untroubled souls which gazed frankly forth, clear-eyed and steady. They drove the dogs of the Queen, wrought fear in the hearts of her enemies, ate of her meagre fare, and were happy. They had seen life, and done deeds, and lived romances; but they did not know it.

And they were very much at home. Two of them were sprawled upon Malemute Kid's bunk, singing chansons which their French forbears sang in the days when first they entered the Northwest-land and mated with its Indian women. Bettles' bunk had suffered a similar invasion, and three or four lusty *voyageurs* worked their toes among its blankets as they listened to the tale of one who had served on the boat brigade with Wolseley when he fought his way to Khartoum.* And when he tired, a cowboy told of courts and kings and lords and ladies he had seen when Buffalo Bill toured the capitals of Europe. In a corner, two half-breeds, ancient comrades in a lost campaign, mended harnesses and talked of the days when the Northwest flamed with insurrection and Louis Reil* was king.

Rough jests and rougher jokes went up and down, and great hazards by trail and river were spoken of in the light of commonplaces, only to be recalled by virtue of some grain of humor or ludicrous happening. Prince was led away by these uncrowned heroes who had seen history made, who regarded the great and the romantic as but the ordinary and the incidental in the routine of life. He passed his precious tobacco among them with lavish disregard, and rusty chains of reminiscence were loosened, and forgotten odysseys resurrected for his especial benefit.

When conversation dropped and the travelers filled the last pipes and unlashed their tight-rolled sleeping-furs, Prince fell back upon his comrade for further information.

'Well, you know what the cowboy is,' Malemute Kid answered, beginning to unlace his moccasins; 'and it's not hard to guess the British blood in his bed-partner. As for the rest, they're all children of the *coureurs du bois*,* mingled with God knows how many other bloods. The two turning in by the door are the regulation "breeds" or *bois brules*.* That lad with the worsted breech scarf—notice his eyebrows and the turn of his jaw—shows a Scotchman wept in his mother's smoky tepee. And that handsome-looking fellow putting the capote under his head is a French half-breed,—you heard him talking; he doesn't like the two Indians turning in next to him. You see, when the "breeds" rose under Reil the full-bloods kept the peace, and they've not lost much love for one another since.'

'But I say, what's that glum-looking fellow by the stove? I'll swear he can't talk English. He hasn't opened his mouth all night.'

'You're wrong. He knows English well enough. Did you follow his eyes when he listened? I did. But he's neither kith nor kin to the others. When they talked their own patois you could see he didn't understand. I've been wondering myself what he is. Let's find out.'

'Fire a couple of sticks into the stove!' Malemute Kid

commanded, raising his voice and looking squarely at the man in question.

He obeyed at once.

'Had discipline knocked into him somewhere,' Prince commented in a low tone.

Malemute Kid nodded, took off his socks, and picked his way among the recumbent men to the stove. There he hung his damp footgear among a score or so of mates.

'When do you expect to get to Dawson?' he asked tentatively.

The man studied him a moment before replying. 'They say seventy-five mile. So? Maybe two days.'

The very slightest accent was perceptible, while there was no awkward hesitancy or groping for words.

'Been in the country before?'

'No.'

'Northwest Territory?'

'Yes.'

'Born there?'

'No.'

'Well, where the devil were you born? You're none of these.' Malemute Kid swept his hand over the dog-drivers, even including the two policemen who had turned into Prince's bunk. 'Where did you come from? I've seen faces like yours before, though I can't remember just where.'

'I know you,' he irrelevantly replied, at once turning the drift of Malemute Kid's questions.

'Where? Ever see me?'

'No; your partner, him priest, Pastilik,* long time ago. Him ask me if I see you, Malemute Kid. Him give me grub. I no stop long. You hear him speak 'bout me?'

'Oh! you're the fellow that traded the otter skins for the dogs?'

The man nodded, knocked out his pipe, and signified his disinclination for conversation by rolling up in his furs. Malemute Kid blew out the slush-lamp and crawled under the blankets with Prince.

'Well, what is he?'

'Don't know—turned me off, somehow, and then shut up

like a clam. But he's a fellow to whet your curiosity. I've heard of him. All the Coast wondered about him eight years ago. Sort of mysterious, you know. He came down out of the North, in the dead of winter, many a thousand miles from here, skirting Bering Sea and traveling as though the devil were after him. No one ever learned where he came from, but he must have come far. He was badly travel-worn when he got food from the Swedish missionary on Golovin Bay and asked the way south. We heard of this afterward. Then he abandoned the shore-line, heading right across Norton Sound. Terrible weather, snowstorms and high winds, but he pulled through where a thousand other men would have died, missing St Michael's and making the land at Pastilik. He'd lost all but two dogs, and was nearly gone with starvation.

'He was so anxious to go on that Father Roubeau fitted him out with grub; but he couldn't let him have any dogs, for he was only waiting my arrival to go on a trip himself. Mr Ulysses* knew too much to start on without animals, and fretted around for several days. He had on his sled a bunch of beautifully cured otter skins, sea-otters, you know, worth their weight in gold. There was also at Pastilik an old Shylock* of a Russian trader, who had dogs to kill. Well, they didn't dicker very long, but when the Strange One headed south again, it was in the rear of a spanking dog-team. Mr Shylock, by the way, had the otter skins. I saw them, and they were magnificent. We figured it up and found the dogs brought him at least five hundred apiece. And it wasn't as if the Strange One didn't know the value of sea-otter; he was an Indian of some sort, and what little he talked showed he'd been among white men.

'After the ice passed out of the Sea, word came up from Nunivak Island that he'd gone in there for grub. Then he dropped from sight, and this is the first heard of him in eight years. Now where did he come from? and what was he doing there? and why did he come from there? He's Indian, he's been nobody knows where, and he's had discipline, which is unusual for an Indian. Another mystery of the North for you to solve, Prince.'

'Thanks, awfully; but I've got too many on hand as it is,' he replied.

Malemute Kid was already breathing heavily; but the young mining engineer gazed straight up through the thick darkness, waiting for the strange orgasm which stirred his blood to die away. And when he did sleep, his brain worked on, and for the nonce he, too, wandered through the white unknown, struggled with the dogs on endless trails, and saw men live, and toil, and die like men.

The next morning, hours before daylight, the dog-drivers and policemen pulled out for Dawson. But the powers that saw to her Majesty's interests, and ruled the destinies of her lesser creatures, gave the mailmen little rest; for a week later they appeared at Stuart River, heavily burdened with letters for Salt Water. However, their dogs had been replaced by fresh ones; but then, they were dogs.

The men had expected some sort of a lay-over in which to rest up; besides, this Klondike was a new section of the Northland, and they had wished to see a little something of the Golden City where dust flowed like water, and dance halls rang with never ending revelry. But they dried their socks and smoked their evening pipes with much the same gusto as on their former visit, though one or two bold spirits speculated on desertion and the possibility of crossing the unexplored Rockies to the east, and thence, by the Mackenzie Valley, of gaining their old stamping-grounds in the Chippewyan Country. Two or three even decided to return to their homes by that route when their terms of service had expired, and they began to lay plans forthwith, looking forward to the hazardous undertaking in much the same way a city-bred man would to a day's holiday in the woods.

He of the Otter Skins seemed very restless, though he took little interest in the discussion, and at last he drew Malemute Kid to one side and talked for some time in low tones. Prince cast curious eyes in their direction, and the mystery deepened when they put on caps and mittens, and went outside. When they returned, Malemute Kid placed his gold-scales on the table, weighed out the matter of sixty ounces, and transferred them to the Strange One's sack. Then the chief of the dog-drivers joined the conclave, and certain business was transacted with him. The next day the gang went on up river, but He of the Otter Skins took several pounds of grub and turned his steps back toward Dawson.

'Didn't know what to make of it,' said Malemute Kid in response to Prince's queries; 'but the poor beggar wanted to be quit of the service for some reason or other—at least it seemed a most important one to him, though he wouldn't let on what. You see, it's just like the army; he signed for two years, and the only way to get free was to buy himself out. He couldn't desert and then stay here, and he was just wild to remain in the country. Made up his mind when he got to Dawson, he said; but no one knew him, hadn't a cent, and I was the only one he'd spoken two words with. So he talked it over with the Lieutenant-Governor, and made arrangements in case he could get the money from me—loan, you know. Said he'd pay back in the year, and if I wanted, would put me onto something rich. Never'd seen it, but knew it was rich.

'And talk! why, when he got me outside he was ready to weep. Begged and pleaded; got down in the snow to me till I hauled him out of it. Palavered around like a crazy man. Swore he's worked to this very end for years and years, and couldn't bear to be disappointed now. Asked him what end, but he wouldn't say. Said they might keep him on the other half of the trail and he wouldn't get to Dawson in two years, and then it would be too late. Never saw a man take on so in my life. And when I said I'd let him have it, had to yank him out of the snow again. Told him to consider it in the light of a grub-stake. Think he'd have it? No, sir! Swore he'd give me all he found, make me rich beyond the dreams of avarice, and all such stuff. Now a man who puts his life and time against a grub-stake ordinarily finds it hard enough to turn over half of what he finds. Something behind all this, Prince; just you make a note of it. We'll hear of him if he stays in the country'—

'And if he doesn't?'

'Then my good nature gets a shock, and I'm sixty some odd ounces out.'

The cold weather had come on with the long nights, and the sun had begun to play his ancient game of peekaboo along the southern snow-line ere aught was heard of Malemute Kid's grub-stake. And then, one bleak morning in early January, a heavily laden dog-train pulled into his cabin below Stuart River. He of the Otter Skins was there, and with him walked a man such as the gods have almost forgotten how to fashion. Men never talked of luck and pluck and five-hundred-dollar dirt without bringing in the name of Axel Gunderson;* nor could tales of nerve or strength or daring pass up and down the camp-fire without the summoning of his presence. And when the conversation flagged, it blazed anew at mention of the woman who shared his fortunes.

As has been noted, in the making of Axel Gunderson the gods had remembered their old-time cunning, and cast him after the manner of men who were born when the world was young. Full seven feet he towered in his picturesque costume which marked a king of Eldorado. His chest, neck, and limbs were those of a giant. To bear his three hundred pounds of bone and muscle, his snowshoes were greater by a generous yard than those of other men. Rough-hewn, with rugged brow and massive jaw and unflinching eyes of palest blue, his face told the tale of one who knew but the law of might. Of the yellow of ripe corn silk, his frost-incrusted hair swept like day across the night, and fell far down his coat of bearskin. A vague tradition of the sea seemed to cling about him, as he swung down the narrow trail in advance of the dogs; and he brought the butt of his dog-whip against Malemute Kid's door as a Norse sea rover, on southern foray, might thunder for admittance at the castle gate.

Prince bared his womanly arms and kneaded sour-dough bread, casting, as he did so, many a glance at the three guests,—three guests the like of which might never come under a man's roof in a lifetime. The Strange One, whom Malemute Kid had surnamed Ulysses, still fascinated him; but his interest chiefly gravitated between Axel Gunderson and Axel Gunderson's wife. She felt the day's journey, for she had softened in comfortable cabins during the many days since her husband mastered the wealth of frozen pay-streaks, and she was tired. She rested against his great breast like a slender flower against a wall, replying lazily to Male-mute Kid's good-natured banter, and stirring Prince's blood strangely with an occasional sweep of her deep, dark eyes. For Prince was a man, and healthy, and had seen few women in many months. And she was older than he, and an Indian besides. But she was different from all native wives he had met: she had traveled,—had been in his country among others, he gathered from the conversation; and she knew most of the things the women of his own race knew, and much more that it was not in the nature of things for them to know. She could make a meal of sun-dried fish or a bed in the snow; yet she teased them with tantalizing details of many-course dinners, and caused strange internal dissen-sions to arise at the mention of various quondam dishes which they had well-nigh forgotten. She knew the ways of the moose, the bear, and the little blue fox, and of the wild amphibians of the Northern seas;* she was skilled in the lore of the woods and the streams, and the tale writ by man and bird and beast upon the delicate snow crust was to her an open book; yet Prince caught the appreciative twinkle in her eye as she read the Rules of the Camp. These rules had been fathered by the Unquenchable Bettles at a time when his blood ran high, and were remarkable for the terse simplicity of their humor. Prince always turned them to the wall before the arrival of ladies; but who could suspect that this native wife—Well, it was too late now.

This, then, was the wife of Axel Gunderson, a woman whose name and fame had traveled with her husband's, hand in hand, through all the Northland. At table, Malemute Kid baited her with the assurance of an old friend, and Prince shook off the shyness of first acquaintance and joined in. But she held her own in the unequal contest, while her husband, slower in wit, ventured naught but applause. And he was very proud of her; his every look and action revealed the magnitude of the place she occupied in his life. He of the Otter Skins ate in silence, forgotten in the merry battle; and long ere the others were done he pushed back from the table and went out among the dogs. Yet all too soon his fellow travelers drew on their mittens and *parkas*, and followed him.

There had been no snow for many days, and the sleds slipped along the hard-packed Yukon trail as easily as if it had been glare ice. Ulysses led the first sled; with the second came Prince and Axel Gunderson's wife; while Malemute Kid and the yellow-haired giant brought up the third.

'It's only a "hunch," Kid,' he said; 'but I think it's straight. He's never been there, but he tells a good story, and shows a map I heard of when I was in the Kootenay country,* years ago. I'd like to have you go along; but he's a strange one, and swore point-blank to throw it up if any one was brought in. But when I come back you'll get first tip, and I'll stake you next to me, and give you a half share in the town site besides.

'No! no!' he cried, as the other strove to interrupt. 'I'm running this, and before I'm done it'll need two heads. If it's all right, why it'll be a second Cripple Creek,* man; do you hear?—a second Cripple Creek! It's quartz, you know, not placer; and if we work it right we'll corral the whole thing, —millions upon millions. I've heard of the place before, and so have you. We'll build a town—thousands of workmen— good waterways—steamship lines—big carrying trade— light-draught steamers for head-reaches—survey a railroad, perhaps—sawmills—electric-light plant—do our own banking —commercial company—syndicate—Say! just you hold your hush till I get back!'

The sleds came to a halt where the trail crossed the mouth of Stuart River. An unbroken sea of frost, its wide expanse stretched away into the unknown east. The snow-shoes were withdrawn from the lashings of the sleds. Axel Gunderson shook hands and stepped to the fore, his great webbed shoes sinking a fair half yard into the feathery surface and packing the snow so the dogs should not wallow. His wife fell in behind the last sled, betraying long practice in the art of handling the awkward footgear. The stillness was broken with cheery farewells; the dogs whined; and He of the Otter Skins talked with his whip to a recalcitrant wheeler.

An hour later, the train had taken on the likeness of a black pencil crawling in a long, straight line across a mighty sheet of foolscap.

II

One night, many weeks later, Malemute Kid and Prince fell to solving chess problems from the torn page of an ancient magazine. The Kid had just returned from his Bonanza properties, and was resting up preparatory to a long moose hunt. Prince too had been on creek and trail nearly all winter, and had grown hungry for a blissful week of cabin life.

'Interpose the black knight, and force the king. No, that won't do. See, the next move'—

'Why advance the pawn two squares? Bound to take it in transit, and with the bishop out of the way'—

'But hold on! That leaves a hole, and'—

'No; it's protected. Go ahead! You'll see it works.'

It was very interesting. Somebody knocked at the door a second time before Malemute Kid said, 'Come in.' The door swung open. Something staggered in. Prince caught one square look, and sprang to his feet. The horror in his eyes caused Malemute Kid to whirl about; and he too was startled, though he had seen bad things before. The thing tottered blindly toward them. Prince edged away till he reached the nail from which hung his Smith & Wesson.

'My God! what is it?' he whispered to Malemute Kid.

'Don't know. Looks like a case of freezing and no grub,' replied the Kid, sliding away in the opposite direction. 'Watch out! It may be mad,' he warned, coming back from closing the door.

The thing advanced to the table. The bright flame of the slush-lamp caught its eye. It was amused, and gave voice to eldritch cackles which betokened mirth. Then, suddenly, he —for it was a man—swayed back, with a hitch to his skin trousers, and began to sing a chanty, such as men lift when they swing around the capstan circle and the sea snorts in their ears:—

> Yan-kee ship come down de ri-ib-er,
> Pull! my bully boys! Pull!
> D'yeh want—to know de captain ru-uns her?
> Pull! my bully boys! Pull!
> Jon-a-than Jones ob South Caho-li-in-a,
> Pull! my bully—

He broke off abruptly, tottered with a wolfish snarl to the meat-shelf, and before they could intercept was tearing with his teeth at a chunk of raw bacon. The struggle was fierce between him and Malemute Kid; but his mad strength left him as suddenly as it had come, and he weakly surrendered the spoil. Between them they got him upon a stool, where he sprawled with half his body across the table. A small dose of whiskey strengthened him, so that he could dip a spoon into the sugar caddy which Malemute Kid placed before him. After his appetite had been somewhat cloyed, Prince, shuddering as he did so, passed him a mug of weak beef tea.

The creature's eyes were alight with a sombre frenzy, which blazed and waned with every mouthful. There was very little skin to the face. The face, for that matter, sunken and emaciated, bore very little likeness to human countenance. Frost after frost had bitten deeply, each depositing its stratum of scab upon the half-healed scar that went before. This dry, hard surface was of a bloody-black color, serrated by grievous cracks wherein the raw red flesh peeped forth. His skin garments were dirty and in tatters, and the fur of one side was singed and burned away, showing where he had lain upon his fire.

Malemute Kid pointed to where the sun-tanned hide had been cut away, strip by strip,—the grim signature of famine.

'Who—are—you?' slowly and distinctly enunciated the Kid.

The man paid no heed.

'Where do you come from?'

'Yan-kee ship come down de ri-ib-er,' was the quavering response.

'Don't doubt the beggar came down the river,' the Kid

said, shaking him in an endeavor to start a more lucid flow
of talk.

But the man shrieked at the contact, clapping a hand to
his side in evident pain. He rose slowly to his feet, half
leaning on the table.

'She laughed at me—so—with the hate in her eye; and
she—would—not—come.'

His voice died away, and he was sinking back when
Malemute Kid gripped him by the wrist, and shouted, 'Who?
Who would not come?'

'She, Unga. She laughed, and struck at me, so, and so.
And then'—

'Yes?'

'And then'—

'And then what?'

'And then he lay very still, in the snow, a long time. He
is—still in—the—snow.'

The two men looked at each other helplessly.

'Who is in the snow?'

'She, Unga. She looked at me with the hate in her eye,
and then'—

'Yes, yes.'

'And then she took the knife, so; and once, twice—she was
weak. I traveled very slow. And there is much gold in that
place, very much gold.'

'Where is Unga?' For all Malemute Kid knew, she might
be dying a mile away. He shook the man savagely, repeating
again and again, 'Where is Unga? Who is Unga?'

'She—is—in—the—snow.'

'Go on!' The Kid was pressing his wrist cruelly.

'So—I—would—be—in—the snow—but—I—had—a—
debt—to—pay. It—was—heavy—I—had—a—debt—to—
pay—a—debt—to—pay—I—had'—The faltering monosyll-
ables ceased, as he fumbled in his pouch and drew forth a
buckskin sack. 'A—debt—to—pay—five—pounds—of—
gold—grub—stake—Mal—e—mute—Kid—I'—The exhausted head dropped upon the table; nor could Malemute
Kid rouse it again.

'It's Ulysses,' he said quietly, tossing the bag of dust on

the table. 'Guess it's all day with Axel Gunderson and the woman. Come on, let's get him between the blankets. He's Indian; he'll pull through, and tell a tale besides.'

As they cut his garments from him, near his right breast could be seen two unhealed, hard-lipped knife thrusts.

III

'I will talk of the things which were, in my own way; but you will understand. I will begin at the beginning, and tell of myself and the woman, and, after that, of the man.'

He of the Otter Skins drew over to the stove as do men who have been deprived of fire and are afraid the Promethean gift may vanish at any moment. Malemute Kid pricked up the slush-lamp, and placed it so its light might fall upon the face of the narrator. Prince slid his body over the edge of the bunk and joined them.

'I am Naass, a chief, and the son of a chief, born between a sunset and a rising, on the dark seas, in my father's oomiak.* All of a night the men toiled at the paddles, and the women cast out the waves which threw in upon us, and we fought with the storm. The salt spray froze upon my mother's breast till her breath passed with the passing of the tide. But I,— I raised my voice with the wind and the storm, and lived.

'We dwelt in Akatan'—

'Where?' asked Malemute Kid.

'Akatan, which is in the Aleutians;* Akatan, beyond Chignik, beyond Kardalak, beyond Unimak. As I say, we dwelt in Akatan, which lies in the midst of the sea on the edge of the world. We farmed the salt seas for the fish, the seal, and the otter; and our homes shouldered about one another on the rocky strip between the rim of the forest and the yellow beach where our kayaks lay. We were not many, and the world was very small. There were strange lands to the east,—islands like Akatan; so we thought all the world was islands, and did not mind.

'I was different from my people. In the sands of the beach were the crooked timbers and wave-warped planks of a boat such as my people never built; and I remember on the point of the island which overlooked the ocean three ways there stood a pine tree which never grew there, smooth and straight and tall. It is said the two men came to that spot, turn about, through many days, and watched with the passing of the light. These two men came from out of the sea in the boat which lay in pieces on the beach. And they were white like you, and weak as the little children when the seal have gone away and the hunters come home empty. I know of these things from the old men and the old women, who got them from their fathers and mothers before them. These strange white men did not take kindly to our ways at first, but they grew strong, what of the fish and the oil, and fierce. And they built them each his own house, and took the pick of our women, and in time children came. Thus he was born who was to become the father of my father's father.

'As I said, I was different from my people, for I carried the strong, strange blood of this white man who came out of the sea. It is said we had other laws in the days before these men; but they were fierce and quarrelsome, and fought with our men till there were no more left who dared to fight. Then they made themselves chiefs, and took away our old laws and gave us new ones, insomuch that the man was the son of his father, and not his mother, as our way had been. They also ruled that the son, firstborn, should have all things which were his father's before him, and that the brothers and sisters should shift for themselves. And they gave us other laws. They showed us new ways in the catching of fish and the killing of bear which were thick in the woods; and they taught us to lay by bigger stores for the time of famine. And these things were good.

'But when they had become chiefs, and there were no more men to face their anger, they fought, these strange white men, each with the other. And the one whose blood I carry drove his seal spear the length of an arm through the other's body. Their children took up the fight, and their children's children; and there was great hatred between them, and black doings, even to my time, so that in each family but one lived to pass down the blood of them that went before. Of my blood I was alone; of the other man's there was but a girl, Unga, who lived with her mother. Her father and my father did not come back from the fishing one night; but afterward they washed up to the beach on the big tides, and they held very close to each other.

'The people wondered, because of the hatred between the houses, and the old men shook their heads and said the fight would go on when children were born to her and children to me. They told me this as a boy, till I came to believe, and to look upon Unga as a foe, who was to be the mother of children which were to fight with mine. I thought of these things day by day, and when I grew to a stripling I came to ask why this should be so. And they answered, 'We do not know, but that in such way your fathers did.' And I marveled that those which were to come should fight the battles of those that were gone, and in it I could see no right. But the people said it must be, and I was only a stripling.

'And they said I must hurry, that my blood might be the older and grow strong before hers. This was easy, for I was head man, and the people looked up to me because of the deeds and the laws of my fathers, and the wealth which was mine. Any maiden would come to me, but I found none to my liking. And the old men and the mothers of maidens told me to hurry, for even then were the hunters bidding high to the mother of Unga; and should her children grow strong before mine, mine would surely die.

'Nor did I find a maiden till one night coming back from the fishing. The sunlight was lying, so, low and full in the eyes, the wind free, and the kayaks racing with the white seas. Of a sudden the kayak of Unga came driving past me, and she looked upon me, so, with her black hair flying like a cloud of night and the spray wet on her cheek. As I say, the sunlight was full in the eyes, and I was a stripling; but somehow it was all clear, and I knew it to be the call of kind to kind. As she whipped ahead she looked back within the space of two strokes,—looked as only the woman Unga could look,—and again I knew it as the call of kind. The people shouted as we ripped past the lazy oomiaks and left them far behind. But she was quick at the paddle, and my heart was like the belly of a sail, and I did not gain. The wind freshened, the sea whitened, and, leaping like the seals on the windward breech, we roared down the golden pathway of the sun.'

Naass was crouched half out of his stool, in the attitude of one driving a paddle, as he ran the race anew. Somewhere across the stove he beheld the tossing kayak and the flying hair of Unga. The voice of the wind was in his ears, and its salt beat fresh upon his nostrils.

'But she made the shore, and ran up the sand, laughing, to the house of her mother. And a great thought came to me that night,—a thought worthy of him that was chief over all the people of Akatan. So, when the moon was up, I went down to the house of her mother, and looked upon the goods of Yash-Noosh, which were piled by the door,—the goods of Yash-Noosh, a strong hunter who had it in mind to be the father of the children of Unga. Other young men had piled their goods there, and taken them away again; and each young man had made a pile greater than the one before.

'And I laughed to the moon and the stars, and went to my own house where my wealth was stored. And many trips I made, till my pile was greater by the fingers of one hand than the pile of Yash-Noosh. There were fish, dried in the sun and smoked; and forty hides of the hair seal, and half as many of the fur, and each hide was tied at the mouth and big-bellied with oil; and ten skins of bear which I killed in the woods when they came out in the spring. And there were beads and blankets and scarlet cloths, such as I got in trade from the people who lived to the east, and who got them in trade from the people who lived still beyond in the east. And I looked upon the pile of Yash-Noosh and laughed; for I was head man in Akatan, and my wealth was greater than the wealth of all my young men, and my fathers had done deeds, and given laws, and put their names for all time in the mouths of the people.

'So, when the morning came, I went down to the beach, casting out of the corner of my eye at the house of the mother of Unga. My offer yet stood untouched. And the women smiled, and said sly things one to the other. I wondered, for never had such a price been offered; and that night I added more to the pile, and put beside it a kayak of well-tanned skins which never yet had swam in the sea. But in the day it was yet there, open to the laughter of all men. The mother of Unga was crafty, and I grew angry at the shame in which I stood before my people. So that night I added till it became a great pile, and I hauled up my oomiak, which was of the value of twenty kayaks. And in the morning there was no pile.

'Then made I preparation for the wedding, and the people that lived even to the east came for the food of the feast and the *potlach* token. Unga was older than I by the age of four suns in the way we reckoned the years. I was only a stripling; but then I was a chief, and the son of a chief, and it did not matter.

'But a ship shoved her sails above the floor of the ocean, and grew larger with the breath of the wind. From her scuppers she ran clear water, and the men were in haste and worked hard at the pumps. On the bow stood a mighty man, watching the depth of the water and giving commands with a voice of thunder. His eyes were of the pale blue of the deep waters, and his head was maned like that of a sea lion. And his hair was yellow, like the straw of a southern harvest or the manila rope-yarns which sailormen plait.

'Of late years we had seen ships from afar, but this was the first to come to the beach of Akatan. The feast was broken, and the women and children fled to the houses, while we men strung our bows and waited with spears in hand. But when the ship's forefoot smelt the beach the strange men took no notice of us, being busy with their own work. With the falling of the tide they careened the schooner and patched a great hole in her bottom. So the women crept back, and the feast went on.

'When the tide rose, the sea wanderers kedged the schooner to deep water, and then came among us. They bore presents and were friendly; so I made room for them, and out of the largeness of my heart gave them tokens such as I gave all the guests; for it was my wedding day, and I was head man in Akatan. And he with the mane of the sea lion was there, so tall and strong that one looked to see the earth shake with the fall of his feet. He looked much and straight at Unga, with his arms folded, so, and stayed till the sun went away and the stars came out. Then he went down to his ship. After that I took Unga by the hand and led her to my own house. And there was singing and great laughter, and the women said sly things, after the manner of women at such times. But we did not care. Then the people left us alone and went home.

'The last noise had not died away, when the chief of the sea wanderers came in by the door. And he had with him black bottles, from which we drank and made merry. You see, I was only a stripling, and had lived all my days on the edge of the world. So my blood became as fire, and my heart as light as the froth that flies from the surf to the cliff. Unga sat silent among the skins in the corner, her eyes wide, for she seemed to fear. And he with the mane of the sea lion looked upon her straight and long. Then his men came in with bundles of goods, and he piled before me wealth such as was not in all Akatan. There were guns, both large and small, and powder and shot and shell, and bright axes and knives of steel, and cunning tools, and strange things the like of which I had never seen. When he showed me by sign that it was all mine, I thought him a great man to be so free; but he showed me also that Unga was to go away with him in his ship. Do you understand?—that Unga was to go away with him in his ship. The blood of my fathers flamed hot on the sudden, and I made to drive him through with my spear. But the spirit of the bottles had stolen the life from my arm, and he took me by the neck, so, and knocked my head against the wall of the house. And I was made weak like a newborn child, and my legs would no more stand under me. Unga screamed, and she laid hold of the things of the house with her hands, till they fell all about us as he dragged her to the door. Then he took her in his great arms, and when she tore at his yellow hair laughed with a sound like that of the big bull seal in the rut.

'I crawled to the beach and called upon my people; but they were afraid. Only Yash-Noosh was a man, and they struck him on the head with an oar, till he lay with his face in the sand and did not move. And they raised the sails to the sound of their songs, and the ship went away on the wind.

'The people said it was good, for there would be no more war of the bloods in Akatan; but I said never a word, waiting till the time of the full moon, when I put fish and oil in my kayak, and went away to the east. I saw many islands and many people, and I, who had lived on the edge, saw that the world was very large. I talked by signs; but they had not seen a schooner nor a man with the mane of a sea lion, and they pointed always to the east. And I slept in queer places, and ate odd things, and met strange faces. Many laughed, for they thought me light of head; but sometimes old men turned my face to the light and blessed me, and the eyes of the young women grew soft as they asked me of the strange ship, and Unga, and the men of the sea.

'And in this manner, through rough seas and great storms, I came to Unalaska.* There were two schooners there, but neither was the one I sought. So I passed on to the east, with the world growing ever larger, and in the Island of Unamok there was no word of the ship, nor in Kadiak, nor in Atognak. And so I came one day to a rocky land, where men dug great holes in the mountain. And there was a schooner, but not my schooner, and men loaded upon it the rocks which they dug. This I thought childish, for all the world was made of rocks; but they gave me food and set me to work. When the schooner was deep in the water, the captain gave me money and told me to go; but I asked which way he went, and he pointed south. I made signs that I would go with him; and he laughed at first, but then, being short of men, took me to help work the ship. So I came to talk after their manner, and to heave on ropes, and to reef the stiff sails in sudden squalls, and to take my turn at the wheel. But it was not strange, for the blood of my fathers was the blood of the men of the sea.

'I had thought it an easy task to find him I sought, once I got among his own people; and when we raised the land one day, and passed between a gateway of the sea to a port, I looked for perhaps as many schooners as there were fingers to my hands. But the ships lay against the wharves for miles, packed like so many little fish; and when I went among them to ask for a man with the mane of a sea lion, they laughed, and answered me in the tongues of many peoples. And I found that they hailed from the uttermost parts of the earth.

'And I went into the city to look upon the face of every man. But they were like the cod when they run thick on the banks, and I could not count them. And the noise smote upon me till I could not hear, and my head was dizzy with much movement. So I went on and on, through the lands which sang in the warm sunshine; where the harvests lay rich on the plains; and where great cities were fat with men that lived like women, with false words in their mouths and their hearts black with the lust of gold. And all the while my people of Akatan hunted and fished, and were happy in the thought that the world was small.

'But the look in the eyes of Unga coming home from the fishing was with me always, and I knew I would find her when the time was met. She walked down quiet lanes in the dusk of the evening, or led me chases across the thick fields wet with the morning dew, and there was a promise in her eyes such as only the woman Unga could give.

'So I wandered through a thousand cities. Some were gentle and gave me food, and others laughed, and still others cursed; but I kept my tongue between my teeth, and went strange ways and saw strange sights. Sometimes, I, who was a chief and the son of a chief, toiled for men,—men rough of speech and hard as iron, who wrung gold from the sweat and sorrow of their fellow men. Yet no word did I get of my quest, till I came back to the sea like a homing seal to the rookeries. But this was at another port, in another country which lay to the north. And there I heard dim tales of the yellow-haired sea wanderer, and I learned that he was a hunter of seals, and that even then he was abroad on the ocean.

'So I shipped on a seal schooner with the lazy Siwashes, and followed his trackless trail to the north where the hunt was then warm. And we were away weary months, and spoke many of the fleet, and heard much of the wild doings of him I sought; but never once did we raise him above the sea. We went north, even to the Pribyloffs,* and killed the seals in herds on the beach, and brought their warm bodies aboard till our scuppers ran grease and blood and no man could stand upon the deck. Then were we chased by a ship of slow steam, which fired upon us with great guns. But we put on sail till the sea was over our decks and washed them clean, and lost ourselves in a fog.

'It is said, at this time, while we fled with fear at our hearts, that the yellow-haired sea wanderer put into the Pribyloffs, right to the factory, and while the part of his men held the servants of the company, the rest loaded ten thousand green skins from the salt-houses. I say it is said, but I believe; for in the voyages I made on the coast with never a meeting, the northern seas rang with his wildness and daring, till the three nations which have lands there sought him with their ships. And I heard of Unga, for the captains sang loud in her praise, and she was always with him. She had learned the ways of his people, they said, and was happy. But I knew better,—knew that her heart harked back to her own people by the yellow beach of Akatan.

'So, after a long time, I went back to the port which is by a gateway of the sea, and there I learned that he had gone across the girth of the great ocean to hunt for the seal to the east of the warm land which runs south from the Russian Seas. And I, who was become a sailorman, shipped with men of his own race, and went after him in the hunt of the seal. And there were few ships off that new land; but we hung on the flank of the seal pack and harried it north through all the spring of the year. And when the cows were heavy with pup and crossed the Russian line, our men grumbled and were afraid. For there was much fog, and every day men were lost in the boats. They would not work, so the captain turned the ship back toward the way it came. But I knew the yellow-haired sea wanderer was unafraid, and would hang by the pack, even to the Russian Isles, where few men go. So I took a boat, in the black of night, when the lookout dozed on the fok'slehead, and went alone to the warm, long land. And I journeyed south to meet the men by Yeddo Bay, who are wild and unafraid. And the Yoshiwara* girls were small, and bright like steel, and good to look upon; but I could not stop, for I knew that Unga rolled on the tossing floor by the rookeries of the north.

'The men by Yeddo Bay had met from the ends of the earth, and had neither gods nor homes, sailing under the flag of the Japanese. And with them I went to the rich beaches of Copper Island,* where our salt-piles became high with skins. And in that silent sea we saw no man till we were ready to come away. Then, one day, the fog lifted on the edge of a heavy wind, and there jammed down upon us a schooner, with close in her wake the cloudy funnels of a Russian man-of-war. We fled away on the beam of the wind, with the schooner jamming still closer and plunging ahead three feet to our two. And upon her poop was the man with the mane of the sea lion, pressing the rails under with the canvas and laughing in his strength of life. And Unga was there,—I knew her on the moment,—but he sent her below when the cannons began to talk across the sea. As I say, with three feet to our two, till we saw the rudder lift green at every jump,—and I swinging on to the wheel and cursing, with my back to the Russian shot. For we knew he had it in mind to run before us, that he might get away while we were caught. And they knocked our masts out of us till we dragged into the wind like a wounded gull; but he went on over the edge of the sky-line,—he and Unga.

'What could we? The fresh hides spoke for themselves. So they took us to a Russian port, and after that to a lone country, where they set us to work in the mines to dig salt. And some died, and—and some did not die.'

Naass swept the blanket from his shoulders, disclosing the gnarled and twisted flesh, marked with the unmistakable striations of the knout. Prince hastily covered him, for it was not nice to look upon.

'We were there a weary time; and sometimes men got away to the south, but they always came back. So, when we who hailed from Yeddo Bay rose in the night and took the guns from the guards, we went to the north. And the land was very large, with plains, soggy with water, and great forests. And the cold came, with much snow on the ground, and no man knew the way. Weary months we journeyed through the endless forest,—I do not remember, now, for there was little food and often we lay down to die. But at last we came to the cold sea, and but three were left to look upon it. One had shipped from Yeddo as captain, and he knew in his head the lay of the great lands, and of the place where men may cross from one to the other on the ice. And he led us,—I do not know, it was so long,—till there were but two. When we came to that place we found five of the strange people which live in that country, and they had dogs and skins, and we were very poor. We fought in the snow till they died, and the captain died, and the dogs and skins were mine. Then I crossed on the ice, which was broken, and once I drifted till a gale from the west put me upon the shore. And after that, Golovin Bay, Pastilik, and the priest. Then south, south, to the warm sunlands where first I wandered.

'But the sea was no longer fruitful, and those who went upon it after the seal went to little profit and great risk. The fleets scattered, and the captains and the men had no word of those I sought. So I turned away from the ocean which never rests, and went among the lands, where the trees, the houses, and the mountains sit always in one place and do not move. I journeyed far, and came to learn many things, even to the way of reading and writing from books. It was well I should do this, for it came upon me that Unga must know these things, and that some day, when the time was met—we—you understand, when the time was met.

'So I drifted, like those little fish which raise a sail to the wind, but cannot steer. But my eyes and my ears were open always, and I went among men who traveled much, for I knew they had but to see those I sought, to remember. At last there came a man, fresh from the mountains, with pieces of rock in which the free gold stood to the size of peas, and he had heard, he had met, he knew them. They were rich, he said, and lived in the place where they drew the gold from the ground.

'It was in a wild country, and very far away; but in time I came to the camp, hidden between the mountains, where men worked night and day, out of the sight of the sun. Yet the time was not come. I listened to the talk of the people. He had gone away,—they had gone away,—to England, it was said, in the matter of bringing men with much money together to form companies. I saw the house they had lived in; more like a palace, such as one sees in the old countries. In the nighttime I crept in through a window that I might see in what manner he treated her. I went from room to room, and in such way thought kings and queens must live, it was all so very good. And they all said he treated her like a queen, and many marveled as to what breed of woman she was; for there was other blood in her veins, and she was different from the women of Akatan, and no one knew her for what she was. Ay, she was a queen; but I was a chief, and the son of a chief, and I had paid for her an untold price of skin and boat and bead.

'But why so many words? I was a sailorman, and knew the way of the ships on the seas. I followed to England, and then to other countries. Sometimes I heard of them by word of mouth, sometimes I read of them in the papers; yet never once could I come by them, for they had much money, and traveled fast, while I was a poor man. Then came trouble upon them, and their wealth slipped away, one day, like a curl of smoke. The papers were full of it at the time; but after that nothing was said, and I knew they had gone back where more gold could be got from the ground.

'They had dropped out of the world, being now poor; and so I wandered from camp to camp, even north to the Kootenay Country, where I picked up the cold scent. They had come and gone, some said this way, and some that, and still others that they had gone to the Country of the Yukon. And I went this way, and I went that, ever journeying from place to place, till it seemed I must grow weary of the world which was so large. But in the Kootenay I traveled a bad trail, and a long trail, with a "breed" of the Northwest, who saw fit to die when the famine pinched. He had been to the Yukon by an unknown way over the mountains, and when he knew his time was near gave me the map and the secret of a place where he swore by his gods there was much gold.

'After that all the world began to flock into the north. I

was a poor man; I sold myself to be a driver of dogs. The rest you know. I met him and her in Dawson. She did not know me, for I was only a stripling, and her life had been large, so she had no time to remember the one who had paid for her an untold price.

'So? You bought me from my term of service. I went back to bring things about in my own way; for I had waited long, and now that I had my hand upon him was in no hurry. As I say, I had it in mind to do my own way; for I read back in my life, through all I had seen and suffered, and remembered the cold and hunger of the endless forest by the Russian Seas. As you know, I led him into the east,—him and Unga,—into the east where many have gone and few returned. I led them to the spot where the bones and the curses of men lie with the gold which they may not have.

'The way was long and the trail unpacked. Our dogs were many and ate much; nor could our sleds carry till the break of spring. We must come back before the river ran free. So here and there we cached grub, that our sleds might be lightened and there be no chance of famine on the back trip. At the McQuestion there were three men, and near them we built a cache, as also did we at the Mayo,* where was a hunting-camp of a dozen Pellys* which had crossed the divide from the south. After that, as we went on into the east, we saw no men; only the sleeping river, the moveless forest, and the White Silence of the North. As I say, the way was long and the trail unpacked. Sometimes, in a day's toil, we made no more than eight miles, or ten, and at night we slept like dead men. And never once did they dream that I was Naass, head man of Akatan, the righter of wrongs.

'We now made smaller caches, and in the nighttime it was a small matter to go back on the trail we had broken, and change them in such way that one might deem the wolverines the thieves. Again, there be places where there is a fall to the river, and the water is unruly, and the ice makes above and is eaten away beneath. In such a spot the sled I drove broke through, and the dogs; and to him and Unga it was ill luck, but no more. And there was much grub on that sled, and the dogs the strongest. But he laughed, for he was strong of life, and gave the dogs that were left little grub till we cut them from the harnesses, one by one, and fed them to their mates. We would go home light, he said, traveling and eating from cache to cache, with neither dogs nor sleds; which was true, for our grub was very short, and the last dog died in the traces the night we came to the gold and the bones and the curses of men.

'To reach that place,—and the map spoke true,—in the heart of the great mountains, we cut ice steps against the wall of a divide. One looked for a valley beyond, but there was no valley; the snow spread away, level as the great harvest plains, and here and there about us mighty mountains shoved their white heads among the stars. And midway on that strange plain which should have been a valley, the earth and the snow fell away, straight down toward the heart of the world. Had we not been sailormen our heads would have swung round with the sight; but we stood on the dizzy edge that we might see a way to get down. And on one side, and one side only, the wall had fallen away till it was like the slope of the decks in a topsail breeze. I do not know why this thing should be so, but it was so. "It is the mouth of hell," he said; "let us go down." And we went down.

'And on the bottom there was a cabin, built by some man, of logs which he had cast down from above. It was a very old cabin; for men had died there alone at different times, and on pieces of birch bark which were there we read their last words and their curses. One had died of scurvy; another's partner had robbed him of his last grub and powder and stolen away; a third had been mauled by a bald-face grizzly; a fourth had hunted for game and starved,—and so it went, and they had been loath to leave the gold, and had died by the side of it in one way or another. And the worthless gold they had gathered yellowed the floor of the cabin like in a dream.

'But his soul was steady, and his head clear, this man I had led thus far. "We have nothing to eat," he said, "and we will only look upon this gold, and see whence it comes and how much there be. Then we will go away quick, before it gets into our eyes and steals away our judgment. And in this way we may return in the end, with more grub, and possess it all." So we looked upon the great vein, which cut the wall of the pit as a true vein should; and we measured it, and traced it from above and below, and drove the stakes of the claims and blazed the trees in token of our rights. Then, our knees shaking with lack of food, and a sickness in our bellies, and our hearts chugging close to our mouths, we climbed the mighty wall for the last time and turned our faces to the back trip.

'The last stretch we dragged Unga between us, and we fell often, but in the end we made the cache. And lo, there was no grub. It was well done, for he thought it the wolverines, and damned them and his gods in the one breath. But Unga was brave, and smiled, and put her hand in his, till I turned away that I might hold myself. "We will rest by the fire," she said, "till morning, and we will gather strength from our moccasins." So we cut the tops of our moccasins in strips, and boiled them half of the might, that we might chew them and swallow them. And in the morning we talked of our chance. The next cache was five days' journey; we could not make it. We must find game.

'"We will go forth and hunt," he said.

'"Yes," said I, "we will go forth and hunt."

'And he ruled that Unga stay by the fire and save her strength. And we went forth, he in quest of the moose, and I to the cache I had changed. But I ate little, so they might not see in me much strength. And in the night he fell many times as he drew into camp. And I too made to suffer great weakness, stumbling over my snow-shoes as though each step might be my last. And we gathered strength from our moccasins.

'He was a great man. His soul lifted his body to the last; nor did he cry aloud, save for the sake of Unga. On the second day I followed him, that I might not miss the end. And he lay down to rest often. That night he was near gone; but in the morning he swore weakly and went forth again. He was like a drunken man, and I looked many times for him to give up; but his was the strength of the strong, and his soul the soul of a giant, for he lifted his body through all the weary day. And he shot two ptarmigan, but would not eat them. He needed no fire; they meant life; but his thought was for Unga, and he turned toward camp. He no longer walked, but crawled on hand and knee through the snow. I came to him, and read death in his eyes. Even then it was not too late to eat of the ptarmigan. He cast away his rifle, and carried the birds in his mouth like a dog. I walked by his side, upright. And he looked at me during the moments he rested, and wondered that I was so strong. I could see it, though he no longer spoke; and when his lips moved, they moved without sound. As I say, he was a great man, and my heart spoke for softness; but I read back in my life, and remembered the cold and hunger of the endless forest by the Russian Seas. Besides, Unga was mine, and I had paid for her an untold price of skin and boat and bead.

'And in this manner we came through the white forest, with the silence heavy upon us like a damp sea mist. And the ghosts of the past were in the air and all about us; and I saw the yellow beach of Akatan, and the kayaks racing home from the fishing, and the houses on the rim of the forest. And the men who had made themselves chiefs were there, the lawgivers whose blood I bore, and whose blood I had wedded in Unga. Ay, and Yash-Noosh walked with me, the wet sand in his hair, and his war spear, broken as he fell upon it, still in his hand. And I knew the time was met, and saw in the eyes of Unga the promise.

'As I say, we came thus through the forest, till the smell of the camp smoke was in our nostrils. And I bent above him, and tore the ptarmigan from his teeth. He turned on his side and rested, the wonder mounting in his eyes, and the hand which was under slipping slow toward the knife at his hip. But I took it from him, smiling close in his face. Even then he did not understand. So I made to drink from black bottles, and to build high upon the snow a pile of goods, and to live again the things which happened on the night of my marriage. I spoke no word, but he understood. Yet was he unafraid. There was a sneer to his lips, and cold anger, and he gathered new strength with the knowledge. It was not far, but the snow was deep, and he dragged himself very slow.

Once, he lay so long, I turned him over and gazed into his eyes. And sometimes he looked forth, and sometimes death. And when I loosed him he struggled on again. In this way we came to the fire. Unga was at his side on the instant. His lips moved, without sound; then he pointed at me, that Unga might understand. And after that he lay in the snow, very still, for a long while, Even now is he there in the snow.

'I said no word till I had cooked the ptarmigan. Then I spoke to her, in her own tongue, which she had not heard in many years. She straightened herself, so, and her eyes were wonder-wide, and she asked who I was, and where I had learned that speech.

'"I am Naass," I said.

'"You?" she said. "You?" And she crept close that she might look upon me.

'"Yes," I answered; "I am Naass, head man of Akatan, the last of the blood, as you are the last of the blood."

'And she laughed. By all the things I have seen and the deeds I have done, may I never hear such a laugh again. It put the chill to my soul, sitting there in the White Silence, alone with death and this woman who laughed.

'"Come!" I said, for I thought she wandered. "Eat of the food and let us be gone. It is a far fetch from here to Akatan."

'But she shoved her face in his yellow mane, and laughed till it seemed the heavens must fall about our ears. I had thought she would be overjoyed at the sight of me, and eager to go back to the memory of old times; but this seemed a strange form to take.

'"Come!" I cried, taking her strong by the hand. "The way is long and dark. Let us hurry!"

'"Where?" she asked, sitting up, and ceasing from her strange mirth.

'"To Akatan," I answered, intent on the light to grow on her face at the thought. But it became like his, with a sneer to the lips, and cold anger.

'"Yes," she said; "we will go, hand in hand, to Akatan, you and I. And we will live in the dirty huts, and eat of the fish and oil, and bring forth a spawn,—a spawn to be proud of all the days of our life. We will forget the world and be happy, very happy. It is good, most good. Come! Let us hurry. Let us go back to Akatan."

'And she ran her hand through his yellow hair, and smiled in a way which was not good. And there was no promise in her eyes.

'I sat silent, and marveled at the strangeness of woman. I went back to the night when he dragged her from me, and she screamed and tore at his hair,—at his hair which now she played with and would not leave. Then I remembered the price and the long years of waiting; and I gripped her close, and dragged her away as he had done. And she held back, even as on that night, and fought like a she-cat for its whelp. And when the fire was between us and the man, I loosed her, and she sat and listened. And I told her of all that lay between, of all that had happened me on strange seas, of all that I had done in strange lands; of my weary quest, and the hungry years, and the promise which had been mine from the first. Ay, I told all, even to what had passed that day between the man and me, and in the days yet young. And as I spoke I saw the promise grow in her eyes, full and large like the break of dawn. And I read pity there, the tenderness of woman, the love, the heart and the soul of Unga. And I was a stripling again, for the look was the look of Unga as she ran up the beach, laughing, to the home of her mother. The stern unrest was gone, and the hunger, and the weary waiting. The time was met. I felt the call of her breast, and it seemed there I must pillow my head and forget. She opened her arms to me, and I came against her. Then, sudden, the hate flamed in her eye, her hand was at my hip. And once, twice, she passed the knife.

'"Dog!" she sneered, as she flung me into the snow. "Swine!" And then she laughed till the silence cracked, and went back to her dead.

'As I say, once she passed the knife, and twice; but she was weak with hunger, and it was not meant that I should die. Yet was I minded to stay in that place, and to close my eyes in the last long sleep with those whose lives had crossed with mine and led my feet on unknown trails. But there lay a debt upon me which would not let me rest.

'And the way was long, the cold bitter, and there was little grub. The Pellys had found no moose, and had robbed my cache. And so had the three white men; but they lay thin and dead in their cabin as I passed. After that I do not remember, till I came here, and found food and fire,—much fire.'

As he finished, he crouched closely, even jealously, over the stove. For a long while the slush-lamp shadows played tragedies upon the wall.

'But Unga!' cried Prince, the vision still strong upon him.

'Unga? She would not eat of the ptarmigan. She lay with her arms about his neck, her face deep in his yellow hair. I drew the fire close, that she might not feel the frost; but she crept to the other side. And I built a fire there; yet it was little good, for she would not eat. And in this manner they still lie up there in the snow.'

'And you?' asked Malemute Kid.

'I do not know; but Akatan is small, and I have little wish to go back and live on the edge of the world. Yet is there small use in life. I can go to Constantine, and he will put irons upon me, and one day they will tie a piece of rope, so, and I will sleep good. Yet—no; I do not know.'

'But, Kid,' protested Prince, 'this is murder!'

'Hush!' commanded Malemute Kid. 'There be things greater than our wisdom, beyond our justice. The right and the wrong of this we cannot say, and it is not for us to judge.'

Naass drew yet closer to the fire. There was a great silence, and in each man's eyes many pictures came and went.

SELECTED NORTHLAND TALES

GRIT OF WOMEN

A wolfish head, wistful-eyed and frost-rimed, thrust aside the tent-flaps.

'Hi! Chook!* Siwash! Chook, you limb of Satan!' chorused the protesting inmates. Bettles rapped the dog sharply with a tin plate, and it withdrew hastily. Louis Savoy refastened the flaps, kicked a frying-pan over against the bottom, and warmed his hands. It was very cold without. Forty-eight hours gone, the spirit thermometer had burst at sixty-eight below, and since that time it had grown steadily and bitterly colder. There was no telling when the snap would end. And it is poor policy, unless the gods will it, to venture far from a stove at such times, or to increase the quantity of cold atmosphere one must breathe. Men sometimes do it, and sometimes they chill their lungs. This leads up to a dry, hacking cough, noticeably irritable when bacon is being fried. After that, somewhere along in the spring or summer, a hole is burned in the frozen muck. Into this a man's carcass is dumped, covered over with moss, and left with the assurance that it will rise on the crack of Doom, wholly and frigidly intact. For those of little faith, sceptical of material integration on that fateful day, no fitter country than the Klondike can be recommended to die in. But it is not to be inferred from this that it is a fit country for living purposes.

It was very cold without, but it was not over-warm within. The only article which might be designated furniture was the stove, and for this the men were frank in displaying their preference. Upon half of the floor pine boughs had been cast; above this were spread the sleeping-furs, beneath lay the winter's snowfall. The remainder of the floor was moccasin-packed snow, littered with pots and pans and the general *impedimenta* of an Arctic camp. The stove was red and roaring hot, but only a bare three feet away lay a block of ice, as sharp-edged and dry as when first quarried from the creek bottom. The pressure of the outside cold forced the inner

heat upward. Just above the stove, where the pipe penetrated
the roof, was a tiny circle of dry canvas; next, with the pipe
always as centre, a circle of steaming canvas; next a damp
and moisture-exuding ring; and finally, the rest of the tent,
sidewalls and top, coated with a half-inch of dry, white,
crystal-encrusted frost.

'*Oh!* OH! OH!' A young fellow, lying asleep in the furs,
bearded and wan and weary, raised a moan of pain, and
without waking increased the pitch and intensity of his anguish. His body half-lifted from the blankets, and quivered
and shrank spasmodically, as though drawing away from a
bed of nettles.

'Roll'm over!' ordered Bettles. 'He's crampin'.'

And thereat, with pitiless good-will, he was pitched upon
and rolled and thumped and pounded by half-a-dozen willing comrades.

'Damn the trail,' he muttered softly, as he threw off the
robes and sat up. 'I've run across country, played quarter
three seasons hand-running,* and hardened myself in all
manner of ways; and then I pilgrim it into this God-forsaken
land and find myself an effeminate Athenian without the
simplest rudiments of manhood!' He hunched up to the fire
and rolled a cigarette. 'Oh, I'm not whining. I can take my
medicine all right, all right; but I'm just decently ashamed of
myself, that's all. Here I am, on top of a dirty thirty miles,
as knocked up and stiff and sore as a pink-tea degenerate*
after a five-mile walk on a country turnpike. Bah! It makes
me sick! Got a match?'

'Don't git the tantrums, youngster.' Bettles passed over
the required fire-stick and waxed patriarchal. 'Ye've gotter
'low some for the breakin'-in. Sufferin' cracky! don't I recollect the first time I hit the trail! Stiff? I've seen the time
it'd take me ten minutes to git my mouth from the waterhole
an' come to my feet—every jint crackin' an' kickin' fit to
kill. Cramp? In sech knots it'd take the camp half a day to
untangle me. You're all right, for a cub, an' ye've the true
sperrit. Come this day year, you'll walk all us old bucks into
the ground any time. An' best in your favor, you hain't got
that streak of fat in your make-up which has sent many a

husky man to the bosom of Abraham afore his right and
proper time.'

'Streak of fat?'

'Yep. Comes along of bulk. 'Tain't the big men as is the
best when it comes to the trail.'

'Never heard of it.'

'Never heered of it, eh? Well, it's a dead straight, open-
an'-shut fact, an' no gittin' round. Bulk's all well enough for
a mighty big effort, but 'thout stayin' powers it ain't worth
a continental whoop; an' stayin' powers an' bulk ain't runnin'
mates. Takes the small, wiry fellows when it comes to gittin'
right down an' hangin' on like a lean-jowled dog to a bone.
Why, hell's fire, the big men they ain't in it!'

'By gar!' broke in Louis Savoy, 'dat is no, vot you call,
josh! I know one mans, so vaire beeg like ze buffalo. Wit
him, on ze Sulphur Creek stampede, go one small mans,
Lon McFane. You know dat Lon McFane, dat leetle Irisher
wit ze red hair and ze grin. An' dey walk an' walk an' walk,
all ze day long an' ze night long. And beeg mans, him become vaire tired, an' lay down mooch in ze snow. And leetle
mans keek beeg mans, an' him cry like, vot you call—ah! vot
you call ze kid. And leetle mans keek an' keek an' keek, an'
bime by, long time, long way, keek beeg mans into my cabin.
Tree days 'fore him crawl out my blankets. Nevaire I see
beeg squaw like him. No nevaire. Him haf vot you call ze
streak of fat. You bet.'

'But there was Axel Gunderson,'* Prince spoke up. The
great Scandinavian, with the tragic events which shadowed
his passing, had made a deep mark on the mining engineer.
'He lies up there, somewhere.' He swept his hand in the
vague direction of the mysterious east.

'Biggest man that ever turned his heels to Salt Water or
run a moose down with sheer grit,' supplemented Bettles;
'but he's the prove-the-rule exception. Look at his woman,
Unga,—tip the scales at a hundred an' ten, clean meat an'
nary ounce to spare. She'd bank grit 'gainst his for all there
was in him, an' see him, an' go him better* if it was possible.
Nothing over the earth, or in it, or under it, she wouldn't 'a'
done.'

'But she loved him,' objected the engineer.

''Tain't that. It—'

'Look you, brothers,' broke in Sitka Charley from his seat on the grub-box. 'Ye have spoken of the streak of fat that runs in big men's muscles, of the grit of women and the love, and ye have spoken fair; but I have in mind things which happened when the land was young and the fires of men apart as the stars. It was then I had concern with a big man, and a streak of fat, and a woman. And the woman was small; but her heart was greater than the beef-heart of the man, and she had grit. And we traveled a weary trail, even to the Salt Water, and the cold was bitter, the snow deep, the hunger great. And the woman's love was a mighty love—no more can man say than this.'

He paused, and with the hatchet broke pieces of ice from the large chunk beside him. These he threw into the gold pan on the stove, where the drinking-water thawed. The men drew up closer, and he of the cramps sought greater comfort vainly for his stiffened body.

'Brothers, my blood is red with Siwash, but my heart is white. To the faults of my fathers I owe the one, to the virtues of my friends the other. A great truth came to me when I was yet a boy. I learned that to your kind and you was given the earth; that the Siwash could not withstand you, and like the caribou and the bear, must perish in the cold. So I came into the warm and sat among you, by your fires; and behold, I became one of you. I have seen much in my time. I have known strange things, and bucked big, on big trails, with men of many breeds. And because of these things, I measure deeds after your manner, and judge men, and think thoughts. Wherefore, when I speak harshly of one of your own kind, I know you will not take it amiss; and when I speak high of one of my father's people, you will not take it upon you to say, "Sitka Charley is Siwash, and there is a crooked light in his eyes and small honor to his tongue." Is it not so?'

Deep down in throat, the circle vouchsafed its assent.

'The woman was Passuk. I got her in fair trade from her people, who were of the Coast and whose Chilcat totem* stood at the head of a salt arm of the sea. My heart did not go out to the woman, nor did I take stock of her looks. For she scarce took her eyes from the ground, and she was timid and afraid, as girls will be when cast into a stranger's arms whom they have never seen before. As I say, there was no place in my heart for her to creep, for I had a great journey in mind, and stood in need of one to feed my dogs and to lift a paddle with me through the long river days. One blanket would cover the twain; so I chose Passuk.

'Have I not said I was a servant to the Government? If not, it is well that ye know. So I was taken on a warship, sleds and dogs and evaporated foods, and with me came Passuk. And we went north, to the winter ice-rim of Bering Sea, where we were landed,—myself, and Passuk, and the dogs. I was also given moneys of the Government, for I was its servant, and charts of lands which the eyes of man had never dwelt upon, and messages. These messages were sealed, and protected shrewdly from the weather, and I was to deliver them to the whale-ships of the Arctic, ice-bound by the great Mackenzie. Never was there so great a river, forgetting only our own Yukon, the Mother of all Rivers.

'All of which is neither here nor there, for my story deals not with the whale-ships, nor the berg-bound winter I spent by the Mackenzie. Afterward, in the spring, when the days lengthened and there was a crust to the snow, we came south, Passuk and I, to the Country of the Yukon. A weary journey, but the sun pointed out the way of our feet. It was a naked land then, as I have said, and we worked up the current, with pole and paddle, till we came to Forty Mile. Good it was to see white faces once again, so we put into the bank. And that winter was a hard winter. The darkness and the cold drew down upon us, and with them the famine. To each man the agent of the Company gave forty pounds of flour and twenty of bacon. There were no beans. And the dogs howled always, and there were flat bellies and deep-lined faces, and strong men became weak, and weak men died. There was also much scurvy.

'Then came we together in the store one night, and the empty shelves made us feel our own emptiness the more. We talked low, by the light of the fire, for the candles had been set aside for those who might yet gasp in the spring. Discussion was held, and it was said that a man must go forth to the Salt Water and tell to the world our misery. At this all eyes turned to me, for it was understood that I was a great traveler. "It is seven hundred miles," said I, "to Haines Mission by the sea, and every inch of it snowshoe work. Give me the pick of your dogs and the best of your grub, and I will go. And with me shall go Passuk."

'To this they were agreed. But there arose one, Long Jeff, a Yankee-man, big-boned and big-muscled. Also his talk was big. He, too, was a mighty traveler, he said, born to the snowshoe and bred up on buffalo milk. He would go with me, in case I fell by the trail, that he might carry the word on to the Mission. I was young, and I knew not Yankee-men. How was I to know that big talk betokened the streak of fat, or that Yankee-men who did great things kept their teeth together? So we took the pick of the dogs and the best of the grub, and struck the trail, we three,—Passuk, Long Jeff, and I.

'Well, ye have broken virgin snow, labored at the gee-pole, and are not unused to the packed river-jams; so I will talk little of the toil, save that on some days we made ten miles, and on others thirty, but more often ten. And the best of the grub was not good, while we went on stint from the start. Likewise the pick of the dogs was poor, and we were hard put to keep them on their legs. At the White River our three sleds became two sleds, and we had only come two hundred miles. But we lost nothing; the dogs that left the traces went into the bellies of those that remained.

'Not a greeting, not a curl of smoke, till we made Pelly. Here I had counted on grub; and here I had counted on leaving Long Jeff, who was whining and trail-sore. But the factor's lungs were wheezing, his eyes bright, his cache nigh empty; and he showed us the empty cache of the missionary, also his grave with the rocks piled high to keep off the dogs. There was a bunch of Indians there, but babies and old men there were none, and it was clear that few would see the spring.

'So we pulled on, light-stomached and heavy-hearted, with half a thousand miles of snow and silence between us and Haines Mission by the sea. The darkness was at its worst, and at midday the sun could not clear the sky-line to the south. But the ice-jams were smaller, the going better; so I pushed the dogs hard and traveled late and early. As I said at Forty Mile, every inch of it was snow-shoe work. And the shoes made great sores on our feet, which cracked and scabbed but would not heal. And every day these sores grew more grievous, till in the morning, when we girded on the shoes, Long Jeff cried like a child. I put him at the fore of the light sled to break trail, but he slipped off the shoes for comfort. Because of this the trail was not packed, his moccasins made great holes, and into these holes the dogs wallowed. The bones of the dogs were ready to break through their hides, and this was not good for them. So I spoke hard words to the man, and he promised, and broke his word. Then I beat him with the dog-whip, and after that the dogs wallowed no more. He was a child, what of the pain and the streak of fat.

'But Passuk. While the man lay by the fire and wept, she cooked, and in the morning helped lash the sleds, and in the evening to unlash them. And she saved the dogs. Ever was she to the fore, lifting the webbed shoes and making the way easy. Passuk—how shall I say?—I took it for granted that she should do these things, and thought no more about it. For my mind was busy with other matters, and besides, I was young in years and knew little of woman. It was only on looking back that I came to understand.

'And the man became worthless. The dogs had little strength in them, but he stole rides on the sled when he lagged behind. Passuk said she would take the one sled, so the man had nothing to do. In the morning I gave him his fair share of grub and started him on the trail alone. Then the woman and I broke camp, packed the sleds, and harnessed the dogs. By midday, when the sun mocked us,* we would overtake the man, with the tears frozen on his cheeks, and pass him. In the night we made camp, set aside his fair share of grub, and spread his furs. Also we made a big fire, that he might see. And hours afterward he would come limping in, and eat his grub with moans and groans, and sleep. He was not sick, this man. He was only trail-sore and tired, and weak with hunger. But Passuk and I were trail-sore and tired, and weak with hunger; and we did all the work and he did none. But he had the streak of fat of which our brother Bettles has spoken. Further, we gave the man always his fair share of grub.

'Then one day we met two ghosts journeying through the Silence. They were a man and a boy, and they were white. The ice had opened on Lake Le Barge, and through it had gone their main outfit. One blanket each carried about his shoulders. At night they built a fire and crouched over it till morning. They had a little flour. This they stirred in warm water and drank. The man showed me eight cups of flour— all they had, and Pelly, stricken with famine, two hundred miles away. They said, also, that there was an Indian behind; that they had whacked fair,* but that he could not keep up. I did not believe they had whacked fair, else would the Indian have kept up. But I could give them no grub. They strove to steal a dog—the fattest, which was very thin—but I shoved my pistol in their faces and told them begone. And they went away, like drunken men, through the Silence toward Pelly.

'I had three dogs now, and one sled, and the dogs were only bones and hair. When there is little wood, the fire burns low and the cabin grows cold. So with us. With little grub the frost bites sharp, and our faces were black and frozen till our own mothers would not have known us. And our feet were very sore. In the morning, when I hit the trail, I sweated to keep down the cry when the pain of the snowshoes smote me. Passuk never opened her lips, but stepped to the fore to break the way. The man howled.

'The Thirty Mile was swift, and the current ate away the ice from beneath, and there were many air-holes and cracks, and much open water. One day we came upon the man, resting, for he had gone ahead, as was his wont, in the morning. But between us was open water. This he had passed around by taking to the rim-ice where it was too narrow for a sled. So we found an ice-bridge. Passuk weighed little, and went first, with a long pole crosswise in her hands in chance she broke through. But she was light, and her shoes large, and she passed over. Then she called the dogs. But they had neither poles nor shoes, and they broke through and were swept under by the water. I held tight to the sled from behind, till the traces broke and the dogs went on down under the ice. There was little meat to them, but I had counted on them for a week's grub, and they were gone.

'The next morning I divided all the grub, which was little, into three portions. And I told Long Jeff that he could keep up with us, or not, as he saw fit; for we were going to travel light and fast. But he raised his voice and cried over his sore feet and his troubles, and said harsh things against comradeship. Passuk's feet were sore, and my feet were sore—ay, sorer than his, for we had worked with the dogs; also, we looked to see. Long Jeff swore he would die before he hit the trail again; so Passuk took a fur robe, and I a cooking pot and an axe, and we made ready to go. But she looked on the man's portion, and said, 'It is wrong to waste good food on a baby. He is better dead.' I shook my head and said no— that a comrade once was a comrade always. Then she spoke of the men of Forty Mile, that they were many men and good; and that they looked to me for grub in the spring. But when I still said no, she snatched the pistol from my belt, quick, and as our brother Bettles has spoken, Long Jeff went to the bosom of Abraham before his time. I chided Passuk for this; but she showed no sorrow, nor was she sorrowful. And in my heart I knew she was right.'

Sitka Charley paused and threw pieces of ice into the gold pan on the stove. The men were silent, and their backs chilled to the sobbing cries of the dogs as they gave tongue to their misery in the outer cold.

'And day by day we passed in the snow the sleeping-places of the two ghosts—Passuk and I—and we knew we would be glad for such ere we made Salt Water. Then we came to the Indian, like another ghost, with his face set toward Pelly. They had not whacked up fair, the man and the boy, he said, and he had had no flour for three days. Each night he boiled pieces of his moccasins in a cup, and ate them. He did not have much moccasins left. And he was a Coast Indian, and told us these things through Passuk, who talked his tongue. He was a stranger in the Yukon, and he knew not the way, but his face was set to Pelly. How far was it? Two sleeps? ten? a hundred?—he did not know, but he was going to Pelly. It was too far to turn back; he could only keep on.

'He did not ask for grub, for he could see we, too, were hard put. Passuk looked at the man, and at me, as though she were of two minds, like a mother partridge whose young are in trouble. So I turned to her and said, "This man has been dealt unfair. Shall I give him of our grub a portion?" I saw her eyes light, as with quick pleasure; but she looked long at the man and at me, and her mouth drew close and hard, and she said, "No. The Salt Water is afar off, and Death lies in wait. Better it is that he take this stranger man and let my man Charley pass." So the man went away in the Silence toward Pelly. That night she wept. Never had I seen her weep before. Nor was it the smoke of the fire, for the wood was dry wood. So I marveled at her sorrow, and thought her woman's heart had grown soft at the darkness of the trail and the pain.

'Life is a strange thing. Much have I thought on it, and pondered long, yet daily the strangeness of it grows not less, but more. Why this longing for Life? It is a game which no man wins. To live is to toil hard, and to suffer sore, till Old Age creeps heavily upon us and we throw down our hands on the cold ashes of dead fires. It is hard to live. In pain the babe sucks his first breath, in pain the old man gasps his last, and all his days are full of trouble and sorrow; yet he goes down to the open arms of Death, stumbling, falling, with head turned backward, fighting to the last. And Death is kind. It is only Life, and the things of Life that hurt. Yet we love Life, and we hate Death. It is very strange.

'We spoke little, Passuk and I, in the days which came. In the night we lay in the snow like dead people, and in the morning we went on our way, walking like dead people. And all things were dead. There were no ptarmigan, no squirrels, no snowshoe rabbits,—nothing. The river made no sound beneath its white robes. The sap was frozen in the forest. And it became cold, as now; and in the night the stars drew near and large, and leaped and danced; and in the day the sun-dogs mocked us till we saw many suns, and all the air flashed and sparkled, and the snow was diamond dust. And there was no heat, no sound, only the bitter cold and the Silence. As I say, we walked like dead people, as in a dream, and we kept no count of time. Only our faces were set to Salt Water, our souls strained for Salt Water, and our feet carried us toward Salt Water. We camped by the Tahkeena, and knew it not. Our eyes looked upon the White Horse, but we saw it not. Our feet trod the portage of the Canyon, but they felt it not. We felt nothing. And we fell often by the way, but we fell, always, with our faces toward Salt Water.

'Our last grub went, and we had shared fair, Passuk and I, but she fell more often, and at Caribou Crossing her strength left her. And in the morning we lay beneath the one robe and did not take the trail. It was in my mind to stay there and meet Death hand-in-hand with Passuk; for I had grown old, and had learned the love of woman. Also, it was eighty miles to Haines Mission, and the great Chilcoot, far above the timber-line, reared his storm-swept head between. But Passuk spoke to me, low, with my ear against her lips that I might hear. And now, because she need not fear my anger, she spoke her heart, and told me of her love, and of many things which I did not understand.

'And she said: "You are my man, Charley, and I have been a good woman to you. And in all the days I have made your fire, and cooked your food, and fed your dogs, and lifted paddle or broken trail, I have not complained. Nor did I say that there was more warmth in the lodge of my father, or that there was more grub on the Chilcat. When you have spoken, I have listened. When you have ordered, I have obeyed. Is it not so, Charley?"

'And I said: "Ay, it is so."

'And she said: "When first you came to the Chilcat, nor looked upon me, but bought me as a man buys a dog, and took me away, my heart was hard against you and filled with bitterness and fear. But that was long ago. For you were kind to me, Charley, as a good man is kind to his dog. Your heart was cold, and there was no room for me; yet you dealt me fair and your ways were just. And I was with you when you did bold deeds and led great ventures, and I measured you against the men of other breeds, and I saw you stood among them full of honor, and your word was wise, your tongue true. And I grew proud of you, till it came that you filled all my heart, and all my thought was of you. You were as the midsummer sun, when its golden trail runs in a circle and never leaves the sky. And whatever way I cast my eyes I beheld the sun. But your heart was ever cold, Charley, and there was no room."

'And I said: "It is so. It was cold, and there was no room. But that is past. Now my heart is like the snowfall in the spring, when the sun has come back. There is a great thaw and a bending, a sound of running waters, and a budding and sprouting of green things. And there is drumming of partridges, and songs of robins, and great music, for the winter is broken, Passuk, and I have learned the love of woman."

'She smiled and moved for me to draw her closer. And she said, "I am glad." After that she lay quiet for a long time, breathing softly, her head upon my breast. Then she whispered: "The trail ends here, and I am tired. But first I would speak of other things. In the long ago, when I was a girl on the Chilcat, I played alone among the skin bales of my father's lodge; for the men were away on the hunt, and the women and boys were dragging in the meat. It was in the spring, and I was alone. A great brown bear, just awake from his winter's sleep, hungry, his fur hanging to the bones in flaps of leanness, shoved his head within the lodge and said, 'Oof!' My brother came running back with the first sled of meat. And he fought the bear with burning sticks from the fire, and the dogs in their harnesses, with the sled behind them, fell upon the bear. There was a great battle and much noise. They rolled in the fire, the skin bales were scattered, the lodge overthrown. But in the end the bear lay dead, with the fingers of my brother in his mouth and the marks of his claws upon my brother's face. Did you mark the Indian by the Pelly trail, his mitten which had no thumb, his hand which he warmed by our fire? He was my brother. And I said he should have no grub. And he went away in the Silence without grub."

'This, my brothers, was the love of Passuk, who died in the snow, by the Caribou Crossing. It was a mighty love, for she denied her brother for the man who led her away on weary trails to a bitter end. And, further, such was this woman's love, she denied herself. Ere her eyes closed for the last time she took my hand and slipped it under her squirrel-skin *parka* to her waist. I felt there a well-filled pouch, and learned the secret of her lost strength. Day by day we had shared fair, to the last least bit; and day by day but half her share had she eaten. The other half had gone into the well-filled pouch.

'And she said: "This is the end of the trail for Passuk; but your trail, Charley, leads on and on, over the great Chilcoot, down to Haines Mission and the sea. And it leads on and on, by the light of many suns, over unknown lands and strange waters, and it is full of years and honors and great glories. It leads you to the lodges of many women, and good women, but it will never lead you to a greater love than the love of Passuk."

'And I knew the woman spoke true. But a madness came upon me, and I threw the well-filled pouch from me, and swore that my trail had reached an end, till her tired eyes grew soft with tears, and she said: "Among men has Sitka Charley walked in honor, and ever has his word been true. Does he forget that honor now, and talk vain words by the Caribou Crossing? Does he remember no more the men of Forty Mile, who gave him of their grub the best, of their dogs the pick? Ever has Passuk been proud of her man. Let him lift himself up, gird on his snow-shoes, and begone, that she may still keep her pride."

'And when she grew cold in my arms I arose, and sought out the well-filled pouch, and girt on my snowshoes, and staggered along the trail; for there was a weakness in my knees, and my head was dizzy, and in my ears there was a roaring, and a flashing of fire upon my eyes. The forgotten trails of boyhood came back to me. I sat by the full pots of the *potlach* feast, and raised my voice in song, and danced to the chanting of the men and maidens and the booming of the walrus drums. And Passuk held my hand and walked by my side. When I laid down to sleep, she waked me. When I stumbled and fell, she raised me. When I wandered in the deep snow, she led me back to the trail. And in this wise, like a man bereft of reason, who sees strange visions and whose thoughts are light with wine, I came to Haines Mission by the sea.'

Sitka Charley threw back the tent-flaps. It was midday. To the south, just clearing the bleak Henderson Divide, poised the cold-disked sun. On either hand the sun-dogs blazed. The air was a gossamer of glittering frost. In the foreground, beside the trail, a wolf-dog, bristling with frost, thrust a long snout heavenward and mourned.

THE GREAT INTERROGATION

I

To say the least, Mrs Sayther's career in Dawson was mete-
oric. She arrived in the spring, with dog sleds and French-
Canadian *voyageurs*, blazed gloriously for a brief month, and
departed up the river as soon as it was free of ice. Now
womanless Dawson never quite understood this hurried
departure, and the local Four Hundred* felt aggrieved and
lonely till the Nome strike* was made and old sensations
gave way to new. For it had delighted in Mrs Sayther, and
received her wide-armed. She was pretty, charming, and,
moreover, a widow. And because of this she at once had at
heel any number of Eldorado Kings, officials, and adventur-
ing younger sons, whose ears were yearning for the frou-frou
of a woman's skirts.

The mining engineers revered the memory of her husband, the late Colonel Sayther, while the syndicate and pro-
moter representatives spoke awesomely of his deals and
manipulations; for he was known down in the States as a
great mining man, and as even a greater one in London.
Why his widow, of all women, should have come into the
country, was the great interrogation. But they were a practical breed, the men of the Northland, with a wholesome
disregard for theories and a firm grip on facts. And to not a
few of them Karen Sayther was a most essential fact. That
she did not regard the matter in this light, is evidenced by
the neatness and celerity with which refusal and proposal
tallied off during her four weeks' stay. And with her vanished
the fact, and only the interrogation remained.

To the solution, Chance vouchsafed one clew. Her last
victim, Jack Coughran, having fruitlessly laid at her feet both
his heart and a five-hundred-foot creek claim on Bonanza,
celebrated the misfortune by walking all of a night with the
gods. In the midwatch of this night he happened to rub

shoulders with Pierre Fontaine, none other than head man of Karen Sayther's *voyageurs*. This rubbing of shoulders led to recognition and drinks, and ultimately involved both men in a common muddle of inebriety.

'Heh?' Pierre Fontaine later on gurgled thickly. 'Vot for Madame Sayther mak visitation to thees country? More better you spik wit her. I know no t'ing 'tall, only all de tam her ask one man's name. "Pierre," her spik wit me; "Pierre, you moos' find thees mans, and I gif you mooch—one thousand dollar you find thees mans." Thees mans? Ah, *oui*. Thees man's name—vot you call—Daveed Payne. *Oui*, m'sieu, Daveed Payne. All de tam her spik das name. And all de tam I look rount vaire mooch, work lak hell, but no can find das dam mans, and no get one thousand dollar 'tall. By dam!

'Heh? Ah, *oui*. One tam dose mens vot come from Circle City, dose mens know thees mans. Him Birch Creek, dey spik. And madame? Her say "*Bon!*" and look happy lak anyt'ing. And her spik wit me. "Pierre," her spik, "harness de dogs. We go queek. We find thees mans I gif you one thousand dollar more." And I say, "*Oui*, queek! *Allons, madame!*"

'For sure, I t'ink, das two thousand dollar mine. Bully boy! Den more mens come from Circle City, and dey say no, das thees mans, Daveed Payne, come Dawson leel tam back. So madame and I go not 'tall.

'*Oui, m'sieu*. Thees day madame spik. "Pierre," her spik, and gif me five hundred dollar, "go buy poling-boat. To-morrow we go up de river." Ah, *oui*, to-morrow, up de river, and das dam Sitka Charley mak me pay for de poling-boat five hundred dollar. Dam!'

Thus it was, when Jack Coughran unburdened himself next day, that Dawson fell to wondering who was this David Payne, and in what way his existence bore upon Karen Sayther's. But that very day, as Pierre Fontaine had said, Mrs Sayther and her barbaric crew of *voyageurs* towed up the east bank to Klondike City, shot across to the west bank to escape the bluffs, and disappeared amid the maze of islands to the south.

II

'*Oui, madame,* thees is de place. One, two, t'ree island below Stuart River. Thees is t'ree island.'

As he spoke, Pierre Fontaine drove his pole against the bank and held the stern of the boat against the current. This thrust the bow in, till a nimble breed* climbed ashore with the painter and made fast.

'One leel tam, madame, I go look see.'

A chorus of dogs marked his disappearance over the edge of the bank, but a minute later he was back again.

'*Oui, madame,* thees is de cabin. I mak investigation. No can find mans at home. But him no go vaire far, vaire long, or him no leave dogs. Him come queek, you bet!'

'Help me out, Pierre. I'm tired all over from the boat. You might have made it softer, you know.'

From a nest of furs amidships, Karen Sayther rose to her full height of slender fairness. But if she looked lily-frail in her elemental environment, she was belied by the grip she put upon Pierre's hand, by the knotting of her woman's biceps as it took the weight of her body, by the splendid effort of her limbs as they held her out from the perpendicular bank while she made the ascent. Though shapely flesh clothed delicate frame, her body was a seat of strength.

Still, for all the careless ease with which she had made the landing, there was a warmer color than usual to her face, and a perceptibly extra beat to her heart. But then, also, it was with a certain reverent curiousness that she approached the cabin, while the flush on her cheek showed a yet riper mellowness.

'Look, see!' Pierre pointed to the scattered chips by the woodpile. 'Him fresh—two, t'ree day, no more.'

Mrs Sayther nodded. She tried to peer through the small window, but it was made of greased parchment which admitted light while it blocked vision. Failing this, she went round to the door, half lifted the rude latch to enter, but changed her mind and let it fall back into place. Then she suddenly dropped on one knee and kissed the rough-hewn threshold. If Pierre Fontaine saw, he gave no sign, and the memory in the time to come was never shared. But the next instant, one of the boatmen, placidly lighting his pipe, was startled by an unwonted harshness in his captain's voice.

'Hey! You! Le Goire! You mak 'm soft more better,' Pierre commanded. 'Plenty bear-skin; plenty blanket. Dam!'

But the nest was soon after disrupted, and the major portion tossed up to the crest of the shore, where Mrs Sayther lay down to wait in comfort. Reclining on her side, she looked out and over the wide-stretching Yukon. Above the mountains which lay beyond the further shore, the sky was murky with the smoke of unseen forest fires, and through this the afternoon sun broke feebly, throwing a vague radiance to earth, and unreal shadows. To the sky-line of the four quarters—spruce-shrouded islands, dark waters, and ice-scarred rocky ridges—stretched the immaculate wilderness. No sign of human existence broke the solitude; no sound the stillness. The land seemed bound under the unreality of the unknown, wrapped in the brooding mystery of great spaces.

Perhaps it was this which made Mrs Sayther nervous; for she changed her position constantly, now to look up the river, now down, or to scan the gloomy shores for the half-hidden mouths of back channels. After an hour or so the boatmen were sent ashore to pitch camp for the night, but Pierre remained with his mistress to watch.

'Ah! him come thees tam,' he whispered, after a long silence, his gaze bent up the river to the head of the island.

A canoe, with a paddle flashing on either side, was slipping down the current. In the stern a man's form, and in the bow a woman's, swung rhythmically to the work. Mrs Sayther had no eyes for the woman till the canoe drove in closer and her bizarre beauty peremptorily demanded notice. A close-fitting blouse of moose-skin, fantastically beaded, outlined faithfully the well-rounded lines of her body, while a silken kerchief, gay of color and picturesquely draped, partly covered great masses of blue-black hair. But it was the face, cast belike in copper bronze, which caught and held Mrs Sayther's fleeting glance. Eyes, piercing and black and large, with a traditionary hint of obliqueness, looked forth from under clear-stencilled, clean-arching brows. Without suggesting cadaverousness, though high-boned and prominent, the cheeks fell away and met in a mouth, thin-lipped and softly strong. It was a face which advertised the dimmest trace of ancient Mongol blood, a reversion, after long centuries of wandering, to the parent stem. This effect was heightened by the delicately aquiline nose with its thin trembling nostrils, and by the general air of eagle wildness which seemed to characterize not only the face but the creature herself. She was, in fact, the Tartar type modified to idealization, and the tribe of Red Indian is lucky that breeds such a unique body once in a score of generations.

Dipping long strokes and strong, the girl, in concert with the man, suddenly whirled the tiny craft about against the current and brought it gently to the shore. Another instant and she stood at the top of the bank, heaving up by rope, hand under hand, a quarter of fresh-killed moose. Then the man followed her, and together, with a swift rush, they drew up the canoe. The dogs were in a whining mass about them, and as the girl stooped among them caressingly, the man's gaze fell upon Mrs Sayther, who had arisen. He looked, brushed his eyes unconsciously as though his sight were deceiving him, and looked again.

'Karen,' he said simply, coming forward and extending his hand, 'I thought for the moment I was dreaming. I went snow-blind for a time, this spring, and since then my eyes have been playing tricks with me.'

Mrs Sayther, whose flush had deepened and whose heart was urging painfully, had been prepared for almost anything save this coolly extended hand; but she tactfully curbed herself and grasped it heartily with her own.

'You know, Dave, I threatened often to come, and I would have, too, only—only—'

'Only I didn't give the word.' David Payne laughed and watched the Indian girl disappearing into the cabin.

'Oh, I understand, Dave, and had I been in your place I'd most probably have done the same. But I have come—now.'

'Then come a little bit farther, into the cabin and get something to eat,' he said genially, ignoring or missing the feminine suggestion of appeal in her voice. 'And you must be tired too. Which way are you travelling? Up? Then you wintered in Dawson, or came in on the last ice. Your camp?' He glanced at the *voyageurs* circled about the fire in the open, and held back the door for her to enter.

'I came up on the ice from Circle City last winter,' he continued, 'and settled down here for a while. Am prospecting some on Henderson Creek, and if that fails, have been thinking of trying my hand this fall up the Stuart River.'

'You aren't changed much, are you?' she asked irrelevantly, striving to throw the conversation upon a more personal basis.

'A little less flesh, perhaps, and a little more muscle. How did *you* mean?'

'But she shrugged her shoulders and peered through the dim light at the Indian girl, who had lighted the fire and was frying great chunks of moose meat, alternated with thin ribbons of bacon.

'Did you stop in Dawson long?' The man was whittling a stave of birchwood into a rude axe-handle, and asked the question without raising his head.

'Oh, a few days,' she answered, following the girl with her eyes, and hardly hearing. 'What were you saying? In Dawson? A month, in fact, and glad to get away. The arctic male is elemental, you know, and somewhat strenuous in his feelings.'

'Bound to be when he gets right down to the soil. He leaves convention with the spring bed at home. But you were wise in your choice of time for leaving. You'll be out of the country before mosquito season, which is a blessing your lack of experience will not permit you to appreciate.'

'I suppose not. But tell me about yourself, about your life. What kind of neighbors have you? Or have you any?'

While she queried she watched the girl grinding coffee in the corner of a flower sack upon the hearthstone. With a steadiness and skill which predicated nerves as primitive as the method, she crushed the imprisoned berries with a heavy fragment of quartz. David Payne noted his visitor's gaze, and the shadow of a smile drifted over his lips.

'I did have some,' he replied. 'Missourian chaps, and a couple of Cornishmen, but they went down to Eldorado to work at wages for a grubstake.'

Mrs Sayther cast a look of speculative regard upon the girl. 'But of course there are plenty of Indians about?'

'Every mother's son of them down to Dawson long ago. Not a native in the whole country, barring Winapie here, and she's a Koyokuk lass,—comes from a thousand miles or so down the river.'

Mrs Sayther felt suddenly faint; and though the smile of interest in no wise waned, the face of the man seemed to draw away to a telescopic distance, and the tiered logs of the cabin to whirl drunkenly about. But she was bidden draw up to the table, and during the meal discovered time and space in which to find herself. She talked little, and that principally about the land and weather, while the man wandered off into a long description of the difference between the shallow summer diggings of the Lower Country and the deep winter diggings of the Upper Country.

'You do not ask why I came north?' she asked. 'Surely you know.' They had moved back from the table, and David Payne had returned to his axe-handle. 'Did you get my letter?'

'A last one? No, I don't think so. Most probably it's trailing around the Birch Creek Country or lying in some trader's shack on the Lower River. The way they run the mails in here is shameful. No order, no system, no—'

'Don't be wooden, Dave! Help me!' She spoke sharply now, with an assumption of authority which rested upon the past. 'Why don't you ask me about myself? About those we knew in the old times? Have you no longer any interest in the world? Do you know that my husband is dead?'

'Indeed, I am sorry. How long—'

'David!' She was ready to cry with vexation, but the reproach she threw into her voice eased her.

'Did you get any of my letters? You must have got some of them, though you never answered.'

'Well, I didn't get the last one, announcing, evidently, the death of your husband, and most likely others went astray; but I did get some. I—er—read them aloud to Winapie as a warning—that is, you know, to impress upon her the wickedness of her white sisters. And I—er—think she profited by it. Don't you?'

She disregarded the sting, and went on. 'In the last letter, which you did not receive, I told, as you have guessed, of Colonel Sayther's death. That was a year ago. I also said that if you did not come out to me, I would go in to you. And as I had often promised, I came.'

'I know of no promise.'

'In the earlier letters?'

'Yes, you promised, but as I neither asked nor answered, it was unratified. So I do not know of any such promise. But I do know of another, which you, too, may remember. It was very long ago.' He dropped the axe-handle to the floor and raised his head. 'It was so very long ago, yet I remember it distinctly, the day, the time, every detail. We were in a rose garden, you and I,—your mother's rose garden. All things were budding, blossoming, and the sap of spring was in our blood. And I drew you over—it was the first—and kissed you full on the lips. Don't you remember?'

'Don't go over it, Dave, don't! I know every shameful line of it. How often have I wept! If you only knew how I have suffered—'

'You promised me then—ay, and a thousand times in the sweet days that followed. Each look of your eyes, each touch of your hand, each syllable that fell from your lips, was a promise. And then—how shall I say?—there came a man. He was old—old enough to have begotten you—and not nice to look upon, but as the world goes, clean. He had done no wrong, followed the letter of the law, was respectable. Further, and to the point, he possessed some several paltry mines,— a score; it does not matter: and he owned a few miles of lands, and engineered deals, and clipped coupons. He—'

'But there were other things,' she interrupted, 'I told you. Pressure—money matters—want—my people—trouble. You understood the whole sordid situation. I could not help it. It was not my will. I was sacrificed, or I sacrificed, have it as you wish. But, my God! Dave, I gave you up! You never did *me* justice. Think what I have gone through!'

'It was not your will? Pressure? Under high heaven there was no thing to will you to this man's bed or that.'

'But I cared for you all the time,' she pleaded.

'I was unused to your way of measuring love. I am still unused. I do not understand.'

'But now! now!'

'We were speaking of this man you saw fit to marry. What manner of man was he? Wherein did he charm your soul? What potent virtues were his? True, he had a golden grip,— an almighty golden grip. He knew the odds. He was versed in cent per cent.* He had a narrow wit and excellent judgment of the viler parts, whereby he transferred this man's money to his pockets, and that man's money, and the next man's. And the law smiled. In that it did not condemn, our Christian ethics approved. By social measure he was not a bad man. But by your measure, Karen, by mine, by ours of the rose garden, what was he?'

'Remember, he is dead.'

'The fact is not altered thereby. What was he? A great, gross, material creature, deaf to song, blind to beauty, dead to the spirit. He was fat with laziness, and flabby-cheeked, and the round of his belly witnessed his gluttony—'

'But he is dead. It is we who are now—now! now! Don't you hear? As you say, I have been inconstant. I have sinned. Good. But should not you, too, cry *peccavi*? If I have broken promises, have not you? Your love of the rose garden was of all time, or so you said. Where is it now?'

'It is here! now!' he cried, striking his breast passionately with clenched hand. 'It has always been.'

'And your love was a great love; there was none greater,' she continued; 'or so you said in the rose garden. Yet it is not fine enough, large enough, to forgive me here, crying now at your feet?'

The man hesitated. His mouth opened; words shaped vainly on his lips. She had forced him to bare his heart and speak truths which he had hidden from himself. And she was good to look upon, standing there in a glory of passion, calling back old associations and warmer life. He turned away his head that he might not see, but she passed around and fronted him.

'Look at me, Dave! Look at me! I am the same, after all. And so are you, if you would but see. We are not changed.'

Her hand rested on his shoulder, and his had half-passed, roughly, about her, when the sharp crackle of a match startled him to himself. Winapie, alien to the scene, was lighting the slow wick of the slush lamp. She appeared to start out against a background of utter black, and the flame, flaring suddenly up, lighted her bronze beauty to royal gold.

'You see, it is impossible,' he groaned, thrusting the fair-haired woman gently from him. 'It is impossible,' he repeated. 'It is impossible.'

'I am not a girl, Dave, with a girl's illusions,' she said softly, though not daring to come back to him. 'It is as a woman that I understand. Men are men. A common custom of the country. I am not shocked. I divined it from the first. But—ah!—it is only a marriage of the country—not a real marriage?'

'We do not ask such questions in Alaska,' he interposed feebly.

'I know, but—'

'Well, then, it is only a marriage of the country—nothing else.'

'And there are no children?'

'No.'

'Nor—'

'No, no; nothing—but it is impossible.'

'But it is not.' She was at his side again, her hand touching lightly, caressingly, the sunburned back of his. 'I know the custom of the land too well. Men do it every day. They do not care to remain here, shut out from the world, for all their days; so they give an order on the P. C. C. Company for a year's provisions, some money in hand, and the girl is content. By the end of that time, a man—' She shrugged her shoulders. 'And so with the girl here. We will give her an order upon the company, not for a year, but for life. What was she when you found her? A raw, meat-eating savage; fish in summer, moose in winter, feasting in plenty, starving in famine. But for you that is what she would have remained. For your coming she was happier; for your going, surely, with a life of comparative splendor assured, she will be happier than if you had never been.'

'No, no,' he protested. 'It is not right.'

'Come, Dave, you must see. She is not your kind. There is no race affinity. She is an aborigine, sprung from the soil, yet close to the soil, and impossible to lift from the soil. Born savage, savage she will die. But we—you and I—the dominant, evolved race—the salt of the earth and the masters thereof! We are made for each other. The supreme call is of kind, and we are of kind. Reason and feeling dictate it. Your very instinct demands it. That you cannot deny. You cannot escape the generations behind you. Yours is an ancestry which has survived for a thousand centuries, and for a hundred thousand centuries, and your line must not stop here. It cannot. Your ancestry will not permit it. Instinct is stronger than the will. The race is mightier than you. Come, Dave, let us go. We are young yet, and life is good. Come.'

Winapie, passing out of the cabin to feed the dogs, caught his attention and caused him to shake his head and weakly to reiterate. But the woman's hand slipped about his neck, and her cheek pressed to his. His bleak life rose up and smote him,—the vain struggle with pitiless forces; the dreary years of frost and famine; the harsh and jarring contact with elemental life; the aching void which mere animal existence could not fill. And there, seduction by his side, whispering of brighter, warmer lands, of music, light, and joy, called the old times back again. He visioned it unconsciously. Faces rushed in upon him; glimpses of forgotten scenes, memories of merry hours; strains of song and trills of laughter—

'Come, Dave, come. I have for both. The way is soft.' She looked about her at the bare furnishings of the cabin. 'I have for both. The world is at our feet, and all joy is ours. Come! come!'

She was in his arms, trembling, and he held her tightly. He rose to his feet. . . . But the snarling of hungry dogs, and the shrill cries of Winapie bringing about peace between the combatants, came muffled to his ear through the heavy logs. And another scene flashed before him. A struggle in the forest,—a bald-face grizzly, broken-legged, terrible; the snarling of the dogs and the shrill cries of Winapie as she urged them to the attack; himself in the midst of the crush, breathless, panting, striving to hold off red death; boken-backed, entrail-ripped dogs howling in impotent anguish and desecrating the snow; the virgin white running scarlet with the blood of man and beast; the bear, ferocious, irresistible, crunching, crunching down to the core of his life; and Winapie, at the last, in the thick of the frightful muddle, hair flying, eyes flashing, fury incarnate, passing the long hunting knife again and again—Sweat started to his forehead. He shook off the clinging woman and staggered back to the wall. And she, knowing that the moment had come, but unable to divine what was passing within him, felt all she had gained slipping away.

'Dave! Dave!' she cried. 'I will not give you up! I will not give you up! If you do not wish to come, we will stay. I will stay with you. The world is less to me than are you. I will be a Northland wife to you. I will cook your food, feed your dogs, break trail for you, lift a paddle with you. I can do it. Believe me, I am strong.'

Nor did he doubt it, looking upon her and holding her off from him; but his face had grown stern and gray, and the warmth had died out of his eyes.

'I will pay off Pierre and the boatmen, and let them go. And I will stay with you, priest or no priest, minister or no minister; go with you, now, anywhere! Dave! Dave! Listen to me! You say I did you wrong in the past—and I did—let me make up for it, let me atone. If I did not rightly measure love before, let me show that I can now.'

She sank to the floor and threw her arms about his knees, sobbing. 'And you *do* care for me. You *do* care for me. Think! The long years I have waited, suffered! You can never know!'

He stooped and raised her to her feet.

'Listen,' he commanded, opening the door and lifting her bodily outside. 'It cannot be. We are not alone to be considered. You must go. I wish you a safe journey. You will find it tougher work when you get up by the Sixty Mile, but you have the best boatmen in the world, and will get through all right. Will you say good-by?'

Though she already had herself in hand, she looked at him hopelessly. 'If—if—if Winapie should—' She quavered and stopped.

But he grasped the unspoken thought, and answered, 'Yes.' Then struck with the enormity of it, 'It cannot be conceived. There is no likelihood. It must not be entertained.'

'Kiss me,' she whispered, her face lighting. Then she turned and went away.

'Break camp, Pierre,' she said to the boatman, who alone had remained awake against her return. 'We must be going.'

By the firelight his sharp eyes scanned the woe in her face, but he received the extraordinary command as though it were the most usual thing in the world. '*Oui, madame*,' he assented. 'Which way? Dawson?'

'No,' she answered, lightly enough; 'up; out; Dyea.'

Whereat he fell upon the sleeping *voyageurs*, kicking them, grunting, from their blankets, and buckling them down to the work, the while his voice, vibrant with action, shrilling through all the camp. In a trice Mrs Sayther's tiny tent had been struck, pots and pans were being gathered up, blankets rolled, and the men staggering under the loads to the boat. Here, on the banks, Mrs Sayther waited till the luggage was made ship-shape and her nest prepared.

'We line up to de head of de island,' Pierre explained to her while running out the long tow rope. 'Den we tak to das back channel, where de water not queek, and I t'ink we mak good tam.'

A scuffling and pattering of feet in the last year's dry grass caught his quick ear, and he turned his head. The Indian girl, circled by a bristling ring of wolf dogs, was coming toward them. Mrs Sayther noted that the girl's face, which had been apathetic throughout the scene in the cabin, had now quickened into blazing and wrathful life.

'What you do my man?' she demanded abruptly of Mrs Sayther. 'Him lay on bunk, and him look bad all the time. I say, "What the matter, Dave? You sick?" But him no say nothing. After that him say, "Good girl Winapie, go way. I be all right bimeby." What you do my man, eh? I think you bad woman.'

Mrs Sayther looked curiously at the barbarian woman who shared the life of this man, while she departed alone in the darkness of night.

'I think you bad woman,' Winapie repeated in the slow, methodical way of one who gropes for strange words in an alien tongue. 'I think better you go way, no come no more. Eh? What you think? I have one man. I Indian girl. You 'Merican woman. You good to see. You find plenty men. Your eyes blue like the sky. Your skin so white, so soft.'

Coolly she thrust out a brown forefinger and pressed the soft cheek of the other woman. And to the eternal credit of Karen Sayther, she never flinched. Pierre hesitated and half stepped forward; but she motioned him away, though her heart welled to him with secret gratitude. 'It's all right, Pierre,' she said. 'Please go away.'

He stepped back respectfully out of earshot, where he stood grumbling to himself and measuring the distance in springs.

'Um white, um soft, like baby.' Winapie touched the other cheek and withdrew her hand. 'Bimeby mosquito come. Skin get sore in spot; um swell, oh, so big; um hurt, oh, so much. Plenty mosquito; plenty spot. I think better you go now before mosquito come. This way,' pointing down the stream, 'you go St Michael's; that way,' pointing up, 'you go Dyea. Better you go Dyea. Good-by.'

And that which Mrs Sayther then did, caused Pierre to marvel greatly. For she threw her arms around the Indian girl, kissed her, and burst into tears.

'Be good to him,' she cried. 'Be good to him.'

Then she slipped half down the face of the bank, called back 'Good-by,' and dropped into the boat amidships. Pierre followed her and cast off. He shoved the steering oar into place and gave the signal. Le Goire lifted an old French *chanson*; the men, like a row of ghosts in the dim starlight, bent their backs to the tow line; the steering oar cut the black current sharply, and the boat swept out into the night.

THE LAW OF LIFE

Old Koskoosh listened greedily. Though his sight had long since faded, his hearing was still acute, and the slightest sound penetrated to the glimmering intelligence which yet abode behind the withered forehead, but which no longer gazed forth upon the things of the world. Ah! that was Sit-cum-to-ha, shrilly anathematizing the dogs as she cuffed and beat them into the harnesses. Sit-cum-to-ha was his daughter's daughter, but she was too busy to waste a thought upon her broken grandfather, sitting alone there in the snow, forlorn and helpless. Camp must be broken. The long trail waited while the short day refused to linger. Life called her, and the duties of life, not death. And he was very close to death now.

The thought made the old man panicky for the moment, and he stretched forth a palsied hand which wandered tremblingly over the small heap of dry wood beside him. Reassured that it was indeed there, his hand returned to the shelter of his mangy furs, and he again fell to listening. The sulky crackling of half-frozen hides told him that the chief's moose-skin lodge had been struck, and even then was being rammed and jammed into portable compass. The chief was his son, stalwart and strong, head man of the tribesmen, and a mighty hunter. As the women toiled with the camp luggage, his voice rose, chiding them for their slowness. Old Koskoosh strained his ears. It was the last time he would hear that voice. There went Geehow's lodge! And Tusken's! Seven, eight, nine; only the shaman's could be still standing. There! They were at work upon it now. He could hear the shaman grunt as he piled it on the sled. A child whimpered, and a woman soothed it with soft, crooning gutturals. Little Kootee, the old man thought, a fretful child, and not overstrong. It would die soon, perhaps, and they would burn a hole through the frozen tundra and pile rocks above to keep the wolverines away. Well, what did it matter? A few years at best, and as many an empty belly as a full one. And in the end, Death waited, ever-hungry and hungriest of them all.

What was that? Oh, the men lashing the sleds and drawing tight the thongs. He listened, who would listen no more. The whip-lashes snarled and bit among the dogs. Hear them whine! How they hated the work and the trail! They were off! Sled after sled churned slowly away into the silence. They were gone. They had passed out of his life, and he faced the last bitter hour alone. No. The snow crunched beneath a moccasin; a man stood beside him; upon his head a hand rested gently. His son was good to do this thing. He remembered other old men whose sons had not waited after the tribe. But his son had. He wandered away into the past, till the young man's voice brought him back.

'Is it well with you?' he asked.

And the old man answered, 'It is well.'

'There be wood beside you,' the younger man continued, 'and the fire burns bright. The morning is gray, and the cold has broken. It will snow presently. Even now is it snowing.'

'Ay, even now is it snowing.'

'The tribesmen hurry. Their bales are heavy, and their bellies flat with lack of feasting. The trail is long and they travel fast. I go now. It is well?'

'It is well. I am as a last year's leaf, clinging lightly to the stem. The first breath that blows, and I fall. My voice is become like an old woman's. My eyes no longer show me the way of my feet, and my feet are heavy, and I am tired. It is well.'

He bowed his head in content till the last noise of the complaining snow had died away, and he knew his son was beyond recall. Then his hand crept out in haste to the wood. It alone stood between him and the eternity that yawned in upon him. At last the measure of his life was a handful of faggots. One by one they would go to feed the fire, and just so, step by step, death would creep upon him. When the last stick had surrendered up its heat, the frost would begin to gather strength. First his feet would yield, then his hands; and the numbness would travel, slowly, from the extremities to the body. His head would fall forward upon his knees, and he would rest. It was easy. All men must die.

He did not complain. It was the way of life, and it was

just. He had been born close to the earth, close to the earth had he lived, and the law thereof was not new to him. It was the law of all flesh. Nature was not kindly to the flesh. She had no concern for that concrete thing called the individual. Her interest lay in the species, the race. This was the deepest abstraction old Koskoosh's barbaric mind was capable of, but he grasped it firmly. He saw it exemplified in all life. The rise of the sap, the bursting greenness of the willow bud, the fall of the yellow leaf—in this alone was told the whole history. But one task did Nature set the individual. Did he not perform it, he died. Did he perform it, it was all the same, he died. Nature did not care; there were plenty who were obedient, and it was only the obedience in this matter, not the obedient, which lived and lived always. The tribe of Koskoosh was very old. The old men he had known when a boy, had known old men before them. Therefore it was true that the tribe lived, that it stood for the obedience of all its members, way down into the forgotten past, whose very resting-places were unremembered. They did not count; they were episodes. They had passed away like clouds from a summer sky. He also was an episode, and would pass away. Nature did not care. To life she set one task, gave one law. To perpetuate was the task of life, its law was death. A maiden was a good creature to look upon, full-breasted and strong, with spring to her step and light in her eyes. But her task was yet before her. The light in her eyes brightened, her step quickened, she was now bold with the young men, now timid, and she gave them of her own unrest. And ever she grew fairer and yet fairer to look upon, till some hunter, able no longer to withhold himself, took her to his lodge to cook and toil for him and to become the mother of his children. And with the coming of her offspring her looks left her. Her limbs dragged and shuffled, her eyes dimmed and bleared, and only the little children found joy against the withered cheek of the old squaw by the fire. Her task was done. But a little while, on the first pinch of famine or the first long trail, and she would be left, even as he had been left, in the snow, with a little pile of wood. Such was the law.

He placed a stick carefully upon the fire and resumed his

meditations. It was the same everywhere, with all things. The mosquitoes vanished with the first frost. The little tree-squirrel crawled away to die. When age settled upon the rabbit it became slow and heavy, and could no longer out-foot its enemies. Even the big bald-face grew clumsy and blind and quarrelsome, in the end to be dragged down by a handful of yelping huskies. He remembered how he had abandoned his own father on an upper reach of the Klondike one winter, the winter before the missionary came with his talk-books and his box of medicines. Many a time had Koskoosh smacked his lips over the recollection of that box, though now his mouth refused to moisten. The 'painkiller' had been especially good. But the missionary was a bother after all, for he brought no meat into the camp, and he ate heartily, and the hunters grumbled. But he chilled his lungs on the divide by the Mayo, and the dogs afterwards nosed the stones away and fought over his bones.

Koskoosh placed another stick on the fire and harked back deeper into the past. There was the time of the Great Famine, when the old men crouched empty-bellied to the fire, and let fall from their lips dim traditions of the ancient day when the Yukon ran wide open for three winters, and then lay frozen for three summers. He had lost his mother in that famine. In the summer the salmon run had failed, and the tribe looked forward to the winter and the coming of the caribou. Then the winter came, but with it there were no caribou. Never had the like been known, not even in the lives of the old men. But the caribou did not come, and it was the seventh year, and the rabbits had not replenished, and the dogs were naught but bundles of bones. And through the long darkness the children wailed and died, and the women, and the old men; and not one in ten of the tribe lived to meet the sun when it came back in the spring. That *was* a famine!

But he had seen times of plenty, too, when the meat spoiled on their hands, and the dogs were fat and worthless with overeating—times when they let the game go unkilled, and the women were fertile, and the lodges were cluttered with sprawling men-children and women-children. Then it was the men became high-stomached, and revived ancient quarrels, and crossed the divides to the south to kill the Pellys, and to the west that they might sit by the dead fires of the Tananas. He remembered, when a boy, during a time of plenty, when he saw a moose pulled down by the wolves. Zing-ha lay with him in the snow and watched—Zing-ha, who later became the craftiest of hunters, and who, in the end, fell through an air-hole on the Yukon. They found him, a month afterward, just as he had crawled halfway out and frozen stiff to the ice.

But the moose. Zing-ha and he had gone out that day to play at hunting after the manner of their fathers. On the bed of the creek they struck the fresh track of a moose, and with it the tracks of many wolves. 'An old one,' Zing-ha, who was quicker at reading the sign, said—'an old one who cannot keep up with the herd. The wolves have cut him out from his brothers, and they will never leave him.' And it was so. It was their way. By day and by night, never resting, snarling on his heels, snapping at his nose, they would stay by him to the end. How Zing-ha and he felt the blood-lust quicken! The finish would be a sight to see!

Eager-footed, they took the trail, and even he, Koskoosh, slow of sight and an unversed tracker, could have followed it blind, it was so wide. Hot were they on the heels of the chase, reading the grim tragedy, fresh-written, at every step. Now they came to where the moose had made a stand. Thrice the length of a grown man's body, in every direction, had the snow been stamped about and uptossed. In the midst were the deep impressions of the splay-hoofed game, and all about, everywhere, were the lighter footmarks of the wolves. Some, while their brothers harried the kill, had lain to one side and rested. The full-stretched impress of their bodies in the snow was as perfect as though made the moment before. One wolf had been caught in a wild lunge of the maddened victim and trampled to death. A few bones, well picked, bore witness.

Again, they ceased the uplift of their snowshoes at a second stand. Here the great animal had fought desperately. Twice had he been dragged down, as the snow attested, and twice had he shaken his assailants clear and gained footing once more. He had done his task long since, but none the less was life dear to him. Zing-ha said it was a strange thing, a moose once down to get free again; but this one certainly had. The shaman would see signs and wonders in this when they told him.

And yet again, they come to where the moose had made to mount the bank and gain the timber. But his foes had laid on from behind, till he reared and fell back upon them, crushing two deep into the snow. It was plain the kill was at hand, for their brothers had left them untouched. Two more stands were hurried past, brief in time-length and very close together. The trail was red now, and the clean stride of the great beast has grown short and slovenly. Then they heard the first sounds of the battle—not the full-throated chorus of the chase, but the short, snappy bark which spoke of close quarters and teeth to flesh. Crawling up the wind, Zing-ha bellied it through the snow, and with him crept he, Koskoosh, who was to be chief of the tribesmen in the years to come. Together they shoved aside the under branches of a young spruce and peered forth. It was the end they saw.

The picture, like all of youth's impressions, was still strong with him, and his dim eyes watched the end played out as vividly as in that far-off time. Koskoosh marvelled at this, for in the days which followed, when he was a leader of men and a head of councillors, he had done great deeds and made his name a curse in the mouths of the Pellys, to say naught of the strange white man he had killed, knife to knife, in open fight.

For long he pondered on the days of his youth, till the fire died down and the frost bit deeper. He replenished it with two sticks this time, and gauged his grip on life by what remained. If Sit-cum-to-ha had only remembered her grandfather, and gathered a larger armful, his hours would have been longer. It would have been easy. But she was ever a careless child, and honored not her ancestors from the time the Beaver, son of the son of Zing-ha, first cast eyes upon her. Well, what mattered it? Had he not done likewise in his own quick youth? For a while he listened to the silence.

Perhaps the heart of his son might soften, and he would come back with the dogs to take his old father on with the tribe to where the caribou ran thick and the fat hung heavy upon them.

He strained his ears, his restless brain for the moment stilled. Not a stir, nothing. He alone took breath in the midst of the great silence. It was very lonely. Hark! What was that? A chill passed over his body. The familiar, long-drawn howl broke the void, and it was close at hand. Then on his darkened eyes was projected the vision of the moose—the old bull moose—the torn flanks and bloody sides, the riddled mane, and the great branching horns, down low and tossing to the last. He saw the flashing forms of gray, the gleaming eyes, the lolling tongues, the slavered fangs. And he saw the inexorable circle close in till it became a dark point in the midst of the stamped snow.

A cold muzzle thrust against his cheek, and at its touch his soul leaped back to the present. His hand shot into the fire and dragged out a burning faggot. Overcome for the nonce by his hereditary fear of man, the brute retreated, raising a prolonged call to his brothers; and greedily they answered, till a ring of crouching, jaw-slobbered gray was stretched round about. The old man listened to the drawing in of this circle. He waved his brand wildly, and sniffs turned to snarls; but the panting brutes refused to scatter. Now one wormed his chest forward, dragging his haunches after, now a second, now a third; but never a one drew back. Why should he cling to life? he asked, and dropped the blazing stick into the snow. It sizzled and went out. The circle grunted uneasily, but held its own. Again he saw the last stand of the old bull moose, and Koskoosh dropped his head wearily upon his knees. What did it matter after all? Was it not the law of life?

AT THE RAINBOW'S END

I

It was for two reasons that Montana Kid discarded his 'chaps' and Mexican spurs, and shook the dust of the Idaho ranges from his feet. In the first place, the encroachments of a steady, sober, and sternly moral civilization had destroyed the primeval status of the western cattle ranges, and refined society turned the cold eye of disfavor upon him and his ilk. In the second place, in one of its cyclopean moments the race had arisen and shoved back its frontier several thousand miles. Thus, with unconscious foresight, did mature society make room for its adolescent members. True, the new territory was mostly barren; but its several hundred thousand square miles of frigidity at least gave breathing space to those who else would have suffocated at home.

Montana Kid was such a one. Heading for the sea-coast, with a haste several sheriff's posses might possibly have explained, and with more nerve than coin of the realm, he succeeded in shipping from a Puget Sound port, and managed to survive the contingent miseries of steerage seasickness and steerage grub. He was rather sallow and drawn, but still his own indomitable self, when he landed on the Dyea beach one day in the spring of the year. Between the cost of dogs, grub, and outfits, and the customs exactions of the two clashing governments, it speedily penetrated to his understanding that the Northland was anything save a poor man's Mecca. So he cast about him in search of quick harvests. Between the beach and the passes were scattered many thousands of passionate pilgrims. These pilgrims Montana Kid proceeded to farm. At first he dealt faro in a pine-board gambling shack; but disagreeable necessity forced him to drop a sudden period into a man's life, and to move on up trail. Then he effected a corner in horseshoe nails, and they circulated at par with legal tender, four to the dollar, till an unexpected consignment of a hundred barrels or so broke the market and forced him to disgorge his stock at a loss. After that he located at Sheep Camp, organized the professional packers, and jumped the freight ten cents a pound in a single day. In token of their gratitude, the packers patronized his faro and roulette layouts and were mulcted cheerfully of their earnings. But his commercialism was of too lusty a growth to be long endured; so they rushed him one night, burned his shanty, divided the bank, and headed him up the trail with empty pockets.

Ill-luck was his running mate. He engaged with responsible parties to run whisky across the line by way of precarious and unknown trails, lost his Indian guides, and had the very first outfit confiscated by the Mounted Police. Numerous other misfortunes tended to make him bitter of heart and wanton of action, and he celebrated his arrival at Lake Bennett by terrorizing the camp for twenty straight hours. Then a miners' meeting took him in hand, and commanded him to make himself scarce. He had a wholesome respect for such assemblages, and he obeyed in such haste that he inadvertently removed himself at the tail-end of another man's dog team. This was equivalent to horse-stealing in a more mellow clime, so he hit only the high places across Bennett and down Tagish, and made his first camp a full hundred miles to the north.

Now it happened that the break of spring was at hand, and many of the principal citizens of Dawson were travelling south on the last ice. These he met and talked with, noted their names and possessions, and passed on. He had a good memory, also a fair imagination; nor was veracity one of his virtues.

II

Dawson, always eager for news, beheld Montana Kid's sled heading down the Yukon, and went out on the ice to meet him. No, he hadn't any newspapers; didn't know whether Durrant* was hanged yet, nor who had won the Thanksgiving game;* hadn't heard whether the United States and Spain had gone to fighting; didn't know who Dreyfus* was; but

O'Brien? Hadn't they heard? O'Brien, why, he was drowned in the White Horse; Sitka Charley the only one of the party who escaped. Joe Ladue? Both legs frozen and amputated at the Five Fingers. And Jack Dalton? Blown up on the 'Sea Lion' with all hands. And Bettles? Wrecked on the 'Carthagina,' in Seymour Narrows,—twenty survivors out of three hundred. And Swiftwater Bill? Gone through the rotten ice of Lake LeBarge with six female members of the opera troupe he was convoying. Governor Walsh? Lost with all hands and eight sleds on the Thirty Mile. Devereaux? Who was Devereaux? Oh, the courier! Shot by Indians on Lake Marsh.

So it went. The word was passed along. Men shouldered in to ask after friends and partners, and in turn were shouldered out, too stunned for blasphemy. By the time Montana Kid gained the bank he was surrounded by several hundred fur-clad miners. When he passed the Barracks he was the centre of a procession. At the Opera House he was the nucleus of an excited mob, each member struggling for a chance to ask after some absent comrade. On every side he was being invited to drink. Never before had the Klondike thus opened its arms to a *che-cha-qua*. All Dawson was humming. Such a series of catastrophes had never occurred in its history. Every man of note who had gone south in the spring had been wiped out. The cabins vomited forth their occupants. Wild-eyed men hurried down from the creeks and gulches to seek out this man who had told a tale of such disaster. The Russian halfbreed wife of Bettles sought the fireplace, inconsolable, and rocked back and forth, and ever and anon flung white wood-ashes upon her raven hair. The flag at the Barracks flopped dismally at half-mast. Dawson mourned its dead.

Why Montana Kid did this thing no man may know. Nor beyond the fact that the truth was not in him, can explanation be hazarded. But for five whole days he plunged the land in wailing and sorrow, and for five whole days he was the only man in the Klondike. The country gave him its best of bed and board. The saloons granted him the freedom of their bars. Men sought him continuously. The high officials bowed down to him for further information, and he was feasted at the Barracks by Constantine and his brother officers. And then, one day, Devereaux, the government courier, halted his tired dogs before the gold commissioner's office. Dead? Who said so? Give him a moose steak and he'd show them how dead he was. Why, Governor Walsh was in camp on the Little Salmon, and O'Brien coming in on the first water. Dead? Give him a moose steak and he'd show them.

And forthwith Dawson hummed. The Barracks' flag rose to the masthead, and Bettles' wife washed herself and put on clean raiment. The community subtly signified its desire that Montana Kid obliterate himself from the landscape. And Montana Kid obliterated; as usual, at the tailend of some one else's dog team. Dawson rejoiced when he headed down the Yukon, and wished him godspeed to the ultimate destination of the case-hardened sinner. After that the owner of the dogs bestirred himself, made complaint to Constantine, and from him received the loan of a policeman.

III

With Circle City in prospect and the last ice crumbling under his runners, Montana Kid took advantage of the lengthening days and travelled his dogs late and early. Further, he had but little doubt that the owner of the dogs in question had taken his trail, and he wished to make American territory before the river broke. But by the afternoon of the third day it became evident that he had lost in his race with spring. The Yukon was growling and straining at its fetters. Long détours became necessary, for the trail had begun to fall through into the swift current beneath, while the ice, in constant unrest, was thundering apart in great gaping fissures. Through these and through countless airholes, the water began to sweep across the surface of the ice, and by the time he pulled into a woodchopper's cabin on the point of an island, the dogs were being rushed off their feet and were swimming more often than not. He was greeted sourly by the two residents, but he unharnessed and proceeded to cook up.

Donald and Davy were fair specimens of frontier ineffi-
cients. Canadian-born, city-bred Scots, in a foolish moment
they had resigned their counting-house desks, drawn upon
their savings, and gone Klondiking. And now they were feeling the rough edge of the country. Grubless, spiritless, with
a lust for home in their hearts, they had been staked by the
P. C. Company to cut wood for its steamers, with the promise
at the end of a passage home. Disregarding the possibilities
of the ice-run, they had fittingly demonstrated their ineffi-
ciency by their choice of the island on which they located.
Montana Kid, though possessing little knowledge of the
break-up of a great river, looked about him dubiously, and
cast yearning glances at the distant bank where the towering
bluffs promised immunity from all the ice of the Northland.

After feeding himself and dogs, he lighted his pipe and
strolled out to get a better idea of the situation. The island,
like all its river brethren, stood higher at the upper end, and
it was here that Donald and Davy had built their cabin and
piled many cords of wood. The far shore was a full mile
away, while between the island and the near shore lay a
back-channel perhaps a hundred yards across. At first sight
of this, Montana Kid was tempted to take his dogs and
escape to the mainland, but on closer inspection he discovered a rapid current flooding on top. Below, the river twisted
sharply to the west, and in this turn its breast was studded
by a maze of tiny islands.

'That's where she'll jam,' he remarked to himself.

Half a dozen sleds, evidently bound up-stream to Dawson, were splashing through the chill water to the tail of the
island. Travel on the river was passing from the precarious
to the impossible, and it was nip and tuck with them till
they gained the island and came up the path of the wood-
choppers toward the cabin. One of them, snow-blind, towed
helplessly at the rear of a sled. Husky young fellows they were,
rough-garmented and trail-worn, yet Montana Kid had met
the breed before and knew at once that it was not his kind.

'Hello! How's things up Dawson-way?' queried the foremost, passing his eye over Donald and Davy and settling it
upon the Kid.

A first meeting in the wilderness is not characterized by formality. The talk quickly became general, and the news of the Upper and Lower Countries was swapped equitably back and forth. But the little the new-comers had was soon over with, for they had wintered at Minook, a thousand miles below, where nothing was doing. Montana Kid, however, was fresh from Salt Water, and they annexed him while they pitched camp, swamping him with questions concerning the outside, from which they had been cut off for a twelvemonth.

A shrieking split, suddenly lifting itself above the general uproar on the river, drew everybody to the bank. The surface water had increased in depth, and the ice, assailed from above and below, was struggling to tear itself from the grip of the shores. Fissures reverberated into life before their eyes, and the air was filled with multitudinous crackling, crisp and sharp, like the sound that goes up on a clear day from the firing line.

From up the river two men were racing a dog team toward them on an uncovered stretch of ice. But even as they looked, the pair struck the water and began to flounder through. Behind, where their feet had sped the moment before, the ice broke up and turned turtle. Through this opening the river rushed out upon them to their waists, burying the sled and swinging the dogs off at right angles in a drowning tangle. But the men stopped their flight to give the animals a fighting chance, and they groped hurriedly in the cold confusion, slashing at the detaining traces with their sheath-knives. Then they fought their way to the bank through swirling water and grinding ice, where, foremost in leaping to the rescue among the jarring fragments, was the Kid.

'Why, blime me, if it ain't Montana Kid!' exclaimed one of the men whom the Kid was just placing upon his feet at the top of the bank. He wore the scarlet tunic of the Mounted Police and jocularly raised his right hand in salute.

'Got a warrant for you, Kid,' he continued, drawing a bedraggled paper from his breast pocket, 'an' I 'ope as you'll come along peaceable.'

Montana Kid looked at the chaotic river and shrugged his shoulders, and the policeman, following his glance, smiled.

'Where are the dogs?' his companion asked.

'Gentlemen,' interrupted the policeman, 'this 'ere mate o' mine is Jack Sutherland, owner of Twenty-Two Eldorado—'

'Not Sutherland of '92?' broke in the snow-blinded Minook man, groping feebly toward him.

'The same.' Sutherland gripped his hand. 'And you?'

'Oh, I'm after your time, but I remember you in my freshman year,—you were doing P. G. work* then. Boys,' he called, turning half about, 'this is Sutherland, Jack Sutherland, erstwhile full-back on the 'Varsity. Come up, you gold-chasers, and fall upon him! Sutherland, this is Greenwich, —played quarter two seasons back.'

'Yes, I read of the game,' Sutherland said, shaking hands. 'And I remember that big run of yours for the first touch-down.'

Greenwich flushed darkly under his tanned skin and awkwardly made room for another.

'And here's Matthews,—Berkeley man. And we've got some Eastern cracks knocking about, too. Come up, you Princeton men! Come up! This is Sutherland, Jack Sutherland!'

Then they fell upon him heavily, carried him into camp, and supplied him with dry clothes and numerous mugs of black tea.

Donald and Davy, overlooked, had retired to their nightly game of crib. Montana Kid followed them with the policeman.

'Here, get into some dry togs,' he said, pulling them from out his scanty kit. 'Guess you'll have to bunk with me, too.'

'Well, I say, you're a good 'un,' the policeman remarked as he pulled on the other man's socks. 'Sorry I've got to take you back to Dawson, but I only 'ope they won't be 'ard on you.'

'Not so fast.' The Kid smiled curiously. 'We ain't under way yet. When I go I'm going down river, and I guess the chances are you'll go along.'

'Not if I know myself—'

'Come on outside, and I'll show you, then. These damn fools,' thrusting a thumb over his shoulder at the two Scots, 'played smash when they located here. Fill your pipe, first— this is pretty good plug—and enjoy yourself while you can. You haven't many smokes before you.'

The policeman went with him wonderingly, while Donald and Davy dropped their cards and followed. The Minook men noticed Montana Kid pointing now up the river, now down, and came over.

'What's up?' Sutherland demanded.

'Nothing much.' Nonchalance sat well upon the Kid. 'Just a case of raising hell and putting a chunk under. See that bend down there? That's where she'll jam millions of tons of ice. Then she'll jam in the bends up above, millions of tons. Upper jam breaks first, lower jam holds, pouf!' He dramatically swept the island with his hand. 'Millions of tons,' he added reflectively.

'And what of the woodpiles?' Davy questioned.

The Kid repeated his sweeping gesture, and Davy wailed, 'The labor of months! It canna be! Na, na, lad, it canna be. I doot not it's a jowk. Ay, say that it is,' he appealed.

But when the Kid laughed harshly and turned on his heel, Davy flung himself upon the piles and began frantically to toss the cordwood back from the bank.

'Lend a hand, Donald!' he cried. 'Can ye no lend a hand? 'Tis the labor of months and the passage home!'

Donald caught him by the arm and shook him, but he tore free. 'Did ye no hear, man? Millions of tons, and the island shall be sweepit clean.'

'Straighten yersel' up, man,' said Donald. 'It's a bit fashed ye are.'

But Davy fell upon the cordwood. Donald stalked back to the cabin, buckled on his money belt and Davy's, and went out to the point of the island where the ground was highest and where a huge pine towered above its fellows.

The men before the cabin heard the ringing of his axe and smiled. Greenwich returned from across the island with the word that they were penned in. It was impossible to cross the back-channel. The blind Minook man began to sing, and the rest joined in with—

> Wonder if it's true?
> Does it seem so to you?
> Seems to me he's lying—
> Oh, I wonder if it's true?

'It's ay sinfu',' Davy moaned, lifting his head and watching them dance in the slanting rays of the sun. 'And my guid wood a' going to waste.'

Oh, I wonder if it's true,

was flaunted back.

The noise of the river ceased suddenly. A strange calm wrapped about them. The ice had ripped from the shores and was floating higher on the surface of the river, which was rising. Up it came, swift and silent, for twenty feet, till the huge cakes rubbed softly against the crest of the bank. The tail of the island, being lower, was overrun. Then, without effort, the white flood started down-stream. But the sound increased with the momentum, and soon the whole island was shaking and quivering with the shock of the grinding bergs. Under pressure, the mighty cakes, weighing hundreds of tons, were shot into the air like peas. The frigid anarchy increased its riot, and the men had to shout into one another's ears to be heard. Occasionally the racket from the back channel could be heard above the tumult. The island shuddered with the impact of an enormous cake which drove in squarely upon its point. It ripped a score of pines out by the roots, then swinging around and over, lifted its muddy base from the bottom of the river and bore down upon the cabin, slicing the bank and trees away like a gigantic knife. It seemed barely to graze the corner of the cabin, but the cribbed logs tilted up like matches, and the structure, like a toy house, fell backward in ruin.

'The labor of months! The labor of months, and the passage home!' Davy wailed, while Montana Kid and the policeman dragged him backward from the woodpiles.

'You'll 'ave plenty o' hoppertunity all in good time for yer passage 'ome,' the policeman growled, clouting him alongside the head and sending him flying into safety.

Donald, from the top of the pine, saw the devastating berg sweep away the cordwood and disappear down-stream. As though satisfied with this damage, the ice-flood quickly dropped to its old level and began to slacken its pace. The noise likewise eased down, and the others could hear Donald shouting from his eyrie to look down-stream. As forecast, the jam had come among the islands in the bend, and the ice was piling up in a great barrier which stretched from shore to shore. The river came to a standstill, and the water finding no outlet began to rise. It rushed up till the island was awash, the men splashing around up to their knees, and the dogs swimming to the ruins of the cabin. At this stage it abruptly became stationary, with no perceptible rise or fall.

Montana Kid shook his head. 'It's jammed above, and no more's coming down.'

'And the gamble is, which jam will break first,' Sutherland added.

'Exactly,' the Kid affirmed. 'If the upper jam breaks first, we haven't a chance. Nothing will stand before it.'

The Minook men turned away in silence, but soon 'Rumsky Ho' floated upon the quiet air, followed by 'The Orange and the Black.'* Room was made in the circle for Montana Kid and the policeman, and they quickly caught the ringing rhythm of the choruses as they drifted on from song to song.

'Oh, Donald, will ye no lend a hand?' Davy sobbed at the foot of the tree into which his comrade had climbed. 'Oh, Donald, man, will ye no lend a hand?' he sobbed again, his hands bleeding from vain attempts to scale the slippery trunk.

But Donald had fixed his gaze up river, and now his voice rang out, vibrant with fear:—

'God Almichty, here she comes!'

Standing knee-deep in the icy water, the Minook men, with Montana Kid and the policeman, gripped hands and raised their voices in the terrible 'Battle Hymn of the Republic.'* But the words were drowned in the advancing roar.

And to Donald was vouchsafed a sight such as no man may see and live. A great wall of white flung itself upon the island. Trees, dogs, men, were blotted out, as though the hand of God had wiped the face of nature clean. This much he saw, then swayed an instant longer in his lofty perch and hurtled far out into the frozen hell.

THE STORY OF JEES UCK

There have been renunciations, and renunciations. But, in its essence, renunciation is ever the same. And the paradox of it is that men and women forego the dearest thing in the world for something dearer. It was never otherwise. Thus it was when Abel brought of the firstlings of his flock and of the fat thereof. The firstlings and the fat thereof were to him the dearest things in the world; yet he gave them over that he might be on good terms with God. So it was with Abraham when he prepared to offer up his son Isaac on a stone. Isaac was very dear to him; but God, in incomprehensible ways, was yet dearer. It may be that Abraham feared the Lord. But whether that be true or not, it has since been determined by a few billion people that he loved the Lord and desired to serve Him.

And since it has been determined that love is service, and since to renounce is to serve, then Jees Uck, who was merely a woman of a swart-skinned breed, loved with a great love. She was unversed in history, having learned to read only the signs of weather and of game; so she had never heard of Abel, nor of Abraham; nor, having escaped the good sisters at Holy Cross, had she been told the story of Ruth, the Moabitess,* who renounced her very God for the sake of a stranger woman from a strange land. Jees Uck had learned only one way of renouncing, and that was with a club as the dynamic factor, in much the same manner as a dog is made to renounce a stolen marrow-bone. Yet, when the time came, she proved herself capable of rising to the height of the fair-faced royal races and of renouncing in right regal fashion.

So this is the story of Jees Uck, which is also the story of Neil Bonner, and Kitty Bonner, and a couple of Neil Bonner's progeny. Jees Uck was of a swart-skinned breed, it is true, but she was not an Indian; nor was she an Eskimo; nor even an Innuit. Going backward into mouth tradition, there appears the figure of one Skolkz, a Toyaat Indian of the Yukon, who journeyed down in his youth to the Great Delta where dwell the Innuits, and where he forgathered with a woman remembered as Olillie. Now the woman Olillie had been bred from an Eskimo mother by an Innuit man. And from Skolkz and Olillie came Halie, who was one-half Toyaat Indian, one-quarter Innuit, and one-quarter Eskimo. And Halie was the grandmother of Jees Uck.

Now Halie, in whom three stocks had been bastardized, who cherished no prejudice against further admixture, mated with a Russian fur trader called Shpack, also known in his time as the Big Fat. Shpack is herein classed Russian for lack of a more adequate term; for Shpack's father, a Slavonic convict from the Lower Provinces, had escaped from the quicksilver mines into Northern Siberia, where he knew Zimba, who was a woman of the Deer People and who became the mother of Shpack, who became the grandfather of Jees Uck.

Now had not Shpack been captured in his boyhood by the Sea People, who fringe the rim of the Arctic Sea with their misery, he would not have become the grandfather of Jees Uck and there would be no story at all. But he *was* captured by the Sea People, from whom he escaped to Kamchatka, and thence, on a Norwegian whale-ship, to the Baltic. Not long after that he turned up in St Petersburg, and the years were not many till he went drifting east over the same weary road his father had measured with blood and groans a half-century before. But Shpack was a free man, in the employ of the great Russian Fur Company. And in that employ he fared farther and farther east, until he crossed Bering Sea into Russian America; and at Pastolik, which is hard by the Great Delta of the Yukon, became the husband of Halie, who was the grandmother of Jees Uck. Out of this union came the woman-child, Tukesan.

Shpack, under the orders of the company, made a canoe voyage of a few hundred miles up the Yukon to the post of Nulato. With him he took Halie and the babe Tukesan. This was in 1850, and in 1850 it was that the river Indians fell upon Nulato and wiped it from the face of the earth. And that was the end of Shpack and Halie. On that terrible night Tukesan disappeared. To this day the Toyaats aver they had no hand in the trouble; but, be that as it may, the fact remains that the babe Tukesan grew up among them.

Tukesan was married successively to two Toyaat brothers, to both of whom she was barren. Because of this, other women shook their heads, and no third Toyaat man could be found to dare matrimony with the childless widow. But at this time, many hundred miles above, at Fort Yukon, was a man, Spike O'Brien. Fort Yukon was a Hudson Bay Company post, and Spike O'Brien one of the company's servants. He was a good servant, but he achieved an opinion that the service was bad, and in the course of time vindicated that opinion by deserting. It was a year's journey, by the chain of posts, back to York Factory on Hudson's Bay. Further, being company posts, he knew he could not evade the company's clutches. Nothing remained but to go down the Yukon. It was true no white man had ever gone down the Yukon, and no white man knew whether the Yukon emptied into the Arctic Ocean or Bering Sea; but Spike O'Brien was a Celt, and the promise of danger was a lure he had ever followed.

A few weeks later, somewhat battered, rather famished, and about dead with river-fever, he drove the nose of his canoe into the earth bank by the village of the Toyaats and promptly fainted away. While getting his strength back, in the weeks that followed, he looked upon Tukesan and found her good. Like the father of Shpack, who lived to a ripe old age among the Siberian Deer People, Spike O'Brien might have left his aged bones with the Toyaats. But romance gripped his heart-strings and would not let him stay. As he had journeyed from York Factory to Fort Yukon, so, first among men, might he journey from Fort Yukon to the sea and win the honor of being the first man to make the North-west Passage by land. So he departed down the river, won the honor, and was unannaled and unsung. In after years he ran a sailors' boarding-house in San Francisco, where he became esteemed a most remarkable liar by virtue of the gospel truths he told. But a child was born to Tukesan, who had been childless. And this child was Jees Uck. Her lineage has been traced at length to show that she was neither Indian, nor Eskimo, nor Innuit, nor much of anything else;

also to show what waifs of the generations we are, all of us, and the strange meanderings of the seed from which we spring.

What with the vagrant blood in her and the heritage compounded of many races, Jees Uck developed a wonderful young beauty. Bizarre, perhaps, it was, and Oriental enough to puzzle any passing ethnologist. A lithe and slender grace characterized her. Beyond a quickened lilt to the imagination, the contribution of the Celt was in no wise apparent. It might possibly have put the warm blood under her skin, which made her face less swart and her body fairer; but that, in turn, might have come from Shpack, the Big Fat, who inherited the color of his Slavonic father. And, finally, she had great, blazing black eyes—the half-caste eye, round, full-orbed, and sensuous, which marks the collision of the dark races with the light. Also, the white blood in her, combined with her knowledge that it was in her, made her, in a way, ambitious. Otherwise, by upbringing and in outlook on life, she was wholly and utterly a Toyaat Indian.

One winter, when she was a young woman, Neil Bonner came into her life. But he came into her life, as he had come into the country, somewhat reluctantly. In fact, it was very much against his will, coming into the country. Between a father who clipped coupons and cultivated roses, and a mother who loved the social round, Neil Bonner had gone rather wild. He was not vicious, but a man with meat in his belly and without work in the world has to expend his energy somehow, and Neil Bonner was such a man. And he expended his energy in such fashion and to such extent that when the inevitable climax came, his father, Neil Bonner, senior, crawled out of his roses in a panic and looked on his son with a wondering eye. Then he hied himself away to a crony of kindred pursuits, with whom he was wont to confer over coupons and roses, and between the two the destiny of young Neil Bonner was made manifest. He must go away, on probation, to live down his harmless follies in order that he might live up to their own excellent standard.

This determined upon, and young Neil a little repentant and a great deal ashamed, the rest was easy. The cronies were heavy stockholders in the P. C. Company. The P. C. Company owned fleets of river-steamers and ocean-going craft, and, in addition to farming the sea, exploited a hundred thousand square miles or so of the land that, on the maps of geographers, usually occupies the white spaces. So the P. C. Company sent young Neil Bonner north, where the white spaces are, to do its work and to learn to be good like his father. 'Five years of simplicity, close to the soil and far from temptation, will make a man of him,' said old Neil Bonner, and forthwith crawled back among his roses. Young Neil set his jaw, pitched his chin at the proper angle, and went to work. As an underling he did his work well and gained the commendation of his superiors. Not that he delighted in the work, but that it was the one thing that prevented him from going mad.

The first year he wished he was dead. The second year he cursed God. The third year he was divided between the two emotions, and in the confusion quarrelled with a man in authority. He had the best of the quarrel, though the man in authority had the last word,—a word that sent Neil Bonner into an exile that made his old billet appear as paradise. But he went without a whimper, for the North had succeeded in making him into a man.

Here and there, on the white spaces on the map, little circlets like the letter 'o' are to be found, and, appended to these circlets, on one side or the other, are names such as 'Fort Hamilton,' 'Yanana Station,' 'Twenty Mile,' thus leading one to imagine that the white spaces are plentifully besprinkled with towns and villages. But it is a vain imagining. Twenty Mile, which is very like the rest of the posts, is a log building the size of a corner grocery with rooms to let upstairs. A long-legged cache on stilts may be found in the back yard; also a couple of outhouses. The back yard is unfenced, and extends to the sky-line and an unascertainable bit beyond. There are no other houses in sight, though the Toyaats sometimes pitch a winter camp a mile or two down the Yukon. And this is Twenty Mile, one tentacle of the many-tentacled P. C. Company. Here the agent, with an assistant, barters with the Indians for their furs, and does an erratic trade on a gold-dust basis with the wandering miners. Here, also, the agent and his assistant yearn all winter for the spring, and when the spring comes, camp blasphemously on the roof while the Yukon washes out the establishment. And here, also, in the fourth year of his sojourn in the land, came Neil Bonner to take charge.

He had displaced no agent; for the man that previously ran the post had made away with himself; 'because of the rigors of the place,' said the assistant, who still remained; though the Toyaats, by their fires, had another version. The assistant was a shrunken-shouldered, hollow-chested man, with a cadaverous face and cavernous cheeks that his sparse black beard could not hide. He coughed much, as though consumption gripped his lungs, while his eyes had that mad, fevered light common to consumptives in the last stage. Pentley was his name,—Amos Pentley,—and Bonner did not like him, though he felt a pity for the forlorn and hopeless devil. They did not get along together, these two men who, of all men, should have been on good terms in the face of the cold and silence and darkness of the long winter.

In the end, Bonner concluded that Amos was partly demented, and left him alone, doing all the work himself except the cooking. Even then, Amos had nothing but bitter looks and an undisguised hatred for him. This was a great loss to Bonner; for the smiling face of one of his own kind, the cheery word, the sympathy of comradeship shared with misfortune—these things meant much; and the winter was yet young when he began to realize the added reasons, with such an assistant, that the previous agent had found to impel his own hand against his life.

It was very lonely at Twenty Mile. The bleak vastness stretched away on every side to the horizon. The snow, which was really frost, flung its mantle over the land and buried everything in the silence of death. For days it was clear and cold, the thermometer steadily recording forty to fifty degrees below zero. Then a change came over the face of things. What little moisture had oozed into the atmosphere gathered into dull gray, formless clouds; it became quite warm, the thermometer rising to twenty below; and the moisture fell out of the sky in hard frost-granules that hissed like dry sugar or driving sand when kicked underfoot. After that it became clear and cold again, until enough moisture had gathered to blanket the earth from the cold of outer space. That was all. Nothing happened. No storms, no churning waters and threshing forests, nothing but the machine-like precipitation of accumulated moisture. Possibly the most notable thing that occurred through the weary weeks was the gliding of the temperature up to the unprecedented height of fifteen below. To atone for this, outer space smote the earth with its cold till the mercury froze and the spirit thermometer remained more than seventy below for a fortnight, when it burst. There was no telling how much colder it was after that. Another occurrence, monotonous in its regularity, was the lengthening of the nights, till day became a mere blink of light between the darknesses.

Neil Bonner was a social animal. The very follies for which he was doing penance had been bred of his excessive sociability. And here, in the fourth year of his exile, he found himself in company—which were to travesty the word—with a morose and speechless creature in whose sombre eyes smouldered a hatred as bitter as it was unwarranted. And Bonner, to whom speech and fellowship were as the breath of life, went about as a ghost might go, tantalized by the gregarious revelries of some former life. In the day his lips were compressed, his face stern; but in the night he clenched his hands, rolled about in his blankets, and cried aloud like a little child. And he would remember a certain man in authority and curse him through the long hours. Also, he cursed God. But God understands. He cannot find it in His heart to blame weak mortals who blaspheme in Alaska.

And here, to the post of Twenty Mile, came Jees Uck, to trade for flour and bacon, and beads, and bright scarlet cloths for her fancy work. And further, and unwittingly, she came to the post of Twenty Mile to make a lonely man more lonely, make him reach out empty arms in his sleep. For Neil Bonner was only a man. When she first came into the store, he looked at her long, as a thirsty man may look at a flowing well. And she, with the heritage bequeathed her by

Spike O'Brien, imagined daringly and smiled up into his eyes, not as the swart-skinned peoples should smile at the royal races, but as a woman smiles at a man. The thing was inevitable; only, he did not see it, and fought against her as fiercely and passionately as he was drawn toward her. And she? She was Jees Uck, by upbringing wholly and utterly a Toyaat Indian woman.

She came often to the post to trade. And often she sat by the big wood stove and chatted in broken English with Neil Bonner. And he came to look for her coming; and on the days she did not come he was worried and restless. Sometimes he stopped to think, and then she was met coldly, with a reserve that perplexed and piqued her, and which, she was convinced, was not sincere. But more often he did not dare to think, and then all went well and there were smiles and laughter. And Amos Pentley, gasping like a stranded catfish, his hollow cough a-reek with the grave, looked upon it all and grinned. He, who loved life, could not live, and it rankled his soul that others should be able to live. Wherefore he hated Bonner, who was so very much alive and into whose eyes sprang joy at the sight of Jees Uck. As for Amos, the very thought of the girl was sufficient to send his blood pounding up into a hemorrhage.

Jees Uck, whose mind was simple, who thought elementally and was unused to weighing life in its subtler quantities, read Amos Pentley like a book. She warned Bonner, openly and bluntly, in few words; but the complexities of higher existence confused the situation to him, and he laughed at her evident anxiety. To him, Amos was a poor, miserable devil, tottering desperately into the grave. And Bonner, who had suffered much, found it easy to forgive greatly.

But one morning, during a bitter snap, he got up from the breakfast table and went into the store. Jees Uck was already there, rosy from the trail, to buy a sack of flour. A few minutes later, he was out in the snow lashing the flour on her sled. As he bent over he noticed a stiffness in his neck and felt a premonition of impending physical misfortune. And as he put the last half-hitch into the lashing and attempted to straighten up, a quick spasm seized him and he sank into the snow. Tense and quivering, head jerked back, limbs extended, back arched and mouth twisted and distorted, he appeared as though being racked limb from limb. Without cry or sound, Jees Uck was in the snow beside him; but he clutched both her wrists spasmodically, and as long as the convulsion endured she was helpless. In a few moments the spasm relaxed and he was left weak and fainting, his forehead beaded with sweat, his lips flecked with foam.

'Quick!' he muttered, in a strange, hoarse voice. 'Quick! Inside!'

He started to crawl on hands and knees, but she raised him up, and, supported by her young arm, he made faster progress. As he entered the store the spasm seized him again, and his body writhed irresistibly away from her and rolled and curled on the floor. Amos Pentley came and looked on with curious eyes.

'Oh, Amos!' she cried in an agony of apprehension and helplessness, 'him die, you think?' But Amos shrugged his shoulders and continued to look on.

Bonner's body went slack, the tense muscles easing down and an expression of relief coming into his face. 'Quick!' he gritted between his teeth, his mouth twisting with the on-coming of the next spasm and with his effort to control it. 'Quick, Jees Uck! The medicine! Never mind! Drag me!'

She knew where the medicine-chest stood, at the rear of the room, beyond the stove, and thither, by the legs, she dragged the struggling man. As the spasm passed, he began, very faint and very sick, to overhaul the chest. He had seen dogs die exhibiting symptoms similar to his own, and he knew what should be done. He held up a vial of chloral hydrate, but his fingers were too weak and nerveless to draw the cork. This Jees Uck did for him, while he was plunged into another convulsion. As he came out of it he found the open bottle proffered him and looked into the great black eyes of the woman and read what men have always read in the Mate-woman's eyes. Taking a full dose of the stuff, he sank back until another spasm had passed. Then he raised himself limply on his elbow.

'Listen, Jees Uck!' he said very slowly, as though aware of

the necessity for haste and yet afraid to hasten. 'Do what I say. Stay by my side, but do not touch me. I must be very quiet, but you must not go away.' His jaw began to set and his face to quiver and distort with the forerunning pangs, but he gulped and struggled to master them. 'Do not go away. And do not let Amos go away. Understand! Amos must stay right here.'

She nodded her head, and he passed off into the first of many convulsions, which gradually diminished in force and frequency. Jees Uck hung over him, remembering his injunction and not daring to touch him. Once Amos grew restless and made as though to go into the kitchen; but a quick blaze from her eyes quelled him, and after that, save for his labored breathing and charnel cough, he was very quiet.

Bonner slept. The blink of light that marked the day disappeared. Amos, followed about by the woman's eyes, lighted the kerosene lamps. Evening came on. Through the north window the heavens were emblazoned with an auroral display, which flamed and flared and died down into blackness. Some time after that, Neil Bonner roused. First he looked to see that Amos was still there, then smiled at Jees Uck and pulled himself up. Every muscle was stiff and sore, and he smiled ruefully, pressing and prodding himself as if to ascertain the extent of the ravage. Then his face went stern and businesslike.

'Jees Uck,' he said, 'take a candle. Go into the kitchen. There is food on the table—biscuits and beans and bacon; also, coffee in the pot on the stove. Bring it here on the counter. Also, bring tumblers and water and whiskey, which you will find on the top shelf of the locker. Do not forget the whiskey.'

Having swallowed a stiff glass of the whiskey, he went carefully through the medicine chest, now and again putting aside, with definite purpose, certain bottles and vials. Then he set to work on the food, attempting a crude analysis. He had not been unused to the laboratory in his college days and was possessed of sufficient imagination to achieve results with his limited materials. The condition of tetanus, which had marked his paroxysms, simplified matters, and he made

but one test. The coffee yielded nothing; nor did the beans.
To the biscuits he devoted the utmost care. Amos, who
knew nothing of chemistry, looked on with steady curiosity.
But Jees Uck, who had boundless faith in the white man's
wisdom, and especially in Neil Bonner's wisdom, and who
not only knew nothing but knew that she knew nothing,
watched his face rather than his hands.

Step by step he eliminated possibilities, until he came to
the final test. He was using a thin medicine vial for a tube,
and this he held between him and the light, watching the
slow precipitation of a salt through the solution contained in
the tube. He said nothing, but he saw what he had expected
to see. And Jees Uck, her eyes riveted on his face, saw something, too,—something that made her spring like a tigress
upon Amos and with splendid suppleness and strength bend
his body back across her knee. Her knife was out of its
sheath and uplifted, glinting in the lamplight. Amos was
snarling; but Bonner intervened ere the blade could fall.

'That's a good girl, Jees Uck. But never mind. Let him
go!'

She dropped the man obediently, though with protest writ
large on her face; and his body thudded to the floor. Bonner
nudged him with his moccasined foot.

'Get up, Amos!' he commanded. 'You've got to pack an
outfit yet to-night and hit the trail.'

'You don't mean to say—' Amos blurted savagely.

'I mean to say that you tried to kill me,' Neil went on in
cold, even tones. 'I mean to say that you killed Birdsall, for
all the company believes he killed himself. You used strychnine* in my case. God knows with what you fixed him. Now
I can't hang you. You're too near dead, as it is. But Twenty
Mile is too small for the pair of us, and you've got to mush.
It's two hundred miles to Holy Cross. You can make it if
you're careful not to overexert. I'll give you grub, a sled, and
three dogs. You'll be as safe as if you were in jail, for you
can't get out of the country. And I'll give you one chance.
You're almost dead. Very well. I shall send no word to the
company until the spring. In the meantime, the thing for you
to do is to die. Now, *mush!*'

'You go to bed!' Jees Uck insisted, when Amos had churned away into the night toward Holy Cross. 'You sick man yet, Neil.'

'And you're a good girl, Jees Uck,' he answered. 'And here's my hand on it. But you must go home.'

'You don't like me,' she said simply.

He smiled, helped her on with her *parka*, and led her to the door. 'Only too well, Jees Uck,' he said softly; 'only too well.'

After that the pall of the Arctic night fell deeper and blacker on the land. Neil Bonner discovered that he had failed to put proper valuation upon even the sullen face of the murderous and death-stricken Amos. It became very lonely at Twenty Mile. 'For the love of God, Prentiss, send me a man,' he wrote to the agent at Fort Hamilton, three hundred miles up river. Six weeks later the Indian messenger brought back a reply. It was characteristic: 'Hell. Both feet frozen. Need him myself—Prentiss.'

To make matters worse, most of the Toyaats were in the back country on the flanks of a caribou herd, and Jees Uck was with them. Removing to a distance seemed to bring her closer than ever, and Neil Bonner found himself picturing her, day by day, in camp and on trail. It is not good to be alone. Often he went out of the quiet store, bare-headed and frantic, and shook his fist at the blink of day that came over the southern sky-line. And on still, cold nights he left his bed and stumbled into the frost, where he assaulted the silence at the top of his lungs, as though it were some tangible, sentient thing that he might arouse; or he shouted at the sleeping dogs till they howled and howled again. One shaggy brute he brought into the post, playing that it was the new man sent by Prentiss. He strove to make it sleep decently under blankets at night and to sit at table and eat as a man should; but the beast, mere domesticated wolf that it was, rebelled, and sought out dark corners and snarled and bit him in the leg, and was finally beaten and driven forth.

Then the trick of personification seized upon Neil Bonner and mastered him. All the forces of his environment meta-morphosed into living, breathing entities and came to live with him. He re-created the primitive pantheon; reared an altar to the sun and burned candle fat and bacon grease thereon; and in the unfenced yard, by the long-legged cache, made a frost devil, which he was wont to make faces at and mock when the mercury oozed down into the bulb. All this in play, of course. He said it to himself that it was in play, and repeated it over and over to make sure, unaware that madness is ever prone to express itself in make-believe and play.

One midwinter day, Father Champreau, a Jesuit missionary, pulled into Twenty Mile. Bonner fell upon him and dragged him into the post, and clung to him and wept, until the priest wept with him from sheer compassion. Then Bonner became madly hilarious and made lavish entertainment, swearing valiantly that his guest should not depart. But Father Champreau was pressing to Salt Water on urgent business for his order, and pulled out next morning, with Bonner's blood threatened on his head.

And the threat was in a fair way toward realization, when the Toyaats returned from their long hunt to the winter camp. They had many furs, and there was much trading and stir at Twenty Mile. Also, Jees Uck came to buy beads and scarlet cloths and things, and Bonner began to find himself again. He fought for a week against her. Then the end came one night when she rose to leave. She had not forgotten her repulse, and the pride that drove Spike O'Brien on to complete the Northwest Passage by land was her pride.

'I go now,' she said; 'good night, Neil.'

But he came up behind her. 'Nay, it is not well,' he said.

And as she turned her face toward his with a sudden joyful flash, he bent forward, slowly and gravely, as it were a sacred thing, and kissed her on the lips. The Toyaats had never taught her the meaning of a kiss upon the lips, but she understood and was glad.

With the coming of Jees Uck, at once things brightened up. She was regal in her happiness, a source of unending delight. The elemental workings of her mind and her naïve little ways made an immense sum of pleasurable surprise to the overcivilized man that had stooped to catch her up. Not alone was she solace to his loneliness, but her primitiveness rejuvenated his jaded mind. It was as though, after long wandering, he had returned to pillow his head in the lap of Mother Earth. In short, in Jees Uck he found the youth of the world—the youth and the strength and the joy.

And to fill the full round of his need, and that they might not see overmuch of each other, there arrived at Twenty Mile one Sandy MacPherson, as companionable a man as ever whistled along the trail or raised a ballad by a camp-fire. A Jesuit priest had run into his camp, a couple of hundred miles up the Yukon, in the nick of time to say a last word over the body of Sandy's partner. And on departing, the priest had said, 'My son, you will be lonely now.' And Sandy had bowed his head brokenly. 'At Twenty Mile,' the priest added, 'there is a lonely man. You have need of each other, my son.'

So it was that Sandy became a welcome third at the post, brother to the man and woman that resided there. He took Bonner moose-hunting and wolf-trapping; and, in return, Bonner resurrected a battered and way-worn volume and made him friends with Shakespeare, till Sandy declaimed iambic pentameters to his sled-dogs whenever they waxed mutinous. And of the long evenings they played cribbage and talked and disagreed about the universe, the while Jees Uck rocked matronly in an easy-chair and darned their moccasins and socks.

Spring came. The sun shot up out of the south. The land exchanged its austere robes for the garb of a smiling wanton. Everywhere light laughed and life invited. The days stretched out their balmy length and the nights passed from blinks of darkness to no darkness at all. The river bared its bosom, and snorting steamboats challenged the wilderness. There were stir and bustle, new faces, and fresh facts. An assistant arrived at Twenty Mile, and Sandy MacPherson wandered off with a bunch of prospectors to invade the Koyokuk country. And there were newspapers and magazines and letters for Neil Bonner. And Jees Uck looked on in worriment, for she knew his kindred talked with him across the world.

Without much shock, it came to him that his father was dead. There was a sweet letter of forgiveness, dictated in his last hours. There were official letters from the company, graciously ordering him to turn the post over to the assistant and permitting him to depart at his earliest pleasure. A long, legal affair from the lawyers informed him of interminable lists of stocks and bonds, real estate, rents, and chattels that were his by his father's will. And a dainty bit of stationery, sealed and monogrammed, implored dear Neil's return to his heart-broken and loving mother.

Neil Bonner did some swift thinking, and when the *Yukon Belle* coughed in to the bank on her way down to Bering Sea, he departed—departed with the ancient lie of quick return young and blithe on his lips.

'I'll come back, dear Jees Uck, before the first snow flies,' he promised her, between the last kisses at the gang-plank.

And not only did he promise, but, like the majority of men under the same circumstances, he really meant it. To John Thompson, the new agent, he gave orders for the extension of unlimited credit to his wife, Jees Uck. Also, with his last look from the deck of the *Yukon Belle*, he saw a dozen men at work rearing the logs that were to make the most comfortable house along a thousand miles of river front—the house of Jees Uck, and likewise the house of Neil Bonner—ere the first flurry of snow. For he fully and fondly meant to come back. Jees Uck was dear to him, and, further, a golden future awaited the North. With his father's money he intended to verify that future. An ambitious dream allured him. With his four years of experience, and aided by the friendly coöperation of the P. C. Company, he would return to become the Rhodes of Alaska.* And he would return, fast as steam could drive, as soon as he had put into shape the affairs of his father, whom he had never known, and comforted his mother, whom he had forgotten.

There was much ado when Neil Bonner came back from the Arctic. The fires were lighted and the fleshpots slung, and he took of it all and called it good. Not only was he bronzed and creased, but he was a new man under his skin, with a grip on things and a seriousness and control. His old companions were amazed when he declined to hit up the pace in the good old way, while his father's crony rubbed hands gleefully, and became an authority upon the reclamation of wayward and idle youth.

For four years Neil Bonner's mind had lain fallow. Little that was new had been added to it, but it had undergone a process of selection. It had, so to say, been purged of the trivial and superfluous. He had lived quick years, down in the world; and, up in the wilds, time had been given him to organize the confused mass of his experiences. His superficial standards had been flung to the winds and new standards erected on deeper and broader generalizations. Concerning civilization, he had gone away with one set of values, had returned with another set of values. Aided, also, by the earth smells in his nostrils and the earth sights in his eyes, he laid hold of the inner significance of civilization, beholding with clear vision its futilities and powers. It was a simple little philosophy he evolved. Clean living was the way to grace. Duty performed was sanctification. One must live clean and do his duty in order that he might work. Work was salvation. And to work toward life abundant, and more abundant, was to be in line with the scheme of things and the will of God.

Primarily, he was of the city. And his fresh earth grip and virile conception of humanity gave him a finer sense of civilization and endeared civilization to him. Day by day the people of the city clung closer to him and the world loomed more colossal. And, day by day, Alaska grew more remote and less real. And then he met Kitty Sharon—a woman of his own flesh and blood and kind; a woman who put her hand into his hand and drew him to her, till he forgot the day and hour and the time of the year the first snow flies on the Yukon.

Jees Uck moved into her grand log-house and dreamed away three golden summer months. Then came the autumn, post-haste before the down rush of winter. The air grew thin and sharp, the days thin and short. The river ran sluggishly, and skin ice formed in the quiet eddies. All migratory life departed south, and silence fell upon the land. The first snow flurries came, and the last homing steamboat bucked desperately into the running mush ice. Then came the hard ice, solid cakes and sheets, till the Yukon ran level with its banks. And when all this ceased the river stood still and the blinking days lost themselves in the darkness.

John Thompson, the new agent, laughed; but Jees Uck had faith in the mischances of sea and river. Neil Bonner might be frozen in anywhere between Chilkoot Pass and St Michael's, for the last travellers of the year are always caught by the ice, when they exchange boat for sled and dash on through the long hours behind the flying dogs.

But no flying dogs came up the trail, nor down the trail, to Twenty Mile. And John Thompson told Jees Uck, with a certain gladness ill concealed, that Bonner would never come back again. Also, and brutally, he suggested his own eligibility. Jees Uck laughed in his face and went back to her grand log-house. But when midwinter came, when hope dies down and life is at its lowest ebb, Jees Uck found she had no credit at the store. This was Thompson's doing, and he rubbed his hands, and walked up and down, and came to his door and looked up at Jees Uck's house, and waited. And he continued to wait. She sold her dog-team to a party of miners and paid cash for her food. And when Thompson refused to honor even her coin, Toyaat Indians made her purchases, and sledded them up to her house in the dark.

In February the first post came in over the ice, and John Thompson read in the society column of a five months' old paper of the marriage of Neil Bonner and Kitty Sharon. Jees Uck held the door ajar and him outside while he imparted the information; and, when he had done, laughed pridefully and did not believe. In March, and all alone, she gave birth to a man-child, a brave bit of new life at which she marvelled. And at that hour, a year later, Neil Bonner sat by another bed, marvelling at another bit of new life that had fared into the world.

The snow went off the ground and the ice broke out of the Yukon. The sun journeyed north, and journeyed south again; and, the money from the dogs being spent, Jees Uck went back to her own people. Oche Ish, a shrewd hunter, proposed to kill the meat for her and her babe, and catch the salmon, if she would marry him. And Imego and Hah Yo and Wy Nooch, husky young hunters all, made similar proposals. But she elected to live alone and seek her own meat and fish. She sewed moccasins and *parkas* and mittens—warm, serviceable things, and pleasing to the eye, withal, what of the ornamental hair-tufts and bead work. These she sold to the miners, who were drifting faster into the land each year. And not only did she win food that was good and plentiful, but she laid money by, and one day took passage on the *Yukon Belle* down the river.

At St Michael's she washed dishes in the kitchen of the post. The servants of the company wondered at the remarkable woman with the remarkable child, though they asked no questions and she vouchsafed nothing. But just before Bering Sea closed in for the year, she bought a passage south on a strayed sealing schooner. That winter she cooked for Captain Markheim's household at Unalaska, and in the spring continued south to Sitka on a whiskey sloop. Later, she appeared at Metlakahtla, which is near to St Mary's on the end of the Pan-Handle, where she worked in the cannery through the salmon season. When autumn came and the Siwash fishermen prepared to return to Puget Sound, she embarked with a couple of families in a big cedar canoe; and with them she threaded the hazardous chaos of the Alaskan and Canadian coasts, till the Straits of Juan de Fuca were passed and she led her boy by the hand up the hard pave of Seattle.

There she met Sandy MacPherson, on a windy corner, very much surprised and, when he had heard her story, very wroth—not so wroth as he might have been, had he known of Kitty Sharon; but of her Jees Uck breathed no word, for she had never believed. Sandy, who read commonplace and sordid desertion into the circumstance, strove to dissuade her from her trip to San Francisco, where Neil Bonner was supposed to live when he was at home. And, having striven, he made her comfortable, bought her tickets and saw her off, the while smiling in her face and muttering 'damshame' into his beard.

With roar and rumble, through daylight and dark, swaying and lurching between the dawns, soaring into the winter snows and sinking to summer valleys, skirting depths, leaping chasms, piercing mountains, Jees Uck and her boy were hurled south. But she had no fear of the iron stallion; nor was she stunned by this masterful civilization of Neil Bonner's people. It seemed, rather, that she saw with greater clearness the wonder that a man of such godlike race had held her in his arms. The screaming medley of San Francisco, with its restless shipping, belching factories, and thundering traffic, did not confuse her; instead, she comprehended swiftly the pitiful sordidness of Twenty Mile and the skin-lodged Toyaat village. And she looked down at the boy that clutched her hand and wondered that she had borne him by such a man.

She paid the hack-driver five prices and went up the stone steps to Neil Bonner's front door. A slant-eyed Japanese parleyed with her for a fruitless space, then led her inside and disappeared. She remained in the hall, which to her simple fancy seemed to be the guest room—the show-place wherein were arrayed all the household treasures with the frank purpose of parade and dazzlement. The walls and ceiling were of oiled and panelled redwood. The floor was more glassy than glare ice, and she sought standing place on one of the great skins that gave a sense of security to the polished surface. A huge fireplace—an extravagant fireplace, she deemed it—yawned in the farther wall. A flood of light, mellowed by stained glass, fell across the room, and from the far end came the white gleam of a marble figure.

This much she saw, and more, when the slant-eyed servant led the way past another room—of which she caught a fleeting glance—and into a third, both of which dimmed the brave show of the entrance hall. And to her eyes the great house seemed to hold out a promise of endless similar rooms. There was such length and breadth to them, and the ceilings were so far away! For the first time since her advent into the white man's civilization, a feeling of awe laid hold of her. Neil, her Neil, lived in this house, breathed the air of it, and lay down at night and slept! It was beautiful, all this that she saw, and it pleased her; but she felt, also, the wisdom and mastery behind. It was the concrete expression of power in terms of beauty, and it was the power that she unerringly divined.

And then came a woman, queenly tall, crowned with a glory of hair that was like a golden sun. She seemed to come toward Jees Uck as a ripple of music across still water; her sweeping garment itself a song, her body playing rhythmically beneath. Jees Uck was herself a man compeller. There were Oche Ish and Imego and Hah Yo and Wy Nooch, to say nothing of Neil Bonner and John Thompson and other white men that had looked upon her and felt her power. But she gazed upon the wide blue eyes and rose-white skin of this woman that advanced to meet her, and she measured her with woman's eyes looking through man's eyes; and as a man compeller she felt herself diminish and grow insignificant before this radiant and flashing creature.

'You wish to see my husband?' the woman asked; and Jees Uck gasped at the liquid silver of a voice that had never sounded harsh cries at snarling wolf dogs, nor moulded itself to a guttural speech, nor toughened in storm and frost and camp smoke.

'No,' Jees Uck answered slowly and gropingly, in order that she might do justice to her English. 'I come to see Neil Bonner.'

'He is my husband,' the woman laughed.

Then it was true! John Thompson had not lied that bleak February day, when she laughed pridefully and shut the door in his face. As once she had thrown Amos Pentley across her knee and ripped her knife into the air, so now she felt impelled to spring upon this woman and bear her back and down, and tear the life out of her fair body. But Jees Uck was thinking quickly and gave no sign, and Kitty Bonner little dreamed how intimately she had for an instant been related with sudden death.

Jees Uck nodded her head that she understood, and Kitty Bonner explained that Neil was expected at any moment. Then they sat down on ridiculously comfortable chairs, and Kitty sought to entertain her strange visitor, and Jees Uck strove to help her.

'You knew my husband in the North?' Kitty asked, once.

'Sure, I wash um clothes,' Jees Uck had answered, her English abruptly beginning to grow atrocious.

'And this is your boy? I have a little girl.'

Kitty caused her daughter to be brought, and while the children, after their manner, struck an acquaintance, the mothers indulged in the talk of mothers and drank tea from cups so fragile that Jees Uck feared lest hers should crumble to pieces between her fingers. Never had she seen such cups, so delicate and dainty. In her mind she compared them with the woman who poured the tea, and there uprose in contrast the gourds and pannikins of the Toyaat village and the clumsy mugs of Twenty Mile, to which she likened herself. And in such fashion and such terms the problem presented itself. She was beaten. There was a woman other than herself better fitted to bear and upbring Neil Bonner's children. Just as his people exceeded her people, so did his womenkind exceed her. They were the man compellers as their men were the world compellers. She looked at the rose-white tenderness of Kitty Bonner's skin and remembered the sun-beat on her own face. Likewise she looked from brown hand to white —the one, work-worn and hardened by whip handle and paddle, the other as guiltless of toil and soft as a new-born babe's. And, for all the obvious softness and apparent weakness, Jees Uck looked into the blue eyes and saw the mastery she had seen in Neil Bonner's eyes and in the eyes of Neil Bonner's people.

'Why, it's Jees Uck!' Neil Bonner said, when he entered. He said it calmly, with even a ring of joyful cordiality, coming over to her and shaking both her hands, but looking into her eyes with a worry in his own that she understood.

'Hello, Neil!' she said. 'You look much good.'

'Fine, fine, Jees Uck,' he answered heartily, though secretly studying Kitty for some sign of what had passed between the two. Yet he knew his wife too well to expect, even though the worst had passed, such a sign.

'Well, I can't say how glad I am to see you,' he went on. 'What's happened? Did you strike a mine? And when did you get in?'

'Oo-a, I get in to-day,' she replied, her voice instinctively seeking its guttural parts. 'I no strike it, Neil. You know Cap'n Markheim, Unalaska? I cook, his house, long time.

No spend money. Bime-by, plenty. Pretty good, I think, go down and see White Man's Land. Very fine, White Man's Land, very fine,' she added. Her English puzzled him, for Sandy and he had sought, constantly, to better her speech, and she had proved an apt pupil. Now it seemed that she had sunk back into her race. Her face was guileless, stolidly guileless, giving no cue. Kitty's untroubled brow likewise baffled him. What had happened? How much had been said? and how much guessed?

While he wrestled with these questions and while Jees Uck wrestled with her problem—never had he looked so wonderful and great—a silence fell.

'To think that you knew my husband in Alaska!' Kitty said softly.

Knew him! Jees Uck could not forbear a glance at the boy she had borne him, and his eyes followed hers mechanically to the window where played the two children. An iron band seemed to tighten across his forehead. His knees went weak and his heart leaped up and pounded like a fist against his breast. His boy! He had never dreamed it!

Little Kitty Bonner, fairylike in gauzy lawn, with pinkest of cheeks and bluest of dancing eyes, arms outstretched and lips puckered in invitation, was striving to kiss the boy. And the boy, lean and lithe, sunbeaten and browned, skinclad and in hair-fringed and hair-tufted *muclucs* that showed the wear of the sea and rough work, coolly withstood her advances, his body straight and stiff with the peculiar erectness common to children of savage people. A stranger in a strange land, unabashed and unafraid, he appeared more like an untamed animal, silent and watchful, his black eyes flashing from face to face, quiet so long as quiet endured, but prepared to spring and fight and tear and scratch for life, at the first sign of danger.

The contrast between boy and girl was striking, but not pitiful. There was too much strength in the boy for that, waif that he was of the generations of Shpack, Spike O'Brien, and Bonner. In his features, clean cut as a cameo and almost classic in their severity, there were the power and achievement of his father, and his grandfather, and the one known as the Big Fat, who was captured by the Sea People and escaped to Kamchatka.

Neil Bonner fought his emotion down, swallowed it down, and choked over it, though his face smiled with good humor and the joy with which one meets a friend.

'Your boy, eh, Jees Uck?' He said. And then turning to Kitty: 'Handsome fellow! He'll do something with those two hands of his in this our world.'

Kitty nodded concurrence. 'What is your name?' she asked.

The young savage flashed his quick eyes upon her and dwelt over her for a space, seeking out, as it were, the motive beneath the question.

'Neil,' he answered deliberately when the scrutiny had satisfied him.

'Injun talk,' Jees Uck interposed, glibly manufacturing languages on the spur of the moment. 'Him Injun talk, *nee-al*, all the same "cracker." Him baby, him like cracker; him cry for cracker. Him say, "*Nee-al, nee-al*," all time him say, "*Nee-al*." Then I say that um name. So um name all time Nee-al.'

Never did sound more blessed fall upon Neil Bonner's ear than that lie from Jees Uck's lips. It was the cue, and he knew there was reason for Kitty's untroubled brow.

'And his father?' Kitty asked. 'He must be a fine man.'

'Oo-a, yes,' was the reply. 'Um father fine man. Sure!'

'Did you know him, Neil?' queried Kitty.

'Know him? Most intimately,' Neil answered, and harked back to dreary Twenty Mile and the man alone in the silence with his thoughts.

And here might well end the story of Jees Uck, but for the crown she put upon her renunciation. When she returned to the North to dwell in her grand log-house, John Thompson found that the P. C. Company could make a shift somehow to carry on its business without his aid. Also, the new agent and the succeeding agents received instructions that the woman Jees Uck should be given whatsoever goods and grub she desired, in whatsoever quantities she ordered, and that no charge should be placed upon the books. Further, the company paid yearly to the woman Jees Uck a pension of five thousand dollars.

When he had attained suitable age, Father Champreau laid hands upon the boy, and the time was not long when Jees Uck received letters regularly from the Jesuit college in Maryland. Later on these letters came from Italy, and still later from France. And in the end there returned to Alaska one Father Neil, a man mighty for good in the land, who loved his mother and who ultimately went into a wider field and rose to high authority in the order.

Jees Uck was a young woman when she went back into the North, and men still looked upon her and yearned. But she lived straight, and no breath was ever raised save in commendation. She stayed for a while with the good sisters at Holy Cross, where she learned to read and write and became versed in practical medicine and surgery. After that she returned to her grand log-house and gathered about her the young girls of the Toyaat village, to show them the way of their feet in the world. It is neither Protestant nor Catholic, this school in the house built by Neil Bonner for Jees Uck, his wife; but the missionaries of all the sects look upon it with equal favor. The latch-string is always out, and tired prospectors and trail-weary men turn aside from the flowing river or frozen trail to rest there for a space and be warm by her fire. And, down in the States, Kitty Bonner is pleased at the interest her husband takes in Alaskan education and the large sums he devotes to that purpose; and, though she often smiles and chaffs, deep down and secretly she is but the prouder of him.

THE LEAGUE OF THE OLD MEN

At the Barracks a man was being tried for his life. He was an old man, a native from the Whitefish River, which empties into the Yukon below Lake Le Barge. All Dawson was wrought up over the affair, and likewise the Yukon-dwellers for a thousand miles up and down. It has been the custom of the land-robbing and sea-robbing Anglo-Saxon to give the law to conquered peoples, and ofttimes this law is harsh. But in the case of Imber the law for once seemed inadequate and weak. In the mathematical nature of things, equity did not reside in the punishment to be accorded him. The punishment was a foregone conclusion, there could be no doubt of that; and though it was capital, Imber had but one life, while the tale against him was one of scores.

In fact, the blood of so many was upon his hands that the killings attributed to him did not permit of precise enumeration. Smoking a pipe by the trail-side or lounging around the stove, men made rough estimates of the numbers that had perished at his hand. They had been whites, all of them, these poor murdered people, and they had been slain singly, in pairs, and in parties. And so purposeless and wanton had been these killings, that they had long been a mystery to the mounted police, even in the time of the captains, and later, when the creeks realized, and a governor came from the Dominion to make the land pay for its prosperity.

But more mysterious still was the coming of Imber to Dawson to give himself up. It was in the late spring, when the Yukon was growling and writhing under its ice, that the old Indian climbed painfully up the bank from the river trail and stood blinking on the main street. Men who had witnessed his advent, noted that he was weak and tottery, and that he staggered over to a heap of cabin-logs and sat down. He sat there a full day, staring straight before him at the unceasing tide of white men that flooded past. Many a head jerked curiously to the side to meet his stare, and more than one remark was dropped anent the old Siwash with so strange a look upon his face. No end of men remembered afterward that they had been struck by his extraordinary figure, and forever afterward prided themselves upon their swift discernment of the unusual.

But it remained for Dickensen, Little Dickensen, to be the hero of the occasion. Little Dickensen had come into the land with great dreams and a pocketful of cash; but with the cash the dreams vanished, and to earn his passage back to the States he had accepted a clerical position with the brokerage firm of Holbrook and Mason. Across the street from the office of Holbrook and Mason was the heap of cabin-logs upon which Imber sat. Dickensen looked out of the window at him before he went to lunch; and when he came back from lunch he looked out of the window, and the old Siwash was still there.

Dickensen continued to look out of the window, and he, too, forever afterward prided himself upon his swiftness of discernment. He was a romantic little chap, and he likened the immobile old heathen to the genius of the Siwash race, gazing calm-eyed upon the hosts of the invading Saxon. The hours swept along, but Imber did not vary his posture, did not by a hair's-breadth move a muscle; and Dickensen remembered the man who once sat upright on a sled in the main street where men passed to and fro. They thought the man was resting, but later, when they touched him, they found him stiff and cold, frozen to death in the midst of the busy street. To undouble him, that he might fit into a coffin, they had been forced to lug him to a fire and thaw him out a bit. Dickensen shivered at the recollection.

Later on, Dickensen went out on the sidewalk to smoke a cigar and cool off; and a little later Emily Travis happened along. Emily Travis was dainty and delicate and rare, and whether in London or Klondike she gowned herself as befitted the daughter of a millionnaire mining engineer. Little Dickensen deposited his cigar on an outside window ledge where he could find it again, and lifted his hat.

They chatted for ten minutes or so, when Emily Travis, glancing past Dickensen's shoulder, gave a startled little scream. Dickensen turned about to see, and was startled, too. Imber had crossed the street and was standing there, a gaunt and hungry-looking shadow, his gaze riveted upon the girl.

'What do you want?' Little Dickensen demanded, tremulously plucky.

Imber grunted and stalked up to Emily Travis. He looked her over, keenly and carefully, every square inch of her. Especially did he appear interested in her silky brown hair, and in the color of her cheek, faintly sprayed and soft, like the downy bloom of a butterfly wing. He walked around her, surveying her with the calculating eye of a man who studies the lines upon which a horse or a boat is builded. In the course of his circuit the pink shell of her ear came between his eye and the westering sun, and he stopped to contemplate its rosy transparency. Then he returned to her face and looked long and intently into her blue eyes. He grunted and laid a hand on her arm midway between the shoulder and elbow. With his other hand he lifted her forearm and doubled it back. Disgust and wonder showed in his face, and he dropped her arm with a contemptuous grunt. Then he muttered a few guttural syllables, turned his back upon her, and addressed himself to Dickensen.

Dickensen could not understand his speech, and Emily Travis laughed. Imber turned from one to the other, frowning, but both shook their heads. He was about to go away, when she called out:

'Oh, Jimmy! Come here!'

Jimmy came from the other side of the street. He was a big, hulking Indian clad in approved white-man style, with an Eldorado king's sombrero on his head. He talked with Imber, haltingly, with throaty spasms. Jimmy was a Sitkan, possessed of no more than a passing knowledge of the interior dialects.

'Him Whitefish man,' he said to Emily Travis. 'Me savve um talk no very much. Him want to look see chief white man.'

'The Governor,' suggested Dickensen.

Jimmy talked some more with the Whitefish man, and his face went grave and puzzled.

'I t'ink um want Cap'n Alexander,' he explained. 'Him say

um kill white man, white woman, white boy, plenty kill um white people. Him want to die.'

'Insane, I guess,' said Dickensen.

'What you call dat?' queried Jimmy.

Dickensen thrust a finger figuratively inside his head and imparted a rotary motion thereto.

'Mebbe so, mebbe so,' said Jimmy, returning to Imber, who still demanded the chief man of the white men.

A mounted policeman (unmounted for Klondike service) joined the group and heard Imber's wish repeated. He was a stalwart young fellow, broad-shouldered, deep-chested, legs cleanly built and stretched wide apart, and tall though Imber was, he towered above him by half a head. His eyes were cool, and gray, and steady, and he carried himself with the peculiar confidence of power that is bred of blood and tradition. His splendid masculinity was emphasized by his excessive boyishness,—he was a mere lad,—and his smooth cheek promised a blush as willingly as the cheek of a maid.

Imber was drawn to him at once. The fire leaped into his eyes at sight of a sabre slash that scarred his cheek. He ran a withered hand down the young fellow's leg and caressed the swelling thew. He smote the broad chest with his knuckles, and pressed and prodded the thick muscle-pads that covered the shoulders like a cuirass. The group had been added to by curious passers-by—husky miners, mountaineers, and frontiersmen, sons of the long-legged and broad-shouldered generations. Imber glanced from one to another, then he spoke aloud in the Whitefish tongue.

'What did he say?' asked Dickensen.

'Him say um all the same one man, dat p'liceman,' Jimmy interpreted.

Little Dickensen was little, and what of Miss Travis, he felt sorry for having asked the question.

The policeman was sorry for him and stepped into the breach. 'I fancy there may be something in his story. I'll take him up to the captain for examination. Tell him to come along with me, Jimmy.'

Jimmy indulged in more throaty spasms, and Imber grunted and looked satisfied.

'But ask him what he said, Jimmy, and what he meant when he took hold of my arm.'

So spoke Emily Travis, and Jimmy put the question and received the answer.

'Him say you no afraid,' said Jimmy.

Emily Travis looked pleased.

'Him say you no *skookum*, no strong, all the same very soft like little baby. Him break you, in um two hands, to little pieces. Him t'ink much funny, very strange, how you can be mother of men so big, so strong, like dat p'liceman.'

Emily Travers kept her eyes up and unfaltering, but her cheeks were sprayed with scarlet. Little Dickensen blushed and was quite embarrassed. The policeman's face blazed with his boy's blood.

'Come along, you,' he said gruffly, setting his shoulder to the crowd and forcing a way.

Thus it was that Imber found his way to the Barracks, where he made full and voluntary confession, and from the precincts of which he never emerged.

Imber looked very tired. The fatigue of hopelessness and age was in his face. His shoulders drooped depressingly, and his eyes were lack-lustre. His mop of hair should have been white, but sun and weatherbeat had burned and bitten it so that it hung limp and lifeless and colorless. He took no interest in what went on around him. The courtroom was jammed with the men of the creeks and trails, and there was an ominous note in the rumble and grumble of their low-pitched voices, which came to his ears like the growl of the sea from deep caverns.

He sat close by a window, and his apathetic eyes rested now and again on the dreary scene without. The sky was overcast, and a gray drizzle was falling. It was flood-time on the Yukon. The ice was gone, and the river was up in the town. Back and forth on the main street, in canoes and poling-boats, passed the people that never rested. Often he saw these boats turn aside from the street and enter the flooded square that marked the Barracks' parade-ground. Sometimes they disappeared beneath him, and he heard them jar against the house-logs and their occupants scramble in through the window. After that came the slush of water against men's legs as they waded across the lower room and mounted the stairs. Then they appeared in the doorway, with doffed hats and dripping sea-boots, and added themselves to the waiting crowd.

And while they centred their looks on him, and in grim anticipation enjoyed the penalty he was to pay, Imber looked at them, and mused on their ways, and on their Law that never slept, but went on unceasing, in good times and bad, in flood and famine, through trouble and terror and death, and which would go on unceasing, it seemed to him, to the end of time.

A man rapped sharply on a table, and the conversation droned away into silence. Imber looked at the man. He seemed one in authority, yet Imber divined the square-browed man who sat by a desk farther back to be the one chief over them all and over the man who had rapped. Another man by the same table uprose and began to read aloud from many fine sheets of paper. At the top of each sheet he cleared his throat, at the bottom moistened his fingers. Imber did not understand his speech, but the others did, and he knew that it made them angry. Sometimes it made them very angry, and once a man cursed him, in single syllables, stinging and tense, till a man at the table rapped him to silence.

For an interminable period the man read. His monotonous, sing-song utterance lured Imber to dreaming, and he was dreaming deeply when the man ceased. A voice spoke to him in his own Whitefish tongue, and he roused up, without surprise, to look upon the face of his sister's son, a young man who had wandered away years agone to make his dwelling with the whites.

'Thou dost not remember me,' he said by way of greeting.

'Nay,' Imber answered. 'Thou art Howkan who went away. Thy mother be dead.'

'She was an old woman,' said Howkan.

But Imber did not hear, and Howkan, with hand upon his shoulder, roused him again.

'I shall speak to thee what the man has spoken, which is

the tale of the troubles thou hast done and which thou hast told, O fool, to the Captain Alexander. And thou shalt understand and say if it be true talk or talk not true. It is so commanded.'

Howkan had fallen among the mission folk and been taught by them to read and write. In his hands he held the many fine sheets from which the man had read aloud, and which had been taken down by a clerk when Imber first made confession, through the mouth of Jimmy, to Captain Alexander. Howkan began to read. Imber listened for a space, when a wonderment rose up in his face and he broke in abruptly.

'That be my talk, Howkan. Yet from thy lips it comes when thy ears have not heard.'

Howkan smirked with self-appreciation. His hair was parted in the middle. 'Nay, from the paper it comes, O Imber. Never have my ears heard. From the paper it comes, through my eyes, into my head, and out of my mouth to thee. Thus it comes.'

'Thus it comes? It be there in the paper?' Imber's voice sank in whisperful awe as he crackled the sheets 'twixt thumb and finger and stared at the charactery scrawled thereon. 'It be a great medicine, Howkan, and thou art a worker of wonders.'

'It be nothing, it be nothing,' the young man responded carelessly and pridefully. He read at hazard from the document: '*In that year, before the break of the ice, came an old man, and a boy who was lame of one foot. These also did I kill, and the old man made much noise—*'

'It be true,' Imber interrupted breathlessly. 'He made much noise and would not die for a long time. But how dost thou know, Howkan? The chief man of the white men told thee, mayhap? No one beheld me, and him alone have I told.'

Howkan shook his head with impatience. 'Have I not told thee it be there in the paper, O fool?'

Imber stared hard at the ink-scrawled surface. 'As the hunter looks upon the snow and says, Here but yesterday there passed a rabbit; and here by the willow scrub it stood and listened, and heard, and was afraid; and here it turned upon its trail; and here it went with great swiftness, leaping wide; and here, with greater swiftness and wider leapings, came a lynx; and here, where the claws cut deep into the snow, the lynx made a very great leap; and here it struck, with the rabbit under and rolling belly up; and here leads off the trail of the lynx alone, and there is no more rabbit,—as the hunter looks upon the markings of the snow and says thus and so and here, dost thou, too, look upon the paper and say thus and so and here be the things old Imber hath done?'

'Even so,' said Howkan. 'And now do thou listen, and keep thy woman's tongue between thy teeth till thou art called upon for speech.'

Thereafter, and for a long time, Howkan read to him the confession, and Imber remained musing and silent. At the end, he said:

'It be my talk, and true talk, but I am grown old, Howkan, and forgotten things come back to me which were well for the head man there to know. First, there was the man who came over the Ice Mountains, with cunning traps made of iron, who sought the beaver of the Whitefish. Him I slew. And there were three men seeking gold on the Whitefish long ago. Them also I slew, and left them to the wolverines. And at the Five Fingers there was a man with a raft and much meat.'

At the moments when Imber paused to remember, Howkan translated and a clerk reduced to writing. The courtroom listened stolidly to each unadorned little tragedy, till Imber told of a red-haired man whose eyes were crossed and whom he had killed with a remarkably long shot.

'Hell,' said a man in the forefront of the onlookers. He said it soulfully and sorrowfully. He was red-haired. 'Hell,' he repeated. 'That was my brother Bill.' And at regular intervals throughout the session, his solemn 'Hell' was heard in the courtroom; nor did his comrades check him, nor did the man at the table rap him to order.

Imber's head drooped once more, and his eyes went dull, as though a film rose up and covered them from the world. And he dreamed as only age can dream upon the colossal futility of youth.

Later, Howkan roused him again, saying: 'Stand up, O Imber. It be commanded that thou tellest why you did these troubles, and slew these people, and at the end journeyed here seeking the Law.'

Imber rose feebly to his feet and swayed back and forth. He began to speak in a low and faintly rumbling voice, but Howkan interrupted him.

'This old man, he is damn crazy,' he said in English to the square-browed man. 'His talk is foolish and like that of a child.'

'We will hear his talk which is like that of a child,' said the square-browed man. 'And we will hear it, word for word, as he speaks it. Do you understand?'

Howkan understood, and Imber's eyes flashed, for he had witnessed the play between his sister's son and the man in authority. And then began the story, the epic of a bronze patriot which might well itself be wrought into bronze for the generations unborn. The crowd fell strangely silent, and the square-browed judge leaned head on hand and pondered his soul and the soul of his race. Only was heard the deep tones of Imber, rhythmically alternating with the shrill voice of the interpreter, and now and again, like the bell of the Lord, the wondering and meditative 'Hell' of the red-haired man.

'I am Imber of the Whitefish people.' So ran the interpretation of Howkan, whose inherent barbarism gripped hold of him, and who lost his mission culture and veneered civilization as he caught the savage ring and rhythm of old Imber's tale. 'My father was Otsbaok, a strong man. The land was warm with sunshine and gladness when I was a boy. The people did not hunger after strange things, nor hearken to new voices, and the ways of their fathers were their ways. The women found favor in the eyes of the young men, and the young men looked upon them with content. Babes hung at the breasts of the women, and they were heavy-hipped with increase of the tribe. Men were men in those days. In peace and plenty, and in war and famine, they were men.

'At that time there was more fish in the water than now, and more meat in the forest. Our dogs were wolves, warm with thick hides and hard to the frost and storm. And as with our dogs so with us, for we were likewise hard to the frost and storm. And when the Pellys came into our land we slew them and were slain. For we were men, we Whitefish, and our fathers and our fathers' fathers had fought against the Pellys and determined the bounds of the land.

'As I say, with our dogs, so with us. And one day came the first white man. He dragged himself, so, on hand and knee, in the snow. And his skin was stretched tight, and his bones were sharp beneath. Never was such a man, we thought, and we wondered of what strange tribe he was, and of its land. And he was weak, most weak, like a little child, so that we gave him a place by the fire, and warm furs to lie upon, and we gave him food as little children are given food.

'And with him was a dog, large as three of our dogs, and very weak. The hair of this dog was short, and not warm, and the tail was frozen so that the end fell off. And this strange dog we fed, and bedded by the fire, and fought from it our dogs, which else would have killed him. And what of the moose meat and the sun-dried salmon, the man and dog took strength to themselves; and what of the strength they became big and unafraid. And the man spoke loud words and laughed at the old men and young men, and looked boldly upon the maidens. And the dog fought with our dogs, and for all of his short hair and softness slew three of them in one day.

'When we asked the man concerning his people, he said, "I have many brothers," and laughed in a way that was not good. And when he was in his full strength he went away, and with him went Noda, daughter to the chief. First, after that, was one of our bitches brought to pup. And never was there such a breed of dogs,—big-headed, thick-jawed, and short-haired, and helpless. Well do I remember my father, Otsbaok, a strong man. His face was black with anger at such helplessness, and he took a stone, so, and so, and there was no more helplessness. And two summers after that came Noda back to us with a man-child in the hollow of her arm.

'And that was the beginning. Came a second white man, with short-haired dogs, which he left behind him when he went. And with him went six of our strongest dogs, for which, in trade, he had given Koo-So-Tee, my mother's brother, a wonderful pistol that fired with great swiftness six times. And Koo-So-Tee was very big, what of the pistol, and laughed at our bows and arrows. "Woman's things," he called them, and went forth against the bald-face grizzly, with the pistol in his hand. Now it be known that it is not good to hunt the bald-face with a pistol, but how were we to know? and how was Koo-So-Tee to know? So he went against the bald-face, very brave, and fired the pistol with great swiftness six times; and the bald-face but grunted and broke in his breast like it were an egg, and like honey from a bee's nest dripped the brains of Koo-So-Tee upon the ground. He was a good hunter, and there was no one to bring meat to his squaw and children. And we were bitter, and we said, "That which for the white men is well, is for us not well." And this be true. There be many white men and fat, but their ways have made us few and lean.

'Came the third white man, with great wealth of all manner of wonderful foods and things. And twenty of our strongest dogs he took from us in trade. Also, what of presents and great promises, ten of our young hunters did he take with him on a journey which fared no man knew where. It is said they died in the snow of the Ice Mountains where man has never been, or in the Hills of Silence which are beyond the edge of the earth. Be that as it may, dogs and young hunters were seen never again by the Whitefish people.

'And more white men came with the years, and ever, with pay and presents, they led the young men away with them. And sometimes the young men came back with strange tales of dangers and toils in the lands beyond the Pellys, and sometimes they did not come back. And we said: "If they be unafraid of life, these white men, it is because they have many lives; but we be few by the Whitefish, and the young men shall go away no more." But the young men did go away; and the young women went also; and we were very wroth.

'It be true, we ate flour, and salt pork, and drank tea which was a great delight; only, when we could not get tea, it was very bad and we became short of speech and quick of anger. So we grew to hunger for the things the white men brought in trade. Trade! trade! all the time was it trade! One winter we sold our meat for clocks that would not go, and watches with broken guts, and files worn smooth, and pistols without cartridges and worthless. And then came famine, and we were without meat, and two score died ere the break of spring.

'"Now are we grown weak," we said; "and the Pellys will fall upon us, and our bounds be overthrown." But as it fared with us, so had it fared with the Pellys, and they were too weak to come against us.

'My father, Otsbaok, a strong man, was now old and very wise. And he spoke to the chief, saying: "Behold, our dogs be worthless. No longer are they thick-furred and strong, and they die in the frost and harness. Let us go into the village and kill them, saving only the wolf ones, and these let us tie out in the night that they may mate with the wild wolves of the forest. Thus shall we have dogs warm and strong again."

'And his word was harkened to, and we Whitefish became known for our dogs, which were the best in the land. But known we were not for ourselves. The best of our young men and women had gone away with the white men to wander on trail and river to far places. And the young women came back old and broken, as Noda had come, or they came not at all. And the young men came back to sit by our fires for a time, full of ill speech and rough ways, drinking evil drinks and gambling through long nights and days, with a great unrest always in their hearts, till the call of the white men came to them and they went away again to the unknown places. And they were without honor and respect, jeering the old-time customs and laughing in the faces of chief and shamans.

'As I say, we were become a weak breed, we Whitefish. We sold our warm skins and furs for tobacco and whiskey and thin cotton things that left us shivering in the cold. And the coughing sickness* came upon us, and men and women coughed and sweated through the long nights, and the hunters on trail spat blood upon the snow. And now one, and now another, bled swiftly from the mouth and died. And the women bore few children, and those they bore were weak and given to sickness. And other sicknesses came to us from the white men, the like of which we had never known and could not understand. Smallpox, likewise measles, have I heard these sicknesses named, and we died of them as die the salmon in the still eddies when in the fall their eggs are spawned and there is no longer need for them to live.

'And yet, and here be the strangeness of it, the white men come as the breath of death; all their ways lead to death, their nostrils are filled with it; and yet they do not die. Theirs the whiskey, and tobacco, and short-haired dogs; theirs the many sicknesses, the smallpox and measles, the coughing and mouth-bleeding; theirs the white skin, and softness to the frost and storm; and theirs the pistols that shoot six times very swift and are worthless. And yet they grow fat on their many ills, and prosper, and lay a heavy hand over all the world and tread mightily upon its peoples. And their women, too, are soft as little babes, most breakable and never broken, the mothers of men. And out of all this softness, and sickness, and weakness, come strength, and power, and authority. They be gods, or devils, as the case may be. I do not know. What do I know, I, old Imber of the Whitefish? Only do I know that they are past understanding, these white men, far-wanderers and fighters over the earth that they be.

'As I say, the meat in the forest became less and less. It be true, the white man's gun is most excellent and kills a long way off; but of what worth the gun, when there is no meat to kill? When I was a boy on the Whitefish there was moose on every hill, and each year came the caribou un-countable. But now the hunter may take the trail ten days and not one moose gladden his eyes, while the caribou un-countable come no more at all. Small worth the gun, I say, killing a long way off, when there be nothing to kill.

'And I, Imber, pondered upon these things, watching the while the Whitefish, and the Pellys, and all the tribes of the land, perishing as perished the meat of the forest. Long I pondered. I talked with the shamans and the old men who were wise. I went apart that the sounds of the village might not disturb me, and I ate no meat so that my belly should not press upon me and make me slow of eye and ear. I sat long and sleepless in the forest, wide-eyed for the sign, my ears patient and keen for the word that was to come. And I wandered alone in the blackness of night to the river bank, where was wind-moaning and sobbing of water, and where I sought wisdom from the ghosts of old shamans in the trees and dead and gone.

'And in the end, as in a vision, came to me the short-haired and detestable dogs, and the way seemed plain. By the wisdom of Otsbaok, my father and a strong man, had the blood of our own wolf-dogs been kept clean, wherefore had they remained warm of hide and strong in the harness. So I returned to my village and made oration to the men. "This be a tribe, these white men," I said. "A very large tribe, and doubtless there is no longer meat in their land, and they are come among us to make a new land for themselves. But they weaken us, and we die. They are a very hungry folk. Already has our meat gone from us, and it were well, if we would live, that we deal by them as we have dealt "by their dogs."

'And further oration I made, counselling fight. And the men of the Whitefish listened, and some said one thing, and some another, and some spoke of other and worthless things, and no man made brave talk of deeds and war. But while the young men were weak as water and afraid, I watched that the old men sat silent, and that in their eyes fires came and went. And later, when the village slept and no one knew, I drew the old men away into the forest and made more talk. And now we were agreed, and we remembered the good young days, and the free land, and the times of plenty, and the gladness and sunshine; and we called ourselves brothers, and swore great secrecy, and a mighty oath to cleanse the land of the evil breed that had come upon it. It be plain we were fools, but how were we to know, we old men of the Whitefish?

'And to hearten the others, I did the first deed. I kept guard upon the Yukon till the first canoe came down. In it were two white men, and when I stood upright upon the bank and raised my hand they changed their course and drove in to me. And as the man in the bow lifted his head, so, that he might know wherefore I wanted him, my arrow sang through the air straight to his throat, and he knew. The second man, who held paddle in the stern, had his rifle half to his shoulder when the first of my three spear-casts smote him.

' "These be the first," I said, when the old men had gathered to me. "Later we will bind together all the old men of all the tribes, and after that the young men who remain strong, and the work will become easy."

'And then the two dead white men we cast into the river. And of the canoe, which was a very good canoe, we made a fire, and a fire, also, of the things within the canoe. But first we looked at the things, and they were pouches of leather which we cut open with our knives. And inside these pouches were many papers, like that from which thou hast read, O Howkan, with markings on them which we marvelled at and could not understand. Now, I am become wise, and I know them for the speech of men as thou hast told me.'

A whisper and buzz went around the courtroom when Howkan finished interpreting the affair of the canoe, and one man's voice spoke up: 'That was the lost '91 mail, Peter James and Delaney bringing it in and last spoken at Le Barge by Matthews going out.' The clerk scratched steadily away, and another paragraph was added to the history of the North.

'There be little more,' Imber went on slowly. 'It be there on the paper, the things we did. We were old men, and we did not understand. Even I, Imber, do not now understand. Secretly we slew, and continued to slay, for with our years we were crafty and we had learned the swiftness of going without haste. When white men came among us with black looks and rough words, and took away six of the young men with irons binding them helpless, we knew we must slay wider and farther. And one by one we old men departed up river and down to the unknown lands. It was a brave thing. Old we were, and unafraid, but the fear of far places is a terrible fear to men who are old.

'So we slew, without haste and craftily. On the Chilcoot and in the Delta we slew, from the passes to the sea, wherever the white men camped or broke their trails. It be true, they died, but it was without worth. Ever did they come over the mountains, ever did they grow and grow, while we, being old, became less and less. I remember, by the Caribou Crossing, the camp of a white man. He was a very little white man, and three of the old men came upon him in his sleep. And the next day I came upon the four of them. The white man alone still breathed, and there was breath in him to curse me once and well before he died.

'And so it went, now one old man, and now another. Sometimes the word reached us long after of how they died, and sometimes it did not reach us. And the old men of the other tribes were weak and afraid, and would not join with us. As I say, one by one, till I alone was left. I am Imber, of the Whitefish people. My father was Otsbaok, a strong man. There are no Whitefish now. Of the old men I am the last. The young men and young women are gone away, some to live with the Pellys, some with the Salmons, and more with the white men. I am very old, and very tired, and it being vain fighting the Law, as thou sayest, Howkan, I am come seeking the Law.'

'O Imber, thou art indeed a fool,' said Howkan.

But Imber was dreaming. The square-browed judge likewise dreamed, and all his race rose up before him in a mighty phantasmagoria—his steel-shod, mail-clad race, the lawgiver and world-maker among the families of men. He saw it dawn red-flickering across the dark forests and sullen seas; he saw it blaze, bloody and red, to full and triumphant noon; and down the shaded slope he saw the blood-red sands dropping into night. And through it all he observed the Law, pitiless and potent, ever unswerving and ever ordaining, greater than the motes of men who fulfilled it or were crushed by it, even as it was greater than he, his heart speaking for softness.

THE MARRIAGE OF LIT-LIT

When John Fox came into a country where whiskey freezes solid and may be used as a paper-weight for a large part of the year, he came without the ideals and illusions that usually hamper the progress of more delicately nurtured adventurers. Born and reared on the frontier fringe of the United States, he took with him into Canada a primitive cast of mind, an elemental simplicity and grip on things, as it were, that insured him immediate success in his new career. From a mere servant of the Hudson's Bay Company, driving a paddle with the voyageurs and carrying goods on his back across the portages, he swiftly rose to a Factorship and took charge of a trading post at Fort Angelus.

Here, because of his elemental simplicity, he took to himself a native wife, and, by reason of the connubial bliss that followed, he escaped the unrest and vain longings that curse the days of more fastidious men, spoil their work, and conquer them in the end. He lived contentedly, was at single purposes with the business he was set there to do, and achieved a brilliant record in the service of the Company. About this time his wife died, was claimed by her people, and buried with savage circumstance in a tin trunk in the top of a tree.

Two sons she had borne him, and when the Company promoted him, he journeyed with them still deeper into the vastness of the Northwest Territory to a place called Sin Rock, where he took charge of a new post in a more important fur field. Here he spent several lonely and depressing months, eminently disgusted with the unprepossessing appearance of the Indian maidens, and greatly worried by his growing sons who stood in need of a mother's care. Then his eyes chanced upon Lit-lit.

'Lit-lit—well, she is Lit-lit,' was the fashion in which he despairingly described her to his chief clerk, Alexander McLean.

McLean was too fresh from his Scottish upbringing—'not

dry behind the ears yet,' John Fox put it—to take to the marriage customs of the country. Nevertheless he was not averse to the Factor's imperilling his own immortal soul, and, especially, feeling an ominous attraction himself for Lit-lit, he was sombrely content to clinch his own soul's safety by seeing her married to the Factor.

Nor is it to be wondered that McLean's austere Scotch soul stood in danger of being thawed in the sunshine of Lit-lit's eyes. She was pretty, and slender, and willowy, without the massive face and temperamental stolidity of the average squaw. 'Lit-lit,' so called from her fashion, even as a child, of being fluttery, of darting about from place to place like a butterfly, of being inconsequent and merry, and of laughing as lightly as she darted and danced about.

Lit-lit was the daughter of Snettishane, a prominent chief in the tribe, by a half-breed mother, and to him the Factor fared casually one summer day to open negotiations of marriage. He sat with the chief in the smoke of a mosquito smudge before his lodge, and together they talked about everything under the sun, or, at least, everything that in the Northland is under the sun, with the sole exception of marriage. John Fox had come particularly to talk of marriage; Snettishane knew it, and John Fox knew he knew it, wherefore the subject was religiously avoided. This is alleged to be Indian subtlety. In reality it is transparent simplicity.

The hours slipped by, and Fox and Snettishane smoked interminable pipes, looking each other in the eyes with a guilelessness superbly histrionic. In the mid-afternoon McLean and his brother clerk, McTavish, strolled past, innocently uninterested, on their way to the river. When they strolled back again an hour later, Fox and Snettishane had attained to a ceremonious discussion of the condition and quality of the gunpowder and bacon which the Company was offering in trade. Meanwhile Lit-lit, divining the Factor's errand, had crept in under the rear wall of the lodge and through the front flap was peeping out at the two logomachists by the mosquito smudge. She was flushed and happy-eyed, proud that no less a man than the Factor (who stood next to God in the Northland hierarchy) had singled

her out, femininely curious to see at close range what manner of man he was. Sun-glare on the ice, camp smoke, and
weather beat had burned his face to a copper-brown, so that
her father was as fair as he, while she was fairer. She was
remotely glad of this, and more immediately glad that he was
large and strong, though his great black beard half frightened
her, it was so strange.

Being very young, she was unversed in the ways of men.
Seventeen times she had seen the sun travel south and lose
itself beyond the sky-line, and seventeen times she had seen
it travel back again and ride the sky day and night till there
was no night at all. And through these years she had been
cherished jealously by Snettishane, who stood between her
and all suitors, listening disdainfully to the young hunters as
they bid for her hand, and turning them away as though she
were beyond price. Snettishane was mercenary. Lit-lit was to
him an investment. She represented so much capital, from
which he expected to receive, not a certain definite interest,
but an incalculable interest.

And having thus been reared in a manner as near to that
of the nunnery as tribal conditions would permit,* it was
with a great and maidenly anxiety that she peeped out at the
man who had surely come for her, at the husband who was
to teach her all that was yet unlearned of life, at the masterful being whose word was to be her law, and who was to
mete and bound her actions and comportment for the rest of
her days.

But, peeping through the front flap of the lodge, flushed
and thrilling at the strange destiny reaching out for her, she
grew disappointed as the day wore along, and the Factor and
her father still talked pompously of matters concerning other
things and not pertaining to marriage things at all. As the
sun sank lower and lower toward the north and midnight
approached, the Factor began making unmistakable preparations for departure. As he turned to stride away Lit-lit's
heart sank; but it rose again as he halted, half turning on one
heel.

'Oh, by the way, Snettishane,' he said, 'I want a squaw to
wash for me and mend my clothes.'

Snettishane grunted and suggested Wanidani, who was an old woman and toothless.

'No, no,' interposed the Factor. 'What I want is a wife. I've been kind of thinking about it, and the thought just struck me that you might know of some one that would suit.'

Snettishane looked interested, whereupon the Factor retraced his steps, casually and carelessly to linger and discuss this new and incidental topic.

'Kattou?' suggested Snettishane.

'She has but one eye,' objected the Factor.

'Laska?'

'Her knees be wide apart when she stands upright. Kips, your biggest dog, can leap between her knees when she stands upright.'

'Senatee?' went on the imperturbable Snettishane.

But John Fox feigned anger, crying: 'What foolishness be this? Am I old, that thou shouldst mate me with old women? Am I toothless? lame of leg? blind of eye? Or am I poor that no bright-eyed maiden may look with favor upon me? Behold! I am the Factor, both rich and great, a power in the land, whose speech makes men tremble and is obeyed!'

Snettishane was inwardly pleased, though his sphinxlike visage never relaxed. He was drawing the Factor, and making him break ground. Being a creature so elemental as to have room for but one idea at a time, Snettishane could pursue that one idea a greater distance than could John Fox. For John Fox, elemental as he was, was still complex enough to entertain several glimmering ideas at a time, which debarred him from pursuing the one as single-heartedly or as far as did the chief.

Snettishane calmly continued calling the roster of eligible maidens, which, name by name, as fast as uttered, were stamped ineligible by John Fox, with specified objections appended. Again he gave it up and started to return to the Fort. Snettishane watched him go, making no effort to stop him, but seeing him, in the end, stop himself.

'Come to think of it,' the Factor remarked, 'we both of us forgot Lit-lit. Now I wonder if she'll suit me?'

Snettishane met the suggestion with a mirthless face,

behind the mask of which his soul grinned wide. It was a distinct victory. Had the Factor gone but one step farther, perforce Snettishane would himself have mentioned the name of Lit-lit, but—the Factor had not gone that one step farther.

The chief was non-committal concerning Lit-lit's suitability, till he drove the white man into taking the next step in order of procedure.

'Well,' the Factor meditated aloud, 'the only way to find out is to make a try of it.' He raised his voice. 'So I will give for Lit-lit ten blankets and three pounds of tobacco which is good tobacco.'

Snettishane replied with a gesture which seemed to say that all the blankets and tobacco in all the world could not compensate him for the loss of Lit-lit and her manifold virtues. When pressed by the Factor to set a price, he coolly placed it at five hundred blankets, ten guns, fifty pounds of tobacco, twenty scarlet cloths, ten bottles of rum, a music-box, and lastly the good-will and best offices of the Factor, with a place by his fire.

The Factor apparently suffered a stroke of apoplexy, which stroke was successful in reducing the blankets to two hundred and in cutting out the place by the fire—an unheard-of condition in the marriages of white men with the daughters of the soil. In the end, after three hours more of chaffering, they came to an agreement. For Lit-lit Snettishane was to receive one hundred blankets, five pounds of tobacco, three guns, and a bottle of rum, good-will and best offices included, which, according to John Fox, was ten blankets and a gun more than she was worth. And as he went home through the wee sma' hours, the three o'clock sun blazing in the due northeast, he was unpleasantly aware that Snettishane had bested him over the bargain.

Snettishane, tired and victorious, sought his bed, and discovered Lit-lit before she could escape from the lodge.

He grunted knowingly: 'Thou hast seen. Thou hast heard. Wherefore it be plain to thee thy father's very great wisdom and understanding. I have made for thee a great match. Heed my words and walk in the way of my words, go when I say go, come when I bid thee come, and we shall grow fat with the wealth of this big white man who is a fool according to his bigness.'

The next day no trading was done at the store. The Factor opened whiskey before breakfast to the delight of McLean and McTavish, gave his dogs double rations, and wore his best moccasins. Outside the Fort preparations were under way for a *potlatch*. Potlatch means 'a giving,' and John Fox's intention was to signalize his marriage with Lit-lit by a potlatch as generous as she was good-looking. In the afternoon the whole tribe gathered to the feast. Men, women, children, and dogs gorged to repletion, nor was there one person, even among the chance visitors and stray hunters from other tribes, who failed to receive some token of the bridegroom's largess.

Lit-lit, tearfully shy and frightened, was bedecked by her bearded husband with a new calico dress, splendidly beaded moccasins, a gorgeous silk handkerchief over her raven hair, a purple scarf about her throat, brass earrings and finger-rings, and a whole pint of pinchbeck jewellery, including a Waterbury watch. Snettishane could scarce contain himself at the spectacle, but watching his chance drew her aside from the feast.

'Not this night, nor the next night,' he began ponderously, 'but in the nights to come, when I shall call like a raven by the river bank, it is for thee to rise up from thy big husband who is a fool and come to me.

'Nay, nay,' he went on hastily, at sight of the dismay in her face at turning her back upon her wonderful new life. 'For no sooner shall this happen than thy big husband who is a fool will come wailing to my lodge. Then it is for thee to wail likewise, claiming that this thing is not well, and that the other thing thou dost not like, and that to be the wife of the Factor is more than thou didst bargain for, only wilt thou be content with more blankets, and more tobacco, and more wealth of various sorts for thy poor old father Snettishane. Remember well, when I call in the night, like a raven, from the river bank.'

Lit-lit nodded; for to disobey her father was a peril she knew well; and, furthermore, it was a little thing he asked, a short separation from the Factor, who would know only greater gladness at having her back. She returned to the feast, and, midnight being well at hand, the Factor sought her out and led her away to the Fort amid joking and outcry in which the squaws were especially conspicuous.

Lit-lit quickly found that married life with the head-man of a fort was even better than she had dreamed. No longer did she have to fetch wood and water and wait hand and foot upon cantankerous menfolk. For the first time in her life she could lie abed till breakfast was on the table. And what a bed!—clean and soft, and comfortable as no bed she had ever known. And such food! Flour, cooked into biscuits, hot-cakes and bread, three times a day and every day, and all one wanted! Such prodigality was hardly believable.

To add to her contentment, the Factor was cunningly kind. He had buried one wife, and he knew how to drive with a slack rein that went firm only on occasion, and then went very firm. 'Lit-lit is boss of this place,' he announced significantly at the table the morning after the wedding. 'What she says goes. Understand?' And McLean and McTavish understood. Also, they knew that the Factor had a heavy hand.

But Lit-lit did not take advantage. Taking a leaf from the book of her husband, she at once assumed charge of his two growing sons, giving them added comforts and a measure of freedom like to that which he gave her. The two sons were loud in the praise of their new mother; McLean and McTavish lifted their voices; and the Factor bragged of the joys of matrimony till the story of her good behavior and her husband's satisfaction became the property of all the dwellers in the Sin Rock district.

Whereupon Snettishane, with visions of his incalculable interest keeping him awake of nights, thought it time to bestir himself. On the tenth night of her wedded life Lit-lit was awakened by the croaking of a raven, and she knew that Snettishane was waiting for her by the river bank. In her great happiness she had forgotten her pact, and now it came back to her with behind it all the childish terror of her father. For a time she lay in fear and trembling, loath to go, afraid to stay. But in the end the Factor won the silent victory, and his kindness, plus his great muscles and square jaw, nerved her to disregard Snettishane's call.

But in the morning she arose very much afraid, and went about her duties in momentary fear of her father's coming. As the day wore along, however, she began to recover her spirits. John Fox, soundly berating McLean and McTavish for some petty dereliction of duty, helped her to pluck up courage. She tried not to let him go out of her sight, and when she followed him into the huge cache and saw him twirling and tossing great bales around as though they were feather pillows, she felt strengthened in her disobedience to her father. Also (it was her first visit to the warehouse, and Sin Rock was the chief distributing point to several chains of lesser posts), she was astounded at the endlessness of the wealth there stored away.

This sight, and the picture in her mind's eye of the bare lodge of Snettishane, put all doubts at rest. Yet she capped her conviction by a brief word with one of her stepsons. 'White daddy good?' was what she asked, and the boy answered that his father was the best man he had ever known. That night the raven croaked again. On the night following the croaking was more persistent. It awoke the Factor, who tossed restlessly for a while. Then he said aloud, 'Damn that raven,' and Lit-lit laughed quietly under the blankets.

In the morning, bright and early, Snettishane put in an ominous appearance, and was set to breakfast in the kitchen with Wanidani. He refused 'squaw food,' and a little later bearded his son-in-law in the store where the trading was done. Having learned, he said, that his daughter was such a jewel, he had come for more blankets, more tobacco, and more guns—especially more guns. He had certainly been cheated in her price, he held, and he had come for justice. But the Factor had neither blankets nor justice to spare. Whereupon he was informed that Snettishane had seen the missionary at Three Forks, who had notified him that such marriages were not made in heaven, and that it was his father's duty to demand his daughter back.

'I am good Christian man now,' Snettishane concluded. 'I want my Lit-lit to go to heaven.'

The Factor's reply was short and to the point; for he directed his father-in-law to go to the heavenly antipodes, and by the scruff of the neck and the slack of the blanket propelled him on that trail as far as the door.

But Snettishane sneaked around and in by the kitchen, cornering Lit-lit in the great living-room of the Fort.

'Mayhap thou didst sleep oversound last night when I called by the river bank,' he began, glowering darkly.

'Nay, I was awake and heard.' Her heart was beating as though it would choke her, but she went on steadily, 'And the night before I was awake and heard, and yet again the night before.'

And thereat, out of her great happiness and out of the fear that it might be taken from her, she launched into an original and glowing address upon the status and rights of woman—the first new-woman lecture delivered north of Fifty-three.

But it fell on unheeding ears. Snettishane was still in the dark ages. As she paused for breath, he said threateningly, 'To-night I shall call again like the raven.'

At this moment the Factor entered the room and again helped Snettishane on his way to the heavenly antipodes.

That night the raven croaked more persistently than ever. Lit-lit, who was a light sleeper, heard and smiled. John Fox tossed restlessly. Then he awoke and tossed about with greater restlessness. He grumbled and snorted, swore under his breath and over his breath, and finally flung out of bed. He groped his way to the great living-room and from the rack took down a loaded shot-gun—loaded with bird shot, left therein by the careless McTavish.

The Factor crept carefully out of the Fort and down to the river. The croaking had ceased, but he stretched out in the long grass and waited. The air seemed a chilly balm, and the earth, after the heat of the day, now and again breathed soothingly against him. The Factor, gathered into the rhythm of it all, dozed off, with his head upon his arm, and slept.

Fifty yards away, head resting on knees, and with his back to John Fox, Snettishane likewise slept, gently conquered by the quietude of the night. An hour slipped by and then he awoke, and, without lifting his head, set the night vibrating with the hoarse gutturals of the raven call.

The Factor roused, not with the abrupt start of civilized man, but with the swift and comprehensive glide from sleep to waking of the savage. In the night light he made out a dark object in the midst of the grass and brought his gun to bear upon it. A second croak began to rise, and he pulled the trigger. The crickets ceased from their sing-song chant, the wild fowl from their squabbling, and the raven croak broke midmost and died away in gasping silence.

John Fox ran to the spot and reached for the thing he had killed, but his fingers closed on a coarse mop of hair and he turned Snettishane's face upward to the starlight. He knew how a shot-gun scattered at fifty yards, and he knew that he had peppered Snettishane across the shoulders and in the small of the back. And Snettishane knew that he knew, but neither referred to it.

'What dost thou here?' the Factor demanded. 'It were time old bones should be in bed.'

But Snettishane was stately in spite of the bird shot burning under his skin.

'Old bones will not sleep,' he said solemnly. 'I weep for my daughter, for my daughter Lit-lit, who liveth and who yet is dead, and who goeth without doubt to the white man's hell.'

'Weep henceforth on the far bank, beyond earshot of the fort,' said John Fox, turning on his heel, 'for the noise of thy weeping is exceeding great and will not let one sleep of nights.'

'My heart is sore,' Snettishane answered, 'and my days and nights be black with sorrow.'

'As the raven is black,' said John Fox.

'As the raven is black,' Snettishane said.

Never again was the voice of the raven heard by the river bank. Lit-lit grows matronly day by day and is very happy. Also, there are sisters to the sons of John Fox's first wife who lies buried in a tree. Old Snettishane is no longer a visitor at the Fort, and spends long hours raising a thin, aged voice against the filial ingratitude of children in general and of his daughter Lit-lit in particular. His declining years are embittered by the knowledge that he was cheated, and even John Fox has withdrawn the assertion that the price for Lit-lit was too much by ten blankets and a gun.

LOVE OF LIFE

This out of all will remain—
They have lived and have tossed:
So much of the game will be gain,
Though the gold of the dice has been lost.

They limped painfully down the bank, and once the foremost of the two men staggered among the rough-strewn rocks. They were tired and weak, and their faces had the drawn expression of patience which comes of hardship long endured. They were heavily burdened with blanket packs which were strapped to their shoulders. Head-straps, passing across the forehead, helped support these packs. Each man carried a rifle. They walked in a stooped posture, the shoulders well forward, the head still farther forward, the eyes bent upon the ground.

'I wish we had just about two of them cartridges that's layin' in that cache of ourn,' said the second man.

His voice was utterly and drearily expressionless. He spoke without enthusiasm; and the first man, limping into the milky stream that foamed over the rocks, vouchsafed no reply.

The other man followed at his heels. They did not remove their foot-gear, though the water was icy cold—so cold that their ankles ached and their feet went numb. In places the water dashed against their knees, and both men staggered for footing.

The man who followed slipped on a smooth boulder, nearly fell, but recovered himself with a violent effort, at the same time uttering a sharp exclamation of pain. He seemed faint and dizzy and put out his free hand while he reeled, as though seeking support against the air. When he had steadied himself he stepped forward, but reeled again and nearly fell. Then he stood still and looked at the other man, who had never turned his head.

The man stood still for fully a minute, as though debating with himself. Then he called out:

'I say, Bill, I've sprained my ankle.'

Bill staggered on through the milky water. He did not look around. The man watched him go, and though his face was expressionless as ever, his eyes were like the eyes of a wounded deer.

The other man limped up the farther bank and continued straight on without looking back. The man in the stream watched him. His lips trembled a little, so that the rough thatch of brown hair which covered them was visibly agitated. His tongue even strayed out to moisten them.

'Bill!' he cried out.

It was the pleading cry of a strong man in distress, but Bill's head did not turn. The man watched him go, limping grotesquely and lurching forward with stammering gait up the slow slope toward the soft sky-line of the low-lying hill. He watched him go till he passed over the crest and disappeared. Then he turned his gaze and slowly took in the circle of the world that remained to him now that Bill was gone.

Near the horizon the sun was smouldering dimly, almost obscured by formless mists and vapors, which gave an impression of mass and density without outline or tangibility. The man pulled out his watch, the while resting his weight on one leg. It was four o'clock, and as the season was near the last of July or first of August,—he did not know the precise date within a week or two,—he knew that the sun roughly marked the northwest. He looked to the south and knew that somewhere beyond those bleak hills lay the Great Bear Lake; also, he knew that in that direction the Arctic Circle cut its forbidding way across the Canadian Barrens. This stream in which he stood was a feeder to the Coppermine River, which in turn flowed north and emptied into Coronation Gulf and the Arctic Ocean. He had never been there, but he had seen it, once, on a Hudson Bay Company chart.

Again his gaze completed the circle of the world about him. It was not a heartening spectacle. Everywhere was soft sky-line. The hills were all low-lying. There were no trees, no shrubs, no grasses—naught but a tremendous and terrible desolation that sent fear swiftly dawning into his eyes.

'Bill!' he whispered, once and twice; 'Bill!'

He cowered in the midst of the milky water, as though the

vastness were pressing in upon him with overwhelming force, brutally crushing him with its complacent awfulness. He began to shake as with an ague-fit, till the gun fell from his hand with a splash. This served to rouse him. He fought with his fear and pulled himself together, groping in the water and recovering the weapon. He hitched his pack farther over on his left shoulder, so as to take a portion of its weight from off the injured ankle. Then he proceeded, slowly and carefully, wincing with pain, to the bank.

He did not stop. With a desperation that was madness, unmindful of the pain, he hurried up the slope to the crest of the hill over which his comrade had disappeared—more grotesque and comical by far than that limping, jerking comrade. But at the crest he saw a shallow valley, empty of life. He fought with his fear again, overcame it, hitched the pack still farther over on his left shoulder, and lurched on down the slope.

The bottom of the valley was soggy with water, which the thick moss held, spongelike, close to the surface. This water squirted out from under his feet at every step, and each time he lifted a foot the action culminated in a sucking sound as the wet moss reluctantly released its grip. He picked his way from muskeg to muskeg, and followed the other man's footsteps along and across the rocky ledges which thrust like islets through the sea of moss.

Though alone, he was not lost. Farther on he knew he would come to where dead spruce and fir, very small and weazened, bordered the shore of a little lake, the *titchin-nichilie*, in the tongue of the country, the 'land of little sticks.' And into that lake flowed a small stream, the water of which was not milky. There was rush-grass on that stream—this he remembered well—but no timber, and he would follow it till its first trickle ceased at a divide. He would cross this divide to the first trickle of another stream, flowing to the west, which he would follow until it emptied into the river Dease, and here he would find a cache under an upturned canoe and piled over with many rocks. And in this cache would be ammunition for his empty gun, fish-hooks and lines, a small net—all the utilities for the killing and snaring of food. Also, he would find flour,—not much,—a piece of bacon, and some beans.

Bill would be waiting for him there, and they would paddle away south down the Dease to the Great Bear Lake. And south across the lake they would go, ever south, till they gained the Mackenzie. And south, still south, they would go, while the winter raced vainly after them, and the ice formed in the eddies, and the days grew chill and crisp, south to some warm Hudson Bay Company post, where timber grew tall and generous and there was grub without end.

These were the thoughts of the man as he strove onward. But hard as he strove with his body, he strove equally hard with his mind, trying to think that Bill had not deserted him, that Bill would surely wait for him at the cache. He was compelled to think this thought, or else there would not be any use to strive, and he would have lain down and died. And as the dim ball of the sun sank slowly into the northwest he covered every inch—and many times—of his and Bill's flight south before the downcoming winter. And he conned the grub of the cache and the grub of the Hudson Bay Company post over and over again. He had not eaten for two days; for a far longer time he had not had all he wanted to eat. Often he stooped and picked pale muskeg berries, put them into his mouth, and chewed and swallowed them. A muskeg berry is a bit of seed enclosed in a bit of water. In the mouth the water melts away and the seed chews sharp and bitter. The man knew there was no nourishment in the berries, but he chewed them patiently with a hope greater than knowledge and defying experience.

At nine o'clock he stubbed his toe on a rocky ledge, and from sheer weariness and weakness staggered and fell. He lay for some time, without movement, on his side. Then he slipped out of the pack-straps and clumsily dragged himself into a sitting posture. It was not yet dark, and in the lingering twilight he groped about among the rocks for shreds of dry moss. When he had gathered a heap he built a fire,—a smouldering, smudgy fire,— and put a tin pot of water on to boil.

He unwrapped his pack and the first thing he did was to

count his matches. There were sixty-seven. He counted them three times to make sure. He divided them into several portions, wrapping them in oil paper, disposing of one bunch in his empty tobacco pouch, of another bunch in the inside band of his battered hat, of a third bunch under his shirt on the chest. This accomplished, a panic came upon him, and he unwrapped them all and counted them again. There were still sixty-seven.

He dried his wet foot-gear by the fire. The moccasins were in soggy shreds. The blanket socks were worn through in places, and his feet were raw and bleeding. His ankle was throbbing, and he gave it an examination. It had swollen to the size of his knee. He tore a long strip from one of his two blankets and bound the ankle tightly. He tore other strips and bound them about his feet to serve for both moccasins and socks. Then he drank the pot of water, steaming hot, wound his watch, and crawled between his blankets.

He slept like a dead man. The brief darkness around midnight came and went. The sun arose in the northeast— at least the day dawned in that quarter, for the sun was hidden by gray clouds.

At six o'clock he awoke, quietly lying on his back. He gazed straight up into the gray sky and knew that he was hungry. As he rolled over on his elbow he was startled by a loud snort, and saw a bull caribou regarding him with alert curiosity. The animal was not more than fifty feet away, and instantly into the man's mind leaped the vision and the savor of a caribou steak sizzling and frying over a fire. Mechanically he reached for the empty gun, drew a bead, and pulled the trigger. The bull snorted and leaped away, his hoofs rattling and clattering as he fled across the ledges.

The man cursed and flung the empty gun from him. He groaned aloud as he started to drag himself to his feet. It was a slow and arduous task. His joints were like rusty hinges. They worked harshly in their sockets, with much friction, and each bending or unbending was accomplished only through a sheer exertion of will. When he finally gained his feet, another minute or so was consumed in straightening up, so that he could stand erect as a man should stand.

He crawled up a small knoll and surveyed the prospect.
There were no trees, no bushes, nothing but a gray sea of
moss scarcely diversified by gray rocks, gray lakelets, and
gray streamlets. The sky was gray. There was no sun nor
hint of sun. He had no idea of north, and he had forgotten
the way he had come to this spot the night before. But he
was not lost. He knew that. Soon he would come to the land
of the little sticks. He felt that it lay off to the left somewhere, not far—possibly just over the next low hill.

He went back to put his pack into shape for travelling. He
assured himself of the existence of his three separate parcels
of matches, though he did not stop to count them. But he
did linger, debating, over a squat moose-hide sack. It was
not large. He could hide it under his two hands. He knew
that it weighed fifteen pounds,—as much as all the rest of
the pack,—and it worried him. He finally set it to one side
and proceeded to roll the pack. He paused to gaze at the
squat moose-hide sack. He picked it up hastily with a defiant
glance about him, as though the desolation were trying to
rob him of it; and when he rose to his feet to stagger on into
the day, it was included in the pack on his back.

He bore away to the left, stopping now and again to eat
muskeg berries. His ankle had stiffened, his limp was more
pronounced, but the pain of it was as nothing compared
with the pain of his stomach. The hunger pangs were sharp.
They gnawed and gnawed until he could not keep his mind
steady on the course he must pursue to gain the land of little
sticks. The muskeg berries did not allay this gnawing, while
they made his tongue and the roof of his mouth sore with
their irritating bite.

He came upon a valley where rock ptarmigan rose on
whirring wings from the ledges and muskegs. Ker—ker—ker
was the cry they made. He threw stones at them, but could
not hit them. He placed his pack on the ground and stalked
them as a cat stalks a sparrow. The sharp rocks cut through
his pants' legs till his knees left a trail of blood; but the hurt
was lost in the hurt of his hunger. He squirmed over the wet
moss, saturating his clothes and chilling his body; but he was
not aware of it, so great was his fever for food. And always

the ptarmigan rose, whirring, before him, till their ker—ker—ker became a mock to him, and he cursed them and cried aloud at them with their own cry.

Once he crawled upon one that must have been asleep. He did not see it till it shot up in his face from its rocky nook. He made a clutch as startled as was the rise of the ptarmigan, and there remained in his hand three tail-feathers. As he watched its flight he hated it, as though it had done him some terrible wrong. Then he returned and shouldered his pack.

As the day wore along he came into valleys or swales where game was more plentiful. A band of caribou passed by, twenty and odd animals, tantalizingly within rifle range. He felt a wild desire to run after them, a certitude that he could run them down. A black fox came toward him, carrying a ptarmigan in his mouth. The man shouted. It was a fearful cry, but the fox, leaping away in fright, did not drop the ptarmigan.

Late in the afternoon he followed a stream, milky with lime, which ran through sparse patches of rush-grass. Grasping these rushes firmly near the root, he pulled up what resembled a young onion-sprout no larger than a shingle-nail. It was tender, and his teeth sank into it with a crunch that promised deliciously of food. But its fibers were tough. It was composed of stringy filaments saturated with water, like the berries, and devoid of nourishment. He threw off his pack and went into the rush-grass on hands and knees, crunching and munching, like some bovine creature.

He was very weary and often wished to rest—to lie down and sleep; but he was continually driven on—not so much by his desire to gain the land of little sticks as by his hunger. He searched little ponds for frogs and dug up the earth with his nails for worms, though he knew in spite that neither frogs nor worms existed so far north.

He looked into every pool of water vainly, until, as the long twilight came on, he discovered a solitary fish, the size of a minnow, in such a pool. He plunged his arm in up to the shoulder, but it eluded him. He reached for it with both hands and stirred up the milky mud at the bottom. In his excitement he fell in, wetting himself to the waist. Then the water was too muddy to admit of his seeing the fish, and he was compelled to wait until the sediment had settled.

The pursuit was renewed, till the water was again muddied. But he could not wait. He unstrapped the tin bucket and began to bale the pool. He baled wildly at first, splashing himself and flinging the water so short a distance that it ran back into the pool. He worked more carefully, striving to be cool, though his heart was pounding against his chest and his hands were trembling. At the end of half an hour the pool was nearly dry. Not a cupful of water remained. And there was no fish. He found a hidden crevice among the stones through which it had escaped to the adjoining and larger pool—a pool which he could not empty in a night and a day. Had he known of the crevice, he could have closed it with a rock at the beginning and the fish would have been his.

Thus he thought, and crumpled up and sank down upon the wet earth. At first he cried softly to himself, then he cried loudly to the pitiless desolation that ringed him around; and for a long time after he was shaken by great dry sobs.

He built a fire and warmed himself by drinking quarts of hot water, and made camp on a rocky ledge in the same fashion he had the night before. The last thing he did was to see that his matches were dry and to wind his watch. The blankets were wet and clammy. His ankle pulsed with pain. But he knew only that he was hungry, and through his restless sleep he dreamed of feasts and banquets and of food served and spread in all imaginable ways.

He awoke chilled and sick. There was no sun. The gray of earth and sky had become deeper, more profound. A raw wind was blowing, and the first flurries of snow were whitening the hilltops. The air about him thickened and grew white while he made a fire and boiled more water. It was wet snow, half rain, and the flakes were large and soggy. At first they melted as soon as they came in contact with the earth, but ever more fell, covering the ground, putting out the fire, spoiling his supply of moss-fuel.

This was a signal for him to strap on his pack and stumble

onward, he knew not where. He was not concerned with the land of little sticks, nor with Bill and the cache under the up-turned canoe by the river Dease. He was mastered by the verb 'to eat.' He was hunger-mad. He took no heed of the course he pursued, so long as that course led him through the swale bottoms. He felt his way through the wet snow to the watery muskeg berries, and went by feel as he pulled up the rush-grass by the roots. But it was tasteless stuff and did not satisfy. He found a weed that tasted sour and he ate all he could find of it, which was not much, for it was a creeping growth, easily hidden under the several inches of snow.

He had no fire that night, nor hot water, and crawled under his blanket to sleep the broken hunger-sleep. The snow turned into a cold rain. He awakened many times to feel it falling on his upturned face. Day came—a gray day and no sun. It had ceased raining. The keenness of his hunger had departed. Sensibility, as far as concerned the yearning for food, had been exhausted. There was a dull, heavy ache in his stomach, but it did not bother him so much. He was more rational, and once more he was chiefly interested in the land of little sticks and the cache by the river Dease.

He ripped the remnant of one of his blankets into strips and bound his bleeding feet. Also, he recinched the injured ankle and prepared himself for a day of travel. When he came to his pack, he paused long over the squat moose-hide sack, but in the end it went with him.

The snow had melted under the rain, and only the hilltops showed white. The sun came out, and he succeeded in locat-ing the points of the compass, though he knew now that he was lost. Perhaps, in his previous days' wanderings, he had edged away too far to the left. He now bore off to the right to counteract the possible deviation from his true course.

Though the hunger pangs were no longer so exquisite, he realized that he was weak. He was compelled to pause for frequent rests, when he attacked the muskeg berries and rush-grass patches. His tongue felt dry and large, as though covered with a fine hairy growth, and it tasted bitter in his mouth. His heart gave him a great deal of trouble. When he had travelled a few minutes it would begin a remorseless thump, thump, thump, and then leap up and away in a painful flutter of beats that choked him and made him go faint and dizzy.

In the middle of the day he found two minnows in a large pool. It was impossible to bale it, but he was calmer now and managed to catch them in his tin bucket. They were no longer than his little finger, but he was not particularly hungry. The dull ache in his stomach had been growing duller and fainter. It seemed almost that his stomach was dozing. He ate the fish raw, masticating with painstaking care, for the eating was an act of pure reason. While he had no desire to eat, he knew that he must eat to live.

In the evening he caught three more minnows, eating two and saving the third for breakfast. The sun had dried stray shreds of moss, and he was able to warm himself with hot water. He had not covered more than ten miles that day; and the next day, travelling whenever his heart permitted him, he covered no more than five miles. But his stomach did not give him the slightest uneasiness. It had gone to sleep. He was in a strange country, too, and the caribou were growing more plentiful, also the wolves. Often their yelps drifted across the desolation, and once he saw three of them slinking away before his path.

Another night; and in the morning, being more rational, he untied the leather string that fastened the squat moosehide sack. From its open mouth poured a yellow stream of coarse gold-dust and nuggets. He roughly divided the gold in halves, caching one half on a prominent ledge, wrapped in a piece of blanket, and returning the other half to the sack. He also began to use strips of the one remaining blanket for his feet. He still clung to his gun, for there were cartridges in that cache by the river Dease.

This was a day of fog, and this day hunger awoke in him again. He was very weak and was afflicted with a giddiness which at times blinded him. It was no uncommon thing now for him to stumble and fall; and stumbling once, he fell squarely into a ptarmigan nest. There were four newly hatched chicks, a day old—little specks of pulsating life no more than a mouthful; and he ate them ravenously, thrusting them alive into his mouth and crunching them like egg-shells between his teeth. The mother ptarmigan beat about him with great outcry. He used his gun as a club with which to knock her over, but she dodged out of reach. He threw stones at her and with one chance shot broke a wing. Then she fluttered away, running, trailing the broken wing, with him in pursuit.

The little chicks had no more than whetted his appetite. He hopped and bobbed clumsily along on his injured ankle, throwing stones and screaming hoarsely at times; at other times hopping and bobbing silently along, picking himself up grimly and patiently when he fell, or rubbing his eyes with his hand when the giddiness threatened to overpower him.

The chase led him across swampy ground in the bottom of the valley, and he came upon footprints in the soggy moss. They were not his own—he could see that. They must be Bill's. But he could not stop, for the mother ptarmigan was running on. He would catch her first, then he would return and investigate.

He exhausted the mother ptarmigan; but he exhausted himself. She lay panting on her side. He lay panting on his side, a dozen feet away, unable to crawl to her. And as he recovered she recovered, fluttering out of reach as his hungry hand went out to her. The chase was resumed. Night settled down and she escaped. He stumbled from weakness and pitched head foremost on his face, cutting his cheek, his pack upon his back. He did not move for a long while; then he rolled over on his side, wound his watch, and lay there until morning.

Another day of fog. Half of his last blanket had gone into foot-wrappings. He failed to pick up Bill's trail. It did not matter. His hunger was driving him too compellingly—only— only he wondered if Bill, too, were lost. By midday the irk of his pack became too oppressive. Again he divided the gold, this time merely spilling half of it on the ground. In the afternoon he threw the rest of it away, there remaining to him only the half-blanket, the tin bucket, and the rifle.

An hallucination began to trouble him. He felt confident that one cartridge remained to him. It was in the chamber of the rifle and he had overlooked it. On the other hand, he knew all the time that the chamber was empty. But the hallucination persisted. He fought it off for hours, then threw his rifle open and was confronted with emptiness. The disappointment was as bitter as though he had really expected to find the cartridge.

He plodded on for half an hour, when the hallucination arose again. Again he fought it, and still it persisted, till for very relief he opened his rifle to unconvince himself. At times his mind wandered farther afield, and he plodded on, a mere automaton, strange conceits and whimsicalities gnawing at his brain like worms. But these excursions out of the real were of brief duration, for ever the pangs of the hunger-bite called him back. He was jerked back abruptly once from such an excursion by a sight that caused him nearly to faint. He reeled and swayed, doddering like a drunken man to keep from falling. Before him stood a horse. A horse! He could not believe his eyes. A thick mist was in them, intershot with sparkling points of light. He rubbed his eyes savagely to clear his vision, and beheld, not a horse, but a great brown bear. The animal was studying him with bellicose curiosity.

The man had brought his gun halfway to his shoulder before he realized. He lowered it and drew his hunting-knife from its beaded sheath at his hip. Before him was meat and life. He ran his thumb along the edge of his knife. It was sharp. The point was sharp. He would fling himself upon the bear and kill it. But his heart began its warning thump, thump, thump. Then followed the wild upward leap and tattoo of flutters, the pressing as of an iron band about his forehead, the creeping of the dizziness into his brain.

His desperate courage was evicted by a great surge of fear. In his weakness, what if the animal attacked him? He drew himself up to his most imposing stature, gripping the knife and staring hard at the bear. The bear advanced clumsily a couple of steps, reared up, and gave vent to a tentative growl. If the man ran, he would run after him; but the man did not run. He was animated now with the courage of fear. He, too, growled, savagely, terribly, voicing the fear that is to life germane and that lies twisted about life's deepest roots.

The bear edged away to one side, growling menacingly, himself appalled by this mysterious creature that appeared upright and unafraid. But the man did not move. He stood like a statue till the danger was past, when he yielded to a fit of trembling and sank down into the wet moss.

He pulled himself together and went on, afraid now in a new way. It was not the fear that he should die passively from lack of food, but that he should be destroyed violently before starvation had exhausted the last particle of the endeavor in him that made toward surviving. There were the wolves. Back and forth across the desolation drifted their howls, weaving the very air into a fabric of menace that was so tangible that he found himself, arms in the air, pressing it back from him as it might be the walls of a wind-blown tent.

Now and again the wolves, in packs of two and three, crossed his path. But they sheered clear of him. They were not in sufficient numbers, and besides they were hunting the caribou, which did not battle, while this strange creature that walked erect might scratch and bite.

In the late afternoon he came upon scattered bones where the wolves had made a kill. The débris had been a caribou calf an hour before, squawking and running and very much alive. He contemplated the bones, clean-picked and polished, pink with the cell-life in them which has not yet died. Could it possibly be that he might be that ere the day was done! Such was life, eh? A vain and fleeting thing. It was only life that pained. There was no hurt in death. To die was to sleep. It meant cessation, rest. Then why was he not content to die?

But he did not moralize long. He was squatting in the moss, a bone in his mouth, sucking at the shreds of life that still dyed it faintly pink. The sweet meaty taste, thin and elusive almost as a memory, maddened him. He closed his jaws on the bones and crunched. Sometimes it was the bone that broke, sometimes his teeth. Then he crushed the bones between rocks, pounded them to a pulp, and swallowed them. He pounded his fingers, too, in his haste, and yet found a moment in which to feel surprise at the fact that his fingers did not hurt much when caught under the descending rock.

Came frightful days of snow and rain. He did not know when he made camp, when he broke camp. He travelled in the night as much as in the day. He rested wherever he fell, crawled on whenever the dying life in him flickered up and burned less dimly. He, as a man, no longer strove. It was the life in him, unwilling to die, that drove him on. He did not suffer. His nerves had become blunted, numb, while his mind was filled with weird visions and delicious dreams.

But ever he sucked and chewed on the crushed bones of the caribou calf, the least remnants of which he had gathered up and carried with him. He crossed no more hills or divides, but automatically followed a large stream which flowed through a wide and shallow valley. He did not see this stream nor this valley. He saw nothing save visions. Soul and body walked or crawled side by side, yet apart, so slender was the thread that bound them.

He awoke in his right mind, lying on his back on a rocky ledge. The sun was shining bright and warm. Afar off he heard the squawking of caribou calves. He was aware of vague memories of rain and wind and snow, but whether he had been beaten by the storm for two days or two weeks he did not know.

For some time he lay without movement, the genial sunshine pouring upon him and saturating his miserable body with its warmth. A fine day, he thought. Perhaps he could manage to locate himself. By a painful effort he rolled over on his side. Below him flowed a wide and sluggish river. Its unfamiliarity puzzled him. Slowly he followed it with his eyes, winding in wide sweeps among the bleak, bare hills, bleaker and barer and lower-lying than any hills he had yet encountered. Slowly, deliberately, without excitement or more than the most casual interest, he followed the course of the strange stream toward the sky-line and saw it emptying into a bright and shining sea. He was still unexcited. Most unusual, he thought, a vision or a mirage—more likely a vision, a trick of his disordered mind. He was confirmed in this by sight of a ship lying at anchor in the midst of the shining sea. He closed his eyes for a while, then opened them. Strange how the vision persisted! Yet not strange. He knew there were no seas or ships in the heart of the barren lands, just as he had known there was no cartridge in the empty rifle.

He heard a snuffle behind him—a half-choking gasp or cough. Very slowly, because of his exceeding weakness and stiffness, he rolled over on his other side. He could see nothing near at hand, but he waited patiently. Again came the snuffle and cough, and outlined between two jagged rocks not a score of feet away he made out the gray head of a wolf. The sharp ears were not pricked so sharply as he had seen them on other wolves; the eyes were bleared and bloodshot, the head seemed to droop limply and forlornly. The animal blinked continually in the sunshine. It seemed sick. As he looked it snuffled and coughed again.

This, at least, was real, he thought, and turned on the other side so that he might see the reality of the world which had been veiled from him before by the vision. But the sea still shone in the distance and the ship was plainly discernible. Was it reality, after all? He closed his eyes for a long while and thought, and then it came to him. He had been making north by east, away from the Dease Divide and into the Coppermine Valley. This wide and sluggish river was the Coppermine. That shining sea was the Arctic Ocean. That ship was a whaler, strayed east, far east, from the mouth of the Mackenzie, and it was lying at anchor in Coronation Gulf. He remembered the Hudson Bay Company chart he had seen long ago, and it was all clear and reasonable to him.

He sat up and turned his attention to immediate affairs. He had worn through the blanket-wrappings, and his feet were shapeless lumps of raw meat. His last blanket was gone. Rifle and knife were both missing. He had lost his hat somewhere, with the bunch of matches in the band, but the matches against his chest were safe and dry inside the tobacco pouch and oil paper. He looked at his watch. It marked eleven o'clock and was still running. Evidently he had kept it wound.

He was calm and collected. Though extremely weak, he had no sensation of pain. He was not hungry. The thought of food was not even pleasant to him, and whatever he did was done by his reason alone. He ripped off his pants' legs to the knees and bound them about his feet. Somehow he had succeeded in retaining the tin bucket. He would have some hot water before he began what he foresaw was to be a terrible journey to the ship.

His movements were slow. He shook as with a palsy. When he started to collect dry moss, he found he could not rise to his feet. He tried again and again, then contented himself with crawling about on hands and knees. Once he crawled near to the sick wolf. The animal dragged itself reluctantly out of his way, licking its chops with a tongue which seemed hardly to have the strength to curl. The man noticed that the tongue was not the customary healthy red. It was a yellowish brown and seemed coated with a rough and half-dry mucus.

After he had drunk a quart of hot water the man found he was able to stand, and even to walk as well as a dying man might be supposed to walk. Every minute or so he was compelled to rest. His steps were feeble and uncertain, just as the wolf's that trailed him were feeble and uncertain; and that night, when the shining sea was blotted out by blackness, he knew he was nearer to it by no more than four miles.

Throughout the night he heard the cough of the sick wolf, and now and then the squawking of the caribou calves. There was life all around him, but it was strong life, very much alive and well, and he knew the sick wolf clung to the sick man's trail in the hope that the man would die first. In the morning, on opening his eyes, he beheld it regarding him with a wistful and hungry stare. It stood crouched, with tail between its legs, like a miserable and woe-begone dog. It shivered in the chill morning wind, and grinned dispiritedly when the man spoke to it in a voice that achieved no more than a hoarse whisper.

The sun rose brightly, and all morning the man tottered and fell toward the ship on the shining sea. The weather was perfect. It was the brief Indian Summer of the high latitudes. It might last a week. To-morrow or next day it might be gone.

In the afternoon the man came upon a trail. It was of another man, who did not walk, but who dragged himself on

all fours. The man thought it might be Bill, but he thought
in a dull, uninterested way. He had no curiosity. In fact,
sensation and emotion had left him. He was no longer sus-
ceptible to pain. Stomach and nerves had gone to sleep. Yet
the life that was in him drove him on. He was very weary,
but it refused to die. It was because it refused to die that he
still ate muskeg berries and minnows, drank his hot water,
and kept a wary eye on the sick wolf.

He followed the trail of the other man who dragged himself along, and soon came to the end of it—a few fresh-
picked bones where the soggy moss was marked by the
foot-pads of many wolves. He saw a squat moose-hide sack,
mate to his own, which had been torn by sharp teeth. He
picked it up, though its weight was almost too much for his
feeble fingers. Bill had carried it to the last. Ha! ha! He
would have the laugh on Bill. He would survive and carry it
to the ship in the shining sea. His mirth was hoarse and
ghastly, like a raven's croak, and the sick wolf joined him,
howling lugubriously. The man ceased suddenly. How could
he have the laugh on Bill if that were Bill; if those bones, so
pinky-white and clean, were Bill?

He turned away. Well, Bill had deserted him; but he would
not take the gold, nor would he suck Bill's bones. Bill would
have, though, had it been the other way around, he mused
as he staggered on.

He came to a pool of water. Stooping over in quest of
minnows, he jerked his head back as though he had been
stung. He had caught sight of his reflected face. So horrible
was it that sensibility awoke long enough to be shocked.
There were three minnows in the pool, which was too large
to drain; and after several ineffectual attempts to catch them
in the tin bucket he forbore. He was afraid, because of his
great weakness, that he might fall in and drown. It was for
this reason that he did not trust himself to the river astride
one of the many drift-logs which lined its sand-spits.

That day he decreased the distance between him and the
ship by three miles; the next day by two—for he was crawling now as Bill had crawled; and the end of the fifth day
found the ship still seven miles away and him unable to

make even a mile a day. Still the Indian Summer held on, and he continued to crawl and faint, turn and turn about; and ever the sick wolf coughed and wheezed at his heels. His knees had become raw meat like his feet, and though he padded them with the shirt from his back it was a red track he left behind him on the moss and stones. Once, glancing back, he saw the wolf licking hungrily his bleeding trail, and he saw sharply what his own end might be—unless—unless he could get the wolf. Then began as grim a tragedy of existence as was ever played—a sick man that crawled, a sick wolf that limped, two creatures dragging their dying carcasses across the desolation and hunting each other's lives.

Had it been a well wolf, it would not have mattered so much to the man; but the thought of going to feed the maw of that loathsome and all but dead thing was repugnant to him. He was finicky. His mind had begun to wander again, and to be perplexed by hallucinations, while his lucid intervals grew rarer and shorter.

He was awakened once from a faint by a wheeze close in his ear. The wolf leaped lamely back, losing its footing and falling in its weakness. It was ludicrous, but he was not amused. Nor was he even afraid. He was too far gone for that. But his mind was for the moment clear, and he lay and considered. The ship was no more than four miles away. He could see it quite distinctly when he rubbed the mists out of his eyes, and he could see the white sail of a small boat cutting the water of the shining sea. But he could never crawl those four miles. He knew that, and was very calm in the knowledge. He knew that he could not crawl half a mile. And yet he wanted to live. It was unreasonable that he should die after all he had undergone. Fate asked too much of him. And, dying, he declined to die. It was stark madness, perhaps, but in the very grip of Death he defied Death and refused to die.

He closed his eyes and composed himself with infinite precaution. He steeled himself to keep above the suffocating languor that lapped like a rising tide through all the wells of his being. It was very like a sea, this deadly languor, that rose and rose and drowned his consciousness bit by bit. Sometimes he was all but submerged, swimming through oblivion with a faltering stroke; and again, by some strange alchemy of soul, he would find another shred of will and strike out more strongly.

Without movement he lay on his back, and he could hear, slowly drawing near and nearer, the wheezing intake and output of the sick wolf's breath. It drew closer, ever closer, through an infinitude of time, and he did not move. It was at his ear. The harsh dry tongue grated like sandpaper against his cheek. His hands shot out—or at least he willed them to shoot out. The fingers were curved like talons, but they closed on empty air. Swiftness and certitude require strength, and the man had not this strength.

The patience of the wolf was terrible. The man's patience was no less terrible. For half a day he lay motionless, fighting off unconsciousness and waiting for the thing that was to feed upon him and upon which he wished to feed. Sometimes the languid sea rose over him and he dreamed long dreams; but ever through it all, waking and dreaming, he waited for the wheezing breath and the harsh caress of the tongue.

He did not hear the breath, and he slipped slowly from some dream to the feel of the tongue along his hand. He waited. The fangs pressed softly; the pressure increased; the wolf was exerting its last strength in an effort to sink teeth in the food for which it had waited so long. But the man had waited long, and the lacerated hand closed on the jaw. Slowly, while the wolf struggled feebly and the hand clutched feebly, the other hand crept across to a grip. Five minutes later the whole weight of the man's body was on top of the wolf. The hands had not sufficient strength to choke the wolf, but the face of the man was pressed close to the throat of the wolf and the mouth of the man was full of hair. At the end of half an hour the man was aware of a warm trickle in his throat. It was not pleasant. It was like molten lead being forced into his stomach, and it was forced by his will alone. Later the man rolled over on his back and slept.

There were some members of a scientific expedition on the whale-ship *Bedford*. From the deck they remarked a strange object on the shore. It was moving down the beach toward the water. They were unable to classify it, and, being scientific men, they climbed into the whale-boat alongside and went ashore to see. And they saw something that was alive but which could hardly be called a man. It was blind, unconscious. It squirmed along the ground like some monstrous worm. Most of its efforts were ineffectual, but it was persistent, and it writhed and twisted and went ahead perhaps a score of feet an hour.

Three weeks afterward the man lay in a bunk on the whaleship *Bedford*, and with tears streaming down his wasted cheeks told who he was and what he had undergone. He also babbled incoherently of his mother, of sunny Southern California, and a home among the orange groves and flowers.

The days were not many after that when he sat at table with the scientific men and ship's officers. He gloated over the spectacle of so much food, watching it anxiously as it went into the mouths of others. With the disappearance of each mouthful an expression of deep regret came into his eyes. He was quite sane, yet he hated those men at mealtime. He was haunted by a fear that the food would not last. He inquired of the cook, the cabin-boy, the captain, concerning the food stores. They reassured him countless times; but he could not believe them, and pried cunningly about the lazarette to see with his own eyes.

It was noticed that the man was getting fat. He grew stouter with each day. The scientific men shook their heads and theorized. They limited the man at his meals, but still his girth increased and he swelled prodigiously under his shirt.

The sailors grinned. They knew. And when the scientific man set a watch on the man, they knew too. They saw him slouch for'ard after breakfast, and, like a mendicant, with outstretched palm, accost a sailor. The sailor grinned and passed him a fragment of sea biscuit. He clutched it avariciously, looked at it as a miser looks at gold, and thrust it into his shirt bosom. Similar were the donations from other grinning sailors.

The scientific men were discreet. They let him alone. But

they privily examined his bunk. It was lined with hardtack; the mattress was stuffed with hardtack; every nook and cranny was filled with hardtack. Yet he was sane. He was taking precautions against another possible famine—that was all. He would recover from it, the scientific men said; and he did, ere the *Bedford*'s anchor rumbled down in San Francisco Bay.

THE WHITE MAN'S WAY

'To cook by your fire and to sleep under your roof for the night,' I had announced on entering old Ebbits's cabin; and he had looked at me blear-eyed and vacuous, while Zilla had favored me with a sour face and a contemptuous grunt. Zilla was his wife, and no more bitter-tongued, implacable old squaw dwelt on the Yukon. Nor would I have stopped there had my dogs been less tired or had the rest of the village been inhabited. But this cabin alone had I found occupied, and in this cabin, perforce, I took my shelter.

Old Ebbits now and again pulled his tangled wits together, and hints and sparkles of intelligence came and went in his eyes. Several times during the preparation of my supper he even essayed hospitable inquiries about my health, the condition and number of my dogs, and the distance I had travelled that day. And each time Zilla had looked sourer than ever and grunted more contemptuously.

Yet I confess that there was no particular call for cheerfulness on their part. There they crouched by the fire, the pair of them, at the end of their days, old and withered and helpless, racked by rheumatism, bitten by hunger, and tantalized by the frying-odors of my abundance of meat. They rocked back and forth in a slow and hopeless way, and regularly, once every five minutes, Ebbits emitted a low groan. It was not so much a groan of pain, as of pain-weariness. He was oppressed by the weight and the torment of this thing called life, and still more was he oppressed by the fear of death. His was that eternal tragedy of the aged, with whom the joy of life has departed and the instinct for death has not come.

When my moose-meat spluttered rowdily in the frying-pan, I noticed old Ebbits's nostrils twitch and distend as he caught the food-scent. He ceased rocking for a space and forgot to groan, while a look of intelligence seemed to come into his face.

Zilla, on the other hand, rocked more rapidly, and for the first time, in sharp little yelps, voiced her pain. It came to me that their behavior was like that of hungry dogs, and in the fitness of things I should not have been astonished had Zilla suddenly developed a tail and thumped it on the floor in right doggish fashion. Ebbits drooled a little and stopped his rocking very frequently to lean forward and thrust his tremulous nose nearer to the source of gustatory excitement.

When I passed them each a plate of the fried meat, they ate greedily, making loud mouth-noises—champings of worn teeth and sucking intakes of the breath, accompanied by a continuous spluttering and mumbling. After that, when I gave them each a mug of scalding tea, the noises ceased. Easement and content came into their faces. Zilla relaxed her sour mouth long enough to sigh her satisfaction. Neither rocked any more, and they seemed to have fallen into placid meditation. Then a dampness came into Ebbits's eyes, and I knew that the sorrow of self-pity was his. The search required to find their pipes told plainly that they had been without tobacco a long time, and the old man's eagerness for the narcotic rendered him helpless, so that I was compelled to light his pipe for him.

'Why are you all alone in the village?' I asked. 'Is everybody dead? Has there been a great sickness? Are you alone left of the living?'

Old Ebbits shook his head, saying: 'Nay, there has been no great sickness. The village has gone away to hunt meat. We be too old, our legs are not strong, nor can our backs carry the burdens of camp and trail. Wherefore we remain here and wonder when the young men will return with meat.'

'What if the young men do return with meat?' Zilla demanded harshly.

'They may return with much meat,' he quavered hopefully.

'Even so, with much meat,' she continued, more harshly than before. 'But of what worth to you and me? A few bones to gnaw in our toothless old age. But the back-fat, the kidneys, and the tongues—these shall go into other mouths than thine and mine, old man.'

Ebbits nodded his head and wept silently.

'There be no one to hunt meat for us,' she cried, turning fiercely upon me.

There was accusation in her manner, and I shrugged my shoulders in token that I was not guilty of the unknown crime imputed to me.

'Know, O White Man, that it is because of thy kind, because of all white men, that my man and I have no meat in our old age and sit without tobacco in the cold.'

'Nay,' Ebbits said gravely, with a stricter sense of justice. 'Wrong has been done us, it be true; but the white men did not mean the wrong.'

'Where be Moklan?' she demanded. 'Where be thy strong son, Moklan, and the fish he was ever willing to bring that you might eat?'

The old man shook his head.

'And where be Bidarshik, thy strong son? Ever was he a mighty hunter, and ever did he bring thee the good back-fat and the sweet dried tongues of the moose and the caribou. I see no back-fat and no sweet dried tongues. Your stomach is full with emptiness through the days, and it is for a man of a very miserable and lying people to give you to eat.'

'Nay,' old Ebbits interposed in kindliness, 'the white man's is not a lying people. The white man speaks true. Always does the white man speak true.' He paused, casting about him for words wherewith to temper the severity of what he was about to say. 'But the white man speaks true in different ways. To-day he speaks true one way, to-morrow he speaks true another way, and there is no understanding him nor his way.'

'To-day speak true one way, to-morrow speak true another way, which is to lie,' was Zilla's dictum.

'There is no understanding the white man,' Ebbits went on doggedly.

The meat, and the tea, and the tobacco seemed to have brought him back to life, and he gripped tighter hold of the idea behind his age-bleared eyes. He straightened up somewhat. His voice lost its querulous and whimpering note, and became strong and positive. He turned upon me with dignity, and addressed me as equal addresses equal.

'The white man's eyes are not shut,' he began. 'The white man sees all things, and thinks greatly, and is very wise. But the white man of one day is not the white man of next day, and there is no understanding him. He does not do things always in the same way. And what way his next way is to be, one cannot know. Always does the Indian do the one thing in the one way. Always does the moose come down from the high mountains when the winter is here. Always does the salmon come in the spring when the ice has gone out of the river. Always does everything do all things in the same way, and the Indian knows and understands. But the white man does not do all things in the same way, and the Indian does not know nor understand.

'Tobacco be very good. It be food to the hungry man. It makes the strong man stronger, and the angry man to forget that he is angry. Also is tobacco of value. It is of very great value. The Indian gives one large salmon for one leaf of tobacco, and he chews the tobacco for a long time. It is the juice of the tobacco that is good. When it runs down his throat it makes him feel good inside. But the white man! When his mouth is full with the juice, what does he do? That juice, that juice of great value, he spits it out in the snow and it is lost. Does the white man like tobacco? I do not know. But if he likes tobacco, why does he spit out its value and lose it in the snow? It is a great foolishness and without understanding.'

He ceased, puffed at the pipe, found that it was out, and passed it over to Zilla, who took the sneer at the white man off her lips in order to pucker them about the pipe-stem. Ebbits seemed sinking back into his senility with the tale untold, and I demanded:

'What of thy sons, Moklan and Bidarshik? And why is it that you and your old woman are without meat at the end of your years?'

He roused himself as from sleep, and straightened up with an effort.

'It is not good to steal,' he said. 'When the dog takes your meat you beat the dog with a club. Such is the law. It is the law the man gave to the dog, and the dog must live to the law, else will it suffer the pain of the club. When man takes your meat, or your canoe, or your wife, you kill that man.

That is the law, and it is a good law. It is not good to steal, wherefore it is the law that the man who steals must die. Whoso breaks the law must suffer hurt. It is a great hurt to die.'

'But if you kill the man, why do you not kill the dog?' I asked.

Old Ebbits looked at me in childlike wonder, while Zilla sneered openly at the absurdity of my question.

'It is the way of the white man,' Ebbits mumbled with an air of resignation.

'It is the foolishness of the white man,' snapped Zilla.

'Then let old Ebbits teach the white man wisdom,' I said softly.

'The dog is not killed, because it must pull the sled of the man. No man pulls another man's sled, wherefore the man is killed.'

'Oh,' I murmured.

'That is the law,' old Ebbits went on. 'Now listen, O White Man, and I will tell you of a great foolishness. There is an Indian. His name is Mobits. From white man he steals two pounds of flour. What does the white man do? Does he beat Mobits? No. Does he kill Mobits? No. What does he do to Mobits? I will tell you, O White Man. He has a house. He puts Mobits in that house. The roof is good. The walls are thick. He makes a fire that Mobits may be warm. He gives Mobits plenty grub to eat. It is good grub. Never in his all days does Mobits eat so good grub. There is bacon, and bread, and beans without end. Mobits have very good time.

'There is a big lock on door so that Mobits does not run away. This also is a great foolishness. Mobits will not run away. All the time is there plenty grub in that place, and warm blankets, and a big fire. Very foolish to run away. Mobits is not foolish. Three months Mobits stop in that place. He steal two pounds of flour. For that, white man take plenty good care of him. Mobits eat many pounds of flour, many pounds of sugar, of bacon, of beans without end. Also, Mobits drink much tea. After three months white man open door and tell Mobits he must go. Mobits does not want to go. He is like dog that is fed long time in one place.

He want to stay in that place, and the white man must drive Mobits away. So Mobits come back to this village, and he is very fat. That is the white man's way, and there is no understanding it. It is a foolishness, a great foolishness.'

'But thy sons?' I insisted. 'Thy very strong sons and thine old-age hunger?'

'There was Moklan,' Ebbits began.

'A strong man,' interrupted the mother. 'He could dip paddle all of a day and night and never stop for the need of rest. He was wise in the way of the salmon and in the way of the water. He was very wise.'

'There was Moklan,' Ebbits repeated, ignoring the interruption. 'In the spring, he went down the Yukon with the young men to trade at Cambell Fort.* There is a post there, filled with the goods of the white man, and a trader whose name is Jones. Likewise is there a white man's medicine man, what you call missionary. Also is there bad water at Cambell Fort, where the Yukon goes slim like a maiden, and the water is fast, and the currents rush this way and that and come together, and there are whirls and sucks, and always are the currents changing and the face of the water changing, so at any two times it is never the same. Moklan is my son, wherefore he is brave man—'

'Was not my father brave man?' Zilla demanded.

'Thy father was brave man,' Ebbits acknowledged, with the air of one who will keep peace in the house at any cost. 'Moklan is thy son and mine, wherefore he is brave. Mayhap, because of thy very brave father, Moklan is too brave. It is like when too much water is put in the pot it spills over. So too much bravery is put into Moklan, and the bravery spills over.

'The young men are much afraid of the bad water at Cambell Fort. But Moklan is not afraid. He laughs strong, Ho! ho! and he goes forth into the bad water. But where the currents come together the canoe is turned over. A whirl takes Moklan by the legs, and he goes around and around, and down and down, and is seen no more.'

'Ai! ai!' wailed Zilla. 'Crafty and wise was he, and my first-born!'

'I am the father of Moklan,' Ebbits said, having patiently

given the woman space for her noise. 'I get into canoe and journey down to Cambell Fort to collect the debt!'

'Debt!' I interrupted. 'What debt?'

'The debt of Jones, who is chief trader,' came the answer. 'Such is the law of travel in a strange country.'

I shook my head in token of my ignorance, and Ebbits looked compassion at me, while Zilla snorted her customary contempt.

'Look you, O White Man,' he said. 'In thy camp is a dog that bites. When the dog bites a man, you give that man a present because you are sorry and because it is thy dog. You make payment. Is it not so? Also, if you have in thy country bad hunting, or bad water, you must make payment. It is just. It is the law. Did not my father's brother go over into the Tanana Country and get killed by a bear? And did not the Tanana tribe pay my father many blankets and fine furs? It was just. It was bad hunting, and the Tanana people made payment for the bad hunting.

'So I, Ebbits, journeyed down to Cambell Fort to collect the debt. Jones, who is chief trader, looked at me, and he laughed. He made great laughter, and would not give payment. I went to the medicine-man, what you call missionary, and had large talk about the bad water and the payment that should be mine. And the missionary made talk about other things. He talk about where Moklan has gone, now he is dead. There be large fires in that place, and if missionary make true talk, I know that Moklan will be cold no more. Also the missionary talk about where I shall go when I am dead. And he say bad things. He say that I am blind. Which is a lie. He say that I am in great darkness. Which is a lie. And I say that the day come and the night come for everybody just the same, and that in my village it is no more dark than at Cambell Fort. Also, I say that darkness and light and where we go when we die be different things from the matter of payment of just debt for bad water. Then the missionary make large anger, and call me bad names of darkness, and tell me to go away. And so I come back from Cambell Fort, and no payment has been made, and Moklan is dead, and in my old age I am without fish and meat.'

'Because of the white man,' said Zilla.

'Because of the white man,' Ebbits concurred. 'And other things because of the white man. There was Bidarshik. One way did the white man deal with him; and yet another way for the same thing did the white man deal with Yamikan. And first must I tell you of Yamikan, who was a young man of this village and who chanced to kill a white man. It is not good to kill a man of another people. Always is there great trouble. It was not the fault of Yamikan that he killed the white man. Yamikan spoke always soft words and ran away from wrath as a dog from a stick. But this white man drank much whiskey, and in the night-time came to Yamikan's house and made much fight. Yamikan cannot run away, and the white man tries to kill him. Yamikan does not like to die, so he kills the white man.

'Then is all the village in great trouble. We are much afraid that we must make large payment to the white man's people, and we hide our blankets, and our furs, and all our wealth, so that it will seem that we are poor people and can make only small payment. After long time white men come. They are soldier white men, and they take Yamikan away with them. His mother make great noise and throw ashes in her hair, for she knows Yamikan is dead. And all the village knows that Yamikan is dead, and is glad that no payment is asked.

'That is in the spring when the ice has gone out of the river. One year go by, two years go by. It is spring-time again, and the ice has gone out of the river. And then Yamikan, who is dead, comes back to us, and he is not dead, but very fat, and we know that he has slept warm and had plenty grub to eat. He has much fine clothes and is all the same white man, and he has gathered large wisdom so that he is very quick head man in the village.

'And he has strange things to tell of the way of the white man, for he has seen much of the white man and done a great travel into the white man's country. First place, soldier white men take him down the river long way. All the way do they take him down the river to the end, where it runs into a lake which is larger than all the land and large as the sky.

I do not know the Yukon is so big river, but Yamikan has seen with his own eyes. I do not think there is a lake larger than all the land and large as the sky, but Yamikan has seen. Also, he has told me that the waters of this lake be salt, which is a strange thing and beyond understanding.

'But the White Man knows all these marvels for himself, so I shall not weary him with the telling of them. Only will I tell him what happened to Yamikan. The white man give Yamikan much fine grub. All the time does Yamikan eat, and all the time is there plenty more grub. The white man lives under the sun, so said Yamikan, where there be much warmth, and animals have only hair and no fur, and the green things grow large and strong and become flour, and beans, and potatoes. And under the sun there is never famine. Always is there plenty grub. I do not know. Yamikan has said.

'And here is a strange thing that befell Yamikan. Never did the white man hurt him. Only did they give him warm bed at night and plenty fine grub. They take him across the salt lake which is big as the sky. He is on white man's fire-boat, what you call steamboat, only he is on boat maybe twenty times bigger than steamboat on Yukon. Also, it is made of iron, this boat, and yet does it not sink. This I do not understand, but Yamikan has said, "I have journeyed far on the iron boat; behold! I am still alive." It is a white man's soldier-boat with many soldier men upon it.

'After many sleeps of travel, a long, long time, Yamikan comes to a land where there is no snow. I cannot believe this. It is not in the nature of things that when winter comes there shall be no snow. But Yamikan has seen. Also have I asked the white men, and they have said yes, there is no snow in that country. But I cannot believe, and now I ask you if snow never come in that country. Also, I would hear the name of that country. I have heard the name before, but I would hear it again, if it be the same—thus will I know if I have heard lies or true talk.'

Old Ebbits regarded me with a wistful face. He would have the truth at any cost, though it was his desire to retain his faith in the marvel he had never seen.

'Yes,' I answered, 'it is true talk that you have heard. There is no snow in that country, and its name is California.'

'Cal-ee-forn-ee-yeh,' he mumbled twice and thrice, listening intently to the sound of the syllables as they fell from his lips. He nodded his head in confirmation. 'Yes, it is the same country of which Yamikan made talk.'

I recognized the adventure of Yamikan as one likely to occur in the early days when Alaska first passed into the possession of the United States. Such a murder case, occurring before the instalment of territorial law and officials, might well have been taken down to the United States for trial before a Federal court.

'When Yamikan is in this country where there is no snow,' old Ebbits continued, 'he is taken to large house where many men make much talk. Long time men talk. Also many questions do they ask Yamikan. By and by they tell Yamikan he have no more trouble. Yamikan does not understand, for never has he had any trouble. All the time have they given him warm place to sleep and plenty grub.

'But after that they give him much better grub, and they give him money, and they take him many places in white man's country, and he see many strange things which are beyond the understanding of Ebbits, who is an old man and has not journeyed far. After two years, Yamikan comes back to this village, and he is head man, and very wise until he dies.

'But before he dies, many times does he sit by my fire and make talk of the strange things he has seen. And Bidarshik, who is my son, sits by the fire and listens; and his eyes are very wide and large because of the things he hears. One night, after Yamikan has gone home, Bidarshik stands up, so, very tall, and he strikes his chest with his fist, and says, "When I am a man, I shall journey in far places, even to the land where there is no snow, and see things for myself."'

'Always did Bidarshik journey in far places,' Zilla interrupted proudly.

'It be true,' Ebbits assented gravely. 'And always did he return to sit by the fire and hunger for yet other and unknown far places.'

'And always did he remember the salt lake as big as the sky and the country under the sun where there is no snow,' quoth Zilla.

'And always did he say, "When I have the full strength of a man, I will go and see for myself if the talk of Yamikan be true talk,"' said Ebbits.

'But there was no way to go to the white man's country,' said Zilla.

'Did he not go down to the salt lake that is big as the sky?' Ebbits demanded.

'And there was no way for him across the salt lake,' said Zilla.

'Save in the white man's fire-boat which is of iron and is bigger than twenty steamboats on the Yukon,' said Ebbits. He scowled at Zilla, whose withered lips were again writhing into speech, and compelled her to silence. 'But the white man would not let him cross the salt lake in the fire-boat, and he returned to sit by the fire and hunger for the country under the sun where there is no snow.'

'Yet on the salt lake had he seen the fire-boat of iron that did not sink,' cried out Zilla the irrepressible.

'Ay,' said Ebbits, 'and he saw that Yamikan had made true talk of the things he had seen. But there was no way for Bidarshik to journey to the white man's land under the sun, and he grew sick and weary like an old man and moved not away from the fire. No longer did he go forth to kill meat—'

'And no longer did he eat the meat placed before him,' Zilla broke in. 'He would shake his head and say, "Only do I care to eat the grub of the white man and grow fat after the manner of Yamikan."'

'And he did not eat the meat,' Ebbits went on. 'And the sickness of Bidarshik grew into a great sickness until I thought he would die. It was not a sickness of the body, but of the head. It was a sickness of desire. I, Ebbits, who am his father, make a great think. I have no more sons and I do not want Bidarshik to die. It is a head-sickness, and there is but one way to make it well. Bidarshik must journey across the lake as large as the sky to the land where there is no snow,

else will he die. I make a very great think, and then I see the
way for Bidarshik to go.

'So, one night when he sits by the fire, very sick, his head
hanging down, I say, "My son, I have learned the way for
you to go to the white man's land." He looks at me, and his
face is glad. "Go," I say, "even as Yamikan went." But
Bidarshik is sick and does not understand. "Go forth," I say,
"and find a white man, and, even as Yamikan, do you kill
that white man. Then will the soldier white men come and
get you, and even as they took Yamikan will they take you
across the salt lake to the white man's land. And then, even
as Yamikan, will you return very fat, your eyes full of the
things you have seen, your head filled with wisdom."

'And Bidarshik stands up very quick, and his hand is reaching out for his gun. "Where do you go?" I ask. "To kill the
white man," he says. And I see that my words have been
good in the ears of Bidarshik and that he will grow well
again. Also do I know that my words have been wise.

'There is a white man come to this village. He does not
seek after gold in the ground, nor after furs in the forest. All
the time does he seek after bugs and flies. He does not eat
the bugs and flies, then why does he seek after them? I do
not know. Only do I know that he is a funny white man.
Also does he seek after the eggs of birds. He does not eat the
eggs. All that is inside he takes out, and only does he keep
the shell. Eggshell is not good to eat. Nor does he eat the
eggshells, but puts them away in soft boxes where they will
not break. He catch many small birds. But he does not eat
the birds. He takes only the skins and puts them away in
boxes. Also does he like bones. Bones are not good to eat.
And this strange white man likes best the bones of long time
ago which he digs out of the ground.

'But he is not a fierce white man, and I know he will die
very easy; so I say to Bidarshik, "My son, there is the white
man for you to kill." And Bidarshik says that my words be
wise. So he goes to a place he knows where are many bones
in the ground. He digs up very many of these bones and
brings them to the strange white man's camp. The white
man is made very glad. His face shines like the sun, and he

smiles with much gladness as he looks at the bones. He bends his head over, so, to look well at the bones, and then Bidarshik strikes him hard on the head, with axe, once, so, and the strange white man kicks and is dead.

'"Now," I say to Bidarshik, "will the white soldier men come and take you away to the land under the sun, where you will eat much and grow fat." Bidarshik is happy. Already has his sickness gone from him, and he sits by the fire and waits for the coming of the white soldier men.

'How was I to know the way of the white man is never twice the same?' the old man demanded, whirling upon me fiercely. 'How was I to know that what the white man does yesterday he will not do to-day, and that what he does to-day he will not do to-morrow?' Ebbits shook his head sadly. 'There is no understanding the white man. Yesterday he takes Yamikan to the land under the sun and makes him fat with much grub. To-day he takes Bidarshik and—what does he do with Bidarshik? Let me tell you what he does with Bidarshik.

'I, Ebbits, his father, will tell you. He takes Bidarshik to Cambell Fort, and he ties a rope around his neck, so, and, when his feet are no more on the ground, he dies.'

'Ai! ai!' wailed Zilla. 'And never does he cross the lake large as the sky, nor see the land under the sun where there is no snow.'

'Wherefore,' old Ebbits said with grave dignity, 'there be no one to hunt meat for me in my old age, and I sit hungry by my fire and tell my story to the White Man who has given me grub, and strong tea, and tobacco for my pipe.'

'Because of the lying and very miserable white people,' Zilla proclaimed shrilly.

'Nay,' answered the old man with gentle positiveness. 'Because of the way of the white man, which is without understanding and never twice the same.'

FINIS*

It was the last of Morganson's bacon. In all his life he had never pampered his stomach. In fact, his stomach had been a sort of negligible quantity that bothered him little, and about which he thought less. But now, in the long absence of wonted delights, the keen yearning of his stomach was tickled hugely by the sharp, salty bacon.

His face had a wistful, hungry expression. The cheeks were hollow, and the skin seemed stretched a trifle tightly across the cheek-bones. His pale blue eyes were troubled. There was that in them that showed the haunting imminence of something terrible. Doubt was in them, and anxiety and foreboding. The thin lips were thinner than they were made to be, and they seemed to hunger towards the polished frying-pan.

He set back and drew forth a pipe. He looked into it with sharp scrutiny, and tapped it emptily on his open palm. He turned the hair-seal tobacco pouch inside out and dusted the lining, treasuring carefully each flake and mite of tobacco that his efforts gleaned. The result was scarce a thimbleful. He searched in his pockets, and brought forward, between thumb and forefinger, tiny pinches of rubbish. Here and there in this rubbish were crumbs of tobacco. These he segregated with microscopic care, though he occasionally permitted small particles of foreign substance to accompany the crumbs to the hoard in his palm. He even deliberately added small, semi-hard woolly fluffs, that had come originally from the coat lining, and that had lain for long months in the bottoms of the pockets.

At the end of fifteen minutes he had the pipe part filled. He lighted it from the camp fire, and sat forward on the blankets, toasting his moccasined feet and smoking parsimoniously. When the pipe was finished he sat on, brooding into the dying flame of the fire. Slowly the worry went out of his eyes and resolve came in. Out of the chaos of his fortunes he had finally achieved a way. But it was not a

pretty way. His face had become stern and wolfish, and the
thin lips were drawn very tightly.

With resolve came action. He pulled himself stiffly to his
feet and proceeded to break camp. He packed the rolled
blankets, the frying-pan, rifle, and axe on the sled, and passed
a lashing around the load. Then he warmed his hands at the
fire and pulled on his mittens. He was foot-sore, and limped
noticeably as he took his place at the head of the sled. When
he put the looped haul-rope over his shoulder, and leant his
weight against it to start the sled, he winced. His flesh was
galled by many days of contact with the haul-rope.

The trail led along the frozen breast of the Yukon. At the
end of four hours he came around a bend and entered the
town of Minto. It was perched on top of a high earth bank
in the midst of a clearing, and consisted of a road house, a
saloon, and several cabins. He left his sled at the door and
entered the saloon.

'Enough for a drink?' he asked, laying an apparently empty
gold sack upon the bar.

The barkeeper looked sharply at it and him, then set out
a bottle and a glass.

'Never mind the dust,' he said.

'Go on and take it,' Morganson insisted.

The barkeeper held the sack mouth downward over the
scales and shook it, and a few flakes of gold dust fell out.
Morganson took the sack from him, turned it inside out,
and dusted it carefully.

'I thought there was half-a-dollar in it,' he said.

'Not quite,' answered the other, 'but near enough. I'll get
it back with the down weight on the next comer.'

Morganson shyly poured the whisky into the glass, partly
filling it.

'Go on, make it a man's drink,' the barkeeper encouraged.

Morganson tilted the bottle and filled the glass to the
brim. He drank the liquor slowly, pleasuring in the fire of it
that bit his tongue, sank hotly down his throat, and with
warm, gentle caresses permeated his stomach.

'Scurvy, eh?' the barkeeper asked.

'A touch of it,' he answered. 'But I haven't begun to swell

yet. Maybe I can get to Dyea and fresh vegetables, and beat it out.'

'Kind of all in, I'd say,' the other laughed sympathetically. 'No dogs, no money, and the scurvy. I'd try spruce tea if I was you.'

At the end of half-an-hour, Morganson said good-bye and left the saloon. He put his galled shoulder to the haul-rope and took the river-trail south. An hour later he halted. An inviting swale left the river and led off to the right at an acute angle. He left his sled and limped up the swale for half a mile. Between him and the river was three hundred yards of flat ground covered with cottonwoods. He crossed the cottonwoods to the bank of the Yukon. The trail went by just beneath, but he did not descend to it. South toward Selkirk he could see the trail widen its sunken length through the snow for over a mile. But to the north, in the direction of Minto, a tree-covered out-jut in the bank a quarter of a mile away screened the trail from him.

He seemed satisfied with the view and returned to the sled the way he had come. He put the haul-rope over his shoulder and dragged the sled up the swale. The snow was unpacked and soft, and it was hard work. The runners clogged and stuck, and he was panting severely ere he had covered the half-mile. Night had come on by the time he had pitched his small tent, set up the sheet-iron stove, and chopped a supply of firewood. He had no candles, and contented himself with a pot of tea before crawling into his blankets.

In the morning, as soon as he got up, he drew on his mittens, pulled the flaps of his cap down over his ears, and crossed through the cottonwoods to the Yukon. He took his rifle with him. As before, he did not descend the bank. He watched the empty trail for an hour, beating his hands and stamping his feet to keep up the circulation, then returned to the tent for breakfast. There was little tea left in the canister —half a dozen drawings at most; but so meagre a pinch did he put in the teapot that he bade fair to extend the lifetime of the tea indefinitely. His entire food supply consisted of half-a-sack of flour and a part-full can of baking powder. He made biscuits, and ate them slowly, chewing each mouthful

with infinite relish. When he had had three he called a halt.
He debated a while, reached for another biscuit, then hesitated. He turned to the part sack of flour, lifted it, and
judged its weight.

'I'm good for a couple of weeks,' he spoke aloud.

'Maybe three,' he added, as he put the biscuits away.

Again he drew on his mittens, pulled down his ear-flaps,
took the rifle, and went out to his station on the river bank.
He crouched in the snow, himself unseen, and watched.
After a few minutes of inaction, the frost began to bite in,
and he rested the rifle across his knees and beat his hands
back and forth. Then the sting in his feet became intolerable,
and he stepped back from the bank and tramped heavily up
and down among the trees. But he did not tramp long at a
time. Every several minutes he came to the edge of the bank
and peered up and down the trail, as though by sheer will
he could materialise the form of a man upon it. The short
morning passed, though it had seemed century-long to him,
and the trail remained empty.

It was easier in the afternoon, watching by the bank. The
temperature rose, and soon the snow began to fall—dry and
fine and crystalline. There was no wind, and it fell straight
down, in quiet monotony. He crouched with eyes closed, his
head upon his knees, keeping his watch upon the trail with
his ears. But no whining of dogs, churning of sleds, nor cries
of drivers broke the silence. With twilight he returned to the
tent, cut a supply of firewood, ate two biscuits, and crawled
into his blankets. He slept restlessly, tossing about and groan-
ing; and at midnight he got up and ate another biscuit.

Each day grew colder. Four biscuits could not keep up the
heat of his body, despite the quantities of hot spruce tea he
drank, and he increased his allowance, morning and evening,
to three biscuits. In the middle of the day he ate nothing,
contenting himself with several cups of excessively weak real
tea. This programme became routine. In the morning three
biscuits, at noon real tea, and at night three biscuits. In
between he drank spruce tea for his scurvy. He caught himself making larger biscuits, and after a severe struggle with
himself went back to the old size.

On the fifth day the trail returned to life. To the south a dark object appeared, and grew larger. Morganson became alert. He worked his rifle, ejecting a loaded cartridge from the chamber, by the same action replacing it with another, and returning the ejected cartridge into the magazine. He lowered the trigger to half-cock, and drew on his mitten to keep the trigger-hand warm. As the dark object came nearer he made it out to be a man, without dogs or sled, travelling light. He grew nervous, cocked the trigger, then put it back to half-cock again. The man developed into an Indian, and Morganson, with a sigh of disappointment, dropped the rifle across his knees. The Indian went on past and disappeared towards Minto behind the out-jutting clump of trees.

But Morganson conceived an idea. He changed his crouching spot to a place where cottonwood limbs projected on either side of him. Into these with his axe he chopped two broad notches. Then in one of the notches he rested the barrel of his rifle and glanced along the sights. He covered the trail thoroughly in that direction. He turned about, rested the rifle in the other notch, and, looking along the sights, swept the trail to the clump of trees behind which it disappeared.

He never descended to the trail. A man travelling the trail could have no knowledge of his lurking presence on the bank above. The snow surface was unbroken. There was no place where his tracks left the main trail.

As the nights grew longer, his periods of daylight watching of the trail grew shorter. Once a sled went by with jingling bells in the darkness, and with sullen resentment he chewed his biscuits and listened to the sounds. Chance conspired against him. Faithfully he had watched the trail for ten days, suffering from the cold all the prolonged torment of the damned, and nothing had happened. Only an Indian, travelling light, had passed in. Now, in the night, when it was impossible for him to watch, men and dogs and a sled loaded with life, passed out, bound south to the sea and the sun and civilisation.

So it was that he conceived of the sled for which he waited. It was loaded with life, his life. His life was fading, fainting, gasping away in the tent in the snow. He was weak from lack of food, and could not travel of himself. But on the sled for which he waited were dogs that would drag him, food that would fan up the flame of his life, money that would furnish sea and sun and civilisation. Sea and sun and civilisation became terms interchangeable with life, his life, and they were loaded there on the sled for which he waited. The idea became an obsession, and he grew to think of himself as the rightful and deprived owner of the sled-load of life.

His flour was running short, and he went back to two biscuits in the morning and two biscuits at night. Because of this his weakness increased and the cold bit in more savagely, and day by day he watched by the dead trail that would not live for him. At last the scurvy entered upon its next stage. The skin was unable longer to cast off the impurity of the blood, and the result was that the body began to swell. His ankles grew puffy, and the ache in them kept him awake long hours at night. Next, the swelling jumped to his knees, and the sum of his pain was more than doubled.

Then there came a cold snap. The temperature went down and down—forty, fifty, sixty degrees below zero. He had no thermometer, but this he knew by the signs and natural phenomena understood by all men in that country—the crackling of water thrown on the snow, the swift sharpness of the bite of the frost, and the rapidity with which his breath froze and coated the canvas walls and roof of the tent. Vainly he fought the cold and strove to maintain his watch on the bank. In his weak condition he was an easy prey, and the frost sank its teeth deep into him before he fled away to the tent and crouched by the fire. His nose and cheeks were frozen and turned black, and his left thumb had frozen inside the mitten. He concluded that he would escape with the loss of the first joint.

Then it was, beaten into the tent by the frost, that the trail, with monstrous irony, suddenly teemed with life. Three sleds went by the first day, and two the second. Once, during each day, he fought his way out to the bank only to succumb and retreat, and each of the two times, within half-an-hour after he retreated, a sled went by.

The cold snap broke, and he was able to remain by the bank once more, and the trail died again. For a week he crouched and watched, and never life stirred along it, not a soul passed in or out. He had cut down to one biscuit night and morning, and somehow he did not seem to notice it. Sometimes he marvelled at the way life remained in him. He never would have thought it possible to endure so much.

When the trail fluttered anew with life it was life with which he could not cope. A detachment of the North-West police went by, a score of them, with many sleds and dogs; and he cowered down on the bank above, and they were unaware of the menace of death that lurked in the form of a dying man beside the trail.

His frozen thumb gave him a great deal of trouble. While watching by the bank he got into the habit of taking his mitten off and thrusting the hand inside his shirt so as to rest the thumb in the warmth of his arm-pit. A mail carrier came over the trail, and Morganson let him pass. A mail carrier was an important person, and was sure to be missed immediately.

On the first day after his last flour had gone it snowed. It was always warm when the snow fell, and he sat out the whole eight hours of daylight on the bank, without movement, terribly hungry and terribly patient, for all the world like a monstrous spider waiting for its prey. But the prey did not come, and he hobbled back to the tent through the darkness, drank quarts of spruce tea and hot water, and went to bed.

The next morning circumstance eased its grip on him. As he started to come out of the tent he saw a huge bull-moose crossing the swale some four hundred yards away. Morganson felt a surge and bound of the blood in him, and then went unaccountably weak. A nausea overpowered him, and he was compelled to sit down a moment to recover. Then he reached for his rifle and took careful aim. The first shot was a hit: he knew it; but the moose turned and broke for the wooded hillside that came down to the swale. Morganson pumped bullets wildly among the trees and brush at the fleeing animal, until it dawned upon him that he was exhausting the ammunition he needed for the sled-load of life for which he waited.

He stopped shooting, and watched. He noted the direction of the animal's flight, and, high up on the hillside in an opening among the trees, saw the trunk of a fallen pine. Continuing the moose's flight in his mind he saw that it must pass the trunk. He resolved on one more shot, and in the empty air above the trunk he aimed and steadied his wavering rifle. The animal sprang into his field of vision, with lifted fore-legs as it took the leap. He pulled the trigger. With the explosion the moose seemed to somersault in the air. It crashed down to earth in the snow beyond and flurried the snow into dust.

Morganson dashed up the hillside—at least he started to dash up. The next he knew he was coming out of a faint and dragging himself to his feet. He went up more slowly, pausing from time to time to breathe and to steady his reeling senses. At last he crawled over the trunk. The moose lay before him. He sat down heavily upon the carcase and laughed. He buried his face in his mittened hands and laughed some more.

He shook the hysteria from him. He drew his hunting knife and worked as rapidly as his injured thumb and weakness would permit him. He did not stop to skin the moose, but quartered it with its hide on. It was a Klondike of meat.

When he had finished he selected a piece of meat weighing a hundred pounds, and started to drag it down to the tent. But the snow was soft, and it was too much for him. He exchanged it for a twenty-pound piece, and, with many pauses to rest, succeeded in getting it to the tent. He fried some of the meat, but ate sparingly. Then, and automatically, he went out to his crouching place on the bank. There were sled-tracks in the fresh snow on the trail. The sled-load of life had passed by while he had been cutting up the moose.

But he did not mind. He was glad that the sled had not passed before the coming of the moose. The moose had changed his plans. Its meat was worth fifty cents a pound, and he was but little more than three miles from Minto. He need no longer wait for the sled-load of life. The moose was the sled-load of life. He would sell it. He would buy a couple of dogs at Minto, some food and some tobacco, and the dogs would haul him south along the trail to the sea, the sun, and civilisation.

He felt hungry. The dull, monotonous ache of hunger had now become a sharp and insistent pang. He hobbled back to the tent and fried a slice of meat. After that he smoked two whole pipefuls of dried tea leaves. Then he fried another slice of moose. He was aware of an unwonted glow of strength, and went out and chopped some firewood. He followed that up with a slice of meat. Teased on by the food, his hunger grew into an inflammation. It became imperative every little while to fry a slice of meat. He tried smaller slices and found himself frying oftener.

In the middle of the day he thought of the wild animals that might eat his meat, and he climbed the hill, carrying along his axe, the haul rope, and a sled lashing. In his weak state the making of the cache and storing of the meat was an all-afternoon task. He cut young saplings, trimmed them, and tied them together into a tall scaffold. It was not so strong a cache as he would have desired to make, but he had done his best. To hoist the meat to the top was heart-breaking. The larger pieces defied him until he passed the rope over a limb above, and, with one end fast to a piece of meat, put all his weight on the other end.

Once in the tent, he proceeded to indulge in a prolonged and solitary orgy. He did not need friends. His stomach and he were company. Slice after slice and many slices of meat he fried and ate. He ate pounds of the meat. He brewed real tea, and brewed it strong. He brewed the last he had. It did not matter. On the morrow he would be buying tea in Minto. When it seemed he could eat no more, he smoked. He smoked all his stock of dried tea leaves. What of it? On the morrow he would be smoking tobacco. He knocked out his pipe, fried a final slice, and went to bed. He had eaten so much he seemed bursting, yet he got out of his blankets and had just one more mouthful of meat.

In the morning he awoke as from the sleep of death. In

his ears were strange sounds. He did not know where he was, and looked about him stupidly until he caught sight of the frying-pan with the last piece of meat in it, partly eaten. Then he remembered all, and with a quick start turned his attention to the strange sounds. He sprang from the blankets with an oath. His scurvy-ravaged legs gave way under him and he winced with the pain. He proceeded more slowly to put on his moccasins and leave the tent.

From the cache up the hillside arose a confused noise of snapping and snarling, punctuated by occasional short, sharp yelps. He increased his speed at much expense of pain, and cried loudly and threateningly. He saw the wolves hurrying away through the snow and underbrush, many of them, and he saw the scaffold down on the ground. The animals were heavy with the meat they had eaten, and they were content to slink away and leave the wreckage.

The way of the disaster was clear to him. The wolves had scented his cache. One of them had leapt from the trunk of the fallen tree to the top of the cache. He could see marks of the brute's paws in the snow that covered the trunk. He had not dreamt a wolf could leap so far. A second had followed the first, and a third and fourth, until the flimsy scaffold had gone down under their weight and movement.

His eyes were hard and savage for a moment as he contemplated the extent of the calamity; then the old look of patience returned into them, and he began to gather together the bones well picked and gnawed. There was marrow in them, he knew; and also, here and there, as he sifted the snow, he found scraps of meat that had escaped the maws of the brutes made careless by plenty.

He spent the rest of the morning dragging the wreckage of the moose down the hillside. In addition, he had at least ten pounds left of the chunk of meat he had dragged down the previous day.

'I'm good for weeks yet,' was his comment as he surveyed the heap.

He had learnt how to starve and live. He cleaned his rifle and counted the cartridges that remained to him. There were seven. He loaded the weapon and hobbled out to his crouching-place on the bank. All day he watched the dead trail. He watched all the week, but no life passed over it.

Thanks to the meat he felt stronger, though his scurvy was worse and more painful. He now lived upon soup, drinking endless gallons of the thin product of the boiling of the moose bones. The soup grew thinner and thinner as he cracked the bones and boiled them over and over; but the hot water with the essence of the meat in it was good for him, and he was more vigorous than he had been previous to the shooting of the moose.

It was in the next week that a new factor entered into Morganson's life. He wanted to know the date. It became an obsession. He pondered and calculated, but his conclusions were rarely twice the same. The first thing in the morning and the last thing at night, and all day as well, watching by the trail, he worried about it. He awoke at night and lay awake for hours over the problem. To have known the date would have been of no value to him; but his curiosity grew until it equalled his hunger and his desire to live. Finally it mastered him, and he resolved to go to Minto and find out.

It was dark when he arrived at Minto, but this served him. No one saw him arrive. Besides, he knew he would have moonlight by which to return. He climbed the bank and pushed open the saloon door. The light dazzled him. The source of it was several candles, but he had been living for long in an unlighted tent. As his eyes adjusted themselves, he saw three men sitting around the stove. They were trail-travellers—he knew it at once; and since they had not passed in, they were evidently bound out. They would go by his tent next morning.

The barkeeper emitted a long and marvelling whistle.

'I thought you was dead,' he said.

'Why?' Morganson asked in a faltering voice.

He had become unused to talking, and he was not acquainted with the sound of his own voice. It seemed hoarse and strange.

'You've been dead for more'n two months, now,' the barkeeper explained. 'You left here going south, and you never arrived at Selkirk. Where have you been?'

'Chopping wood for the steamboat company,' Morganson lied unsteadily.

He was still trying to become acquainted with his own voice. He hobbled across the floor and leant against the bar. He knew he must lie consistently; and while he maintained an appearance of careless indifference, his heart was beating and pounding furiously and irregularly, and he could not help looking hungrily at the three men by the stove. They were the possessors of life—his life.

'But where in hell you been keeping yourself all this time?' the barkeeper demanded.

'I located across the river,' he answered. 'I've got a mighty big stack of wood chopped.'

The barkeeper nodded. His face beamed with understanding.

'I heard sounds of chopping several times,' he said. 'So that was you, eh? Have a drink?'

Morganson clutched the bar tightly. A drink! He could have thrown his arms around the man's legs and kissed his feet. He tried vainly to utter his acceptance; but the barkeeper had not waited and was already passing out the bottle.

'But what did you do for grub?' the latter asked. 'You don't look as if you could chop wood to keep yourself warm. You look terribly bad, friend.'

Morganson yearned towards the delayed bottle and gulped dryly.

'I did the chopping before the scurvy got bad,' he said. 'Then I got a moose right at the start. I've been living high all right. It's the scurvy that's run me down.'

He filled the glass, and added, 'But the spruce tea's knocking it, I think.'

'Have another,' the barkeeper said.

The action of the two glasses of whisky on Morganson's empty stomach and weak condition was rapid. The next he knew he was sitting by the stove on a box, and it seemed as though ages had passed. A tall, broad-shouldered, black-whiskered man was paying for drinks. Morganson's swimming eyes saw him drawing a greenback from a fat roll, and Morganson's swimming eyes cleared on the instant. They were hundred-dollar bills. It was life! His life! He felt an almost irresistible impulse to snatch the money and dash madly out into the night.

The black-whiskered man and one of his companions arose.

'Come on, Oleson,' the former said to the third one of the party, a fair-haired, ruddy-faced giant.

Oleson came to his feet, yawning and stretching.

'What are you going to bed so soon for?' the barkeeper asked plaintively. 'It's early yet.'

'Got to make Selkirk to-morrow,' said he of the black whiskers.

'On Christmas Day!' the barkeeper cried.

'The better the day the better the deed,' the other laughed.

As the three men passed out of the door it came dimly to Morganson that it was Christmas Eve. That was the date. That was what he had come to Minto for. But it was over-shadowed now by the three men themselves, and the fat roll of hundred-dollar bills.

The door slammed.

'That's Jack Thompson,' the barkeeper said. 'Made two millions on Bonanza and Sulphur, and got more coming. I'm going to bed. Have another drink first.'

Morganson hesitated.

'A Christmas drink,' the other urged. 'It's all right. I'll get it back when you sell your wood.'

Morganson mastered his drunkenness long enough to swallow the whisky, say good night, and get out on the trail. It was moonlight, and he hobbled along through the bright, silvery quiet, with a vision of life before him that took the form of a roll of hundred-dollar bills.

He awoke. It was dark, and he was in his blankets. He had gone to bed in his moccasins and mittens, with the flaps of his cap pulled down over his ears. He got up as quickly as his crippled condition would permit, and built the fire and boiled some water. As he put the spruce-twigs into the tea-pot he noted the first glimmer of the pale morning light. He caught up his rifle and hobbled in a panic out to the bank. As he crouched and waited, it came to him that he had forgotten to drink his spruce tea. The only other thought in his mind was the possibility of John Thompson changing his mind and not travelling Christmas Day.

Dawn broke and merged into day. It was cold and clear. Sixty below zero was Morganson's estimate of the frost. Not a breath stirred the chill Arctic quiet. He sat up suddenly, his muscular tensity increasing the hurt of the scurvy. He had heard the far sound of a man's voice and the faint whining of dogs. He began beating his hands back and forth against his sides. It was a serious matter to bare the trigger hand to sixty degrees below zero, and against that time he needed to develop all the warmth of which his flesh was capable.

They came into view around the outjutting clump of trees. To the fore was the third man whose name he had not learnt. Then came eight dogs drawing the sled. At the front of the sled, guiding it by the gee-pole, walked John Thompson. The rear was brought up by Oleson, the Swede. He was certainly a fine man, Morganson thought, as he looked at the bulk of him in his squirrel-skin *parka*. The men and dogs were silhouetted sharply against the white of the landscape. They had the seeming of two dimension, cardboard figures that worked mechanically.

Morganson rested his cocked rifle in the notch in the tree. He became abruptly aware that his fingers were cold, and discovered that his right hand was bare. He did not know that he had taken off the mitten. He slipped it on again hastily. The men and dogs drew closer, and he could see their breaths spouting into visibility in the cold air. When the first man was fifty yards away, Morganson slipped the mitten from his right hand. He placed the first finger on the trigger and aimed low. When he fired the first man whirled half around and went down on the trail.

In the instant of surprise, Morganson pulled the trigger on John Thompson—too low, for the latter staggered and sat down suddenly on the sled. Morganson raised his aim and fired again. John Thompson sank down backward along the top of the loaded sled.

Morganson turned his attention to Oleson. At the same time that he noted the latter running away towards Minto he noted that the dogs, coming to where the first man's body blocked the trail, had halted. Morganson fired at the fleeing man and missed, and Oleson swerved. He continued to swerve back and forth, while Morganson fired twice in rapid succession and missed both shots. Morganson stopped himself just as he was pulling the trigger again. He had fired six shots. Only one more cartridge remained, and it was in the chamber. It was imperative that he should not miss his last shot.

He held his fire and desperately studied Oleson's flight. The giant was grotesquely curving and twisting and running at top speed along the trail, the tail of his *parka* flapping smartly behind. Morganson trained his rifle on the man and with a swaying action followed his erratic flight. Morganson's finger was getting numb. He could scarcely feel the trigger. 'God help me,' he breathed a prayer aloud, and pulled the trigger. The running man pitched forward on his face, rebounded from the hard trail, and slid along, rolling over and over. He threshed for a moment with his arms and then lay quiet.

Morganson dropped his rifle (worthless now that the last cartridge was gone) and slid down the bank through the soft snow. Now that he had sprung the trap, concealment of his lurking-place was no longer necessary. He hobbled along the trail to the sled, his fingers making involuntary gripping and clutching movements inside the mittens.

The snarling of the dogs halted him. The leader, a heavy dog, half Newfoundland and half Hudson Bay, stood over the body of the man that lay on the trail, and menaced Morganson with bristling hair and bared fangs. The other seven dogs of the team were likewise bristling and snarling. Morganson approached tentatively, and the team surged towards him. He stopped again and talked to the animals, threatening and cajoling by turns. He noticed the face of the man under the leader's feet, and was surprised at how quickly it had turned white with the ebb of life and the entrance of the frost. John Thompson lay back along the top of the loaded sled, his head sunk in a space between two sacks and his chin tilted upwards, so that all Morganson could see was the black beard pointing skyward.

Finding it impossible to face the dogs Morganson stepped

off the trail into the deep snow and floundered in a wide circle to the rear of the sled. Under the initiative of the leader, the team swung around in its tangled harness. Because of his crippled condition, Morganson could move only slowly. He saw the animals circling around on him and tried to retreat. He almost made it, but the big leader, with a savage lunge, sank its teeth into the calf of his leg. The flesh was slashed and torn, but Morganson managed to drag himself clear.

He cursed the brutes fiercely, but could not cow them. They replied with neck-bristling and snarling, and with quick lunges against their breastbands. He remembered Oleson, and turned his back upon them and went along the trail. He scarcely took notice of his lacerated leg. It was bleeding freely; the main artery had been torn, but he did not know it.

Especially remarkable to Morganson was the extreme pallor of the Swede, who the preceding night had been so ruddy-faced. Now his face was like white marble. What with his fair hair and lashes he looked like a carved statue rather than something that had been a man a few minutes before. Morganson pulled off his mittens and searched the body. There was no money-belt around the waist next to the skin, nor did he find a gold-sack. In a breast pocket he lit on a small wallet. With fingers that swiftly went numb with the frost, he hurried through the contents of the wallet. There were letters with foreign stamps and postmarks on them, and several receipts and memorandum accounts, and a letter of credit for eight hundred dollars. That was all. There was no money.

He made a movement to start back toward the sled, but found his foot rooted to the trail. He glanced down and saw that he stood in a fresh deposit of frozen red. There was red ice on his torn pants leg and on the moccasin beneath. With a quick effort he broke the frozen clutch of his blood and hobbled along the trail to the sled. The big leader that had bitten him began snarling and lunging, and was followed in this conduct by the whole team.

Morganson wept weakly for a space, and weakly swayed from one side to the other. Then he brushed away the frozen

tears that gemmed his lashes. It was a joke. Malicious chance
was having its laugh at him. Even John Thompson, with his
heaven-aspiring whiskers, was laughing at him.

He prowled around the sled demented, at times weeping
and pleading with the brutes for his life there on the sled, at
other times raging impotently against them. Then calmness
came upon him. He had been making a fool of himself. All
he had to do was to go to the tent, get the axe, and return
and brain the dogs. He'd show them.

In order to get to the tent he had to go wide of the sled
and the savage animals. He stepped off the trail into the soft
snow. Then he felt suddenly giddy and stood still. He was
afraid to go on for fear he would fall down. He stood still for
a long time, balancing himself on his crippled legs that were
trembling violently from weakness. He looked down and saw
the snow reddening at his feet. The blood flowed freely as
ever. He had not thought the bite was so severe. He controlled his giddiness and stooped to examine the wound.
The snow seemed rushing up to meet him, and he recoiled
from it as from a blow. He had a panic fear that he might
fall down, and after a struggle he managed to stand upright
again. He was afraid of that snow that had rushed up to him.

Then the white glimmer turned black, and the next he
knew he was awakening in the snow where he had fallen. He
was no longer giddy. The cobwebs were gone. But he could
not get up. There was no strength in his limbs. His body
seemed lifeless. By a desperate effort he managed to roll over
on his side. In this position he caught a glimpse of the sled
and of John Thompson's black beard pointing skyward. Also
he saw the lead dog licking the face of the man who lay on
the trail. Morganson watched curiously. The dog was nervous and eager. Sometimes it uttered short, sharp yelps, as
though to arouse the man, and surveyed him with ears cocked
forward and wagging tail. At last it sat down, pointed its
nose upward, and began to howl. Soon all the team was
howling.

Now that he was down, Morganson was no longer afraid.
He had a vision of himself being found dead in the snow,
and for a while he wept in self-pity. But he was not afraid.

The struggle had gone out of him. When he tried to open his eyes he found that the wet tears had frozen them shut. He did not try to brush the ice away. It did not matter. He had not dreamed death was so easy. He was even angry that he had struggled and suffered through so many weary weeks. He had been bullied and cheated by the fear of death. Death did not hurt. Every torment he had endured had been a torment of life. Life had defamed death. It was a cruel thing.

But his anger passed. The lies and frauds of life were of no consequence now that he was coming to his own. He became aware of drowsiness, and felt a sweet sleep stealing upon him, balmy with promises of easement and rest. He heard faintly the howling of the dogs, and had a fleeting thought that in the mastering of his flesh the frost no longer bit. Then the light and the thought ceased to pulse beneath the tear-gemmed eyelids, and with a tired sigh of comfort he sank into sleep.

LIKE ARGUS OF THE
ANCIENT TIMES

It was the summer of 1897, and there was trouble in the Tarwater family. Grandfather Tarwater,* after remaining properly subdued and crushed for a quiet decade, had broken out again. This time it was the Klondike fever. His first and one unvarying symptom of such attacks was song. One Chant only he raised, though he remembered no more than the first stanza and but three lines of that. And the family knew his feet were itching and his brain was tingling with the old madness, when he lifted his hoarse-cracked voice, now falsetto-cracked, in:

> Like Argus* of the ancient times,
>   We leave this modern Greece,
> Tum-tum, tum-tum, tum, tum, tum-tum,
>   To shear the Golden Fleece.

Ten years earlier he had lifted the chant, sung to the air of the 'Doxology,' when afflicted with the fever to go goldmining in Patagonia.* The multitudinous family had sat upon him, but had had a hard time doing it. When all else had failed to shake his resolution, they had applied lawyers to him, with the threat of getting out guardianship papers and of confining him in the state asylum for the insane—which was reasonable for a man who had, a quarter of a century before, speculated away all but ten meager acres of a California principality, and who had displayed no better business acumen ever since.

The application of lawyers to John Tarwater was like the application of a mustard plaster. For, in his judgment, they were the gentry, more than any other, who had skinned him out of the broad Tarwater acres. So, at the time of his Patagonian fever, the very thought of so drastic a remedy was sufficient to cure him. He quickly demonstrated he was not crazy by shaking the fever from him and agreeing not to go to Patagonia.

Next, he demonstrated how crazy he really was, by deeding over to his family, unsolicited, the ten acres on Tarwater Flat, the house, barn, out-buildings, and water-rights. Also did he turn over the eight hundred dollars in bank that was the long-saved salvage of his wrecked fortune. But for this the family found no cause for committal to the asylum, since such committal would necessarily invalidate what he had done.

'Grandfather is sure peeved,' said Mary, his oldest daughter, herself a grandmother, when her father quit smoking.

All he had retained for himself was a span of old horses, a mountain buckboard, and his one room in the crowded house. Further, having affirmed that he would be beholden to none of them, he got the contract to carry the United States mail, twice a week, from Kelterville up over Tarwater Mountain to Old Almaden—which was a sporadically worked quicksilver mine in the upland cattle country. With his old horses it took all his time to make the two weekly round trips. And for ten years, rain or shine, he had never missed a trip. Nor had he failed once to pay his week's board into Mary's hand. This board he had insisted on, in the convalescence from his Patagonian fever, and he had paid it strictly though he had given up tobacco in order to be able to do it.

'Huh!' he confided to the ruined water wheel of the old Tarwater Mill, which he had built from the standing timber and which had ground wheat for the first settlers. 'Huh! They'll never put me in the poor farm so long as I support myself. And without a penny to my name it ain't likely any lawyer fellows'll come snoopin' around after me.'

And yet, precisely because of these highly rational acts, it was held that John Tarwater was mildly crazy!

The first time he had lifted the chant of 'Like Argus of the Ancient Times,' had been in 1849, when, twenty-two years of age, violently attacked by the California fever, he had sold two hundred and forty Michigan acres, forty of it cleared, for the price of four yoke of oxen and a wagon, and had started across the Plains.

'And we turned off at Fort Hall, where the Oregon emigration went north'ard, and swung south for Californy,' was his way of concluding the narrative of that arduous journey. 'And Bill Ping and me used to rope grizzlies out of the under-brush of Cache Slough in the Sacramento Valley.'

Years of freighting and mining had followed, and, with a stake gleaned from the Merced placers, he satisfied the land-hunger of his race and time by settling in Sonoma County.*

During the ten years of carrying the mail across Tarwater Township, up Tarwater Valley, and over Tarwater Moun-tain, most all of which land had once been his, he had spent his time dreaming of winning back that land before he died. And now, his huge gaunt form more erect than it had been for years, with a glinting of blue fires in his small and close-set eyes, he was lifting his ancient chant again.

'There he goes now—listen to him,' said William Tarwater.

'Nobody at home,' laughed Harris Topping, day laborer, husband of Annie Tarwater, and father of her nine children.

The kitchen door opened to admit the old man, returning from feeding his horses. The song had ceased from his lips; but Mary was irritable from a burnt hand and a grandchild whose stomach refused to digest properly diluted cow's milk.

'Now there ain't no use you carryin' on that way, father,' she tackled him. 'The time's past for you to cut and run for a place like the Klondike, and singing won't buy you nothing.'

'Just the same,' he answered quietly. 'I bet I could go to that Klondike place and pick up enough gold to buy back the Tarwater lands.'

'Old fool!' Annie contributed.

'You couldn't buy them back for less'n three hundred thou-sand and then some,' was William's effort at squelching him.

'Then I could pick up three hundred thousand, and then some, if I was only there,' the old man retorted placidly.

'Thank God, you can't walk there, or you'd be startin', I know,' Mary cried. 'Ocean travel costs money.'

'I used to have money,' her father said humbly.

'Well, you ain't got any now—so forget it,' William advised. 'Them times is past, like roping bear with Bill Ping. There ain't no more bear.'

'Just the same—'

But Mary cut him off. Seizing the day's paper from the kitchen table, she flourished it savagely under her aged progenitor's nose.

'What do those Klondikers say? There it is in cold print. Only the young and robust can stand the Klondike. It's worse than the north pole. And they've left their dead a-plenty there themselves. Look at their pictures. You're forty years older'n the oldest of them.'

John Tarwater did look, but his eyes strayed to other photographs on the highly sensational front page.

'And look at the photys of them nuggets they brought down,' he said. 'I know gold. Didn't I gopher twenty thousand outa the Merced? And wouldn't it a-ben a hundred thousand if that cloudburst hadn't busted my wing-dam? Now if I was only in the Klondike—'

'Crazy as a loon,' William sneered in open aside to the rest.

'A nice way to talk to your father,' Old Man Tarwater censured mildly. 'My father'd have walloped the tar out of me with a single-tree if I'd spoke to him that way.'

'But you *are* crazy, father—' William began.

'Reckon you're right, son. And that's where my father wasn't crazy. He'd a-done it.'

'The old man's been reading some of them magazine articles about men who succeeded after forty,' Annie gibed.

'And why not, daughter?' he asked. 'And why can't a man succeed after he's seventy? I was only seventy this year. And mebbe I could succeed if only I could get to the Klondike—'

'Which you ain't going to get to,' Mary shut him off.

'Oh, well, then,' he sighed, 'seein's I ain't, I might just as well go to bed.'

He stood up, tall, gaunt, great-boned and gnarled, a splendid ruin of a man. His ragged hair and whiskers were not gray but snowy white, as were the tufts of hair that stood out on the backs of his huge bony fingers. He moved toward the door, opened it, sighed, and paused with a backward look.

'Just the same,' he murmured plaintively, 'the bottoms of my feet is itching something terrible.'

Long before the family stirred next morning, his horses fed and harnessed by lantern light, breakfast cooked and eaten by lamplight, Old Man Tarwater was off and away down Tarwater Valley on the road to Kelterville. Two things were unusual about this usual trip which he had made a thousand and forty times since taking the mail contract. He did not drive to Kelterville, but turned off on the main road south to Santa Rosa. Even more remarkable than this was the paper-wrapped parcel between his feet. It contained his one decent black suit, which Mary had been long reluctant to see him wear any more, not because it was shabby, but because, as he guessed what was at the back of her mind, it was decent enough to bury him in.

And at Santa Rosa, in a second-hand clothes shop, he sold the suit outright for two dollars and a half. From the same obliging shopman he received four dollars for the wedding ring of his long-dead wife. The span of horses and the wagon he disposed of for seventy-five dollars, although twenty-five was all he received down in cash. Chancing to meet Alton Granger on the street, to whom never before had he mentioned the ten dollars loaned him in '74, he reminded Alton Granger of the little affair, and was promptly paid. Also, of all unbelievable men to be in funds, he so found the town drunkard for whom he had bought many a drink in the old and palmy days. And from him John Tarwater borrowed a dollar. Finally, he took the afternoon train to San Francisco.

A dozen days later, carrying a half-empty canvas sack of blankets and old clothes, he landed on the beach of Dyea in the thick of the great Klondike Rush. The beach was screaming bedlam. Ten thousand tons of outfit lay heaped and scattered, and twice ten thousand men struggled with it and clamored about it. Freight, by Indian-back, over Chilcoot to Lake Linderman, had jumped from sixteen to thirty cents a pound, which latter was a rate of six hundred dollars a ton. And the sub-arctic winter gloomed near at hand. All knew it, and all knew that of the twenty thousand of them very few would get across the passes, leaving the rest to winter and wait for the late spring thaw.

Such the beach old John Tarwater stepped upon; and straight across the beach and up the trail toward Chilcoot he headed, cackling his ancient chant, a very Grandfather Argus himself, with no outfit worry in the world, for he did not possess any outfit. That night he slept on the flats, five miles above Dyea, at the head of canoe navigation. Here the Dyea River became a rushing mountain torrent, plunging out of a dark canyon from the glaciers that fed it far above.

And here, early next morning, he beheld a little man weighing no more than a hundred, staggering along a foot-log under all of a hundred pounds of flour strapped on his back. Also, he beheld the little man stumble off the log and fall face-downward in a quiet eddy where the water was two feet deep and proceed quietly to drown. It was no desire of his to take death so easily, but the flour on his back weighed as much as he and would not let him up.

'Thank you, old man,' he said to Tarwater, when the latter had dragged him up into the air and ashore.

While he unlaced his shoes and ran the water out, they had further talk. Next, he fished out a ten-dollar gold-piece and offered it to his rescuer.

Old Tarwater shook his head and shivered, for the ice-water had wet him to his knees.

'But I reckon I wouldn't object to settin' down to a friendly meal with you.'

'Ain't had breakfast?' the little man, who was past forty and who had said his name was Anson, queried with a glance frankly curious.

'Nary bite,' John Tarwater answered.

'Where's your outfit? Ahead?'

'Nary outfit.'

'Expect to buy your grub on the Inside?'

'Nary a dollar to buy it with, friend. Which ain't so important as a warm bite of breakfast right now.'

In Anson's camp, a quarter of a mile on, Tarwater found a slender, red-whiskered young man of thirty cursing over a fire of wet willow wood. Introduced as Charles, he transferred his scowl and wrath to Tarwater, who, genially oblivious, devoted himself to the fire, took advantage of the chill morning breeze to create a draught which the other had left stupidly blocked by stones, and soon developed less smoke and more flame. The third member of the party, Bill Wilson, or Big Bill as they called him, came in with a hundred-and-forty-pound pack; and what Tarwater esteemed to be a very rotten breakfast was dished out by Charles. The mush was half cooked and mostly burnt, the bacon was charred carbon, and the coffee was unspeakable.

Immediately the meal was wolfed down, the three partners took their empty packstraps and headed down trail to where the remainder of their outfit lay at the last camp a mile away. And old Tarwater became busy. He washed the dishes, foraged dry wood, mended a broken packstrap, put an edge on the butcher-knife and camp-ax, and repacked the picks and shovels into a more carryable parcel.

What had impressed him during the brief breakfast was the sort of awe in which Anson and Big Bill stood of Charles. Once, during the morning, while Anson took a breathing spell after bringing in another hundred-pound pack, Tarwater delicately hinted his impression.

'You see, it's this way,' Anson said. 'We've divided our leadership. We've all got specialties. Now I'm a carpenter. When we get to Lake Linderman, and the trees are chopped and whipsawed into planks, I'll boss the building of the boat. Big Jim is a logger and miner. So he'll boss getting out the logs and all mining operations. Most of our outfit's ahead. We went broke paying the Indians to pack that much of it to the top of Chilcoot. Our last partner is up there with it, moving it along by himself down the other side. His name's Liverpool, and he's a sailor. So, when the boat's built, he's the boss of the outfit to navigate the lakes and rapids to Klondike.'

'And Charles—this Mr Clayton—what might his specialty be?' Tarwater asked.

'He's the business man. When it comes to business and organization he's boss.'

'Hum,' Tarwater pondered. 'Very lucky to get such a bunch of specialties into one outfit.'

'More than lucky,' Anson agreed. 'It was all accident, too. Each of us started alone. We met on the steamer coming up from San Francisco, and formed the party.—Well, I got to be goin'. Charles is liable to get kicking because I ain't packing my share. Just the same, you can't expect a hundred-pound man to pack as much as a hundred-and-sixty-pounder.'

'Stick around and cook us something for dinner,' Charles, on his next load in and noting the effects of the old man's handiness, told Tarwater.

And Tarwater cooked a dinner that was a dinner, washed the dishes, had real pork and beans for supper, and bread baked in a frying-pan that was so delectable that the three partners nearly foundered themselves on it. Supper dishes washed, he cut shavings and kindling for a quick and certain breakfast fire, showed Anson a trick with foot-gear that was invaluable to any hiker, sang his 'Like Argus of the Ancient Times,' and told them of the great emigration across the Plains in Forty-nine.

'My goodness, the first cheerful and hearty-like camp since we hit the beach,' Big Jim remarked as he knocked out his pipe and began pulling off his shoes for bed.

'Kind of made things easy, boys, eh?' Tarwater queried genially.

All nodded. 'Well, then, I got a proposition, boys. You can take it or leave it, but just listen kindly to it. You're in a hurry to get in before the freeze-up. Half the time is wasted over the cooking by one of you that he might be puttin' in packin' outfit. If I do the cookin' for you, you all'll get on that much faster. Also, the cookin' 'll be better, and that'll make you pack better. And I can pack quite a bit myself in between times, quite a bit, yes, sir, quite a bit.'

Big Bill and Anson were just beginning to nod their heads in agreement, when Charles stopped them.

'What do you expect of us in return?' he demanded of the old man.

'Oh, I leave it up to the boys.'

'That ain't business,' Charles reprimanded sharply. 'You made the proposition. Now finish it.'

'Well, it's this way—'

'You expect us to feed you all winter, eh?' Charles interrupted.

'No, siree, I don't. All I reckon is a passage to Klondike in your boat would be mighty square of you.'

'You haven't an ounce of grub, old man. You'll starve to death when you get there.'

'I've been feedin' some long time pretty successful,' Old Tarwater replied, a whimsical light in his eyes. 'I'm seventy, and ain't starved to death never yet.'

'Will you sign a paper to the effect that you shift for yourself as soon as you get to Dawson?' the business one demanded.

'Oh, sure,' was the response.

Again Charles checked his two partners' expressions of satisfaction with the arrangement.

'One other thing, old man. We're a party of four, and we all have a vote on questions like this. Young Liverpool is ahead with the main outfit. He's got a say so, and he isn't here to say it.'

'What kind of a party might he be?' Tarwater inquired.

'He's a rough-neck sailor, and he's got a quick, bad temper.'

'Some turbulent,' Anson contributed.

'And the way he can cuss is simply God-awful,' Big Jim testified.

'But he's square,' Big Jim added.

Anson nodded heartily to this appraisal.

'Well, boys,' Tarwater summed up, 'I set out for Californy and I got there. And I'm going to get to Klondike. Ain't a thing can stop me, ain't a thing. I'm going to get three hundred thousand outa the ground, too. Ain't a thing can stop me, ain't a thing, because I just naturally need the money. I don't mind a bad temper so long's the boy is square. I'll take my chance, an' I'll work along with you till we catch up with him. Then, if he says no to the proposition, I reckon I'll lose. But somehow I just can't see 'm sayin' no, because that'd mean too close up to freeze-up and too late for me to find another chance like this. And, as I'm sure going to get to Klondike, it's just plumb impossible for him to say no.'

Old John Tarwater became a striking figure on a trail unusually replete with striking figures. With thousands of men, each back-tripping half a ton of outfit, retracing every mile of the trail twenty times, all came to know him and to hail him as 'Father Christmas.' And as he worked ever he raised his chant with his age-falsetto voice. None of the three men he had joined could complain about his work. True, his joints were stiff—he admitted to a trifle of rheumatism. He moved slowly, and seemed to creak and crackle when he moved; but he kept on moving. Last into the blankets at night, he was first out in the morning, so that the other three had hot coffee before their one before-breakfast pack. And, between breakfast and dinner and between dinner and supper, he always managed to back-trip for several packs himself. Sixty pounds was the limit of his burden, however. He could manage seventy-five, but he could not keep it up. Once, he tried ninety, but collapsed on the trail and was seriously shaky for a couple of days afterward.

Work! On a trail where hard-working men learned for the first time what work was, no man worked harder in proportion to his strength than Old Tarwater. Driven desperately on by the near-thrust of winter, and lured madly on by the dream of gold, they worked to their last ounce of strength and fell by the way. Others, when failure made certain, blew out their brains. Some went mad, and still others, under the irk of the man-destroying strain, broke partnerships and dissolved life-time friendships with fellows just as good as themselves and just as strained and mad.

Work! Old Tarwater could shame them all, despite his creaking and crackling and the nasty hacking cough he had developed. Early and late, on trail or in camp beside the trail, he was ever in evidence, ever busy at something, ever responsive to the hail of 'Father Christmas.' Weary back-trippers would rest their packs on a log or rock alongside of where he rested his, and would say: 'Sing us that song of yourn, dad, about Forty-Nine.' And, when he had wheezingly complied, they would arise under their loads, remark that it was real heartening, and hit the forward trail again.

'If ever a man worked his passage and earned it,' Big Jim confided to his two partners, 'that man's our old Skeezicks.'

'You bet,' Anson confirmed. 'He's a valuable addition to the party, and I, for one, ain't at all disagreeable to the notion of making him a regular partner—'

'None of that!' Charles Crayton cut in. 'When we get to Dawson we're quit of him—that's the agreement. We'd only have to bury him if we let him stay on with us. Besides, there's going to be a famine, and every ounce of grub'll count. Remember, we're feeding him out of our own supply all the way in. And if we run short in the pinch next year, you'll know the reason. Steamboats can't get up grub to Dawson till the middle of June, and that's nine months away.'

'Well, you put as much money and outfit in as the rest of us,' Big Bill conceded, 'and you've a say according.'

'And I'm going to have my say,' Charles asserted with increasing irritability. 'And it's lucky for you with your fool sentiments that you've got somebody to think ahead for you, else you'd all starve to death. I tell you that famine's coming. I've been studying the situation. Flour will be two dollars a pound, or ten, and no sellers. You mark my words.'

Across the rubble-covered flats, up the dark canyon to Sheep Camp, past the overhanging and ever-threatening glaciers to the Scales, and from the Scales up the steep pitches of ice-scoured rock where packers climbed with hands and feet, Old Tarwater camp-cooked and packed and sang. He blew across Chilcoot Pass, above timber-line, in the first swirl of autumn snow. Those below, without firewood, on the bitter rim of Crater Lake, heard from the driving obscurity above them a weird voice chanting:

> Like Argus of the ancient times,
>   We leave this modern Greece,
> Tum-tum, tum-tum, tum, tum, tum-tum,
>   To shear the Golden Fleece.

And out of the snow flurries they saw appear a tall, gaunt form, with whiskers of flying white that blended with the storm, bending under a sixty-pound pack of camp dunnage.

'Father Christmas!' was the hail. And then: 'Three rousing cheers for Father Christmas!'

Two miles beyond Crater Lake lay Happy Camp—so named because here was found the uppermost fringe of the timber line, where men might warm themselves by fire again. Scarcely could it be called timber, for it was a dwarf rock-spruce that never raised its loftiest branches higher than a foot above the moss, and that twisted and groveled like a pig-vegetable under the moss. Here, on the trail leading into Happy Camp, in the first sunshine of half a dozen days, Old Tarwater rested his pack against a huge bowlder and caught his breath. Around this bowlder the trail passed, laden men toiling slowly forward and men with empty pack-straps limping rapidly back for fresh loads. Twice Old Tarwater essayed to rise and go on, and each time, warned by his shakiness, sank back to recover more strength. From around the bowlder he heard voices in greeting, recognized Charles Crayton's voice, and realized that at last they had met up with Young Liverpool. Quickly, Charles plunged into business, and Tarwater heard with great distinctness every word of Charles' unflattering description of him and of the proposition to give him passage to Dawson.

'A damn fool proposition,' was Liverpool's judgment, when Charles had concluded. 'An old granddad of seventy! If he's on his last legs, why in hell did you hook up with him? If there's going to be a famine, and it looks like it, we need every ounce of grub for ourselves. We only outfitted for four, not five.'

'It's all right,' Tarwater heard Charles assuring the other. 'Don't get excited. The old codger agreed to leave the final decision to you when we caught up with you. All you've got to do is put your foot down and say no.'

'You mean it's up to me to turn the old one down, after your encouraging him and taking advantage of his work clear from Dyea here?'

'It's a hard trail, Liverpool, and only the men that are hard will get through,' Charles strove to palliate.

'And I'm to do the dirty work?' Liverpool complained, while Tarwater's heart sank.

'That's just about the size of it,' Charles said. 'You've got the deciding.'

Then Old Tarwater's heart uprose again as the air was rent by a cyclone of profanity, from the midst of which crackled sentences like: 'Dirty skunks! . . . See you in hell first! . . . My mind's made up! . . . Hell's fire and corruption! . . . The old codger goes down the Yukon with us, stack on that, my hearty! . . . Hard? You don't know what hard is unless I show you! . . . I'll bust the whole outfit to hell and gone if any of you try to side-track him! . . . Just try to side-track him, that's all, and you'll think the day of Judgment and all God's blastingness has hit the camp in one chunk!'

Such was the invigoratingness of Liverpool's flow of speech that, quite without consciousness of effort, the old man arose easily under his load and strode on toward Happy Camp.

From Happy Camp to Long Lake, from Long Lake to Deep Lake, and from Deep Lake up over the enormous hog-back and down to Linderman, the man-killing race against winter kept on. Men broke their hearts and backs and wept beside the trail in sheer exhaustion. But winter never faltered. The fall gales blew, and amid bitter soaking rains and ever increasing snow flurries, Tarwater and the party to which he was attached piled the last of their outfit on the beach.

There was no rest. Across the lake, a mile above a roaring torrent, they located a patch of spruce and built their saw-pit. Here, by hand, with an inadequate whipsaw, they sawed the spruce-trunks into lumber. They worked night and day. Thrice, on the night-shift, underneath in the saw-pit, Old Tarwater fainted. By day he cooked as well, and, in the betweenwhiles, helped Anson in the building of the boat beside the torrent as the green planks came down.

The days grew shorter. The wind shifted into the north and blew unending gales. In the mornings the weary men crawled from their blankets and in their socks thawed out their frozen shoes by the fire Tarwater always had burning for them. Ever arose the increasing tale of famine on the Inside. The last grub steamboats up from Bering Sea were stalled by low water at the beginning of the Yukon Flats hundreds of miles north of Dawson. In fact, they lay at the old Hudson Bay Company's post at Fort Yukon inside the Arctic Circle. Flour in Dawson was up to two dollars a pound but no one would sell. Bonanza and Eldorado Kings, with money to burn, were leaving for the Outside because they could buy no grub. Miners' Committees were confiscating all grub and putting the population on strict rations. A man who held out an ounce of grub was shot like a dog. A score had been so executed already.

And, under a strain which had broken so many younger men, Old Tarwater began to break. His cough had become terrible, and had not his exhausted comrades slept like the dead, he would have kept them awake nights. Also, he began to take chills, so that he dressed up to go to bed. When he had finished so dressing, not a rag of garment remained in his clothes bag. All he possessed was on his back and swathed around his gaunt old form.

'Gee!' said Big Bill. 'If he puts all he's got on now, when it ain't lower than twenty above, what'll he do later on when it goes down to fifty and sixty below?'

They lined the rough-made boat down the mountain torrent, nearly losing it a dozen times, and rowed across the south end of Lake Linderman in the thick of a fall blizzard. Next morning they planned to load and start, squarely into the teeth of the north, on their perilous traverse of half a thousand miles of lakes and rapids and box canyons. But before he went to bed that night, Young Liverpool was out over the camp. He returned to find his whole party asleep. Rousing Tarwater, he talked with him in low tones.

'Listen, dad,' he said. 'You've got a passage in our boat, and if ever a man earned a passage you have. But you know yourself you're pretty well along in years, and your health right now ain't exciting. If you go on with us you'll croak surer'n hell.—Now wait till I finish, dad. The price for a passage has jumped to five hundred dollars. I've been throw-

ing my feet and I've hustled a passenger. He's an official of
the Alaska Commercial and just has to get in. He's bid up
to six hundred to go with me in our boat. Now the passage
is yours. You sell it to him, poke the six hundred into your
jeans, and pull South for California while the goin's good.
You can be in Dyea in two days, and in California in a week
more. What d'ye say?'

Tarwater coughed and shivered for a space, ere he could
get freedom of breath for speech.

'Son,' he said, 'I just want to tell you one thing. I drove
my four yoke of oxen across the Plains in Forty-nine and lost
nary a one. I drove them plumb to Californy, and I freighted
with them afterward out of Sutter's Fort to American Bar.
Now I'm going to Klondike. Ain't nothing can stop me, ain't
nothing at all. I'm going to ride that boat, with you at the
steering sweep, clean to Klondike, and I'm going to shake
three hundred thousand out of the moss-roots. That being
so, it's contrary to reason and common sense for me to sell
out my passage. But I thank you kindly, son, I thank you
kindly.'

The young sailor shot out his hand impulsively and gripped
the old man's.

'By God, dad!' he cried. 'You're sure going to go then.
You're the real stuff.' He looked with undisguised contempt
across the sleepers to where Charles Crayton snored in his
red beard. 'They don't seem to make your kind any more,
dad.'

Into the north they fought their way, although old-timers,
coming out, shook their heads and prophesied they would be
frozen in on the lakes. That the freeze-up might come any
day was patent, and delays of safety were no longer considered. For this reason, Liverpool decided to shoot the rapid
stream connecting Linderman to Lake Bennett with the fully
loaded boat. It was the custom to line the empty boats down
and to portage the cargoes across. Even then, many empty
boats had been wrecked. But the time was past for such
precaution.

'Climb out, dad,' Liverpool commanded, as he prepared
to swing from the bank and enter the rapids.

Old Tarwater shook his white head.

'I'm sticking to the outfit,' he declared. 'It's the only way to get through. You see, son, I'm going to Klondike. If I stick by the boat, then the boat just naturally goes to Klondike, too. If I get out, then most likely you'll lose the boat.'

'Well, there's no use in overloading,' Charles announced, springing abruptly out on the bank as the boat cast off.

'Next time you wait for my orders!' Liverpool shouted ashore as the current gripped the boat. 'And there won't be any more walking around rapids and losing time waiting to pick you up!'

What took them ten minutes by river, took Charles half an hour by land, and while they waited for him at the head of Lake Bennett they passed the time of day with several dilapidated old-timers on their way out. The famine news was graver than ever. The Northwest Mounted Police, stationed at the foot of Lake Marsh where the gold-rushers entered Canadian Territory, were refusing to let a man past who did not carry with him seven hundred pounds of grub. In Dawson City a thousand men, with dog-teams, were waiting the freeze-up to come out over the ice. The trading companies could not fill their grub-contracts, and partners were cutting the cards to see which should go and which should stay and work the claims.

'That settles it,' Charles announced, when he learned of the action of the mounted police on the boundary. 'Old Man, you might as well start back now.'

'Climb aboard!' Liverpool commanded. 'We're going to Klondike, and old dad is going along.'

A shift of gale to the south gave them a fair wind down Lake Bennett, before which they ran under a huge sail made by Liverpool. The heavy weight of outfit gave such ballast that he cracked on as a daring sailor should when moments counted. A shift of four points into the southwest, coming just at the right time as they entered upon Caribou Crossing, drove them down that connecting link to lakes Taggish and Marsh. In stormy sunset and twilight they made the dangerous crossing of Great Windy Arm, wherein they beheld two other boat-loads of gold-rushers capsize and drown.

Charles was for beaching for the night, but Liverpool held on, steering down Tagish by the sound of the surf on the shoals and by the occasional shore-fires that advertised wrecked or timid argonauts. At four in the morning, he aroused Charles. Old Tarwater, shiveringly awake, heard Liverpool order Crayton aft beside him at the steering-sweep, and also heard the one-sided conversation.

'Just listen, friend Charles, and keep your own mouth shut,' Liverpool began. 'I want you to get one thing into your head and keep it there: *old dad's going by the police. Understand? He's going by.* When they examine our outfit, old dad's got a fifth share in it, savvee? That'll put us all 'way under what we ought to have, but we can bluff it through. Now get this, and get it hard: *there ain't going to be any fall-down on this bluff—*'

'If you think I'd give away on the old codger—' Charles began indignantly.

'You thought that,' Liverpool checked him, 'because I never mentioned any such thing. Now—get me and get me hard: I don't care what you've been thinking. It's what you're going to think. We'll make the police post some time this afternoon, and we've got to get ready to pull the bluff without a hitch, and a word to the wise is plenty.'

'If you think I've got it in my mind—' Charles began again.

'Look here,' Liverpool shut him off. 'I don't know what's in your mind. I don't want to know. I want you to know what's in my mind. If there's any slip-up, if old dad gets turned back by the police, I'm going to pick out the first quiet bit of landscape and take you ashore on it. And then I'm going to beat you up to the Queen's taste. Get me, and get me hard. It ain't going to be any half-way beating, but a real, two-legged, two-fisted, he-man beating. I don't expect I'll kill you, but I'll come damn near to half-killing you.'

'But what can I do?' Charles almost whimpered.

'Just one thing,' was Liverpool's final word. 'You just pray. You pray so hard that old dad gets by the police that he does get by. That's all. Go back to your blankets.'

* * *

Before they gained Lake Le Barge, the land was sheeted with snow that would not melt for half a year. Nor could they lay their boat at will against the bank, for the rim-ice was already forming. Inside the mouth of the river, just ere it entered Lake Le Barge, they found a hundred storm-bound boats of the argonauts. Out of the north, across the full sweep of the great lake, blew an unending snow gale. Three mornings they put out and fought it and the cresting seas it drove that turned to ice as they fell in-board. While the others broke their hearts at the oars, Old Tarwater managed to keep up just sufficient circulation to survive by chopping ice and throwing it overboard.

Each day for three days, beaten to helplessness, they turned tail on the battle and ran back into the sheltering river. By the fourth day, the hundred boats had increased to three hundred, and the two thousand argonauts on board knew that the great gale heralded the freeze-up of Le Barge. Beyond, the rapid rivers would continue to run for days, but unless they got beyond, and immediately, they were doomed to be frozen in for six months to come.

'This day we go through,' Liverpool announced. 'We turn back for nothing, And those of us that dies at the oars will live again and go on pulling.'

And they went through, winning half the length of the lake by nightfall and pulling on through all the night hours as the wind went down, falling asleep at the oars and being rapped awake by Liverpool, toiling on through an age-long nightmare while the stars came out and the surface of the lake turned to the unruffledness of a sheet of paper and froze skin-ice that tinkled like broken glass as their oar-blades shattered it.

As day broke clear and cold, they entered the river, with behind them a sea of ice. Liverpool examined his aged passenger and found him helpless and almost gone. When he rounded the boat to against the rim-ice to build a fire and warm up Tarwater inside and out, Charles protested against such loss of time.

'This ain't business, so don't you come horning in,' Liverpool informed him. 'I'm running the boat trip. So you just climb out and chop firewood, and plenty of it. I'll take care of dad. You, Anson, make a fire on the bank. And you, Bill, set up the Yukon stove in the boat. Old dad ain't as young as the rest of us, and for the rest of this voyage he's going to have a fire on board to sit by.'

All of which came to pass; and the boat, in the grip of the current, like a river steamer with smoke rising from the two joints of stove-pipe, grounded on shoals, hung up on split currents, and charged rapids and canyons, as it drove deeper into the Northland winter. The Big and Little Salmon rivers were throwing mush-ice into the main river as they passed, and, below the riffles, anchor-ice arose from the river bottom and coated the surface with crystal scum. Night and day the rim-ice grew, till, in quiet places, it extended out a hundred yards from shore. And Old Tarwater, with all his clothes on, sat by the stove and kept the fire going. Night and day, not daring to stop for fear of the imminent freeze-up, they dared to run, an increasing mushiness of ice running with them.

'What ho, old hearty?' Liverpool would call out at times.

'Cheer O,' Old Tarwater had learned to respond.

'What can I ever do for you, son, in payment?' Tarwater, stoking the fire, would sometimes ask Liverpool beating now one released hand and now the other as he fought for circulation where he steered in the freezing stern-sheets.

'Just break out that regular song of yours, old Forty-Niner,' was the invariable reply.

And Tarwater would lift his voice in the cackling chant, as he lifted it at the end, when the boat swung in through driving cake-ice and moored to the Dawson City bank, and all waterfront Dawson pricked its ears to hear the triumphant paean:

> Like Argus of the ancient times,
>   We leave this modern Greece,
> Tum-tum, tum-tum, tum, tum, tum-tum,
>   To shear the Golden Fleece.

Charles did it, but he did it so discreetly that none of his party, least of all the sailor, ever learned of it. He saw two great open barges being filled up with men, and, on inquiry, learned that these were grubless ones being rounded up and sent down the Yukon by the Committee of Safety. The barges were to be towed by the last little steamboat in Dawson, and the hope was that Fort Yukon, where lay the stranded steamboats, would be gained before the river froze. At any rate, no matter what happened to them, Dawson would be relieved of their grub-consuming presence. So to the Committee of Safety Charles went, privily to drop a flea in its ear concerning Tarwater's grubless, moneyless, and aged condition. Tarwater was one of the last gathered in, and when Young Liverpool returned to the boat, from the bank he saw the barges in a run of cake-ice, disappearing around the bend below Moosehide Mountain.

Running in cake-ice all the way, and several times escaping jams in the Yukon Flats, the barges made their hundreds of miles of progress farther into the north and froze up cheek by jowl with the grub-fleet. Here, inside the Arctic Circle Old Tarwater settled down to pass the long winter. Several hours' work a day, chopping firewood for the steamboat companies, sufficed to keep him in food. For the rest of the time there was nothing to do but hibernate in his log cabin.

Warmth, rest, and plenty to eat, cured his hacking cough and put him in as good physical condition as was possible for his advanced years. But, even before Christmas, the lack of fresh vegetables caused scurvy to break out, and disappointed adventurer after disappointed adventurer took to his bunk in abject surrender to this culminating misfortune. Not so Tarwater. Even before the first symptoms appeared on him, he was putting into practice his one prescription, namely, exercise. From the junk of the old trading post he resurrected a number of rusty traps, and from one of the steamboat captains he borrowed a rifle.

Thus equipped, he ceased from wood-chopping, and began to make more than a mere living. Nor was he downhearted when the scurvy broke out on his own body. Ever he ran his trap-lines and sang his ancient chant. Nor could the pessimist shake his surety of the three hundred thousand of Alaskan gold he was going to shake out of the moss-roots.

'But this ain't gold-country,' they told him.

'Gold is where you find it, son, as I should know who was mining before you was born, 'way back in Forty-Nine,' was his reply. 'What was Bonanza Creek but a moose-pasture? No miner'd look at it; yet they washed five-hundred-dollar pans and took out fifty million dollars. Eldorado was just as bad. For all you know, right under this here cabin, or right over the next hill, is millions just waiting for a lucky one like me to come and shake it out.'

At the end of January came his disaster. Some powerful animal that he decided was a bob-cat, managing to get caught in one of his smaller traps, dragged it away. A heavy snowfall put a stop midway to his pursuit, losing the trail for him and losing himself. There were but several hours of daylight each day between the twenty hours of intervening darkness, and his efforts in the gray light and continually falling snow succeeded only in losing him more thoroughly. Fortunately, when winter snow falls in the Northland the thermometer invariably rises; so, instead of the customary forty and fifty and even sixty degrees below zero, the temperature remained fifteen below. Also, he was warmly clad and had a full matchbox. Further to mitigate his predicament, on the fifth day he killed a wounded moose that weighed over half a ton. Making his camp beside it on a spruce-bottom, he was prepared to last out the winter, unless a searching party found him or his scurvy grew worse.

But at the end of two weeks there had been no sign of search, while his scurvy had undeniably grown worse. Against his fire, banked from outer cold by a shelter-wall of spruce-boughs, he crouched long hours in sleep and long hours in waking. But the waking hours grew less, becoming semi-waking or half-dreaming hours as the processes of hibernation worked their way with him. Slowly the sparkle point of consciousness and identity that was John Tarwater sank, deeper and deeper, into the profounds of his being that had been compounded ere man was man, and while he was becoming man, when he, first of all animals regarded himself with an introspective eye and laid the beginnings of morality in foundations of nightmare peopled by the monsters of his own ethic-thwarted desires.

Like a man in fever, waking to intervals of consciousness, so Old Tarwater awoke, cooked his moose-meat, and fed the fire; but more and more time he spent in his torpor, unaware of what was day-dream and what was sleep-dream in the content of his unconsciousness.* And here, in the unforgetable crypts of man's unwritten history, unthinkable and unrealizable, like passages of nightmare or impossible adventures of lunacy, he encountered the monsters created of man's first morality that ever since have vexed him into the spinning of fantasies to elude them or do battle with them.

In short, weighted by his seventy years, in the vast and silent loneliness of the North, Old Tarwater, as in the delirium of drug or anaesthetic, recovered, within himself, the infantile mind of the child-man of the early world. It was in the dusk of Death's fluttery wings that Tarwater thus crouched, and, like his remote forebear, the child-man, went to myth-making, and sun-heroizing, himself hero-maker and the hero in quest of the immemorable treasure difficult of attainment.

Either must he attain the treasure—for so ran the inexorable logic of the shadow-land of the unconscious—or else sink into the all-devouring sea, the blackness eater of the light that swallowed to extinction the sun each night . . . the sun that arose ever in rebirth next morning in the east, and that had become to man man's first symbol of immortality through rebirth. All this, in the deeps of his unconsciousness (the shadowy western land of descending light), was the near dusk of Death down into which he slowly ebbed.

But how to escape this monster of the dark that from within him slowly swallowed him? Too deep-sunk was he to dream of escape or feel the prod of desire to escape. For him reality had ceased. Nor from within the darkened chamber of himself could reality recrudesce. His years were too heavy upon him, the debility of disease and the lethargy and torpor of the silence and the cold were too profound. Only from without could reality impact upon him and reawake within him an awareness of reality. Otherwise he would ooze down through the shadow-realm of the unconscious into the all-darkness of extinction.

But it came, the smash of reality from without, crashing upon his ear drums in a loud, explosive snort. For twenty days, in a temperature that had never risen above fifty below, no breath of wind had blown movement, no slightest sound had broken the silence. Like the smoker on the opium couch refocusing his eyes from the spacious walls of dream to the narrow confines of the mean little room, so Old Tarwater stared vague-eyed before him, across his dying fire, at a huge moose that stared at him in startlement, dragging a wounded leg, manifesting all signs of extreme exhaustion, it, too, had been straying blindly in the shadow-land, and had wakened to reality only just ere it stepped into Tarwater's fire.

He feebly slipped the large fur mitten lined with thick-nesses of wool from his right hand. Upon trial he found the trigger finger too numb for movement. Carefully, slowly, through long minutes, he worked the bare hand inside his blankets, up under his fur *parka*, through the chest openings of his shirts, and into the slightly warm hollow of his left arm-pit. Long minutes passed ere the finger could move, when, with equal slowness of caution, he gathered his rifle to his shoulder and drew bead upon the great animal across the fire.

At the shot, of the two shadow-wanderers, the one reeled downward to the dark and the other reeled upward to the light, swaying drunkenly on his scurvy-ravaged legs, shivering with nervousness and cold, rubbing swimming eyes with shaking fingers, and staring at the real world all about him that had returned to him with such sickening suddenness. He shook himself together, and realized that for long, how long he did not know, he had bedded in the arms of Death. He spat, with definite intention, heard the spittle crackle in the frost, and judged it must be below and far below sixty below. In truth, that day at Fort Yukon, the spirit ther-mometer registered seventy-five degrees below zero, which, since freezing-point is thirty-two above, was equivalent to one hundred and seven degrees of frost.

Slowly Tarwater's brain reasoned to action. Here, in the vast alone, dwelt Death. Here had come two wounded moose. With the clearing of the sky after the great cold came on, he had located his bearings, and he knew that both wounded moose had trailed to him from the east. Therefore, in the east, were men—whites or Indians he could not tell, but at any rate men who might stand by him in his need and help moor him to reality above the sea of dark.

He moved slowly, but he moved in reality, girding himself with rifle, ammunition, matches, and a pack of twenty pounds of moose-meat. Then, an Argus rejuvenated, albeit lame of both legs and tottery, he turned his back on the perilous west and limped into the sun-arising, re-birthing east. . . .

Days later—how many days later he was never to know—dreaming dreams and seeing visions, cackling his old gold-chant of Forty-Nine, like one drowning and swimming feebly to keep his consciousness above the engulfing dark, he came out upon the snow-slope to a canyon and saw below smoke rising and men who ceased from work to gaze at him. He tottered down the hill to them, still singing; and when he ceased from lack of breath they called him variously: Santa Claus, Old Christmas, Whiskers, the Last of the Mohicans, and Father Christmas. And when he stood among them he stood very still, without speech, while great tears welled out of his eyes. He cried silently, a long time, till, as if suddenly bethinking himself, he sat down in the snow with much creaking and crackling of his joints, and from this low vantage point toppled sidewise and fainted calmly and easily away.

In less than a week Old Tarwater was up and limping about the housework of the cabin, cooking and dish-washing for the five men of the creek. Genuine sour-doughs (pioneers) they were, tough and hard-bitten, who had been buried so deeply inside the Circle that they did not know there was a Klondike Strike. The news he brought them was their first word of it. They lived on an almost straight-meat diet of moose, caribou, and smoked salmon, eked out with wild berries and somewhat succulent wild roots they had stocked up with in the summer. They had forgotten the taste of coffee, made fire with a burning glass, carried live fire-sticks with them wherever they traveled, and in their pipes smoked dry leaves that bit the tongue and were pungent to the nostrils.

Three years before, they had prospected from the head-reaches of the Koyokuk northward and clear across to the mouth of the Mackenzie on the Arctic Ocean. Here, on the whaleships, they had beheld their last white men and equipped themselves with the last whiteman's grub, consisting princip-ally of salt and smoking tobacco. Striking south and west on the long traverse to the junction of the Yukon and Por-cupine at Fort Yukon, they had found gold on this creek and remained over to work the ground.

They hailed the advent of Tarwater with joy, never tired of listening to his tales of Forty-Nine, and rechristened him Old Hero. Also, with tea made from spruce needles, with concoctions brewed from the inner willow bark, and with sour and bitter roots and bulbs from the ground, they dosed his scurvy out of him, so that he ceased limping and began to lay on flesh over his bony framework. Further, they saw no reason at all why he should not gather a rich treasure of gold from the ground.

'Don't know about all of three hundred thousand,' they told him one morning, at breakfast, ere they departed to their work, 'but how'd a hundred thousand do, Old Hero? That's what we figure a claim is worth, the ground being badly spotted, and we've already staked your location notices.'

'Well, boys,' Old Tarwater answered, 'and thanking you kindly, all I can say is that a hundred thousand will do nicely, and very nicely, for a starter. Of course, I ain't goin' to stop till I get the full three hundred thousand. That's what I come into the country for.'

They laughed and applauded his ambition and reckoned they'd have to hunt a richer creek for him. And Old Hero reckoned that as the spring came on and he grew spryer, he'd have to get out and do a little snooping around himself.

'For all anybody knows,' he said, pointing to a hillside across the creek bottom, 'the moss under the snow there may be plumb rooted in nugget gold.'

He said no more, but as the sun rose higher and the days

grew longer and warmer, he gazed often across the creek at the definite bench-formation half way up the hill. And, one day, when the thaw was in full swing, he crossed the stream and climbed to the bench. Exposed patches of ground had already thawed an inch deep. On one such patch he stooped, gathered a bunch of moss in his big gnarled hands, and ripped it out by the roots. The sun smoldered on dully glistening yellow. He shook the handful of moss, and coarse nuggets, like gravel, fell to the ground. It was the Golden Fleece ready for the shearing.

Not entirely unremembered in Alaskan annals is the summer stampede of 1898 from Fort Yukon to the bench diggings of Tarwater Hill. And when Tarwater sold his holdings to the Bowdie interests for a sheer half-million and faced for California, he rode a mule over a new-cut trail, with convenient road houses along the way, clear to the steamboat landing at Fort Yukon.

At the first meal on the ocean-going steamship out of St Michaels, a waiter, grayish-haired, pain-ravaged of face, scurvy-twisted of body, served him. Old Tarwater was compelled to look him over twice in order to make certain he was Charles Crayton.

'Got it bad, eh, son?' Tarwater queried.

'Just my luck,' the other complained, after recognition and greeting. 'Only one of the party that the scurvy attacked. I've been through hell. The other three are all at work and healthy, getting grub-stake to prospect up White River this winter. Anson's earning twenty-five a day at carpentering, Liverpool getting twenty logging for the saw-mill, and Big Bill's getting forty a day as chief sawyer. I tried my best, and if it hadn't been for scurvy . . .'

'Sure, son, you done your best, which ain't much, you being naturally irritable and hard from too much business. Now I'll tell you what. You ain't fit to work crippled up this way. I'll pay your passage with the captain in kind remembrance of the voyage you gave me, and you can lay up and take it easy the rest of the trip. And what are your circumstances when you land at San Francisco?'

Charles Crayton shrugged his shoulders.

'Tell you what,' Tarwater continued. 'There's work on the ranch for you till you can start business again.'

'I could manage your business for you—' Charles began eagerly.

'No, siree,' Tarwater declared emphatically. 'But there's always post-holes to dig, and cordwood to chop, and the climate's fine. . . .'

Tarwater arrived home a true prodigal grandfather for whom the fatted calf was killed and ready. But first, ere he sat down at table, he must stroll out and around. And sons and daughters of his flesh and of the law needs must go with him, fulsomely eating out of the gnarled old hand that had half a million to disburse. He led the way, and no opinion he slyly uttered was preposterous or impossible enough to draw dissent from his following. Pausing by the ruined water wheel which he had built from the standing timber, his face beamed as he gazed across the stretches of Tarwater Valley, and on and up the far heights to the summit of Tarwater Mountain—now all his again.

A thought came to him that made him avert his face and blow his nose in order to hide the twinkle in his eyes. Still attended by the entire family, he strolled on to the dilapidated barn. He picked up an age-weathered single-tree from the ground.

'William,' he said. 'Remember that little conversation we had just before I started to Klondike? Sure, William, you remember. You told me I was crazy. And I said my father'd have walloped the tar out of me with a single-tree if I'd spoke to him that way.'

'Aw, but that was only foolin',' William temporized.

William was a grizzled man of forty-five, and his wife and grown sons stood in the group, curiously watching Grandfather Tarwater take off his coat and hand it to Mary to hold.

'William—come here,' he commanded imperatively.

No matter how reluctantly, William came.

'Just a taste, William, son, of what my father give me often enough,' Old Tarwater crooned, as he laid on his son's back and shoulders with the single-tree. 'Observe, I ain't hitting you on the head. My father had a gosh-wollickin' temper and never drew the line at heads when he went after tar.— Don't jerk your elbows back that way! You're likely to get a crack on one by accident. And just tell me one thing, William, son: is there any notion in your head that I'm crazy?'

'No!' William yelped out in pain, as he danced about. 'You ain't crazy, father! Of course you ain't crazy!'

'You said it,' Old Tarwater remarked sententiously, tossing the single-tree aside and starting to struggle into his coat. 'Now let's all go in and eat.'

EXPLANATORY NOTES

3 *Malemute Kid*: like that of Montana Kid in 'At the Rainbow's End', Malemute Kid's name reflects a practice occasionally encountered in the early American West of attaching the cognomen 'Kid' to a young man's place of origin, such as the state of Montana, or to some object with which he was associated: in the present instance the malemute, a breed of Northland sled-dog.

Epworth: the Epworth League, a Methodist religious society.

4 *Hi-yu skookum!*: 'skookum' means 'great' or 'strong' in the Chinook trade jargon in common use at that time among Indians and whites of eastern Alaska and the Yukon Territory.

Fort Yukon . . . Arctic City: outposts in north-central and north-eastern Alaska.

5 *gee-pole*: the long pole with which a dog-sled is guided. 'Gee' is the command to go right, in contrast to 'Haw', the command for left.

9 *Nuklukyeto*: Indian village on the Yukon River in central Alaska.

bench claim: prospector's claim located on land above a river or stream. Gold is extracted from the alluvial deposits exposed by soil erosion and the disintegration of rock through weathering.

11 *the hoary game of natural selection*: Charles Darwin's principle of natural selection, as set forth in *The Origin of Species* (1858), had been widely promoted as an explanation of the theory of biological evolution. Darwin, along with his English proponent Herbert Spencer, was especially in vogue among those European and American writers influenced by the literary 'naturalism' of the French novelist Émile Zola, whose writings stressed the insignificance of the human will in the face of the powerful forces of heredity and environment.

13 *che-cha-quas*: Chinook term for tenderfeet, usually in contrast to *sourdoughs*, Northland veterans who baked their bread without baking powder.

washed the sure-thing bars of the Stuart River for a double grubstake: placer miners, in contrast to those who mined gold out of hard rock, found it in the alluvial deposits along river-banks and in mid-river sandbars. By washing the sand and gravel in pans, rockers, or sluice boxes, they enabled the much heavier gold to precipitate to the bottom while the lighter material was carried away by the water. London spent the winter of 1897/8 in a cabin on Split-Up Island, at the confluence of the Stewart (so spelled) and Yukon rivers, eighty miles south of Dawson City. A grub-stake was a quantity of supplies provided to a prospector at a trading post, usually in exchange for a share in future mining profits.

14 *Forty Mile*: trading outpost at the mouth of Fortymile River, so-called because it was forty miles down the Yukon River from Fort Reliance.

Upper Tanana Sticks: 'Sticks' was a generic term for forest-dwelling Indians of the interior of Alaska and the Yukon Territory, in this case a tribe residing in east-central Alaska in the upper reaches of the Tanana River, a major tributary of the Yukon.

Thling-Tinneh: this chief's name somewhat implausibly combines the then current names of the two major divisions of south-eastern Alaska natives: the coastal Thlingits and the inland Tinneh (now usually rendered as *Dineh* or *Dene*). In the context of this intermittently humorous tale London may have considered the name an inside joke.

potlach: this native term for 'a giving' (usually spelled *potlatch*) designates an elaborate feast at which the host gives away or destroys as many of his possessions as he can afford, thereby gaining prestige within his tribe or even beyond.

21 *Jelchs, the Raven, the Promethean fire-bringer*: like his account of the role of the shaman, London's version of native mythology is approximately correct. The raven or crow designates one of the two lineal divisions in Northland native culture, the other being designated by the wolf. As the creative principle, the raven is the giver of light to the world and thus is appropriately identified with Prometheus, the Titan who in Greek mythology disobeyed the gods and brought fire to humanity. I have found no evidence, however, that the natives identified the wolf with the white man and thus with the 'destructive principle', the 'sneaking interloper and emissary of Satan'. Instead London seems to be drawing on the biblical myth of the Fall, especially as rendered in Milton's *Paradise Lost*, one of the books London brought with him to the Northland.

23 *bald-face*: a grizzly bear.

Chinook: a strong, warm wind common in north-western North America. The Chinooks were a native tribe inhabiting the northern shore of the Columbia River near its mouth on the border between Washington and Oregon.

24 *Innuit*: the native peoples (referred to by whites as Eskimos) inhabiting the coastal regions of northern and western Alaska.

26 *ten thousand years of culture fell from him*: fashionable among the literary naturalists of London's generation was this notion that human beings were fundamentally savages, and that their superficial overlay of civilized culture could not prevent them, under the right conditions, from returning atavistically to their primordial state.

29 *Sitka Charley*: a character who figures more or less prominently in several of London's tales, Charley is a member of the Sitka tribe of the Alaska panhandle.

Fort Reliance: trading outpost six miles down the Yukon River from Dawson City.

31 *Siwash*: in the Chinook jargon, a generic term for an Indian, often used pejoratively.

burning to bed-rock: a winter mining technique that involved lighting a fire to thaw the frozen earth down to the level of solid rock.

32 *the eighth article of the Decalogue*: 'Thou shalt not steal.'

36 *as Pilate might have done after washing his hands*: Pontius Pilate was the Roman governor who, in the biblical account, washed his hands of the innocent blood of Jesus before authorizing his crucifixion (Matt. 27: 24).

39 *Edmonton*: this town in central Alberta promoted itself as the 'back door to the Klondike'; but as the text implies, the journey by this route would have been longer and more difficult than the usual passage from Dyea or Skagway in south-eastern Alaska.

40 *Lake Athabasca*: large lake extending from north-eastern Alberta to north-western Saskatchewan.

pemmican: a form of concentrated food (sometimes spelled *pemican*) developed by American Indians and eventually used also by whites. It was produced by pulverizing dry, lean meat and mixing it with melted fat and sometimes with flour and molasses.

40 *Great Slave . . . Great Bear*: large lakes in the Northwest Territories. The Fort of Good Hope, mentioned below, is west of Great Bear Lake on the Mackenzie River, which flows north-westerly to the Beaufort Sea and thence into the Arctic Ocean.

41 *Sloper*: this character is based on Merritt Sloper, one of the men who travelled with London to the Klondike and with whom he spent the winter of 1897/8 in the cabin at the Stewart River. They eventually got on each other's nerves, quarrelled, and parted company.

43 *Kilkenny cats*: the story goes that soldiers garrisoned at Kilkenny, Ireland, tied two cats together by their tails and flung them over a clothes-line, where they fought until both died. When a soldier cut them down, word got around that the cats had devoured each other, except for their tails.

44 *clip his coupons*: literally, the coupons clipped periodically from bonds and exchanged at a bank or brokerage for interest pay-ments; figuratively implies the easy life of the wealthy.

46 *slush-lamp*: makeshift lamp fuelled by bacon grease.

48 *Caliban*: the subhuman being who inhabits the island on which Prospero, his daughter Miranda, and other companions are shipwrecked in Shakespeare's play *The Tempest*.

Crusoe: Robinson Crusoe, shipwrecked on an island in the 1719 narrative by Daniel Defoe, discovers the presence of another human being when he sees a footprint in the sand.

55 *Lochinvar*: the hero of a ballad in Sir Walter Scott's poem *Marmion* (1808), who abducts his beloved from her wedding feast.

56 *Henry Ward Beecher*: a celebrated American Congregational minister and social crusader (1813–87) whose reputation was damaged by an accusation of adultery and a subsequent law-suit in 1874.

60 *Pelly . . . Five Fingers . . . Thirty Mile River . . . Le Barge*: out-posts or sections of the upper Yukon on the trail south to the port villages of Dyea and Skagway (La Barge is usually spelled *Laberge*). London had taken this trail in the opposite direction in 1897 when he was headed for the Klondike.

61 *Little Salmon . . . Hootalinqua*: the Big and Little Salmon and the Hootalinqua (now known as the Teslin) are eastern tribu-taries of the Yukon River.

61 *P. C. store*: a recurrent institution in London's Northland fiction and often referred to as the P. C. Company, it is apparently a composite of the two trading companies that dominated Dawson's commercial life during the gold rush: the Alaska Commercial Company (A. C. Company) and the North American Trading and Transportation Company (N.A.T. & T.).

62 *Captain Constantine*: Inspector Charles Constantine headed the contingent of Northwest Mounted Police when London was in Dawson in 1897 and 1898.

64 *Golden Fleece*: the prize sought by Jason and other argonauts in a mythical voyage recounted by Apollonius of Rhodes and other Greek and Roman poets.

66 *a mythical quartz-ledge*: a particularly rich vein, or lode, of gold could sometimes be found embedded in hard rock, often quartz.

67 *Henderson Creek*: the creek on which London staked his own claim in the autumn of 1897.

69 *a married woman cannot stake or record a creek, bench, or quartz claim*: this would have been only one of many nineteenth-century laws restricting the right of women to own property independently.

   Eldorado Creek: as its name implies, this small creek—a tributary of Bonanza Creek, which in turn emptied into the Klondike River—was the site of some of the richest deposits mined during the gold rush.

71 *Cleopatra . . . Antony*: the adulterous love affair between the Roman general and the Egyptian queen was the subject of Shakespeare's play *Antony and Cleopatra*.

   The world, and ours to choose from: at the end of Milton's *Paradise Lost*, when Adam and Eve are cast out of Paradise after eating the Forbidden Fruit, 'The world was all before them, where to choose.'

72 *Lucretia, Acte*: Lucretia was the reputedly beautiful and virtuous Roman wife who committed suicide after being raped by the son of King Tarquinius Superbus in the early fifth century BC. Acte was a freedwoman who became the mistress of the Roman emperor Nero in approximately AD 55.

76 *Upper Country . . . Minook . . . Lower Country*: the upper (eastern) section of the Yukon River in the Yukon Territory, including the Klondike region, in contrast to the section in eastern

and central Alaska. Minook, in the Upper Country, is several hundred miles downriver from Dawson.

76 *Great Delta . . . Point Barrow . . . the Porcupine*: the Great Delta is where the Yukon River empties into the Bering Sea in western Alaska; Point Barrow is the northernmost point in Alaska; the Porcupine is a major tributary of the Yukon River in northeastern Alaska.

84 *Chippewyan*: territory of a native group (usually spelled *Chipewyan*) south of Great Slave Lake in the Northwest Territories.

86 *Holy Cross*: the Mission of the Holy Cross was located about 200 miles up the Yukon River from the Bering Sea.

87 *Circle City*: village on the Yukon River in east-central Alaska about forty miles south of the Arctic Circle, hence its name.

88 *'Dan Tucker'*: fiddle tune popular in frontier settlements in nineteenth-century America.

95 *schottisching*: from the German word for *Scottish*, the schottisch is a round-dance similar to a polka.

97 *Opera House*: this combination saloon and dance-hall, a prominent site of the raucous Dawson social life, was destroyed by fire the night before Thanksgiving of 1897 during London's first visit to the town.

Freda: this 'Greek dancer' was based on an actual Freda Moloof, a Turkish belly-dancer whom London met in Dawson and from whom he received two letters after his Northland fiction began to appear in print. He later made her the heroine of his play *Scorn of Women* (1906).

101 *Smith & Wesson*: a pistol made by an American arms-manufacturer of that name.

103 *Wolseley . . . Khartoum*: Lord Wolseley (1833–1913), the British general whose troops in 1885 reached the Sudanese city of Khartoum too late to save the besieged forces of General Gordon.

104 *Louis Reil*: Louis Riel (so spelled) led two rebellions in Western Canada, in 1869 and 1884, by the métis, an independent-minded people of French, Scots, and Indian lineage. Both rebellions were put down by the British-dominated federal government; in the first instance Riel was banished, in the second he was convicted of treason and executed.

coureurs du bois: trappers (French).

104 *bois brules*: French-Canadian term for half-breeds.

105 *Pastilik*: this and the places mentioned on subsequent pages —Golovin Bay, Norton Sound, St Michael's, and Nunivak Island—are located on or near the west coast of Alaska.

106 *Mr Ulysses*: Ulysses, or Odysseus, was the wandering hero of the *Odyssey*, the Greek epic poem of Homer.

Shylock: the miserly protagonist of Shakespeare's play *The Merchant of Venice*.

109 *Axel Gunderson*: a Norwegian by this name was a shipmate of London's on the schooner *Sophia Sutherland*, which took them on a seven-month seal-hunting voyage to Japan and the Bering Sea in 1893.

110 *wild amphibians of the Northern seas*: probably seals and walruses, which technically are not amphibians but mammals.

111 *Kootenay country*: usually spelled *Kootenai*, it extends from northern Idaho and Montana into south-eastern British Columbia.

Cripple Creek: probably refers to the site of a celebrated goldmine in Colorado, although there was also a Cripple Creek in western Alaska.

115 *oomiak*: an Eskimo boat (also spelled *umiak*) similar to a canoe and made of a wood frame covered with hide.

the Aleutians: the long chain of islands extending westward from the Alaskan Peninsula and dividing the Bering Sea from the Pacific Ocean.

121 *Unalaska*: island in the central Aleutians. Subsequently mentioned islands are further east, off the south-western Alaskan coast.

122 *Pribyloffs*: islands in the Bering Sea.

123 *Yeddo Bay . . . Yoshiwara*: during his seal-hunting voyage of 1893 London visited the Japanese port of Yokohama on Yeddo Bay (now called Tokyo Bay) and about seventy-five miles northeast of the town of Yoshiwara on Suruga Bay.

124 *Copper Island*: in the Bering Sea off the Kamchatka Peninsula.

127 *McQuestion . . . Mayo*: the McQuesten (so spelled) and the Mayo are tributaries of the Stewart River east of the Klondike.

Pellys: native tribe inhabiting the Pelly River region in the Yukon Territory south-east of the Klondike.

137 *Chook!*: probably a Chinook term roughly equivalent to 'beat it!'—i.e. 'get away!'

138 *played quarter three seasons hand-running*: i.e. played quarterback on a football team for three successive seasons.

    effeminate Athenian . . . pink-tea degenerate: these references to homosexuals reflect the changes in Western sexual ideology from ancient Athens, where relationships between mature men and young boys were tolerated, to the late nineteenth century, when same-sex relationships entered the medical literature as a form of sexual pathology.

139 *Axel Gunderson*: a central character in London's story 'An Odyssey of the North' (see note to p. 109 above).

    see him, an' go him better: match and then raise the previous bet, in card games such as faro and poker. Bettles means that in courage and tenacity ('grit') Unga could equal and even surpass the much larger Axel.

140 *Chilkat totem*: the emblem—and the elaborately carved pole celebrating it—of the Chilkats, a Thlingit group residing in the vicinity of the Alaska panhandle village of Haines Mission—the destination of the two travellers in the ensuing narrative.

143 *when the sun mocked us*: a parhelic circle, or sun-dog, is a false sun in the form of a luminous circle or halo at the same altitude as the true sun.

144 *whacked fair*: divided the food fairly into equal portions.

151 *the local Four Hundred*: the élite of Dawson society parodying the 400 'best' families of New York high society.

    the Nome strike: gold was discovered at Nome, on the Seward Peninsula of western Alaska, in 1898, two years after the Klondike strike.

153 *a nimble breed*: i.e. a half-breed.

159 *cent per cent*: a hundred for every hundred; a rate of interest equal to the amount of the principal—i.e. a very high rate.

173 *Durrant*: in 1897, the first year of the gold rush, the San Francisco murderer Theodore Durrant, executed in 1898, would still have been alive.

    Thanksgiving game: the football game between Stanford University and the University of California at Berkeley.

    Dreyfus: Alfred Dreyfus (1859–1935), the French army officer whose conviction on a dubious charge of treason in 1894 precipitated a major political controversy that was not resolved until 1906, when he was retried, found not guilty, and restored to his former rank. The names mentioned in the remainder of this paragraph constitute a mix of fictional characters and such actual Klondike personages as Joe Ladue, Jack Dalton, and 'Swiftwater Bill' Gates. 'Governor Walsh' is Major J. M. Walsh, who arrived to become the new Commissioner of the Yukon Territory at exactly the time of London's arrival at Stewart River in early October 1897.

178 *P. G. work*: postgraduate work at a university.

181 *'Rumsky Ho'* and *'The Orange and the Black'*: 'Rumsky Ho' (alternately 'Rumsty Ho') was a drinking song of English origins popular at such colleges as Princeton, one of whose anthems was 'The Orange and the Black'.

'The Battle Hymn of the Republic': the opening lines of Julia Ward Howe's anthem of the Union during the American Civil War have a grim aptness at the end of London's story:

> Mine eyes have seen the glory of the coming of the Lord;
> He is trampling out the vintage where the grapes of wrath are stored;
> He hath loosed the fateful lightning of His terrible swift sword; His truth is marching on.

182 *Ruth, the Moabitess*: the story of Ruth's fidelity to Naomi is told in the Old Testament's Book of Ruth.

192 *strychnine*: strychnine attacks the central nervous system, producing muscle spasms similar to those of the tetanus (lockjaw) mentioned earlier, though the latter is a disease of bacterial origin.

196 *the Rhodes of Alaska*: Cecil Rhodes (1853–1902) was the British developer of South African diamond mines.

217 *coughing sickness*: tuberculosis, which, like the smallpox and measles mentioned below, was unknown among the Indians until the arrival of whites and to which they therefore had little natural immunity—a plight common in remote lands explored and colonized by Europeans.

224 *as near to that of the nunnery as tribal conditions would permit*: Northland native tribes customarily confined a pubescent girl to a tiny cell for up to two years before she was permitted to emerge and become eligible for marriage.

259 *Cambell Fort*: probably Fort Selkirk, at the confluence of the Yukon and Pelly rivers, once under the control of Robert Campbell, a trader for the Hudson's Bay Company.

267 *Finis*: the Latin word for 'the end', formerly used to mark the end of a novel. It appeared, for example—somewhat archaically—at the end of London's *The Call of the Wild*.

285 *Grandfather Tarwater*: in 1897 an old man named Tarwater joined London and his partners a few miles north of Dyea and traveled with them as far as the Stewart River, where they parted company. A thinly disguised version of London appears later in the narrative as the young 'rough-neck sailor' named Liverpool.

Argus: the builder of the ship *Argo* in which Jason voyaged in search of the Golden Fleece. The song—and the protagonist of London's tale—might more accurately have been associated with Jason.

Patagonia: the southern tip of South America.

287 *Merced placers . . . Sonoma County*: the Merced placers were the mines located along the Merced River in the Sierra Nevada in eastern California. Sonoma County, north of San Francisco Bay, was the site of London's own ranch.

306 *the content of his unconsciousness*: this and the following paragraphs reflect London's recent reading of Beatrice M. Hinkle's translation of C. G. Jung's *Psychology of the Unconscious* (1916), with its elaboration of the libido, or vital force, and the collective unconscious with its archetypal symbols.

TROLLOPE IN OXFORD WORLD'S CLASSICS

ANTHONY TROLLOPE

*The
Oxford
World's
Classics
Website*

www.worldsclassics.co.uk

- Information about new titles
- Explore the full range of Oxford World's Classics
- Links to other literary sites and the main OUP webpage
- Imaginative competitions, with bookish prizes
- Peruse *Compass*, the Oxford World's Classics magazine
- Articles by editors
- Extracts from Introductions
- A forum for discussion and feedback on the series
- Special information for teachers and lecturers

www.worldsclassics.co.uk

American Literature

British and Irish Literature

Children's Literature

Classics and Ancient Literature

Colonial Literature

Eastern Literature

European Literature

History

Medieval Literature

Oxford English Drama

Poetry

Philosophy

Politics

Religion

The Oxford Shakespeare